Too Good To Be True
K'Barthan Extras, Hamgeean Misfit: No 4

Too Good To Be True

K'Barthan Extras, Hamgeean Misfit: No 4

by

M T McGuire

Hamgee University Press

First published March 2021 by
Hamgee University Press

ISBN-978-1-907809-36-1

Written by M T McGuire
Edited by Emma Wilkins
Published by Hamgee University Press
Cover design by A Trouble Halved

M T McGuire is over 50 years old now but still checks
inside unfamiliar wardrobes for a gateway to Narnia.
Boringly, she's not found any.

Thank you for buying this book.
If you enjoyed it you can keep up with
news of the author online by
visiting www.hamgee.co.uk

You can also sign up for the
M T McGuire mailing list by visiting
http://www.hamgee.co.uk/freebook
and even buy K'Barthan Series merchandise at
http://bit.ly/UHSUshop

Chapter 1
Chance encounter

The Pan of Hamgee knew it wasn't a smart move to put his feet in the river Dang. But he did it anyway. He'd have to find somewhere to wash the smell off when he was done, but it was too hot to resist. He sat quietly at the end of a decrepit wooden jetty watching the world go by. His trousers were rolled up and his boots and socks sat next to him while his feet dangled in the cool water. He was close to The Planes so presumably the jetty had once been the mooring for someone's private boat. Not anymore.

The Pan wiggled his toes. In the heat, the levels of the river had dropped. The water flowing down it had acquired a certain gloopy texture which could only be achieved when the chemical pollution outweighed the water content. He'd probably wake up tomorrow with green feet and seventeen radioactive toes.

Never mind, he thought as he leaned back and looked up at the blue sky. On days like this, it almost didn't matter that his existence was treason. He was warm, he'd had a decent breakfast and he was fairly confident that, even if he was recognised by a member of the security forces, they were unlikely to bother trying to catch him. It was far too hot for that sort of malarkey. They had to wear stab vests with heavy boots and were armed to the teeth with weighty weaponry, all of which was unbearably hot to wear, and slowed them down. This evening would be a different matter, of course; it would be cool, and all the bad temper and frustration they'd built up over the heat of the day would be vented on the locals in relative comfort.

This evening was a world away though.

The tide was going out, revealing a band of black sticky mud along the bank. It popped and clicked as the water receded and the river Dang's molluscs and worm residents retired to their burrows to await its return. The Pan watched as, a few feet away, a large bubble appeared from one particular hole in the freshly revealed mud and then burst with a watery squelch.

'Mmm,' he said quietly.

He wrinkled his nose. Something was beginning to hum a bit. He wondered if the bubble had been a crab fart. Could crabs even do farts? No, probably not.

Why am I even thinking this?

More likely the smell was the drying mud. Whatever it was, perhaps it was time to return to the bank. The mudlarkers would be out soon and he enjoyed watching them. They also needed someone to look after their stuff while they waded about probing the tide line with ancient rakes and forks. The Pan was always happy to help in that respect, since there was usually a sandwich in it for him, or a few copper coins. However, they tended not to come to this part of the river. Most of the good stuff was found in the centre of the city where there had been a settlement of one form or another for several thousand years. It was only a mile or so downstream but if The Pan wanted to earn anything he'd have to go to them.

'Yep. Time to move on,' he sighed.

He stood up and flapped his feet around, waiting for them to dry in the sun. To his surprise, he noticed that a couple of brave souls were stepping down onto the mud close to the jetty upon which he was standing. Perhaps they were practising. Or maybe they were avoiding the crowds. Mudlarking was popular in the places where pickings were richer; so popular in fact that sometimes fights broke out over territory.

The Pan wondered about having a look himself. It might be dangerous, though. The mudlarkers wore waders for protection and he had none. If he cut his feet on something it was probably curtains if he was up to his ankles in that lot. The Prophet knew what kinds of pathogens lived in that mud, but The Pan was ready to bet there were whole new species of microbes in there, waiting to attack an unwary being's immune system. He could wear his boots, he supposed. No, he only had one pair of boots and a man who's on the run has to avoid detection. Wearing boots steeped in mud from the river Dang in its present form wouldn't help in that respect. They'd smell him hiding a mile off.

He stretched and checked his feet and shins. They were dry but the 'water' had definitely imbued them with a bit of a tang. Never mind—he'd just done a delivery job for Big Merv, so he had a little cash. He smiled to himself. Yes. He'd take a trip to the bath house later for a long luxurious soak.

He put his hat on and watched as the mudlarkers moved nearer. They were looking in a place just before a bend in the river where the currents eddied and whirled and, presumably, dropped things. The Pan continued to watch them for a while and then reluctantly put on his boots and socks.

Arnold's trollies! Something round here really did stink. Was it *just* the river?

He stood up and angled himself so he could use the useful eyes in the back of his head to look up and down stream at the same time. The sluggish brown water slid slowly by, glugging and gurgling as it ran through the wooden beams supporting the jetty beneath him. Then it went 'clonk'.

Hang on; water didn't do that, did it? Not unless the Dang had become so polluted it had achieved sentience and was trying to communicate in—

No, stop already.

There was a second 'clonk', and this time The Pan felt a slight vibration through the wooden slats he was standing on.

Something was down there.

'Curiosity killed the cat,' he muttered to himself and, mudlarkers forgotten for a moment, he lay down on the jetty, braced his feet and leaned over. It took his eyes a moment to adjust to the darker shade underneath. But there *was* something there. Wedged between the wooden supports was a long wooden box about five-and-a-half feet long and maybe two feet wide. It was difficult to gauge how high the box was because it was pretty much submerged. Unfortunately, as well as the box there was something else; the smell that went with it. To be honest, it was more of a stench than a smell and merely moving closer, as he had by lying down and looking at it, caused the intensity of the odour to increase so much that The Pan felt sick. Well, that confirmed it, the box and the stench were definitely a pair. Hiccupping, he shifted himself rapidly back onto the jetty.

'Eugh!' he muttered. 'What in the name of Arnold was that?'

By The Prophet's toenails, of course! A box that size? It was a coffin. The Pan could feel the colour draining from his face. There was a coffin in the river and, if he was a good and decent Nimmist—which all K'Barthans are—he had to fish it out and give it a proper Nimmist burial. In secret, of course, because the Grongles had banned religion and officially practising it was punishable by death. Arnold's toe jam! Now what? The Pan lived hand to mouth. He didn't have the financial resources to pay for a funeral. On the upside, Doing the Right Thing couldn't make his situation any worse since he was a GBI—a Government Blacklisted Individual—so his existence was already punishable by death. On the downside, if he obeyed his conscience, it could lay him open to all the wrong kind of attention if he was caught in the act. Except, an annoying little voice in his head told him, this was his moral duty.

Arse.

OK, so he had time to think about this. The box wasn't going anywhere; it was pretty thoroughly jammed in. Yeh, a quick battle of conscience before the tide went out. Maybe the mudlarkers would help. Good idea. He'd put it to them as a metaphysical conundrum and see what they said.

'Hey, you there,' said a voice, distracting him from his thoughts.

No-one ever crept up on The Pan, or at least not since he'd grown a handy extra set of eyes in the back of his head. Being able to see backwards and forwards at the same time has some advantages, so he knew there was no-one on the jetty.

'I say! Oi!' the voice called again.

The Pan walked over to the side and looked down at the murky water. The riverbed shelved steeply here and the water was deeper under the jetty. At first he saw no-one obvious. Oh no, wait, there she was. The Pan walked a few yards along the jetty, away from the shore. 'Mmm?'

Below him, standing half underneath the supporting wooden piles, and waist deep in the worryingly viscous waters, was a lady. She looked as if she was in her fifties but she had, as Ada might have put it, weathered well. She had smooth skin and the suggestions of a curvaceous figure—although semi-submerged as she was, it was difficult to be certain. Her eyes were bright blue and she wore her long salt and pepper hair piled up under a cap. She was wearing a dark blue t-shirt and chest-high waders. The straps running over her shoulders, holding the waders up like braces, were red. A fire fighter then; or at least, the waders were fire-fighter issue. Whether this lady was actually a member of the fire service, present or previous, was another matter. It was just as likely that the waders had fallen off the back of a fire engine or made their way quietly out of the side door of the fire station to the hands of waiting purchasers on the black market. She had a pipe clamped firmly in her mouth, but it wasn't lit. She appeared to be carrying a billhook of some kind, probably to feel her way in the mud.

'Can you give us a hand?' she said.

'I can try. It depends what you want a hand with,' said The Pan as the woman moved away from the jetty and out into open water, presumably to get a better look at him.

'We're searching for a wooden box; me and Christine, my wife, and Bort, my daughter. Some fellow drove his lorry into the side of Graden End Bridge last night and it shed its load. Word is, some of it fell over the edge. Now, I know it may be just his way of accounting for a couple of boxes he's nicked, but if anything has gone over, I reckon it'll have been carried to around here somewhere. That's if it's still floating of course.' The Pan turned and looked down river to where Graden End Bridge was clearly visible, despite the heat haze, about a mile away. 'King Milo and his crew are after it, along with pretty much everyone else, as well as us.'

'King Milo?'

'Nasty piece of work. Runs most of the operations round here. We like to steer well clear of him. He reckons anything found on the river is his by right. And he has thugs to back him up.'

'I see,' said The Pan. He knew perfectly well who King Milo was. He worked for Big Merv, after all. Even so, he hadn't realised anyone 'ran' the river or lorded it over the mudlarkers. One of the things that had never ceased to amaze him since he was blacklisted, was how few pursuits were free of complications. It seemed there was a gang to run just about anything. He reckoned if he started a business selling children's drawings he'd discover a whole world of shady operatives wanting to put him out of business or muscle their way in for a cut.

'Our colleagues think it sank. That's what the crowd is by Golden Point.' She pointed up the river to where it zigzagged slightly, halfway between Graden End Bridge and the jetty upon which The Pan was standing. Now that the woman had drawn it to his attention, he could see a lot of figures on the bank and others venturing onto the muddy foreshore. 'I know better. I'll bet any money that the real prize has floated down to here,' she continued. 'And if it has, I've got about half an hour to get in first and get gone, before that lot realise what's going on.'

Half an hour wasn't long. Not in the grand scheme of things.

'Was the lorry a hearse? Only, there's a box under here.' The Pan pointed to the jetty, beneath his feet. 'But if you want my honest opinion, I'd say it's a coffin.' How to put this tactfully? 'Probably quite an old one.'

'Is that on account of that it stinks?'

'Like the Devil's own armpit,' said The Pan and immediately felt guilty for describing some poor dead soul like that, even if it was true.

'There! I knew it was round here somewhere,' the woman heaved a sigh of relief. 'That's the box I'm looking for. The smell is the signal.'

Poor dear. It obviously *was* a coffin and she was looking for a dumped relative. Perhaps she'd lobbed it off the bridge the night before herself then had an attack of conscience—or maybe her wife had. Yes. The lorry story must be a cover. Except … The Pan adjusted his hat to shade his eyes better and surveyed the figures at Golden Point.

'Who's in it?' asked The Pan. 'Nobody close, I hope.'

'It's not who, it's what,' said the woman.

'What's in it?' asked The Pan dutifully.

She put a rubber-glove-clad hand to the side of her nose.

'You help me get it ashore, lad, and you'll find out. But we have to be quick.' She turned and called to the others. 'Ahoy! Christine! Bort! Over here!'

The other two figures picked their way through the mud, dumped a sack onto a handcart and started to pull it along the towpath towards the jetty where The Pan was standing.

'What about the others?' asked The Pan, waving a hand at the other two women; Christine and Bort, he now knew they were called.

'Many hands make light work, lad. And speed is the key here.'

'OK. If I help you, am I going to get into trouble?' The Pan asked.

'Not if we're quick.'

Hmm, that wasn't the same as 'no'. 'What's in it for me?'

The woman thought for a moment, contemplating The Pan's tatty boots which were about level with her head. 'Something new for your feet and two Grongolian dollars,' she said.

The Pan raised a cynical eyebrow at her. The Grongolian dollar packed a much weightier punch than the K'Barthan Zloty. It was illegal for K'Barthans to possess them, of course, but there were ways around that, as every K'Barthan knew. If she was willing to dish out a reward like that in return for a little help with a box, there was clearly more cash in this enterprise than she was letting on. He felt guilty haggling, but he knew from experience that a man cannot live by his earnings from Big Merv alone. He therefore ignored his conscience and opened negotiations.

'*Four* Grongolian dollars and a pair of boots.'

The woman glanced nervously up river where the figures around Golden Point seemed to be making their way towards the side, then back at Christine and Bort approaching along the bank. 'My, you drive a hard bargain. Two dollars and two pairs of boots. Good boots though, handmade. They'll last you better than the rubbish you've got on.'

She was talking quickly. She was trying to hide it but she was definitely in a tearing hurry to land the box. Well, of course she was, The Pan reasoned, or she would have waited for her wife and daughter and they'd have dislodged the box themselves, rather than asking him for help. Hmm. Two pairs of boots would be good. And at the current exchange rate two Grongolian dollars was a fair few K'Barthan Zloty. Yeh. Thinking about it, it still seemed an awful lot of reward for helping someone to recover a box. If he held out on her, he could probably get a lot more. Or maybe he should try a different tack. Grongolian dollars were probably a bit of a risk to a blacklisted man and there was always the danger that they were forged. On the other hand, contraband was a different matter entirely. Yep, it might be worth taking a gamble.

'Alright, look, forget the dollars.' A flicker of disappointment crossed the woman's face; the dollars probably were forgeries then. 'How about two pairs of boots and a quarter of the contents of the box? Or, at least, a quarter of whichever bit of the contents it is that you are after,' suggested The Pan, praying to Arnold, The Prophet, that it wasn't a body.

'Done,' she said, just like that. 'Now take this.' She passed The Pan the long pole which was, indeed, a billhook. 'If you go over the other side and give the box a shove, I'll be able to get it round the supports. I'm not strong enough to drag it out on my own. Or at least, if I do, I may not be able to hang onto it. The currents are more powerful than they look round here—I don't want it to be carried away. Once you've pushed it though to me, then if you hook it and help me drag it over to the shallow water, we can beach it on the shore. Chop, chop though, laddio! Let's not dawdle. I'm not the only person who's after this.'

The box was wedged fast, and as The Pan tried to work it free he had to lean out over the water. He stopped for a moment and removed his hat, putting it safely out of the way. It would be a pity if it fell off in the Dang.

'What are you doing?'

'Sorry, give me a minute.' He leaned out again wedging the billhook against the box and pushing. It began to move. He leaned harder, just to check. Yes! Slowly, it was shifting. The Pan noticed that the other two women had parked the handcart and were now making their way through the mud to the water's edge. They waded out a little way, until the water was lapping at the tops of their wellington boots, and waited, billhooks at the ready. He turned his attention back to the matter in hand and felt the box move again.

'I think I've got it!' he said. 'Just a little bit more pressure,' he told her as he leaned out even further to put more force behind the billhook. It would be a pity if it slipped now, he reflected, at which point it did exactly that. He lost his footing and tumbled forward into the stinking water with a splash.

Marvellous. That'd be a trip to the launderette on top of the bath house then. On the upside, he hadn't swallowed any water, so he'd probably live—his head hadn't gone under. It being summer, his cloak and coat were in his wheels along with a change of socks and underwear and his few clothes. Most importantly, his hat was safely on the jetty.

Now that he was actually in the water, he could see where one of the box's rope handles had caught. It took no time to work it free. 'There, that's got it,' he said.

Wading gingerly through the supports under the jetty,

feeling his way with his feet, he moved through to the other side where he joined the lady mudlarker.

'Thank you, young fellow,' she said as they dragged the box to the shore. 'What's your name?'

'I'm The Pan of Hamgee,' he said inclining his head in a bow.

'I'm Terri,' she replied as they reached the waterline. By this time, Christine and Bort were waiting for them.

Christine manhandled the box with consummate ease. She was a petite blonde lady, whose fragility of appearance belied her strength. Bort was also blonde, and heart-stoppingly pretty. The Pan doubted there were many women who could rock waterproof trousers, a vest top and wellingtons but clearly Bort was one. She seemed to be resourceful as well as attractive (a devastating combination, The Pan reflected) as she approached the box with a claw hammer. Swiftly she removed the nails from the lid with casual precision and lined them up on the jetty.

'We have to reseal it and put it back in the river when we're done,' she explained.

'You do? Why?' asked The Pan.

'You'll see,' said Terri.

'There, that's the last of them,' said Bort as she removed the final nail and kicked the lid off.

The box was full of rancid meat, the smell of which was so overpowering that The Pan turned and gagged, much to the amusement of the three women.

By the time he'd composed himself they were delving around in their newly acquired stinking cargo with rubber gloves on. The Pan stood and watched, his soaking clothes clammily sticking to his body. While they were busy he may as well get dry, he decided. After a struggle, he extricated his keys from the sodden embrace of his pockets and pressed the button that would summon his wheels. That was better.

Being a man of no fixed abode, The Pan kept all his possessions in his snurd. It wasn't just his transport that was on its way, it was clean clothes and a towel, too.

He squelched his way back down the jetty to the spot where he'd left his hat. He smelled appalling but it was nothing on the stench of the putrefying meat in the box. He was glad to get away from it for a few moments. As he started back down the jetty, hat in hand, to join the three women, he looked upstream in the direction of Graden End Bridge and Golden Point. A crowd of beings was striding along the towpath in their direction.

There was something about the way they were walking. The Pan knew that walk; it was one of purpose, of intent. People who were looking for him often walked that way, usually when they wanted to thump him. He hurried back to the three women, on the bank.

'Ladies,' he said.

'How many boxes d'you reckon there should be, Terri?' Christine was asking as The Pan joined her and her family.

'Four or five,' Terri was saying as Christine fished out a plastic box from among the reeking meat.

Clearly this was good. The three women were almost shaking, they were so excited about their find. It was a pity to rain on their parade but The Pan felt he'd earned his cut of the contents—and the two pairs of boots. It seemed sensible to make sure that they stayed alive and well, and able to pay him.

'Ladies, you have a problem,' said The Pan as the three women removed more boxes from the stinking meat sludge in which they were hidden.

'Not now, we have to be quick.'

'Yes, you do. That's the problem I'm talking about.' He jerked his head backwards, in the direction of the towpath, where the group of beings he'd seen was approaching. 'You have to leave before they get here.'

Bort stood up and looked past The Pan. As she did so, he turned and looked with her. He couldn't help noticing that the closer it got, the more the group of beings in question was beginning to look like an angry mob.

'Arnold in the skies, they're coming!' she cried.

The women grabbed the plastic boxes, four in all, dunking them in the river to remove the worst of the rancid meat from the outside. The boxes had a strong smell of their own which was prevalent even over the stench of the slurry in which they were packed and the hefty pong of the river.

'Is that Goojan spiced sausage?' asked The Pan, distracted for a moment from the crowd bearing down on them.

Bort rolled her eyes at him. 'Well, duh.'

Goojan spiced sausage was the single most expensive foodstuff in K'Barth. Some incredibly rich and grateful student had given a couple of slices to The Pan's father once, many years ago. It came in a silver presentation box with a green ribbon on it. A year's wages, his mother had said it cost. The Pan doubted it cost that much. And even if it had at the time, it was unlikely that Goojan sausage sold for that much these days—especially if it was contraband or stolen. The amount in the plastic containers probably commanded a decent enough price for the three ladies to retire from mudlarking though. Probably.

'Now help us put this box back in the river.'

'Why?'

'We need to look as if we haven't opened it yet,' said Christine.

'It's our only chance; to pretend we're still hauling it onto the deck so they take the empty box and let us go without realising we have the contents. Quick.'

The Pan held the lid in place while Bort hammered the

nails back. She left some half out, for authenticity, in case the mob moved so fast she had to pretend she was actually opening it when they arrived, he assumed.

'This is not a good plan. You know that, don't you?' he said.

'It's the only one we have. What would you do?'

'I'd run.'

'They'll run too.'

The Pan thought about his snurd SE2. Arnold's snot! Where was the smecking thing? It should be here by now.

'What will they do to you?' he asked. The crowd was getting closer—he could hear shouts and voices now.

'Take the box,' said Christine.

'But we have the stuff,' said Bort.

'And while they're looking in the box, we escape in the melee,' explained Terri.

'What about the smell of the sausage?' asked The Pan. 'They'll know you unpacked it from that.'

'We've got away with worse.'

The approaching crowd was closing fast when The Pan was distracted, for a moment, by a bubbling sound behind him. With a huge eruption of muddy water and unpleasantly taupe-coloured foamy bubbles, his snurd surfaced.

At last.

It morphed half into boat mode but stayed mostly in submariner mode and cruised closer, backing up towards the bank and The Pan. Its top was retracted, ready for a quick getaway.

The three women stared at the snurd and The Pan.

Meanwhile the crowd had arrived and started spilling along the jetty and climbing down the bank, shouting. They were clearly after blood if the stones and bottles they were lobbing with abandon were anything to go by.

'Blimey!' said The Pan. 'You can take your chances with them if you want! I'm not. D'you want a lift?'

The three women hesitated, perhaps wondering about the stuff on their cart.

'Seriously, come with me,' The Pan said.

Still they havered. What were they doing?

'Come on!' he shouted, holding his hand out. 'Go time!'

The leader of the crowd pursuing them started squelching across the mud towards them, his colleagues hot on his heels. They were armed with poles, bill hooks, chains and in one case, a large oar. Luckily the one in front slipped on the slimy mud and fell on his back bringing the advance of the whole party to a temporary halt while some of the others hauled him up again.

The three women finally came to a decision and bundled into The Pan's snurd SE2, Terri in the passenger seat, and Christine and Bort in the space behind. Someone threw a rock which bounced off the top of the windscreen and spun away into the water. Ah yes, the roof. The Pan pressed a button and the polymorphic metal oozed into position over their heads.

'Hold tight,' he said. But as the snurd started forward the crowd of pursuers suddenly halted, the noise of their shouts dying away as an amplified voice came from above.

'Stay where you are! Nobody move.'

Above them a Grongolian police snurd was hovering. For a moment there was silence, broken only by the quiet humming of the SE2's engine as it motored quietly out into the stream.

'I said, nobody move!' shouted the voice. The surface of the water in front of the snurd leapt and boiled as the police snurd sprayed it with machine-gun fire. Warning shots.

Terri screamed.

'I'm really sorry about this but I'm afraid I'm not going

to be able to do what he says,' whispered The Pan.

'They told us to stay put. It's just a check,' said Christine.

'Not for me it isn't.'

'Then let us out,' said Terri.

'Sorry, can't do that.'

'Mum, Christine? We're sinking,' said Bort as very slowly, the snurd started to submerge.

'Actually, we're diving,' said The Pan.

'Then stop! You'll get us killed.'

'No,' said The Pan as the water level began to climb up the windscreen, 'with any luck, we'll be fine. I've done this before.'

At about that moment, a deputation of security forces troops turned up on the towpath and the ones in the hovering snurd above finally noticed that The Pan's wheels were quietly disappearing from sight.

'STOP! Resurface and get out of your vehicle!' ordered the police snurd driver down his megaphone.

'No,' said The Pan. He turned the vehicle's nose downward, accelerated, and in what felt like slow motion, not to mention a hail of laser and machine gun fire, the snurd sank into the murky river.

Chapter 2
Escape ... or not

Luckily the Grongles were rubbish shots, The Pan was glad to see, as the SE2 disappeared into the murky depths. It appeared to be undamaged. Visibility in the River Dang was near zero, so he pressed the button on the dash which turned on the underwater guidance system. For a moment nothing happened but when he thumped it, just above the steering wheel, the snurd finally deigned to project a blurry heads-up display onto the windscreen in front of him. The picture was fuzzy, the vertical hold was rubbish as well and it kept jumping, but it was enough—The Pan could see where he was going now, sort of. As he crept through the murk, he knew that a few yards behind, the police snurd was probably doing the same thing. He accelerated and made his way, as fast as he dared, to the deepest part of the channel. 'Don't worry. Unless I'm mistaken, that's only a series five squad vehicle.'

'They had lasers,' said Bort.

'Yes, but only as an aftermarket add on. The rest of the tech's a bit old and their underwater detection equipment is even worse than the stuff on mine. We'll be home free in a jiffy.'

It was a lie, but somehow, with three passengers on board, The Pan felt a responsibility to provide reassurance. The three women said nothing. Maybe they were in shock. Yes. Probably. Or it might have been the smell, The Pan reflected. What with him and the sausage, the air in the snurd was pretty ripe.

The Pan drove down to Graden End Bridge, turned behind one of the supporting piers until the SE2 was on the other side of it, facing the way he'd come, and then let it sink slowly to the bottom. He dropped the anchor so it would hold position in the current and turned off the engine.

'What are you doing?' asked Terri.

'Shhh! In the name of The Prophet! They may have listening equipment and if they do, they'll hear you,' said The Pan. 'We're pretending to be a rock.'

They waited in the murk where The Pan had stopped. Sitting in silence, the four of them heard the muffled sounds of the police snurd's motor as it passed under the bridge. It didn't stop and as they waited the sound receded into the distance. Good. Now The Pan was as sure as he could be, going by the SE2's temperamental instrumentation, that he'd lost any waterborne pursuit.

'We should probably wait a little while, just in case they think they hit us and that we might resurface. They may realise they've gone past us without noticing. They don't usually, so they're probably miles away, but I like to belt and brace.'

The Pan reckoned fifteen minutes would be enough to let the pursuit cool its heels. He switched the engine back on and the oxygen pump kicked in.

They sat there in silence. The Pan felt a bit of tension in the air. Something was up. He would try and defuse it with conversation. 'Blimey, those sausages hum a bit!' he said cheerfully.

Nothing.

'I didn't realise mudlarking was so dangerous.'

Still nothing. He wasn't sure if they were sulking or in shock. 'We'll give it a minute or two and then we should be able to leave. I can drop you off wherever you like. Have a think and let me know.'

'They'll be watching all the slipways,' said Bort.

'It's alright, we don't need to use them.'

Not all snurds could take off from water, but, despite

being little more than a wreck, The Pan's could … usually.
He explained this to them.

'Thank you for trying to help us,' said Terri.

Trying to help us, as in, not helping us at all, perhaps? She
may have thanked him but her heart wasn't in it, that much
was obvious. The Pan turned to her, sitting beside him. 'I've
cocked it up though haven't I? Something's not right.'

'It was the handcart,' blurted Bort from the back.

'My ID,' said Terri. 'I left it there because I was going
right in. I was worried I'd lose it and now I have. It's in my
bag,' she added.

'On the cart?' asked The Pan, with sinking heart.

'Yes.'

Arnold. That changed everything. Why, why, why did
this have to happen? The Pan knew exactly how to save
Bort and Christine, not to mention his own skin. He should
stay where he was. But the punishment for failing to
produce a valid ID was instant blacklisting so if he did that,
and Terri lost her ID, he was condemning her to a life like
his. Perhaps he already had. How long had it been? He
glanced at his watch. Five minutes? Not more than ten. In
that case maybe all was not lost. Not yet.

'OK. Then we have to get it back. There's still time,' he
said.

His thoughts raced—how to go about this? The
Grongles might leave the cart, but most likely they'd
impound it, in case there was anything interesting the
troopers who'd found it could sell or nick. OK, so The Pan
knew what he was going to do.

'Hang on,' he said as he retracted the anchor. He put the
snurd in gear and surfaced as quickly as he could.

'What are you doing?'

'Getting your ID back.'

He took a cursory glance around for pursuers. No-one at
the moment. But that didn't really mean anything—they

were probably waiting in ambush somewhere. Never mind. Needs must.

'You can't,' said Terri.

'Actually, you're right there, *I* can't. But you, Bort or Christine can,' The Pan said as he selected 'aviator' mode and accelerated.

Even on the small waves of the river the snurd skipped and bounced before finally getting airborne.

'They'll take the cart down the towpath to the nearest street,' he explained. 'They probably have a vehicle waiting for it by now, but if I drop you off ahead of them, you should be able to intercept them before they get there and grab the bag.'

'How?' said Bort.

'We'll just ask them,' said Terri.

'That might not work,' said The Pan.

'It will if two of us distract them with questions and the other gets my bag off the cart.'

'Maybe you should hide yourselves while I bait them somehow. Then, while they're busy shooting at me, one of you can grab the bag.'

'Isn't that dangerous?'

'Not if you're quick.'

'I meant, for you,' said Terri.

'Not really,' lied The Pan. 'I'll just let them run after me for a bit and then hop in the snurd. It has shields.'

'It does?' asked Christine from the back. She sounded dubious.

'Yes.' OK, so they didn't work very well, or at all sometimes, but they were better than nothing. 'How else d'you think we escaped without being shot up just now?'

'I thought they had rubbish aim,' said Bort.

Blimey, she'd got that one bang to rights. 'Well, yes, you're spot on there. Most of them couldn't hit a barn door at point-blank range. I think they only shoot to make you stop, anyway. If you ask me, they prefer to catch their quarry alive and give it a good kicking close to. That's why, in the miraculous event that one of them actually manages to hit the snurd, I'll be fine,' said The Pan. 'Let's see what's happening.'

He flew over the spot where they'd found the box.

'Look! The others are going,' said Christine.

Sure enough, the crowd of angry mudlarkers was dispersing, with a lot of heavy-handed persuasion from the Grongolian security forces.

It seemed that everyone below them was too busy running, or firing, to notice the snurd above them.

'Good riddance!'

The Pan checked the skies around him, there was no sign of the police snurd—it must still be chasing them up river. Meanwhile, further ahead of them, he saw three Grongle security forces troopers pulling the hand cart along the towpath.

'Down there!' he pointed. 'I don't think they've noticed us either. I'll go round and keep out of sight.'

The Pan turned away from the Grongles with the cart and flew a circuitous route just above the trees and buildings to a spot further along the path. Finally, he found a place out of the Grongle's line of sight, behind some trees, and landed his wheels—in an area that was actually designated for the purpose, for once—skidding quickly to a halt. He pressed the button to retract the roof and leapt out of the SE2 so he could help the women to get out too.

The other two ran on in their wellingtons but Terri took a few seconds longer, encumbered as she was, by her chest high waders.

'There's not much time, go!' said The Pan as Bort realised her mother wasn't keeping up and returned for her.

'Quick Mum, they're coming!' she said, and they turned and ran.

'I'll wait here, shall I?' called The Pan to their departing backs. He wasn't sure if they'd heard him. Never mind, he'd wait anyway. They might need some help from him and if he wanted his reward he had no choice. Except ... he sniffed the air. Had they?

He glanced into the footwell and noticed a bag. It was the bag in which the women had stowed the four plastic boxes they'd found.

'That's very trusting of you, ladies,' he said.

He knew what he should do now. He had enough Goojan sausage to make him a millionaire several times over sitting in the footwell of his snurd. Furthermore, the owners of the sausage were embroiled in an encounter from which, if he was honest, they were unlikely to escape. Or at least not without his help.

The Pan knew the sensible course to take, even if it was downright dishonourable. He should look after number one; leave the women to their fate, steal the sausage, sell it, buy a new non-blacklisted ID and retire with the spare millions.

Yeh right. Then again, while dishonourable came easily enough when dying was the alternative, he'd never been big on sensible.

What was he even thinking? There were four Goojan sausages in the footwell and one of them was theoretically his, along with two pairs of boots. One sausage was quite enough. He didn't need three more. Then again, would they *really* give him one of the sausages, even if they'd promised? There was no way to be sure. However, even if they didn't, after what happened to his father, mother, brother and sister he knew he hadn't the stomach to leave them to their fate ... Yeh. And sausage or no sausage, something would go wrong. It always did. Then he'd just end up being responsible for more deaths and still blacklisted. And he'd told these three women he'd help them. He'd talked about providing a distraction. Yeh, and it wasn't as if it would have any dire consequences, was it? Not for him. He was a delivery man for a gangster and his existence was punishable by death. That was about as dire as it got. He could hardly make things worse.

Yep. Decision made.

The Pan got swiftly out of the snurd. If he was going to help Terri, Christine and Bort it would be sensible to go and see how they were getting on. Yeh, and he'd better get a move on and all. They were striding out along the path. They'd meet the Grongles with their cart any moment.

The Pan ran across an open lawn to cut them off. There was enough cover to watch events unseen. Although the cover came in the form of some council planting; a couple of trees and some ornamental shrubs of the incredibly fast-growing, spiky kind beloved only by town planners. It was definitely more at the impenetrable thicket end of the shrubbery spectrum but it was still passable, with care. The Pan sneaked his way carefully in and concealed himself. By the time the women intercepted the Grongles, they were only a few yards away. He waited and listened.

Chapter 3
Back into danger

Bort walked beside Christine and Terri on the towpath. 'What's the plan?' asked Christine as they walked.

Terri stopped. 'Explain that the cart is ours and ask for it back. We'll busk it from there,' she said. 'If we pitch it right, we should get my bag back. We might even get the cart too. Come on! Tally ho, ladies.'

'Shouldn't *you* ask? You're way more eloquent than I am,' said Christine.

'Until I get that bag back I'm a non-being. So you two have to talk to them while I get close to the bag. Then when they ask for ID I can get mine out as if I was carrying it all the time.'

'They're not going to fall for that! Nobody could be that stupid,' whispered Bort.

'Darling, you wouldn't believe how stupid some folks can be.'

'Here's hoping,' muttered Bort as she walked behind them.

'And some Grongles are a great deal pleasanter than others. It'll be luck of the draw.'

Bort hoped she was right. She could feel the butterflies in her stomach on her mother's behalf—less like butterflies to be honest and more like elephants with wings that didn't work very well and had to keep jumping a lot to stay in the air. What if the bag wasn't there? What if the Grongles had taken the ID out of the bag? 'What if?' she whispered.

'You alright, Bort?'

'Yes,' she sighed.

'Come on then, anchors aweigh, girls. Let's get this over with,' said Terri.

'They can only say no,' said Christine.

'That's what I'm afraid of,' muttered Bort.

The Grongles with the handcart were only about twenty yards away now. They slowed and eyed the three women warily.

'Hi,' said Christine and she shuffled timidly towards them.

'What d'you want?' snarled the Grongle who was leading the way. He was speaking his own language, Grongolian.

'I— well the thing is, you see—'

'This is our handcart,' Bort interrupted them. 'We're mudlarkers and we were on the river this morning when we saw a box floating. The others overheard us talking about it as it drifted past and they came to take it off us.'

She stopped. All three Grongles had halted and were staring at her with expressions of blank incomprehension. Of course, none of them spoke Tithian, the language of K'Barth. Bort thought for a moment. She'd had elementary Grongolian lessons at the community school. Mudlarkers didn't usually go for a formal education as such but back in Glardy, where they'd come from, there was education of a sort. Christine hadn't liked the idea of learning Grongolian. She felt that if the Grongles were going to invade a country the least they could do was subjugate the population in a language it could understand. It was a fair point, well made, but Bort was enough of a realist to continue her studies.

'OK.' She switched to Grongolian. 'Kind sirs, cart is ours, mugged we were.' She paused. Was that the right way around? She wasn't sure. 'We were mugged,' she added. Might as well say it both ways, just in case. 'We ran. Kind sirs you are, you are finding our cart, yes?'

There was a pause.

'This cart is evidence,' said the Grongle who was actually pulling the handcart. He moved a couple of steps nearer, bringing the cart with him.

Bort also moved forward with a hopeful expression, her mother and Christine with her, close at her shoulder. 'Cart is ours, we sign for cart?'

'Can you prove you own it?'

'Yes. Christine?'

Bort moved diagonally across the towpath, towards the cart but also towards the river. But as Christine made to follow her Terri put her hand on her wife's arm.

'No, me,' she said

'Mum?' asked Bort. This wasn't part of the plan.

Briefly, Terri looked down at her feet and up at Bort's face, then walked over to join her daughter. The chest-high waders she was wearing made rubbery squeaky creaking noises as she moved.

Good point Mum, you're never going to get to the bag without them noticing, Bort thought.

Amazingly, all three Grongles turned and watched Terri's progress as she joined her daughter. Bort nearly laughed as her mother adopted her best apologetic expression. She'd seen that look on her face so many times and it always seemed to work.

'It's in my boots,' Terri explained.

'What did she say?' demanded the one who'd been leading the others, bad temperedly. The other Grongle, the more polite one who'd been pulling the hand cart, made as if to speak. But the third stepped in front of him and drew his gun.

'No funny business,' he said.

'This is most definitely NOT funny,' said Terri.

'What did she say?' asked the grumpy one again.

Arnold's buttocks, he was like a cracked record! Bort wondered why the Grongles never learned Tithian. Even though she'd made the effort to learn some Grongolian herself, she totally got Christine's viewpoint on that issue. It was smecking rude. Never mind. She took a deep breath.

'Sorry is she,' Bort explained, 'card is in here.' She bent down to point to her mother's wader-clad feet. Bort was what her father, had he been around, might have called a 'comely lass'. Since the Grongles were all male, she made sure she bent down in a manner that was as distracting as possible. They watched her. She noticed the one with the gun nudging the grumpy one doing most of the talking. The third, who'd been pulling the cart, wore a guarded expression. Perhaps he was the odd one out. Could she use that? Difficult to tell but it was worth remembering. For now, her feminine wiles had done the trick—she had all their attention and they didn't appear to notice as, behind them, she caught a glimpse of Christine removing the handbag from the cart and creeping backwards. The ID was back with them and they were home free. As Christine slipped the bag over her shoulder, Bort switched off all her efforts at feminine allure with a great deal of relief.

The Grongle with the laser pistol was still pointing it at her, and the grumpy-sneery one suddenly seemed more animated, more interested. It made her nervous.

'You have papers for that cart?' said the Grongle.

'Mum?' asked Bort.

'No papers, I bought it for cash. But I have proof. My shoes are on the cart,' said Terri. 'All our shoes are on the cart. We wouldn't wear wellies every day and I certainly wouldn't wear waders.'

'Especially in weather like this,' Christine chipped in. 'If we can show you that our feet fit the shoes, will you believe us?'

Bort translated.

'Maybe,' said the Grongle.

'We get shoes now?'

'No.' He turned to the one who'd been pulling the cart. 'Get the shoes and hand them over.'

The cart puller, who was definitely odd-one-out Grongle, did as he was told. He lined up the shoes, in pairs, on the ground in front of the three women. He glanced up at Bort as he did this with a look of warning.

Terri undid the braces on her waders and rolled them down to her waist. The Grongles watched. Underneath she was wearing shorts, a t-shirt and socks. Unfortunately, after a couple of hours trogging about wearing thick, armpit-high rubber waders in the heat the t-shirt and shorts were so damp with sweat that they were sticking to her, outlining every curve.

Bort watched the Grongles looking at her mother. She was way too old to be of interest to them, surely except … were they ogling her? They *were* ogling her! The pervy smeckers! Grumpy Grongle stood with his hands on his hips looking straight at Terri. His eyes travelled slowly down to her feet and back up to her face again. There was something in his manner that struck fear into Bort's heart. Her mum had curves like she did, well, she'd inherited them from somewhere after all, but her mum was fifty, for Arnold's sake. Surely he wasn't going to—

No! He never! Gross! She wasn't even going to think about it.

'If shoes fit, shows cart is ours?' asked Bort.

'Perhaps,' said the grumpy Grongle. The gun-toting one snickered and the odd-one-out fidgeted nervously.

Something was up. Bort could see that, but she wasn't exactly sure what it was, only that she was very afraid it might somehow involve the surly one trying to snog her mum.

Chapter 4
Uh-oh

A few yards up the towpath, The Pan of Hamgee watched from his prickly hiding place. It seemed to be going alright. Christine had got the bag and it looked as if they were in the clear on the ID front, even if they might not get the cart. All the same, he had a feeling he should wait until he was certain. The Pan wasn't a man to ignore his instincts. In his banned existence he was learning to trust them more and more. They seldom let him down.

He shifted position to get more comfortable. Thank The Prophet his clothes were beginning to dry even if his accidental plunge into the river had left him smelling evilly. He was glad that he was in a hiding place that was still near the Dang. At least, here, if the Grongles got a whiff of him, they'd think the strong stench of river water was merely ... well ... the actual river. The Dang honked mightily at the best of times, after all.

As The Pan watched, the three women were still speaking to the Grongles but he couldn't make out everything that was being said. However, what little he could hear didn't sound right. Something was definitely up. Slowly, stealthily, he began to creep a little closer so he could hear more of the conversation.

****

Back at the cart, Terri, Bort and Christine were now wearing their proper footwear. Christine was a cobbler and back at the barge on which they lived she had a small workshop area. She blagged leather scraps and made boots and shoes. In the case of her family, these were good sturdy lace-up boots and shoes which lasted several years, like the pair Bort was wearing.

'See shoes,' said Bort, 'they fit. You believe cart ours. You let us take cart?'

'I'm surprised you care about the cart. I'd have thought you wanted this,' The Grongle put his hand in one of the pouches on his belt, took out Terri's ID card and held it up. As he did so Christine gasped and put her hand to the bag slung over her shoulder. 'Do you really think I didn't notice you take that bag?'

'I'd hoped,' muttered Terri.

'What did she say?'

'She said she knows you kind being and glad you keep her ID safe,' said Bort.

'I bet she does. But now I have a problem. Your mother understands me, yes?'

'We all understand you.'

'Then if they understand Grongolian, maybe your mother and her friend should get off their lazy K'Barthan backsides and learn to speak it like you do.' Bort ached to make a withering retort but decided it would be wiser to say nothing. The Grongle continued. 'I'd like to give you your cart back, but you have no ID.'

'She does!' Bort replied. 'She leave ID on cart while she in river. ID safer on cart than on her in river.'

'She lost her ID though.'

'No! ID always on cart. She leave ID on cart for safety. That not losing ID, that looking after ID. Losing ID is not knowing where ID is.'

'She didn't know where her ID was just now, when she got her friend to take the bag.'

Bort's desperation to help her mother spurred her to argue. 'You moved ID from where she put it.'

The Grongle laughed, a condescending chuckle that left Bort wishing she could thump him.

'Oh dear. Ladies, ladies … I don't think you understand. If she's careless with her ID and lets others steal it, along with her cart, it's not my lookout.'

'Yes it is. It crime. If she has crime done to her, she tell policeman. You policeman,' Bort argued, ignoring the fact that the beings who'd 'stolen' the cart and her mother's ID were these Grongles.

'I am *not* a policeman,' snarled the Grongle. 'I'm a member of the security forces. The police, waste of space that they are, are K'Barthan.'

'That even better then, you better than policeman. You can help us, yes?'

'No. We don't return stolen goods. We keep order.'

'Is the same thing, yes?'

'No. What you natives do to one another is no concern of mine.'

'How can you even—' began Bort, but stopped as she felt the gentle pressure of her mother's hand on her arm.

Terri's Grongolian was worse than Bort's but she had a go anyway. 'You are please to give me the ID,' she said.

'Oh, so you *can* speak my language.'

'Not well. I sorry.'

'Unlucky. I think I'll keep this …' The Grongle held it up for a moment and then put it back in the pouch on his belt. 'Unless you can make it worth my while.'

'OK, you take cart,' said Terri, adding, 'that what you want, yes?'

'No, ladies.' The ironic flourish with which he said the word 'ladies' was unmistakeable. 'It's more complicated than that. You see, you've been very careless. You've left your possessions where they could be stolen and your actions would have sparked a riot if we hadn't been there to stop it. Right, boys?' The Grongle with the gun snickered again. Odd-one-out looked down at the ground. 'If I was less of a compassionate being, I'd charge all three of you with disturbing the peace. That's a serious crime which comes with a custodial sentence.'

Bort took a breath to apologise but he spoke over her.

'As it is, I'm willing to overlook this.' He flashed Terri a nasty smile. 'I'm going to give you back your ID. But if I'm going to show such kindness I want something in return.' He glanced at Bort and licked his lips, like a crocodile sizing up a tasty snack.

'I have cash or—' Terri began, but he spoke over her.

'No. Not cash. Her.' He pointed to Bort.

'What?! She's only eighteen!'

'Then she's over the age of consent. What she does is up to her.' He turned, leering towards Bort. 'Isn't it?'

Bort nearly gagged.

'He can't do this, it's against the law,' said Christine.

'What did she say?'

Bort could hardly speak. All the while the Grongle leered at her, his mouth hooked into a nasty smile.

No. Way. 'Deal like this against law,' she whispered.

'I am the law. I decide what's legal. Listen sweetheart, it's not forever. Twenty-four hours only.' He turned to Terri and Christine and in far too sarcastic a tone for comfort he added, 'We won't hurt her, will we lads? We'll just show her a good time. And we'll give her back at the end. With your ID.'

'Yeh,' the one with the gun agreed.

Behind the two of them, where they couldn't see, their odd-one-out colleague caught Bort's eye and almost imperceptibly, shook his head.

****

A few feet away, listening from behind the nearby bushes, The Pan watched these latest developments in utter horror.

'We,' the Grongle had said. 'We,' The Pan thought. It was a very bad sign. He racked his brains for a way to create a

distraction. But how could he do that from here? These were rubbish odds: three Grongles, all armed, one with his laser pistol already drawn, against one hopelessly inept Hamgeean and some ladies who, though brave, were unlikely to be combat trained. And he couldn't fight. He knew that. Flight was his speciality. What could he do?

The Pan spoke Grongolian a lot more fluently than the three women but there'd be no reasoning with these Grongles. Apart from the fact they were clearly not reasonable, they might recognise him. Even if they didn't, they might ask him for his papers and then recognise him, or realise he didn't have any papers and arrest him, anyway. At the same time, The Pan couldn't condemn Bort to twenty-four hours with those apes. She was only a little younger than he was. She had a lifetime ahead of her to be happy and this ... this would screw her up. The Grongle doing the talking didn't sound like the kind to keep his word. If he didn't kill her he'd certainly hurt her and he was unlikely to set her free.

The Grongle took Terri's ID from the pouch on his belt again. Holding it aloft, he taunted the three females, daring them to try and grab it.

The Pan's hand went to his shirt pocket where he kept a membership card to the lido in Hamgee. It was about the same size and shape as an ID card and made from similar plastic. He kept it in his top pocket in the hope that any members of the police or security forces who noticed him would see its outline under the material, mistake it for a proper, legal form of ID and not bother to ask him to show it.

None of the parties around the cart had noticed him—they were all absorbed in their conversation and most importantly, the Grongles had their backs to him. The Pan hatched a plan, and before he really realised what he was doing, rose quietly to his feet and started to put it into action. It was a rubbish plan, truly abysmal. On the other hand, it was so awful that no-one in their right mind would do anything so stupid. That gave him the element of surprise. Although possibly not quite in the right way. It might work though ... possibly.

He walked quickly and stealthily towards the cart. The three women and the Grongles were too absorbed in their conversation to notice him. Although in two of the Grongles' case it was probably Bort who was commanding most of their attention. Hopelessly inept The Pan may be, but he was quick. And this particular plan was about speed above all else.

****

The Grongle continued to wave Terri's ID card in the air, switching his leering gaze from her, to her daughter and back again. 'If anything were to happen to this you'd be guilty of proceeding without proper identification. I'm sure you know the punishment for that.'

Yes, everyone did. Terri's name would be added to the blacklist and her existence would be illegal. She'd be arrested and dragged off to prison or a labour camp, forever. The Grongle paused theatrically, presumably to give the idea time to sink in, in case it hadn't already.

'So we have your little girl round to the mess on a play date, or I'm going to keep this, in which case, it'll be the end for you anyway.' He and the one with the gun laughed. The other, pale faced and thin lipped, watched on.

'No,' said Terri. 'She's only eighteen.'

'And I told you, that's above the age of consent.'

'She isn't consenting.'

Still holding the ID the Grongle put his other hand in his pocket and pulled out a lighter. 'Think hard about your answer. I don't have to keep my word. I could burn this and take you instead,' he lectured her as Bort watched helplessly

34

on. 'Once this is gone, you cease to exist. I don't have to give *you* back.' He waved the ID.

'Stop!' said Christine.

'Are you threatening to mislay my mum?' demanded Bort. She was surprised at the power in her voice.

'No. I'm making you both an offer, little girl; you or her. Choose.'

'Wait,' said Bort.

'No, Bort,' said Terri.

'Twelve hours and you give back the ID first,' said Bort.

'Twenty four or nothing,' said the Grongle.

'Bort! You're not doing this,' said Terri. 'It's OK, we'll manage. We'll find another way.'

'I've thought of another way,' said the Grongle with the gun. 'Let's take both of them.'

The other started laughing. 'Yeh, I can't be arsed to play nice.'

'No,' said Christine.

'Wait a minute!' snapped Bort. 'You said—'

****

The Pan broke into a run. He reckoned the Grongle who'd been pulling the cart—the odd-one-out—might have heard his last couple of strides, as he reached the metalled towpath and his boots clattered on the asphalt. However, if he did notice The Pan's approach he made no move to intervene. Meanwhile, the heat and their heavy body armour appeared to have made the other two sluggish. They were far too slow to react.

The Pan cannoned into the one with Terri's ID at full tilt. In a tangle of flailing arms and legs the two of them fell to the ground. The Grongle with the ID dropped it and failed to notice as The Pan switched it, and that it was the out-of-date pass to the lido in Hamgee which he picked up and shoved in his pocket in the confusion.

35

As this was happening, the third Grongle, the one who'd been pulling the cart, appeared to try and help the other two. But as he moved towards them he bumped into one of the cart handles, sending the cart cannoning into his other colleague and throwing him off balance. He, too, fell, landing on his prone friend just as *he* was trying to get up. The collision knocked the laser pistol from his hand, and The Pan got away from them, kicking the weapon as he fled. It spun away into the River Dang where it sank into the few inches of muddy water with a feeble electronic fizz.

'Run!' The Pan shouted as he took off.

The three women didn't exactly need telling as they'd already started off—in the other direction.

'No!' There was no cover that way, it would get them killed. 'This way!' shouted The Pan.

The Grongle who'd dropped his gun leapt up to give chase, only to collide with the one who had been pulling the cart for a second time. Down they went, flailing and kicking so much that a stray kick caught the surly one as he started in pursuit of The Pan and the women, bringing him down for a second time, too.

The Pan ran for his life in the direction of the trees and shrubs where he'd been hiding. Christine, Bort and Terri ran too. As they fled, The Pan fumbled his snurd keys from his pocket and pressed the homing button. The three Grongles were following hard on their heels but the women had an impressive turn of speed. The Pan was glad they were wearing their shoes now, rather than wellies and waders. They were keeping up with him and he was faster than most people. The four of them began to gain on the Grongles. The Pan heard his snurd's tyres screech as it answered his call. It headed straight across the middle of the bowling green.

Oh dear. Now every elderly being in this part of town would join the many and varied group of individuals who were after The Pan's neck! Never mind. He and the three women kept running.

'We have to get to the snurd,' he panted, 'they'll stop and shoot soon.'

'You said they can't hit anything!' wheezed Bort.

'I lied.'

'What!'

'Was … trying to … reassure you,' he puffed as he ran.

Through his extra eyes, the ones in the back of his head, The Pan of Hamgee saw the Grongles stop. The one who'd recently been denuded of his weapon had already flipped open his Grongolian army issue smartphone, calling down back-up no doubt, while the others levelled their laser pistols and fired. A bolt of red light fell short, but only just. The asphalt behind them bubbled.

'If we keep this up, we're done for!' shouted Terri.

'Not far to go! You can do it! Keep running!' shouted The Pan.

'Do something!' shouted Bort.

They reached a strip of likely looking hedge and The Pan's snurd crashed through it in an explosion of flying foliage and branches. It spun to a screeching halt front of them, facing the same direction they were headed, with a trail of earth and roots strewn across the path behind it. Thank Arnold for that! Without slowing his pace, The Pan took a running jump into the driver's seat. Terri, Christine and Bort took slightly longer but managed to get inside as another volley of laser fire from the Grongles hit the branch of a nearby tree and brought it down with a crash.

The Pan pressed a button and the roof began to move into position. He didn't wait for it to finish—it was definitely time to go. He accelerated away, selecting 'aviator' mode as he went, and took off. The Grongles below fired half-heartedly at the snurd as it rose into the sky, but let them leave.

Chapter 5
A sharp exit

'Sorry that was a bit of a close shave,' said The Pan as the SE2 rose swiftly into the sky. 'Here.' He handed Terri her ID.

With the metal roof in position, the smell of the sausage, not to mention the river residue on The Pan's (now dry) clothes was strong. He opened a window. 'Also, I'm sorry I fell in. I smell like a sewer.'

'I think we can forgive you,' said Terri as she stuffed her ID down her bra.

'Thank you for waiting for us,' said Bort.

'I should drop you off somewhere.'

'Not here. There are Grongles everywhere now,' said Terri, looking down.

'Mmm,' said The Pan, putting the snurd into a climb. If they had any larger ordnance down there he saw no point in staying in range. 'I should still drop you off as soon I can. The less time you're with me the better. Where do you live?'

'Our barge is moored on the wasteland by the canal.'

'That could be more or less anywhere,' said The Pan. 'There are several canals and the industrial areas are all a bit wrecked.'

'One of the locals said it's where the old power station was,' said Christine. 'Does that help?'

That made it Lower Right, The Pan reckoned. He turned in the other direction, towards Upper Left.

'Where are you going? It's completely the opposite direction to this!' said Bort.

'Exactly. Do any of the many beings we've offended together this morning know where you're parked at the moment?'

'Moored not parked. It's a barge,' said Bort.

The Pan rolled his eyes and noticed Terri, next to him, smiling to herself as he pointedly rephrased his question.

'Do any of them know where you're *moored?*

It was Terri who shrugged and said, 'I doubt it.'

'Then let's keep it that way. Oh and if I were you, I'd take your sausages and move on before anyone finds out.'

'We need to sell them first.'

Fair point, The Pan thought. He wouldn't want to live in a barge with something that hummed that strongly. It was a mouthwatering, heady scent, like truffles, but after a while he suspected the pleasure of smelling it absolutely all the time might wear thin.

'Where do you live?' asked Christine.

'You don't need to know,' said The Pan.

'I do if you want your boots.'

'Ah, right. Well, look, if you need me, leave a message at The Parrot and Screwdriver pub on Turnadot Street. They'll pass it on.'

'What size are your feet?'

'K'Barthan forty four, Grongolian nine.'

They drove on. There was suspiciously little in the way of pursuit, which worried The Pan immensely. There should have been about fifteen police snurds after them by now.

'It looks as if we've got away with it,' said Christine.

'Have we?' asked Terri.

'Well … possibly. But it would be quite unusual. I'll just double check,' said The Pan.

Even though it looked as if they'd evaded any pursuit, The Pan wasn't confident. Something felt wrong. Nothing he could articulate, unfortunately, but he never ignored his hunches. Not when they'd kept him alive thus far. Just in case they were being followed, he zigzagged backwards and forward across the city in giant loops. It wouldn't be wise to take the women home and drop them off near their place—but a couple of miles away would be alright. He should land somewhere public yet secluded, somewhere where they could quickly fade into the masses, even if there was a police presence. But it also needed to be somewhere where nobody would notice them landing.

Hmm ... tricky.

He reached the end of a sweep towards Lower Left, and turned and headed towards Lower Right, bringing the SE2 much lower so it was almost scraping the tops of the buildings. He looked around. Ahead of them was the Arboretum, an off-shoot of the Botanical Gardens. And beyond it, he could see the wasteland where the old power station had been and where his passengers had told him they were living.

'Hmm, this might work,' he said.

'What might?' asked Terri.

'Well, I don't think we're being followed. It's unusual but perhaps it's too hot and they can't be arsed. However, they'll be looking for us, so I was thinking the Arboretum is a very good place to drop you off. Plenty of room to land, yet, at the same time, there's a lot of cover.' He pointed to it, up ahead. 'Shall I drop you here, ladies?'

'What? You mean land in the trees?' said Bort flatly from the back.

'Yes, well, below them.'

'What's wrong with the street?'

'Just because they can't be arsed to follow us in snurds, doesn't mean we're not being tracked from the ground.'

'How do they do that?'

'Easy, they just put out an APB and officers pounding the beat turn their eyes to the skies and report. Then they work out what direction we're taking and wait where they think we might land.'

'Ah, so that's why we've been zigzagging,' said Terri.

'Yes.'

'I did think you were taking us home via the scenic route,' said Christine. 'If you were driving a taxi I'd think you were hiking up the fare.'

'No, just playing safe. Or at least trying to.'

He explained how the Arboretum was an ideal landing spot for anyone who didn't want to be seen from the skies simply because the trees were old and spread out so as to be easily admired. So they were close enough for shade, but far enough apart for The Pan to navigate easily between their trunks, and land. In days gone by, when everyone went about in horse-drawn carriages, Ning Dang Po's wealthy residents had driven between them admiring the scenery and enjoying the shade. From what The Pan had read—in an old history book he'd found on a bomb site—a drive in the Arboretum was quite the thing a few hundred years previously, especially in summer heatwaves like this one. These days, hardly anyone went there and it had an air of faded splendour. It was only a matter of time before the Grongles bulldozed it all and built over it, he supposed. However, for now, it gave almost constant cover—apart from a clearing, in the middle, and the odd small gap in the canopy here and there which a snurd like The Pan's could easily squeeze through. Yes, it would do nicely.

'And … you can land there?'

'Yeh,' said The Pan, although he conceded that not everyone could.

He scoped the trees carefully. There were only a couple of spaces where the snurd would be able squeeze beneath the canopy and the central clearing was probably best avoided, just in case. Pretty much anywhere else in there would do though. It was an ideal place to drop off his passengers without being seen.

'Is it far to the canal from here?' asked Christine.

The Pan thought for a moment. 'About a mile and a half, I'd say. The remains of the power station are over there,' he pointed.

Terri turned to her wife and daughter in the back. The Pan watched them nod with the eyes in the back of his head.

By the time Terri told him they'd agreed with his idea, he was already positioning the snurd. He put the SE2 into a shallow dive, activated the shielding just in case (not that it did much) nipped through a hole and—

'Holy smeck!' he shouted as a wall of fire opened up from the forest below. Then he, Christine, Terri and Bort were all screaming at the tops of their lungs. The branches around them exploded as the Grongles raked them with machine gun and laser fire. The Pan rapidly put the snurd into a climb through the flying debris. A branch bounced off the bonnet with a sickening crack and so much force that the snurd dipped and almost stalled.

'Arnold's nostrils!' The Pan yelled as he hauled on the wheel and somehow managed to keep the SE2 climbing. Once clear of the trees he made a sharp turn so the pursuers below couldn't get a clear shot through the hole they'd blasted in the treetops. But that wasn't going to help them get out of the way of the reception committee now waiting for him above. Suddenly, it seemed as if every police snurd in Ning Dang Po was lining up to attack from all sides. He could see more on their way, too—distant dots rising up from all over the city like angry wasps. Well, there would be. They had radios after all.

'By The Prophet's socks! Where did they come from?' he wailed as he floored the accelerator and fled in blind panic. His hands slippery with sweat on the steering wheel, his stomach churning, he threw the snurd around the sky trying to present as difficult a target as possible. More and more pursuers appeared from between the buildings, or the streets around, or maybe even out of the sun—it was hard for The Pan to tell.

For a few sickening moments he turned, twisted, looped and spun the snurd in a desperate effort not to collect a direct hit. Sweating and screaming, he hurled the SE2 back and forth across the sky when Terri's excited shout broke through his panic-stricken thoughts.

'Shiver me timbers! You got one!' she shouted. The Pan glimpsed a trail of smoke as one of the police snurds ahead of him dropped out of the sky at high speed, crash landing on the street below.

'I never fired!' shouted The Pan as he rolled the snurd over and over. Turning as sharply as he could at the same time, he avoided a round of good old-fashioned machine-gun fire from one of the less up-to-date vehicles in pursuit.

'Well, *someone* hit him!' shouted Christine from the space behind the seats where she was huddled in with Bort.

As if in answer, a volley of laser fire flashed past them from behind.

'Aaaaargh!' yelled everyone as The Pan rolled the snurd again. Bort had lost all traces of colour in her face and was sitting with her hands over her eyes. Christine and Terri sat in a state of barely contained panic, watching as the round that had missed them hit another of the police vehicles homing in on them. Most of the bolts glanced off the shields but enough got through to set one of the tyres on fire. The flames spread and it crash-landed a short distance from the other one, skidding along the street in a shower of sparks until the two collided. As The Pan sped away into the distance, he caught sight of the occupants of both crashed police snurds running for safety just before their vehicles blew up.

'I can't believe this!' he whispered.

The idiots were shooting each other. The Pan felt a small flutter of hope—he might get himself and his passengers out of this. No, he *would* escape, as long as he kept the snurd moving as erratically and quickly as he could. For a moment there, he'd almost let his fear get the upper hand. But now he was calm. It was going to be alright. There were loads of security forces snurds on his tail but they were way too enthusiastic in their pursuit and were working against one another rather than together. A whole host of clumsy sledgehammers, crashing and banging at a single rolling nut, each one trying to bag their quarry. They were just getting in each others' way; all firing at once, filling the skies with smoke, tracer shot and myriad glancing bolts of laser fire until it was almost impossible to see who was who or what was where.

Yeh.

'It's official. We're not going to die,' he muttered to himself, while his passengers screamed extensively. 'Not today.'

Now he knew he could escape, The Pan's panic began to subside. He flipped the snurd upwards and into the area where the numbers of police vehicles were highest. Everyone started firing. The noise and smoke was indescribable but somehow, by the seat of his pants, he managed to fly straight through and out the other side without so much as a scratch.

'Shields down to five percent,' said the electronic voice of the snurd.

OK, probably a fair few scratches then, and a couple of gouges, and some dents, and now he came to think of it, The Pan was pretty sure that crack across the windscreen hadn't been there a few minutes ago. His passengers sat rigid and white faced as he climbed upwards, away from the circling police snurds below; a tiny black speck against the blinding white light of the sun.

Minutes later it was all over. The Pan had completely crossed the city, so he took the snurd down to ground level. He landed on a deserted street. The houses around them were mostly bombed and while there were signs that K'Barthans were regrouping and rebuilding he doubted it was the kind of place where his presence would be reported.

He slowed to a halt, parking the snurd under a tree. His clothes were soaked for the second time that day, but this time, in sweat, rather than river water. His legs were trembling so much he could hardly press the pedals. But he was alive! By The Prophet's sweaty sandals he was alive! He took a quick glance at his passengers. And so were they.

Arnold's toe jam it felt good.

'Ladies.' His voice was shaky. 'I think this is your stop.'

Chapter 6
Now what?

Terri, Christine and Bort stepped out of the snurd. Still shaking, The Pan followed them, partly because he wasn't sure he could drive any further but mainly because the sour smell of his body odour, plus the residual honk from the Dang on his clothes and boots combined with the overriding smell of the sausages, was almost more than he could stand.

'I'm sorry we're so far away—your boat is on the other side of the city. But there'll be security forces personnel crawling all over that part of town.'

'I can't think why,' said Terri.

'Yeh, me neither,' The Pan said, laughing. It sounded a lot more brittle and nervous than he expected.

'We'll find it,' said Christine.

Bort was staring at The Pan with a look of breathless admiration. 'That was amazing,' she said.

'Good or bad amazing?' asked The Pan.

'Bad at the time but now, kind of good,' said Bort. 'You can drive. I mean, you can, like, *really* drive.'

The Pan shrugged. 'No better than anyone else, I shouldn't think.'

'Actually, a lot better than anyone else,' said Terri. Suddenly she seemed worried. 'Are you with the Resistance?'

'Absolutely not,' said The Pan. Just the thought filled him with such utter dread that he thought he might throw up.

'Are you sure?' asked Christine.

He hiccupped. 'Very,' he said.

'But they steal all the drivers! My dad was—' began Bort

before she picked up on the warning look her mother wore and stopped.

'You see why we ask, don't you?' said Terri. 'I'm surprised you've escaped their notice. They're always very interested in recruiting drivers.'

This was true, and the question of unwelcome overtures from the Resistance was often on The Pan's mind. Indeed, he put a lot of time into not being recruited. Their view of resisting was different to his. They were ruthless and fanatical, and many had sworn to rid the world of Grongles. The Pan didn't want to rid the world of Grongles. He might be a young man, but he was wise enough to know that fighting the Grongles' genocidal tendencies with more of the same wasn't the answer. He just wanted them to get bored with K'Barth and go home. 'I doubt I'm up to Resistance standards.'

Bort laughed. 'Believe me, you so are! Isn't he, Mum?'

The Pan understood that he must be a reasonably talented escape man for the simple reason that he was still at large. But he'd never assumed his abilities outstripped those of the actual professionals. This was partly due to lack of confidence but also because without going head-to-head against a professional there was no way to tell. What with the Resistance 'recruiting' them all, there were no professionals anyway. Even if he was a better driver than he thought, it still didn't change his view about the Resistance. It was a military organisation, and as The Pan understood it, that involved a lot of obeying orders—not his strong suit—along with getting up at six am—also not The Pan's forte—not to mention learning to fight and—an insurmountable problem for The Pan—learning to kill. He might be able to shin up the side of a building and leap from roof to roof like a man who'd grown up in the mountains, but that was just a necessity required to stay alive on the blacklist. The Pan knew his limitations. When trouble came he wasn't the type to stay and fight. He turned and ran. He always had, he always would and he certainly couldn't kill.

How to put that succinctly though?

He shrugged. 'I'd say I'm not their type.'

'I'm glad to hear it,' said Christine with obvious relief.

'Yeh.'

'Thank you for helping us,' said Terri.

'Don't mention it.'

'Where will you go now?' asked Bort.

The Pan flashed her a wry smile. 'The public baths. I doubt anyone'll come looking for me there.'

'Bort meant, do you have anywhere to stay?' said Terri.

'We have a spare bunk,' said Christine. 'And you'd make a good mudlarker, I'll bet.'

'You're observant,' said Terri.

'Yeh,' agreed Bort.

'Want to join our team?'

So, so tempting. They were kind, decent people. But harbouring GBIs was a crime. They'd just end up on the blacklist too.

'Thank you all the same, but I work best alone,' he said.

He handed over the cotton bag containing the plastic boxes of sausages. When Terri took it from him, she rummaged about inside it and removed a green plastic box containing the smallest of the smelly cargo. She pressed it into his hands. 'This one's yours,' she said.

'W— what?' stammered The Pan.

Christine nodded and Bort looked up at him and smiled. The Pan thought it might have been the most heart-stoppingly beautiful smile he'd ever seen. He felt a bit weak about the knees, although that wasn't the smile. Of course it wasn't. It was adrenaline, most likely, and also, perhaps, the effects of imagining the kind of untold wealth selling a whole Goojan sausage would bring. No, the sausage had fallen off the back of a lorry—well, the side—and a bridge. He knew the mudlarkers worked on a principle of finders-keepers, but it was probably stolen originally. There'd be a limit to the price it could achieve. It might even be fake. All the same...

'We agreed to two pairs of boots and a quarter of whatever we found. We found four sausages.'

The Pan wasn't sure, but judging by the way his face felt, he reckoned his eyes were bulging. 'You're certain?'

'It's what we agreed.'

'Well ... yes, I know but ... I didn't expect ... I ...' The Pan ran one hand through his hair. 'Goojan spiced sausage is pretty pricy,' he said.

'Four hundred Grongolian dollars an ounce,' said Christine.

The Pan raised an eyebrow. 'You've done your research.'

'Yeh,' said Bort eyeing him, 'we have.'

'We won't get that for it, of course. And neither will you, lad,' said Terri.

'No,' sighed The Pan. They were right. For starters, it might be fake. Even if it wasn't, it wouldn't realise it's true value unless the correct paperwork had fallen off the bridge with it, or The Pan could find a valuer who'd examine it and sign an authentication document. Hmm, this was going to be complicated. Yeh. Complicated but not impossible.

'It'll take us a day or two to shift it as well,' Terri added.

'Yep, we might be here for a while,' said Bort.

'Be careful then,' said The Pan.

He genuinely hoped they could sell the sausage. It would be good if the three of them could retire somewhere together and live out their days in contentment and peace.

They were lucky, having each other to lean on. He closed his eyes as he thought of his own family. No. They were gone, and mooning about it wasn't going to bring them back.

'Are you going to be OK?' asked Christine gently.

'Yeh, in a moment,' The Pan's voice was taut with emotion when he spoke. He took a deep breath and let it out slowly.

'Take care, me hearty,' said Terri. She stepped forward and, apparently oblivious to the way he utterly stank, swept him into her arms in a hug. 'Sell that sausage and buy yourself a new life. That's what we're going to do.'

The Pan looked her in the eye. Yeh, he reckoned she'd seen straight through him. 'Sounds like an excellent plan. Look after yourselves, all of you. I don't want to see you round here again, alright? I want you to be well out of my league.'

'You'll be there with us, whatever league we're in,' said Bort. She gave him another of those smiles; warm, intimate and seemingly just for him. It made him feel a bit giddy. No, that was the shock still. Yes. Of course it was. The smile had nothing to do with it. Although she *was* lovely, Arnold's socks! He couldn't deny that. He summoned up the courage for a brief moment of eye contact. As well as a smile, her green eyes held a hint of something else. Were it not impossible, he might have described the look she was giving him as smouldering. Blimey. Had he got that right? Did Bort like him? No. Get real. She couldn't possibly. She was way out of his league. And it didn't matter anyway. He wasn't going to see her again.

Maybe, in another world and time, before he was blacklisted, before it was impossible, he'd have tried to change that. Anything normal like that was gone now though. Yeh. Don't even think about it. Don't get close to anyone. Anyway, he'd just saved her mother's life, or at least, her mother's ID, which was pretty much the same thing.

Exactly. She's not coming onto you. It's just gratitude, you dork, he thought and answered her question in a manner which he hoped was suave and calm, and belied no hint of his confusion. 'It depends what I spend the money on. By the time I get my life straight, I doubt there'll be much cash left.'

Dare he hope that he could afford a new identity? How much did it cost? A lot, for certain—but surely any sausage-related earnings would cover it. It depended if it was fake, of course. Not to mention if it was stolen, or at least, stolen before it was salvaged from the river, and more to the point, if he could sell it. Best not bank on earning anything from it.

'I hope there is,' said Christine and she hugged him. Then Bort hugged him too.

'Take care, you three,' said The Pan.

They turned and walked a few yards. Then they stopped and Bort ran back. 'Thanks,' she said breathlessly. She made to hug him again but then leaned up and kissed his cheek. A light gentle peck that made his beats per minute pick up alarmingly.

'I wouldn't do that, I've been in the Dang,' he said.

'So have I,' she laughed.

'Not quite in the same way.'

'It doesn't matter. See you at your fitting.'

'My what?'

'For the boots. Those are knackered.' She glanced at his feet then treated him to another of those dazzling just-for-him smiles, before turning and going back to join the other two. Was she sashaying a little bit as she walked away? Possibly. A little further up the street the three women linked arms and started to skip. The Pan chuckled as he watched. When they reached the corner, they stopped, looked back and waved one more time. He waved back. And then they were walking again and disappeared out of sight.

'Well, that's that,' The Pan told the snurd. Even though it was inanimate and couldn't appreciate what he was saying, it seemed to understand. 'Thanks for saving my life again.'

He sat on the boot lid for a moment. He felt far too wobbly to walk, but at the same time, he'd be an idiot to drive anywhere after what he'd just done. He laughed to himself. Arnold's toe jam! It felt good to be alive. He was pumped, restless, full of adrenaline. That would wear off soon enough though and he'd be knackered. Best to get a bath in first. Then he could curl up somewhere clean and warm, and sleep. Maybe, if he sold the sausage, he could spare a few Zloty from his new ID fund to pay for a room in a hotel. Somewhere swanky with an actual bed.

'Yeh,' he said quietly.

He opened the boot of the snurd, which contained his worldly goods, and took out a backpack. He put some clean clothes, a wash bag, a comb and a towel into it. He also added a plastic bag full of dirty washing—first the bath house but then, definitely, the launderette. That done, he put the sausage in the boot, closed the lid, walked round to the driver's door and patted the snurd affectionately on the roof. He looked inside and took in the river mud smeared over the seats. He wasn't the only thing that needed a wash—he'd have to give the inside of the snurd a thorough scrub. If he asked politely, he reckoned Trev might let him use the hose they used to clean out the empty barrels at the Parrot and Screwdriver. Maybe Gladys and Ada would let him have a bath there as well. No, best not push it. He'd be an even more wanted man than usual after this afternoon's events. The fuss would die down again—it always did—but for now, it wasn't fair on them. Although he could probably go to the pub. Thinking about it, he'd have to. Big Merv might need to give him an errand to run. If he wasn't there to receive the instruction it wouldn't go down well.

'That's all I need, to upset Big Merv,' said The Pan to himself. 'Arnold knows what he'd do if I didn't turn up for work.' For a moment he saw a vision in his mind's eye of Finicky Bert the jeweller swinging gently as he hung upside down by his feet. 'Alright, yes, on second thoughts, I know exactly what he'd do,' said The Pan. Yeh. That for starters, and then, probably, something worse.

He bipped the key ring for self-park and watched the snurd drive off down the street. Were those bullet marks down the side? Oh dear.

'Bath time first though,' he said to himself, turned and walked away.

Chapter 7
Regrouping

The Pan of Hamgee sat in a launderette. He'd spent the afternoon there while Grongle patrols tore Ning-Dang-Po apart looking for him. Since they were searching for a man on the run, The Pan reckoned the sensible thing would be to stay put and be very obviously not running.

He'd left the area where he'd landed his snurd and decided to walk to a neighbourhood nearer the Arboretum, dodging patrols as he went. Sure enough, by the time he got there, the whole place had been searched and declared clear. There were roadblocks set up to keep it that way checking anyone going in, but The Pan avoided those with a little creative climbing.

From what he could gather, as he sat in the launderette eavesdropping on other people's conversations, the Grongles hadn't found Terri, Bort and Christine, or the SE2. The events had been on the news and it was pretty much lockdown all over. Most K'Barthans had made a dash for home but some had stayed where they were, including a handful in the launderette with The Pan. He stayed extra vigilant but they carried on chatting to one another and, apart a brief greeting, ignored him. If anyone there had recognised him, they made no sign.

The washing machine cycle took two hours and after twenty minutes or so of heightened awareness, he began to relax. He listened idly to two elderly beings, a human and one of K'Barth's small furry genera, a Spiffle, as they shared their experiences and compared notes. As well as the road blocks, there'd even been house-to-house searches. It was so bad that, according to the Spiffle who was sorting bed linen, there were rumours that Grongles had even been seen walking the roofs. That was almost unheard of. The Pan hadn't noticed any up there himself, but that didn't mean it wasn't true.

The heat of the search was dying down now and the trail cooling meant the worst was over. There were still Grongolian patrols on the streets—there always were—but the inhabitants of Ning Dang Po were cautiously venturing out again. The Grongles would probably give it lip service for another week or so, but they'd soon be turning their energies to other things. The Pan had plenty of laundry to do, so he heaved a grateful sigh, and in so far as he ever could, relaxed.

The launderette ran a book swap and there was a shelf piled with second-hand novels to read. The Pan liked books but they were a luxury he could ill afford, and these days, what with being on the run and all, it wasn't as if he had time to read anyway. Especially after the Grongles had realised that homeless beings were skulking in the city library on cold wet days and installed CCTV. He had to remain reasonably alert but reading a book still felt like a luxury, even though he dared not give it his full attention.

The mundanity of the launderette was intensely unreal. Here he was, washing his clothes all afternoon, while half the police in Ning Dang Po were looking for him. He'd positioned his chair so everything but his legs was hidden from the window. Hopefully he was far enough from the areas where the Grongles were currently searching to be safe, but it was always best to be cautious.

In his favour, none of the security forces had actually seen him, apart from the three grunts with the hand cart. With any luck it was the SE2 that would receive most of the attention. Yeh, if he walked everywhere for a week or two he'd probably be OK. No. He'd *definitely* be OK, and the SE2 had proved time and time again that it was more than able to hide itself. He'd done this often enough and it always ended the same way. With the Grongles giving up. They had too many criminals to choose from and too much to do for The Pan to stay on their radar that long. Sure, he was a wanted man and the price on his head was pretty hefty. But it wasn't *that* high—there were other, far easier, methods for the security forces to earn bonuses, or some cash on the side. On top of that, there were a lot of K'Barthans out there who were much easier to catch than The Pan *and* higher up the wanted list. He'd just have to lie low for a day or two, then it should be alright. It usually was.

The Pan was less adept at blending in than the SE2 but he'd learned to go unnoticed in most places—except in the presence of big beings who wanted to look rock-hard in front of a large group of others by thumping someone.

Yeh, still a nutter magnet, he thought.

The washer beeped, and a light flashed on to tell him the second two-hour wash had finally finished. He put the book down and made his way over to the machine to get his things. But the door was stuck fast. Oh yes, the two-minute pause after it had stopped, in case, by some miracle, it was still spinning and ripped his arm off. He tapped his foot and whistled tunelessly under his breath as his clean clothes sat in perfect stillness in the bottom of the stationary drum, for 120 pointless, boring, seconds.

Right, so that was the plan then; let the snurd do its own thing for a bit, avoid big scary beings who might like to thump him, keep out of the way of the security forces and he should be fine. Oh. Not so much of a plan then, more The Pan's way of life. 'Business as usual then,' he muttered.

Yeh. Hopefully. Escaping from a whole pack of Grongles above the Arboretum would probably mean they wanted him quite a lot more than they had before. Unless ...

'Arnold's conkers,' he muttered thinking about the

bounty on his head. 'I hope they haven't put the price up.'

The Spiffle who'd been folding bed linen and chatting to the little old dears overheard him. 'Oh no, young man, it hasn't changed. It's still three Zloty a wash and two more for a dry.'

'Thank you, that's a relief,' said The Pan because it paid to be polite and he wasn't about to tell her he'd been muttering about the price on his head as opposed to the cost of a wash.

Finally, with a click, the door on the machine released his laundry. The Pan had two Zloty for the dryer—although under normal circumstances he'd just hang his clothes out somewhere, especially in weather this warm. He opened the washing machine and a strong smell hit him, mostly of lemon soap suds, but unfortunately there was a subtle undertone of Goojan spiced sausage. Less than subtle really. Arnold's nasal hair! Still, at least the smell of the Dang was gone. A partial success then.

'Can't win 'em all,' he muttered.

As he stood, damp shirt in hand, the Spiffle shuffled up behind him. She was definitely elderly, her movements a little arthritic. Her orange fur was flecked with white but while her movements might be a bit slow, The Pan suspected her mind was as sharp as ever. Her beady black eyes were alive with an expression of intelligent enquiry. She sniffed the air.

Uh-oh. The Pan tensed, but she flashed him a kindly smile. 'Young man, are you one of Goldy McSpim's boys?'

Who in the name of The Prophet was Goldy McSpim? Better play this carefully, just in case it was a rival gang lord to Big Merv. The Spiffle didn't look like the dangerous type but these days The Pan had learned, to his cost, that trouble could come from the most innocuous-looking sources.

'Why would you think that?' he asked raising a quizzical

eyebrow as if he wasn't worried, or being cagey, at all.

'The smell; Goojan spiced sausage. Goldy is the smartest sausage broker in town.'

The Pan decided she probably was harmless and that it was best to go with the flow. 'I'm guessing that makes you a loyal customer,' he said, silently congratulating himself for giving her such an evasive answer.

She laughed at that, a long drawn-out wheezing chuckle. 'I suppose you could say I am. Goldy's my husband. Mrs Glenda McSpim, at your service.' She held out her small furry paw and The Pan shook it. He tried to make it a firm handshake, but not so firm that it would hurt her if her paws were arthritic.

'Delighted to meet you,' he said.

She gave him a bit of a look. 'Perhaps you're not working for Goldy. Perhaps you have sausage to sell?' She winked.

'I'm not sure I'm selling,' said The Pan. 'But I met some people today who might be interested in a valuation.'

Like all Spiffles, Glenda McSpim wasn't wearing clothes; with a luxuriant coating of long orange fur to keep her cool in the summer and warm in the winter, she didn't need to. However, like all her kind, she did wear an extremely ornate hat—a straw sun hat in this case. She'd attached a number of paper flowers around the band. As she moved her head, paper butterflies on thin, more-or-less invisible wires of different lengths bounced and wobbled above them—as if a cloud of the real insects were following her, seeking nectar. Slung over one shoulder, Glenda also wore a strap with pockets and pouches where she kept the things she needed to carry; essentials such as her ID, wallet, a handkerchief and the like. She opened one of the pouches, and produced a card.

'Give that to your friends,' she said, winking rather theatrically on the word 'friends'. The paper flowers on her hat rustled and the butterflies bobbed and wobbled as she nodded.

'Thank you, I will,' he said.

****

Was this too good to be true? The Pan wondered as he left the launderette. Probably, but he had nothing else to go on, and after his escape with Christine, Terri and Bort something had altered in him. He wasn't confident but he was beginning to realise that when it came to running away, he had talent. It would be arrogant to believe there wasn't someone out there who could catch him, but after today, he understood that if there was, they'd have to be a better hunter than most. Being able to see forward and backwards as the same time definitely gave The Pan an edge. That said, it was sod's law that if ever anyone exceptionally good at chasing people was going to come after him and test his theory it was now, when he had some very expensive merchandise to unload.

Would he get a decent price for the sausage? Who knew? But maybe this Goldy McSpim could sell it for him. The Pan knew he'd never get the going rate on the black market but mainstream? That would be entirely different. He might be able to persuade Mr McSpim that the sausage was legit. After all, it was salvaged rather than stolen … probably.

The Pan imagined what he would do with the kind of cash a Goojan spiced sausage commanded. He could buy a new identity. It would cost him, he understood that, but perhaps then he could do the things normal beings did; rent a flat, get a job and join society. That reminded him, thinking about the sausage—he'd better retrieve it from the boot of his wheels. The snurd might be good at hiding itself, but the smell of Goojan spiced sausage was difficult to hide anywhere. Even the SE2 would have trouble blending in

59

with that thing reeking away on board. 'First thing, stash the sausage.'

That was going to be tricky. Maybe he should go and see if he could find the barge on which Christine, Terri and Bort lived. Possibly. Or he could head for the Parrot and Screwdriver and ask Gladys and Ada if they could stash it in their cellar. As he read and re-read the card Glenda McSpim had given him, he wondered where else he could turn to sell the sausage. He was pretty sure he'd find someone at the Parrot who'd know a bloke who knew someone who could offload Goojan spiced sausage. Except others knew about the sausage too, if the crowd of folks looking for it at Golden Point was anything to go by. They didn't know where it was now but they'd be looking for it.

Then there was his 'job'. Even if he managed to hang onto the sausage, and even if he managed to find a buyer, he'd have to extricate himself from Big Merv's organisation somehow if he really wanted to make a fresh start.

His spirits sank. He hadn't thought this through. Selling the sausage wasn't going to be easy without Big Merv finding out. He'd probably want a cut. Maybe if The Pan got a new ID and just drifted away, the Big Thing and his cohorts wouldn't notice.

'And maybe pigs will fly and the sky will turn green,' he muttered to himself.

Whatever he did, he needed to sell the sausage for the highest price possible. And to do that, risk or not, there was only one logical place to start. He turned the card over in his hands. Yep. Goldy McSpim.

Chapter 8
Goldy McSpim

The following morning, The Pan made his way through the twisty streets of the Goojan Quarter. They were narrow, cobbled and—at street level—dark, while the ancient houses were close together. In times gone by the Goojan Quarter had been prime real estate. Most of the merchants opening businesses there could only afford a small patch of land that expensive. Since it came at such a premium, nobody was going to waste any space on wide boulevards. The streets and alleyways were of sufficient width to let a cart through and that was all. There was also a complicated one-way system, which all beings followed, even now.

Few of those early merchants could afford a home after stumping up for a plot of land in the Goojan Quarter. Many lived above their shops and businesses with their families. To maximise the amount of living space they'd build the floor above jutting out a few feet over the shop window below. As time went by they built more and more floors, each one jutting further out than the ones underneath, until the streets below became darker and darker. At the upper levels, it was often possible to reach out of the window and shake hands with the people living in the property opposite. Because of this, the Goojan Quarter was one of the few places where The Pan couldn't really stick to the roofs, or at least not if he wanted to find somewhere specific. It was impossible to read the house numbers from above.

Luckily it didn't matter the way it might have done as the Grongles didn't venture in here often. Much to The Pan's relief, he only had to look out for any K'Barthans who might be tailing him as he moved through the streets. He wasn't sure why the Grongles left the Goojan K'Barthans relatively alone. It might possibly be something to do with the height of the first floors jutting out at every street corner. The properties in this part of town had been built hundreds of years previously when all the beings using them were universally smaller and shorter. Even The Pan had to duck sometimes and he was a lot less tall than the average Grongle. He could imagine an unwary member of the Security Forces might smack their head on every single building.

Yeh, perhaps that was the reason.

On the other hand, The Pan reflected, it might just as easily have been the smell that kept the Grongles away. Goojans used spices in ways that hadn't even occurred to the Hamgeeans. So a visit to the Goojan Quarter was always an aromatic assault. It made The Pan feel hungry, but since many Grongles preferred plain boring food they probably had a different reaction. Grongles were much like the inhabitants of Ning Dang-Po in that respect.

The mixture of strange and exotic perfumes in the air was particularly strong in the heat; spices, cooking food, aromatic teas and herbs, plus the odd whiff of drains. It was even strong enough to cover the aroma of the spiced sausage in The Pan's bag. Or at least, if anyone noticed the smell as he passed, they made no sign.

At last he found the place. He checked the address on the card in his hand one more time and knocked on the door.

Silence. Maybe Goldy McSpim was out. No, The Pan had rung the number on the card and explained that Mrs McSpim had sent him, without saying why. He'd been invited to visit and he was bang on time. He'd used a payphone for that and hopefully been vague enough not to pique the interest of any Grongles listening in. K'Barthans weren't allowed mobile phones—they were for Grongles.

And the landline system, both private and phone box, was often tapped.

Again, The Pan checked behind him, just in case, but he knew, categorically, that he wasn't being followed. Not at the moment. Then again, The Pan supposed, if *he* was checking for anyone tracking his movements maybe Goldy McSpim was doing the same thing. He wouldn't want trouble brought to his door. If anyone was on The Pan's tail, doubtless Mr McSpim would pretend he wasn't at home.

Finally a window opened far above him. 'Just on my way down!' called a voice.

'Right,' said The Pan. Presumably that was the man, or at least Spiffle, himself. He put the card in his pocket and waited.

Finally The Pan heard the sound of bolts being drawn back behind the door. Clearly Goldy McSpim was careful about security, as there appeared to be about ten of them. After that The Pan listened to a lot of unlocking sounds until the door finally swung open. Two ferocious-looking Blurpons greeted him. Though related to Spiffles—in that they're short and furry—Blurpons are about as different as it's possible to be in other ways. They have red fur, as opposed to the orange fur of Spiffles, and are known for their unsurpassed skill at laundry, a tendency to psychotic violence and the ease with which they take offence. They have one leg but The Pan knew from experience that this didn't present them with a problem if they decided to get antsy.

These Blurpons were obviously Goldy's bodyguards. They had to be employed on account of their violent streak rather than their laundering abilities.

'Ah gentlemen, thank you,' said a voice from inside. 'Do let the young man in.'

The Pan was ushered into the coolness of the interior where he listened to the sounds of the many bolts and locks being re-secured behind him. It suddenly occurred to him that if Goldy wanted to steal the sausage and send him on his way with a flea in his ear, it wasn't going to be difficult. Oh dear, had he walked into a trap? Idiot—he should have left half the sausage in the SE2.

Goldy was wearing a beret, which was surprisingly understated for a Spiffle. It was only when he smiled that The Pan realised why his hat was so restrained. He supposed the traditional Spiffle love of decoration had to come out somewhere, but his teeth? The Pan speculated to himself that Goldy's nickname was probably something to do with the entirely gold contents of his mouth. Not only were his teeth gold but they were studded with precious gems cut cabochon style; emeralds, rubies and the odd diamond. The Pan realised his own mouth had dropped open and closed it quickly.

'If I should ever need to leave here in a hurry, sausage will not travel,' Goldy explained. 'This way,' he flashed The Pan a blinding smile, 'I will always have some assets with me.'

'Won't people notice?'

'Not if I do not smile,' said Goldy, 'and if I am fleeing for my life, I will be worried, very worried, so it is unlikely that I shall. Now, come, come,' he said and headed off down four stairs at the back of the shop, through a large metal safe door and into a back room.

The Pan followed, slightly nervously. Because if there was any trouble, the only way out was past the Blurpons, and he didn't fancy his chances. Goldy took his place on a tall stool behind a table spread with a crisp white damask cloth. In front of the table was a battered antique dining chair with arms and an open back, the seat upholstered in worn leather.

'How is Mrs McSpim?' asked The Pan politely.

'She is very well, yes, yes.'

'Please thank her and send her my best wishes.'

'Ah, I think you should wait until I have valued the goods before you thank either of us, yes?'

The Pan's eyes were drawn to the blinding whiteness of the tablecloth. Maybe the two Blurpons *did* do the laundry as well as the bodyguard duties. Yes, of course they did. And come to think of it, there'd be more than two—they'd be part of a team and someone would always be on duty, round the clock.

The Pan turned in a circle, examining the rest of his surroundings. Ranged along all four walls of the room were glass-fronted shelves. Airtight and climate controlled, they were divided into square units like some huge safety deposit area. Well, yes, The Pan supposed, that was probably what it was. He cast another quick glance at the foot-thick metal door. He was clearly inside a giant safe.

One of the Blurpons flicked a light switch and a dim glow illuminated all the boxes. There were a few empty ones, but most contained sausage; some contained two.

'This is …' what to call it? 'impressive,' said The Pan. 'Are these sausages all yours?'

'Oh no! But as you know, a good sausage is expensive! It needs to be kept securely. A bank vault is not good for that purpose, the air is stale. No-no-no, a sausage is a living thing. Starve it of the correct temperature or humidity and it will pine away and die. The balance of spices will soon fall off and mould will grow.' He shuddered. Clearly that would be bad. 'These storage units are state of the art. For a small fee you can keep your family heirlooms here and my assistants will deliver slices of your precious treat to your door, as and when you require.'

'Heirlooms?'

'Yes, yes! Some of these sausages have been in the same families for centuries. Our climate-controlled storage keeps them at the optimum temperature for years of enjoyment.

And we are fully insured, of course, so it is more cost effective, as well as safer, to keep them here than at home.'

'Yes, I can imagine,' said The Pan.

'The service is very competitively priced, if you are interested.'

'I— well, I suspect I will be selling.'

'You have debts, huh?'

'Something like that.'

Goldy stared at The Pan, a long hard stare. He had the same look of shrewd intelligence as his wife and was clearly missing nothing. He nodded slowly. 'Please sit.'

The Pan did as he was told, seating himself in the chair and placing the bag with the sausage inside on his lap.

'Do these all belong to actual beings?' he asked looking at the shelves around him.

'You are wondering how there can be so many rich people in the world, I would guess. Some are ...' Goldy paused for thought, 'how would you say it? Unclaimed. They belong to the blacklisted, or the mislaid. They will have family, descendants. One day I will find them, or they will find me.' He smiled, almost blinding The Pan with another flash of his bejewelled teeth despite the ambient dimness of the lighting.

'And the others?'

Goldy gave The Pan another long, hard look. 'The richest few percent of the population have ways of surviving anything. Very little changes for them, no matter who is in charge or what is happening to the rest of us. It is all a game to them. Now. You have a sausage to show me.' He held out one paw and wiggled it in the type of beckoning gesture that's the universal sign language for 'gimme-gimme' the world over.

The Pan noticed the two Blurpon bodyguards through the eyes in the back of his head and paused. Goldy guessed the reason for his hesitation. 'I will dismiss John and Smurfit if you require but there is no need. They are the very essence of discretion—you have nothing to fear from them.'

The Pan took a deep breath, removed the plastic box from the bag and placed it on the table.

'Ah ha,' said Goldy softly.

'Here, I'll open it,' said The Pan.

'No, no, no.' Goldy put a paw on his arm. 'Wait a moment.' He leaned over the box and sniffed, a long, long, inhalation. 'Hmm,' he said and was silent for a few moments. 'Yes, yes. I see. That is good. I'm ready. Open it please.'

The Pan undid the plastic fastenings and popped the lid off. The smell that assaulted his nostrils was unique; heady and strong, spicy, aromatic, and pervasive like nothing he'd smelled before.

'This is very good,' said Goldy. 'Very good indeed. Such a pity.'

'A pity?'

'Whoever made this sausage is a most accomplished sausagewright. However, unfortunately, he, or possibly she—but I think it is a he because I think I can detect the identity of the maker here—is no longer able to obtain the correct ingredients. This sausage is made exactly as a Goojan spiced sausage should be, but the turmeric is not the genuine K'Barthan article.'

'It isn't?'

'Alas, my young friend, no. It is a cheaper Grongolian variety, the quarl. Though good, it is not the best. The saffron is from the greatly inferior crocus contrabandi harvested from the plains, rather than the mountainous valleys where they grow the real thing.' He picked up the sausage. 'Here, smell.' He waved it at The Pan, who took it. 'The rosemary and thyme, though of the finest quality, are not imbued with the salt flavour of the Tithian or Hamgeean salt flats from which they should come. They are from the mountains of Driesch. I can almost taste the granite soil in their aroma.'

The Pan gave the sausage a sniff and tried to pick out the scents and flavours Goldy was describing.

'To you it smells of sausage, huh?'

The Pan smiled and looked down. 'I'm afraid so,' he said as he put it back on the table.

'That is natural, yes. But I will show you. Come, come.' Goldy jumped down and trotted over to one of the cabinets. The Pan followed and watched while the little fellow pushed the head of a bronze screw set in the wood next to the lowest box. A small flap opened and a remote control popped out. Goldy removed it and pressed a button. A ladder extended from the top, and The Pan waited as the little Spiffle climbed up to the middle levels, put one furry digit over a print reader on a safe to one side of the ladder and then pressed his eye to a small hole in the surround. With a click it opened. Immediately the smell of the sausage wafted out. Goldy reached in and removed something with reverential awe. He sniffed it before turning and proffering it in The Pan's direction. 'Smell,' he ordered.

The Pan did as he was told. There was definitely a nuance of something, the olfactory equivalent of a bass note perhaps, that wasn't there on the other. 'You're right, it is different.'

'Of course, but you have never smelled the real deal before, huh? So you are not to know. And even if you have, maybe if you like Goojan sausage and you are not so well off, you will be happy with the one you have brought me. It is, undeniably, a fine sausage,' Goldy added as he put the genuine sausage back in the safe and locked it. 'Thank you. Please sit down. John will serve you rosewater coffee—it is very refreshing.'

With a bow, one of the Blurpon bodyguards withdrew and The Pan returned to the chair in front of the table.

'I am sorry, my friend,' he said. The Pan sat in silence. 'You don't believe me when I say that?'

The Pan looked him in the eye, catching him off guard. 'No. I believe you.'

'You are the second person in as many days who has come to me with this. They are the same batch, yes?'

'I couldn't say. I was given it.'

The Spiffle's eyebrows shot up. 'Given?'

'I did someone a favour.'

'Aaaah. Someone who had found some sausages in a box, yes? A box by the River Dang?'

The Pan said nothing as John, the slightly fluffier of Goldy's Blurpon bodyguards, returned with two small cups of thick dark rosewater coffee.

'Ah! Excellent,' said Goldy, taking a sip and waving an encouraging paw at The Pan. 'Try, try.' The Pan sipped the coffee and found that it was, indeed, very good. 'I'm thinking it was a very big favour you did these people for them to give you this?'

'Nothing major,' lied The Pan. 'After all they gave me a fake.'

'It is not a fake, it is a copy, a very good one! There is a difference, no?'

'Maybe.'

'Definitely. It is made the way it is because the sausagewright could not source the correct ingredients, rather than to deceive. He would make a true sausage if he was able. There is no artifice here.'

'Does it change the price?'

'Pshaw!' exclaimed Goldy, waving a theatrical arm. 'There is not a restaurant in Ning Dang Po that wouldn't sell this to its customers as the real thing! They would get away with it too. But yes, it will change the price.' He sealed The Pan's fake sausage back in its green plastic box. 'These people you helped,' he continued, 'I am thinking maybe you have a snurd? You gave them, how shall we say it? A ride home, perhaps?'

For the first time, The Pan felt nervous. 'I think you've mistaken me for someone else.'

Goldy was suddenly serious and leaned forward. 'I doubt that. It's a pity that I don't deal in this sausage. I would take it off your hands, give you a good price and it would be safer for you, I think. People are looking for this sausage. Bad people.' He glanced past The Pan at one of the Blurpons by the door. 'Right, Smurfit?'

'Yer,' said the less fluffy Blurpon from his station. The other one, John, also murmured agreement.

'Smurfit has contacts in the Resistance. They are most interested in a young person with a silver snurd. They think he is a very good driver. Isn't that right, Smurfit?'

'Yer.'

Smeck.

'But it is the sausage they are after. A driver would be, how can I say it? The pretty icing on the bun. They believe there's a lot of capital in that box.' He put his hand on the green plastic in front of him. 'Not as much as you hoped I think, but still a lot. You must be very careful, yes? Or you will lose it. They are watching, always watching and they know you have that sausage, and they know you will come to me.'

'Are you trying to tell me this is a trap?'

'I wish I knew. If it is, none of us here has set it. But they have been here.'

'The Resistance.'

'Yes.'

'They spoke to you?' asked The Pan in horror.

'Oh, nothing so unsubtle! There have been strangers in the street this morning, and they talk to no-one. It is as if they are watching, is that not right, John?'

'Yer,' the other Blurpon assented.

'My clients are very rich. I enjoy some protection from them and as I see you have noted, I provide my own. But sometimes when the wind is too powerful, it breaks the mighty oak. On those occasions, it is only the grass that survives because it bends. I think you know this, yes?'

'What are you trying to say?'

'That, you and I, we may not look alike but I think perhaps we are? I think we bend, no? I walk the line and, my friend, I know you do. That is why I cannot openly give what I would like to offer freely. For example, if I were to hand you this accreditation for that sausage, it would be wrong of me...' He held out a piece of paper.

'I— thanks.'

'Do not thank me. If I were to tell you that the Resistance are waiting for you it would not go well for me. Likewise, if I said that you should avoid the crossroads between Fonkit Alley and Baldimon Street when you leave, I would be in trouble, yes? If I told you that the Resistance do not know your face, that they are searching only for a Goojan spiced sausage and, possibly, a very good escape person...' He tutted. 'It would be very, very detrimental to my health if the wrong beings were to know that.'

Arnold's trousers! 'Then, I can only thank you, wholeheartedly, for not telling me these things.'

Goldy McSpim chuckled. 'I am an old fool, perhaps, but it is a pleasure. You will sell that sausage, I think. It is a very impressive piece of work. If someone asked me what I thought of it, that is what I would tell them, that it is impressive, possibly even exquisite.'

'And a copy.'

Goldy shrugged. 'If they ask the question then, yes. Indeed, if they read the accreditation correctly, it tells them clearly that it is a copy. However, those who do not wish to know the truth may read it differently. That is why I have left the wording ambivalent.'

'I— thank you. With this, might I find a sausage broker who'd sell it?'

'Alas, no.' The Pan sighed. 'But those restaurants I mentioned? If you sell this to certain … less scrupulous establishments you may make a little money.'

'How much? Sorry to ask.'

'A decent amount of Grongolian dollars maybe. You are going to cut it up and sell them slices, yes?'

'Yep. I wondered if I should have cut it up already.'

'If it had been genuine that would not have been such a good idea, my friend. You were wise to leave it whole until you had brought it to me. As it is, now you understand what you have, it is the best way to sell a copy.'

So the sausage wasn't the golden bullet. If The Pan sold it on the black market as stolen goods, there would be a ceiling on the price he could charge. Never mind, it could be worse. He would earn cash and earn well; it was just that it would be the kind of cash that purchased repairs to the SE2 rather than a new ID. It wasn't as if The Pan hadn't prepared himself for this. It had crossed his mind that the sausage being the actual, genuine article was a bit too good to be true. Not in line with the kind of luck he usually experienced. He tried not to be downcast but it was clearly showing in his face because Goldy leaned forward with a sympathetic expression and said, 'I am sorry.'

'It's OK. It's very kind of you to help me.'

'I wish I could do more. My wife trusts you. She is a very good judge of character, my wife! She says you are a good man. And also, you made fools of the entire Grongolian Security Force and I like to have a laugh. We all like to have a laugh. Please do that again for us soon.'

The Pan reflected, privately, that he wouldn't be doing that again, ever, if he could avoid it. 'I think I'd better not. You don't want to laugh too much, the wrong people might see those teeth!'

Goldy threw back his head and guffawed. 'Very good. I like you,' he said. 'I like you a lot! Now,' he drained his coffee cup. 'I regret but it is time for you to leave.'

The Pan swallowed the soupy coffee dregs from his own cup and put it carefully on the table. Then he put the green box and its meaty cargo back in the linen bag and slung it over one shoulder. Goldy trotted to the main door. The Pan followed, with John and Smurfit bringing up the rear. As Goldy reached up to undo the first bolt, there was a sound of shouting in the street outside. Somebody hammered on it, hard. 'This is a search! Open your door, stand to one side and wait for orders.'

'Smeck! The Grongles,' muttered The Pan.

'Tut tut, you have very much annoyed our masters for them to come here, I think.' Goldy winked. 'They do not like to come to the Goojan Quarter. John, please show our guest out through our alternative exit,' he said. Turning to The Pan he added, 'Do not worry, it will take me thirty seconds to unbolt the door.' Smurfit, the other Blurpon, moved a ladder into position so Goldy could access the bolts and locks at the top. 'Go!' He made a shooing movement with his paws.

The Pan didn't need a second invitation. He turned and followed John.

Chapter 9
Another sharp exit

John bounced up the stairs so fast that The Pan had trouble keeping up. Finally they came to a landing and the Blurpon led the way up a rickety ladder to an attic room at the top of the house. He opened a skylight.

'There's two roofs and this gulley runs between them right down to Fonkit Alley and Baldimon Street at the bottom end,' he pointed. 'But the Resistance are waiting there. That means you need to go this way, mate.' He indicated the opposite direction, then pointed to the sky. 'There's a police snurd cruising about up there. Watch out for it.'

'Thanks.'

'Any time, son. Good luck.'

The Pan climbed out into the gulley and waited, squatting low and keeping in the shadow cast by the roof so he wouldn't be seen. Space being such a premium in the Goojan Quarter, there was a lot of living going on up here; tables, awnings, plants in pots, even a couple of small trees. Enough cover.

When the police snurd above was at the other end of the street making a turn, The Pan scurried to safety behind a chimney. He moved along the gulley in this manner as the patrol vehicle above circled, nipping from one piece of cover to the next when he gauged that the officers in the vehicle couldn't see him. Halfway along, using a tree growing in a large dustbin for cover, he risked crawling up the roof a little way and peeping over the ridge tiles to see what was going on below. He couldn't see anything.

He didn't know how the Grongles were conducting the

search. But from the shouts and curses he could hear rising up from the streets below, it sounded as if they were out in force searching blocks of houses at the same time.

Uh-oh. If that's what they were up to then presumably this roof was going to be awash with them very soon.

The Pan listened to the harsh Grongle voices echoing between the buildings. They came in stereo, from both sides of the roof he was on. Each of the streets was being searched then. That usually meant three rows of houses getting the Grongles' attention at once.

'Great! And I'm in the middle one,' he muttered.

He paused, listening to the different groups of Grongles, shouting the odds at one another. Best not go down, then, but it was time to move on. Well ... after a moment to take stock. He didn't want to do anything rash, or at least, not without thinking it over for a second or two first. He took a deep breath. The temptation to summon the SE2 was almost overwhelming, but if there were dents in the polymorphic metal and a giant crack across the windscreen, what other damage was there? Things he couldn't see? Who knew? No, until Gerry at Snurd had ascertained the true extent of the damage The Pan didn't fancy trying to escape with it. It was more than just a vehicle, it was his home. Best not risk totalling it unless he absolutely had to.

Yeh. Let's call that plan B.

He continued his stealthy way up the gulley. The bag containing the sausage was a drawstring fabric affair. He stopped under someone's rooftop pergola to thread his arms through the drawstrings of the bag, arranging it so it was slung over his shoulders and across his back, leaving his arms free. That should keep it out of the way if they chased him and he had to start jumping streets. Sheltered from the police snurds above by vines in pots, he paused for a moment to survey his options.

As he waited for the police snurd to drone past overhead,

he spotted an open skylight in the roof of one of the houses opposite him.

'Ah,' he said, to no-one in particular. *Worth a punt,* he thought.

He crawled a little way up the roof and leaned over as far as he dared to check the activity below. There was a Grongle down there but he was looking to his left and right rather than up. Excellent. The Pan glanced at the open skylight. There wasn't much to hold on to and very little cover, but it should be alright if he timed it right and was quick.

Another glance at the skies to check for the police snurd again then he made a leap for the skylight opposite. He overshot, missed his footing and for a stomach-churning second slid down the roof, out of control, until one scrabbling hand caught the bottom of the skylight and he stopped. He lay still and silent, listening. No shouts from the street; clearly the Grongle below hadn't noticed. Slowly and quietly, he hauled himself up and looked into the room below. It was a bathroom, empty. He lowered himself stealthily into it. The door was ajar so he crept forward and peeped through the crack. No-one about. But he could hear Grongles below, possibly on the ground or first floor. Maybe this wasn't such a good idea.

No, it would work. It had to.

He opened the door and slipped out into the hall. Keeping close to the wall, in a bid to minimise the creaks if he stepped on any loose floorboards, he made his way across to the other side, and the room facing onto the next street over. It took all his courage but he went slowly, to minimise any noise, flattening himself against the ancient plaster. The room was empty but lit with a skylight which was too narrow to squeeze through. However, looking over at the house opposite, he could see that the room on the next floor down had a row of windows, sheltered from the hot sun by its overhanging eaves. Some of the windows were open. Excellent. He knew what to do.

He returned to the hall and made his way to the stairs. There were Grongles coming up them, clattering onto the first floor and into the bedrooms two floors down. The rooms below The Pan, were still, as yet, unsearched.

'Clear!' shouted one of them.

Why do I do these stupid, stupid things? The Pan thought as he skittered down the stairs towards the danger, as quietly as he could. He slipped into the nearest bedroom, the one facing the house with the opened windows opposite. Thank The Prophet this one was similar, with a row of leaded glass panes. He crept quietly inside and closed the door.

Below he could hear the sound of Grongles turning over beds and furniture. He pitied the owners of the house but was glad that the Grongles searching it were the type to have a thorough riffle through for 'evidence' to appropriate or, to put it another way, stuff to nick. Had they been honest, they'd have taken no time at all to conduct their search and would surely have found The Pan skulking around upstairs.

Instead, they were down there searching for jewellery or hidden savings while he stood in front of a row of opened windows trying to see if the house opposite was being searched as well, and if so, what was happening in the room facing him. The wide eaves of the floors and roofs above cut out a lot of light, making it difficult to tell if there was anyone in there. But it looked empty.

Hoorah.

The Pan climbed on to the sill, and pushed the window his side open further. It was three feet to the house opposite, possibly less. He could almost step over the gap, if he could just pull the window on the other side open a little further. He leaned out. That's when he heard heavy footsteps on the stairs.

Smeck. No time to climb across now. What to do?

Chapter 10
Cruel fate

Corporal Minto stomped into the fourth-floor bedroom. These idiots were useless; there was nothing worth nicking. He upended the bed with a crash just in case. 'No!' He swore in Grongolian, causing one of the troopers with him, Private Sayle, who'd been searching the other room on this floor, to come hurrying to his aid.

'What's up, Minto?'

'What's up, *Corporal* Minto, *SIR*.'

'Sorry, what's up, Corporal Minto, sir?'

'Nothing, I'm just ticked off. This is a waste of time.'

'It stinks in here, have you let one go?'

'Don't be a tool, of course I haven't.'

'Sorry sir. It's pretty ripe though, sir.'

'This whole smecking place stinks,' growled Corporal Minto, 'it must have been when I upended the bed.' Corporal Minto heaved a bad-tempered sigh.

'These plebs have nothing worth nicking. I wish they'd just bulldoze this whole dung heap. I hate searching the smecking Goojan Quarter.'

'Yeh. I've smacked my head on their stupid, smecking, midget buildings fifteen times already!'

'The Captain says it's a site of historical significance or something.'

'He would, he's always talking through his arse.'

'Sir.'

'Have Phlange and Wendell finished searching upstairs?'

'Yeh, nothing.'

Corporal Minto blew the air out through his teeth. It was too hot for this crap. 'What a shower. C'mon then, let's see if the vermin across the street have anything worth nicking.'

'Oh, what? We're doing the one opposite?'

'Yeh,' said Minto. 'But don't worry, I told command that if they want any more searched after that they can shove it. And you know what? For once they seemed to be listening.'

****

Outside, braced against the beams under the dark shade of the eaves, The Pan of Hamgee breathed a sigh of relief as he heard them go. From what they'd said if he could get into the house opposite, through that one, and over into the house opposite *that*, he'd be home free. Lucky they'd confused the smell of Goojan spiced sausage with an attack of wind. Well, The Pan supposed, it did smell a bit pungent. Even so, thank The Prophet they were so dumb.

His limbs were shaking with the effort of keeping him in his hiding place. With a great deal of relief he swung his legs slowly down, pushed off the windowsill and caught the gutter of the building opposite. It wasn't a big jump as jumps went, and he was soon slipping through the open window into the room beyond. Once again, he could hear Grongle voices bitching and complaining about having to search the house, but this time, from the rooms above.

Heart hammering, he fled silently across the hall and slipped into a back room, closing the door softly behind him. The window was shut but the ones on the house opposite were open. As he listened to the sounds of boots clumping overhead, he fumbled, hands shaking, with the catch. It seemed to take him forever but he finally managed to fling it open just as the clumping boots started down the stairs.

He leapt and scrambled into the bedroom opposite. As he looked back to the room he'd just left he could dimly make out the door opening, and threw himself to the floor so as not to be seen. He lay still for a moment, listening.

Nobody appeared to be searching this house but The Pan proceeded with caution anyway, slithering across the floor and out onto the landing on his stomach. He dared not stand up for fear of being seen by any Grongles searching the room from which he'd just come. He closed the door, and tiptoed across the third separate hallway in as many minutes. Ahead of him lay another bedroom. Thank The Prophet it was hot and most beings had their windows open. So long as he was careful which way he went when he reached the end of the street, he should be alright from here on. He made his way out and shinned down the building, landing lightly in the cobbled alley below.

As he dropped from the overhang he realised a group of Galorshes was standing in the shadows. They turned towards him with expressions of surprise.

'So sorry, to startle you, do excuse me,' he said, tipping his hat at them and walking swiftly away, as if dropping off the side of a building onto the streets below was a perfectly normal event here in the Goojan Quarter. Let's face it, in some parts of Ning Dang Po, it was. Through the useful eyes in the back of his head The Pan saw them staring after him. Hopefully they wouldn't say anything to anyone but he couldn't be sure—he needed to leave, fast. Despite not wanting to risk using the SE2 he wished he could. No, he told himself, there was hardly any room to manoeuvre and it would be hard for it to find him. He soon came to a crossroads. The quickest way out would be straight over, as far as he could recall, but he should probably put a little more space between himself and the Grongles searching for him. Yes. Definitely. He turned right and doglegged up a smaller back street. The road narrowed very quickly and he found himself in an alley that was small and cramped, even for the Goojan Quarter. Worse, it was a dead end.

Bum!

The door of a nearby building opened as he approached and three unsavoury types stepped out into his path.

Double bum!

'Hello,' said the leader, a woman with pale, piercing green eyes and spiky hair.

'Hi,' squeaked The Pan. Through his useful extra eyes in the back of his head he noticed three Blurpons hopping into the street behind, barring his escape.

Uh-oh, this didn't look good.

The woman sniffed the air. 'What's that smell?'

The Pan attempted a nonchalant shrug, although it was difficult to make it work while shaking with fear. 'I can't smell anything,' he squeaked.

'I can. The river.' The river? Really? Not the sausage? For a moment The Pan wondered if he'd dropped it and put his hand to the strings of the fabric bag sitting tight across his chest. No. She was messing with him, surely. 'That looks like river mud on your boots.'

The others, the Blurpons behind and the two other humans with his female conversant crowded in.

'I— it might be. I do walk along the towpath from time to time.' He took his hat off and slicked one hand through his hair, nervously.

'Like yesterday morning?'

'Er … no. No, no, no. Definitely not yesterday morning.'

'Don't lie to me!' There was a metallic noise, half a scrape and half a metallic ka-ching, which turned out to be the sound of her drawing a knife from the holster strapped to her leg.

Arnold's trousers! She was going to slash him!

The Pan screamed and tried to step swiftly backwards. However, he'd forgotten about the Blurpons behind who were hemming him in so closely that they were below his field of vision. He toppled over one of them and went sprawling onto his back. He leapt up, ready to run, but they were quicker than he was and had circled him again before he could even think about getting started. This was the Resistance. It had to be. No-one else was that fast. Once again, he wished he'd had the wit to cut the sausage up and stash half of it somewhere else—no, because if it'd been real that would have halved its value. Although, if it had been real he could have left it with Goldy McSpim. It was fake anyway. Not that it mattered because he'd be losing it now, all of it. Oh well, at least if he played this right they might be distracted by the sausage and not realise that he was the driver they were after.

'I wouldn't try and run if I were you,' said the woman with the knife as one of the Blurpons produced a lethal-looking crossbow from about its person and pointed it at him.

'Look.' The Pan put his hands out, palms downwards in the universal sign language for 'calm down' the world over. 'I'm K'Barthan, you're K'Barthan. Please. The Grongles kill enough of us as it is. We really don't need to start helping them out by murdering each other.'

'Who said anything about murdering you?' said the woman.

'With the knife and that thing,' The Pan gestured to the crossbow which the Blurpon was still aiming at him, 'it kind of looks, you know, on the cards.'

Her turn to shrug. 'I suppose you might get yourself killed, but only if you try anything stupid.'

'Yeh, like running away from us,' said the Blurpon with the crossbow.

'Right,' said The Pan. 'OK, so how do I get from where we are now to the bit where I walk away, not dead, and everyone's happy?'

'That's difficult. You behave and you'll get "not dead" but you may not get to walk away. I haven't decided yet.'

'How do I convince you?'

'You may not be able to convince me. I may decide you should join us.'

The Pan's stomach turned over. Arnold. No. He couldn't

join the Resistance. Not at any cost. 'No, you don't want that. Seriously, I'm rubbish, I can't kill, I'm clumsy—'

'Not when you climb you're not.'

'No really, I assure you, I am.' There was an awkward silence which The Pan filled, in his fear, by blurting out, 'Why? What on earth would you want me for?'

'If you're the guy we're looking for, you'll know.'

'Yeh, I expect I would, *if I was* but I'm not. I'm really sorry but honestly, I'm just a scrotty little nobody trying to survive.'

'Maybe, but a few streets away, I saw you shin down the side of a building like a pro.'

'This is a police state. A lot of people shin down the sides of buildings.'

'Not respectable people. But we can let that slide. My point is, you've escaped a police search.'

'Oh come on! It was more of a desultory nod to a search than the actual thing. When they're that unenthusiastic, trust me, it doesn't take much.'

'Actually, that's where you're wrong. It does, for most people, unless you're good at it.'

'I'm used to it,' said The Pan.

'Exactly!'

'No, no, no! That's really not the same as being good at—'

'Search him.'

The other two humans stepped up. One took the bag off The Pan's shoulders while the other patted him down for concealed weaponry. He felt his spirits sinking as they removed the snurd keys from his back pocket. They put the bag with the sausage in it and the letter from Goldy McSpim on the ground in front of the woman. She didn't even look at it.

Did she have no sense of smell? Arnold's arm pits, no! Was she after him?

'So you have a snurd,' said the woman, sweetly as one of her acolytes handed her The Pan's keys.

'Yes.' No point lying.

'Is it silver?'

'No.' Of course it wasn't. It was metallic grey, possibly silver-grey; dark and light two-tone, and yes, The Pan supposed, the unwary might easily mistake it as silver from a distance but was it *actual* silver? No.

'It's an SE2 though, isn't it?' She looked at the keys in her hand as if to check.

'I'm sorry, does that mean something?' asked The Pan.

'You're not very clued up, are you?' said one of the humans and they all laughed.

'There was a police chase yesterday. Pretty much everything the Grongle security forces have versus a snurd SE2. Where were you? Under a rock?'

'I was ... in the launderette.'

'Since yesterday?'

'I was ...' The Pan sought desperately for a convincing explanation, 'ill.' Ugh, so lame. 'What happened?' He probably shouldn't have asked her that question.

'It got away.'

'That's good,' said The Pan weakly. He looked at her with his best bemused expression. 'Do your people use SE2s now?'

'No. Our drivers call it a hairdresser's snurd!'

'That's a bit harsh, it's small but it's—' The Pan stopped as he pretended to let the penny drop and stared at her in completely genuine horror. With the possibility of being kidnapped and made to drive for the Resistance in the frame, no real acting was required. 'Hang on ... You don't think it was me, do you?'

'We have to ask ourselves that question,' she said and the beings with her nodded and murmured their assent.

'It could have been anyone—SE2s are two-a-penny.'

'Not exactly two-a-penny,' said the woman.

'OK, no, but there are a fair few. It's not as if mine is going to be the only one, is it?'

'I think it may be the only silver one.'

'I told you, it isn't silver. And do I look as if I can drive like that to you?'

She gave him a disparaging up-and-down glance. 'It's not about what I see or the impression you give. It's about facts.'

'This is insane! D'you want me to summon it and show you how crap I am?' asked The Pan, trying to keep the hope out of his voice. It wouldn't go well, not with the police snurds up there and whatever unspecified, and as yet unknown, damage it had suffered in his previous escape. But he knew he'd get away from these beings in a trice in the SE2. Sure, he'd have to escape the authorities afterwards, but he'd rather attempt that in the SE2 if the alternative was trying to out-run the fierce group of Resistance fighters around him on foot.

'Not here.'

Sensible answer, The Pan conceded. Pity. Now what? These beings were scary but the trick to walking away was surely to hand them something they wanted more than him. That would be the sausage, obviously. Perhaps that was what they were angling for. If they were, he'd happily take it on the chin if the alternative was life in the Resistance. Despite his fear he managed to wait, in silence, for his female aggressor to make the next move.

She bent down and picked up the box. 'What's this?'

'It's just a sausage.'

'Just a sausage?'

'Yep.'

'It's a Goojan spiced sausage.'

Something about her manner had changed. It looked as if it *was* the sausage she was after. Of course it was. All the stuff about the snurd was just scare tactics to make The Pan hand it over in return for his life. Was he meant to ask her to take the sausage and let him go? Possibly. On the other hand, if that wasn't her plan, any attempt at a bribe might insult her. Yeh, and it was never a good idea to insult someone with a patently short fuse when they had a knife that big; especially not when she had a group of friends with her who were as angry and uptight as she was. He eyed the ring of beings gathered around him. Definitely.

It also depended on what she knew about the sausage. Did she realise it was fake or did she think it was the real deal?

'Well, that's the thing ...' he said.

'What d'you mean, that's the thing?' she demanded.

She stood there, knife at the ready, watching, waiting for him to reply. The Pan's thoughts came at the kind of lightning speed they could only achieve when he believed he was about to die.

Should he tell her it was fake? No. Knowing his luck, she'd accuse him of pulling a fast one and cut his throat. On the other hand, if he broke the news to her the right way, he might be able to make it look as if he was pretending. Yeh. And if she got the sausage, he was beginning to think she might leave *him*. Something about the way she so clearly despised him. That wasn't acting. That was real. If she and her gang believed he'd bested the cream of the security forces, surely there would have been a hint of respect. It would have been grudging, for sure, but there'd have been something, wouldn't there? There'd be a feeling, an essence, the faintest whiff ... more than this. Yeh. The Pan heaved a sigh. He knew what to say now, so he took his few reserves of courage in both hands and spoke up. 'I'm afraid that isn't legit. It's a cheap copy. I'm a conman which is why I can escape a police search. But I assure you, that's all I am.'

He waited, but she didn't slash him with the knife and the

Blurpon didn't fire his crossbow. Arnold be praised.

'Where did you get this?' she demanded.

Here came the tricky bit, The Pan thought. He was going to have to tell the truth, or at least enough of it to make his story credible. He was also going to have to admit he'd lied to her, but maybe if he was playing the part of a conman, she'd buy it without killing him. Possibly.

'OK look, to be honest, I got it from the river Dang.'

'When?

'Yesterday. I—'

'What time yesterday?'

'Eleven o'clock in the morning or thereabouts?' said The Pan, picking a time when he'd actually been in the air, in his snurd rather than by the river. 'I reckon someone had stashed it under one of the private jetties up by The Planes, just beyond Golden Point. Word is, a crate of them fell off Graden End Bridge and some mudlarkers picked it up. I reckon they may have hidden it, meaning to come back later.' Was that too much information? Probably.

'How d'you know where it came from?'

'I heard some of the mudlarkers talking while I was lying in one of the shelters along there pretending to be asleep.'

'Which jetty did you find it under?'

'Third one along from Golden Point. There's a nice bit at the end where you can sunbathe and it—'

'Yeh, yeh, we don't need your life story, you jerk. What happened to these mudlarkers?'

'The security forces got them,' The Pan said promptly.

'That's not what I heard. I heard they escaped.'

'That's not what the security forces told me,' The Pan lied. 'We had time for a quick word before I ran away just now.'

'You outran them from a standing start?'

'Are you mad? Of course not! I was at the top of the

stairs. This big hulking great Grongle down at the bottom shouted, "We've got your mates, and the rest of the sausage, there's no point running!"'

'And what did you do?'

'I ran, obviously, but threw a vase down the stairwell at him first, you know, to delay him.'

No, no, no! You idiot! First rule of lying to big scary people; don't make the story too complicated. You may have to remember all this stuff later.

One of the Blurpons opened Goldy McSpim's letter and handed it to the leader. 'I reckon that sausage ain't so fake,' he growled with a glowering look at The Pan.

'No. Really. It is,' The Pan said.

The woman took her time reading the letter and then looked daggers at him over the top of it. 'If it is, how come you have this?'

'I—' began The Pan and stopped. He tried to appear beaten, although to be honest, since he was, thoroughly, it didn't take much effort. 'OK, listen, you have a knife,' The Pan tried not to look at it in case she got the wrong idea and decided to use it on him. 'Can we not cut it in half? An honest conman has to live.'

'You'll find other ways.'

'Please,' The Pan was supposed to be *pretending* to beg but this was embarrassingly close to the real thing.

'No,' the woman put the knife back in a sheath on her thigh. The Pan hardly dared breathe. 'You're going to give us this sausage, aren't you?'

'Look, I really don't—'

'And we're going to sell it to make money for the cause,' she spoke over him. 'Our cause: a noble cause, a fight for freedom from tyranny. You want freedom from the tyranny we live under, don't you?'

'I do, but—'

'You get to live and we've no use for your snurd, or you, so count yourself lucky.'

'You mean you're not taking me with you?'

'As if,' she tossed his keys onto the ground, 'it was the sausage we were after, not you.' Her lip curled in disdain as she said the word 'you'. 'You're no escape man. If you were, we wouldn't have caught you.'

Ouch. But at the same time, kind of, phew.

'Yer. Bit dumb for a conman ain't ya,' said the Blurpon with the crossbow and they all snickered.

Yeh. Ha, smecking ha, thought The Pan but he knew better than to reply.

'Come on lads,' she said, and she and her troops melted away as swiftly as they'd arrived.

Chapter 11
Lying low

The Pan didn't know whether to laugh or cry. He could have done with selling the sausage, in slices, to the wrong kinds of restaurants because the wrong kind of cash—even if there was less than he'd hoped—was better than none. There wouldn't have been enough for a new ID but it would have fixed any damage the security forces might have inflicted on the SE2. As it was he was alive, but unless he got his arse in gear, probably not for long. The Resistance fighters he'd just met were the kinds of gits who'd take everything from him and then earn a few extra Zloty for the cause by reporting him to the nearest Grongolian patrol.

Yeh.

'Because the cause is more important than the actual living beings it's supposed to help, isn't it? You utter, utter smeckers!' he muttered.

He picked up his keys and shoved them in his pocket. Time to get off the street.

The building to his left appeared to be derelict and when he tried the door it swung open. He made his way to the opposite side where he found a window. It only took a small amount of effort to persuade it to open. He looked out. This was the edge of the Goojan Quarter where it bordered the canal and the sheer wall ran down ten or fifteen feet into the water. There wasn't even a path. He sighed. Only one way out then. He looked up but there was no sign of the circling security forces snurds. Maybe it would be OK. With a shrug, he pressed the button on his keys and waited.

It took a while but after a minute or two, in the distance,

he heard the sound of the SE2's engine. It sounded as sweet as a nut; he'd expected it to be missing slightly or showing some signs of the stresses of the chase but no, it seemed fine. Could he be this lucky? Only Gerry at Snurd would be able to tell but it sounded as if the engine, at least, had experienced no ill effects.

He climbed up onto the windowsill and as the snurd cruised by, leapt into the driver's seat. It wasn't the greatest of landings but he'd made worse. Now where? Turnadot Street?

For the first time since he'd started drinking in the Parrot and Screwdriver, The Pan wondered if he should go back there: if it was wise. Should he get close to anyone? Would he lose his edge? More to the point, if there was any kind of manhunt, would his presence there endanger Gladys, Ada, Their Trev and the punters? They were fast becoming like family and The Pan wondered if he should drag them into all of this. Well, no, of course he shouldn't and he had no intention of doing so. That went without saying. Would he though? If he went back there?

Everything about the Parrot and Screwdriver had got under his skin. Badly. He had to accept that. On the other hand, it could hardly have turned him soft the way he feared. More the opposite. He recalled his escape from the Arboretum with Christine, Terri and Bort.

'Yeh,' he told himself. 'You've never flown like that before. It's hardly losing your edge, even if letting those Resistance fighters get to you was a bit stupid.'

Having a safe bolthole seemed to have made him sharper if anything. And if he never went back he would miss the beer. And the company. And the sandwiches. And the punters. But above all, he would miss the old ladies and the reassuring stolidity of Their Trev. He'd even miss Humbert. Probably.

Alright, so if he was honest, becoming a regular there

probably wasn't sensible. But Arnold knew, life on the blacklist was tough enough. Why make it worse? And Big Merv had pretty much told him to become a regular—he had to get hold of The Pan somewhere. Not that that was a bonus exactly, but Big Merv *not* being able to find him and getting upset about it, that would be fairly ugly. A sudden, unwanted mental image of Finicky Bert, the jeweller, swinging upside down, flashed into his head again. He wished that would stop happening. Definitely best not to upset Big Merv though. Which reminded him—

His thoughts were suddenly interrupted by some urgent messages from his nose. 'What *is* that smell?' He sniffed the air. 'Arnold! I know I keep talking to myself, and I know it's not a good sign, but ... I think I would remember if I'd let one go.' He wrinkled his nose. 'Wouldn't I?' Yuk. Something was definitely a bit niffy. 'Blimey.' He sniffed again. It couldn't be the snurd, he'd spent the best part of the morning scrubbing the river mud off the seats. It was minty fresh inside and yet ... there was a smell.

Yes it was definitely coming from the footwell. Of course. The unmistakeable tang of the river Dang, and it was coming from his boots. 'By The Prophet's hair! I smecking scrubbed those as well!'

It probably didn't matter. The sole was coming off one of them anyway. He'd have to 'liberate' a replacement pair from somewhere. They probably wouldn't be black, suede or elastic-sided though, which would be a shame. The Pan liked black, suede, elastic-sided boots.

'It's really not my day, today, is it?' he sighed.

He'd been smart enough to prepare himself for losing the sausage and with it, his chance of a new identity. If that had come off, it would have been the stuff of fairy tales. The Pan was prepared to believe that happy ever afters sometimes happened, but he was also pragmatic enough to accept that, if they did, they were the kind of thing that would happen to other beings. Not him. Even so, it was galling to be down on the job to the tune of a pair of boots and in all probability, some expensive fixing up for his snurd.

'You'll need a new windscreen at any rate,' he told it.

It was equally annoying to think that he'd have come out ahead if he'd accepted the two Grongolian dollars Terri had offered him in the—

'Hang on!' She'd promised him boots as well. And Bort had mentioned them too. In the post-escape euphoria he'd completely forgotten. That settled it then. It wasn't just one pair, either. Terri, Christine and Bort had promised him two.

'I'm going to hold them to that promise,' he said. At the least it would give him an excuse to see Bort again. He was pretty sure he knew where the three women had parked—in his mind's eye he heard Bort correcting him—*moored* their barge.

'Yeh. That.'

Alright then, he'd pop down to Lower Right and scope the canal looking for boats. In particular, Terri, Christine and Bort's boat. 'Sorry, barge,' he corrected himself, as if speaking to an imaginary Bort.

That's if they were still there of course. They might have moved on. Goldy McSpim pretty much said they'd visited him. Would they have already sold the sausage and left? Possibly. Even if they hadn't, he could hardly pay them a visit. Right now he needed to keep a low profile. Except he also needed to check in at the Parrot and Screwdriver to pick up any delivery instructions from Big Merv.

He heaved a sigh. 'Why does it have to be so complicated?' he muttered.

OK, he'd stay incognito for another twenty-four hours, then he'd slip as unobtrusively into the Parrot as he could to check for any messages from his boss.

He flew across the city, keeping his speed and flying as

sedately as possible so as not to draw any unwelcome attention from the security forces or the police. Below him the streets seemed surprisingly quiet. Then again, the Goojan Quarter hadn't been, had it? Yeh well. He supposed that even the Grongles were smart enough to realise that anyone with a stolen sausage would need to have it valued. There probably weren't that many beings in Goldy McSpim's line of work and they were probably all under surveillance. Alright, so the Resistance had the sausage. On the upside it meant they'd give up on him with any luck, and the Grongles ... they'd give up eventually. Or they'd be distracted by someone or something else. Yeh. If he was lucky.

Chapter 12
Off the hook?

Once again it dawned bright, clear and hot. K'Barthans rose, went to work and went about their business. Those without jobs, or retired, loafed about in parks enjoying the sun. Those with dogs, like Mrs Glethewn Prenderghast, went for walks with them. She went out early before it got too warm and let her dog, Wolf, off the lead in a quiet part of the park away from other dogs. She stopped for a moment while Wolf did something nobody could do for him, then she put his disconcertingly warm excrement into a plastic bag and deposited it in a bin specifically designated for the purpose.

Despite his ferocious name, Wolf was a small, mercurial Jack Russell. He immediately disappeared into his favourite row of rhododendron bushes. Mrs Prenderghast watched him. Presumably he was following some dimly—or perhaps not so dimly—remembered instinct to hunt for rabbits. That said, if he found anything there it tended to be litter, or half-eaten burgers. Burgers weren't so bad, so long as there wasn't any chilli sauce. That tended to have an unfortunate effect on Wolf.

In the bushes, unseen by his owner, Wolf snacked briefly on some fox poo before continuing his investigations, only to be brought up short by something far more interesting than a discarded burger. It was more of a burgher in this case. A man. Sleeping. Wolf knew exactly what to do with sleeping humans.

The Pan woke up to discover a small dog helpfully 'washing' his face.

'Do you mind?' The dog seemed friendly. He ruffled its

fur. 'Hello little fellow,' he said which precipitated more enthusiastic licking. He realised that the dog's breath smelled a bit ripe and now so did his face. 'Ugh, what have you been eating?'

He sat up and the sudden movement made the dog run off barking excitedly. The Pan leapt to his feet and made a swift and furtive exit from the other side of the rhododendrons, before the dog's owner or anyone else found him. No-one saw.

It surprised The Pan how well he could sleep in some of the strangest places. Extremely well. The thing about sleeping in the park was that, while it was safe, it was important to be up and away before the gates opened.

On the other side of the rhododendrons he heard someone calling the dog. He looked at his watch. By The Prophet's socks, it was late. He should have been gone ages ago. Never mind, nobody had found him. No-one except the dog at any rate.

Making his way swiftly to the water fountain he washed the slobber off his face. *That was a rude awakening*, he thought. Kind of cute though, or at least it would have been, if he weren't so sure the dog had been eating something grim, which it hadn't really finished chewing, before it licked his face.

He went to the park entrance, summoned the SE2 and retrieved a small rucksack containing clean clothes, his washbag and a towel from the boot. Slinging the rucksack over his shoulder, he pressed the self-park button on the keys and slipped them in his pocket. Better to give it some space. It was now almost two days since he'd escaped from the security forces. Were they still looking? Difficult to tell. But he'd been lying low long enough. Maybe he'd venture into the Parrot for lunch. It was always quieter then.

After I've had a wash, he thought and headed for the baths.

****

'And where do you think you've been, young man?' demanded Ada as The Pan of Hamgee stepped into the bar at The Parrot and Screwdriver.

'Yer, you hasn't been in for two days,' said Gladys.

The Pan ducked a low-flying lunge from Humbert, the eponymous parrot that went with the Screwdriver.

'Arse!' shouted Humbert just as The Pan said,

'Hello.'

'Humbert!' said Ada sternly. 'Leave the poor boy alone!'

The Pan couldn't have stopped the smile that spread across his face if he'd wanted to. He'd narrowly escaped death, twice, and it was only being back in the safe, friendly familiarity of the Parrot and Screwdriver, now, which brought that home.

'It's alright,' he said shakily, which was lucky because Ada's parrot had ignored her, as usual, and landed on his shoulder.

Gladys appeared from the Holy of Holies, behind the bar. 'Where has you been?' she demanded.

'I was just asking him the same question,' said Ada.

'Arnold's Y-fronts! Talk about the third degree, what's got into you two?' asked The Pan.

'We has heard ... things,' said Gladys. He realised that she sounded strained, as if whatever the 'things' were, they'd worried her.

'I'm sorry,' he said. 'I didn't mean to put either of you out.'

'You hasn't. And we knows you can look after yourself. But we worries,' said Gladys.

'Exactly,' Ada chipped in. 'Remember, we *are* old ladies and fretting about things, including our customers, is our job.'

97

'I'm fine.' He flashed the two of them what he hoped was a charming smile.

'Good,' said Ada. She didn't sound convinced.

There weren't many punters in but The Pan noticed the general hubbub of conversation seemed to have gone a bit quieter, as if they were all listening.

'Anything interesting happen since I was last in?' he asked as Gladys put a pint of one of the establishment's home-brewed beers on the bar in front of him. It was a slightly lighter one, suitable for lunchtime drinking. Although it was all relative, and Gladys and Ada's idea of a 'light' beer was only slightly less strong than the others.

'The Grongles arrested the perp— perp— blokes what escaped all them Grongles up at the Arboretum.'

The Pan perked up. 'They have?' Booyacka! That meant he was home free.

'Yer, more's the pity.'

'Who was it?'

'Who were *they*, dear. There was more than one.'

'There was?'

Gladys and Ada exchanged glances. There was a whole world of nuance in those looks, although, as usual, to The Pan, it was totally unreadable.

'Oh yes dear, about five identical snurds apparently,' Ada said.

'Five?' asked The Pan. 'That's not right, surely?' No, no, no, don't say anything.

'Why not, dear?'

'I— I heard there were four.'

'Ner, 's five accordin' to GNN,' said Gladys.

'Although the Free KBC says there were two.'

Blimey, thought The Pan, they'd *both* got it wrong.

Ada continued, apparently oblivious. 'They showed one on the news—'

'Yer it was all mangled and burned up proper,' said Gladys.

'Wow. What kind of snurd?' asked The Pan.

'What model was it? Gladys, can you remember?'

'Yer, 's a silver one.'

Pub-Quiz Alan piped up from a nearby table. 'It was an SE2,' he said. 'We reckoned you got one of them. Dave was concerned it might be yours.'

Psycho Dave, Alan's lantern-jawed drinking buddy, nodded and said, 'Yer.'

'No chance,' said The Pan cheerfully, 'for starters, mine's grey.' Metallic grey, possibly even silver-grey but ... grey. Definitely.

'Weren't the Resistance behind it?' volunteered Betsy, who ran the house of ill repute a few doors down on the opposite side of the street.

''S right,' said Gladys.

'Yeh. They just caught a gang of them in the Quaarl District,' Alan continued. 'It was on GNN. They stole the sausage to sell for funds, some Blurpons and a Tithian woman. They didn't have the sausage on them though. The K'Barthan police captured them all stinking of sausage but then they escaped.'

'Yeh right. I bet they did,' said The Pan.

'Yeh. I'm with you on that,' said Alan. 'I reckon that if they had a sausage in the first place they did a deal. It's what I would've done.'

'Yer, hand over the sausage in return for 'em lookin' the other way for a couple a minutes while I scarpered,' Dave agreed.

'Mmm, Goojan sausage all round at the station tonight,' said The Pan.

'Yep!' said Alan.

OK, so the Resistance gang had gone free. But with any luck they'd be too busy evading the security forces to come looking for The Pan.

'They is sayin' there's three other sausages that was

stolen which has disappeared comple— comple— into thin air,' Gladys added.

The Pan smiled. *At least somebody got something out of it,* he thought.

'Good,' he said. Because, fake or not, the sausage was worth some decent cash.

That was weird. The Grongles appeared to have chalked his escape up to experience and explained it away. OK, so they might secretly be looking for the SE2 that had escaped them ... possibly ... but at the same time, they appeared to have ruled out The Pan's snurd for the moment. He'd changed the number plates of course. That might have helped.

'Here, I is almost forgetting,' said Gladys, and at this point she gave Ada a huge wink. 'A young lass was in looking for you.'

'She was?'

'Yer,' said Gladys with a bit of a look. 'I weren't here when she arrived but Trev says she was disappointed you wasn't in.'

'Yes, dear,' Ada chimed in, 'she seemed to think you live here.'

'Ah ... yes. Sorry, I didn't mean to take any liberties, this seemed as good a place for her to find me as any.'

''Cept you wasn't here.'

'I've been a bit busy the last couple of days.' The Pan tried to sound apologetic.

'Yer, I bets you has,' said Gladys archly. She wasn't buying it. Then again, now he was actually in the pub, he found he couldn't stop smiling. Arnold, it felt good to be there.

'If you asked me, she is rather keen on you,' said Ada.

'Yer. She was blonde.'

The word 'blonde' hung in the air like an accusation. There was silence in the bar as the punters listened.

Arnold's nostril hair they were nosey, thought The Pan, but it just made him smile even more. 'That'd be Bort. I met a family of mudlarkers by the river and helped them out a bit. Bort's the daughter.'

Ada's eyebrows arched. 'Helped them out a bit, dear?'

'It was perfectly innocent. I just gave them a hand with a box.'

Gladys gave him a look. 'I reckons you ought to be careful with them mudlarkers,' she said.

'Yes,' Ada agreed, 'they're a rum lot.'

'I'm pretty rum, myself. It was nothing illegal *and* they can't be much rummer than you lot in here.' He noticed the looks the old ladies were exchanging. 'Will you look at yourselves, you nosey parkers!'

'It's only Gladys and Trev who are the Parkers. I'm a Maddox,' said Ada.

'Ha, ha, very funny.'

'Is that what the smell is, dear?'

'I'm sorry?'

'The smell.'

The Pan sniffed and realised that the eggy tang of the Dang had come into the pub with him. Well, he was wearing his boots, so he supposed it would. 'Yeh, I'm afraid I—' he began and stopped. No need to tell them he fell in. 'My boots got a bit muddy. I'm hoping it'll air out.'

'Good luck with that,' said Alan from across the room.

'Who's the blonde then?' asked Big Psycho Dave.

'I told you. Bort,' The Pan said. 'She's one of the mudlarkers I met. She and her Mum, Terri, and Christine who's Terri's wife. They were by the river and I helped them out.'

'So you said, dear,' said Ada. 'She's in the snug.'

'I'm sorry?'

'The blonde,' Gladys gave him a knowing look. 'Bort?'

'Bort,' The Pan confirmed.

'She's in the snug, dear,' Ada carried on where Gladys had left off. 'She's come all the way from Lower Right, out near the old power station. We really couldn't send her back. At the least we had to feed her. We suggested she wait.'

'So you weren't *that* worried about me then?'

'We were hopeful,' said Ada. 'She said you'd arranged to meet her.'

'Yer, an' I reckons she's been here nearly half an' hour.'

'Exactly, the poor girl was so ravenously hungry—we had to make her some sandwiches.'

The Pan went pale.

'With chutney?'

'Of course not, they're for her, not you', said Ada. 'You really ought to look to your timekeeping, young man. Now off you go and apologise to her. It's very unchivalrous to keep a lady waiting.'

'Yer,' agreed Gladys.

What timekeeping? The Pan thought. How could he be late when he hadn't even known she was going to turn up?

Chapter 13
Surprise visitor

The Pan opened the snug door and Bort looked up suddenly, as if he'd made her jump.

'Hi,' he said, adding, before he could stop himself, 'sorry I'm late.' What was he saying?

She gave him a bit of a look. 'It's not like we arranged anything.' She smiled at him and he felt his heart melting.

'You told *them* you did.' He nodded in the direction of the main bar.

'Well, I had to tell them something. I haven't any cash with me and I was afraid they'd throw me out.'

'I see.' The Pan closed the door, went over to the table and put his beer down. His brother and sister had always teased him about trying to chat up women who were out of his league. Bort was a typical example. He attempted to arrange his features into something approaching a suave expression. He concentrated on looking at her face rather than any of the other bits of Bort, which were even more distracting than he remembered from their previous encounter. He cleared his throat.

OK, there was no need to feel shy. 'She's just another human who happens to be female.' That's what his sister always said.

But this was a female who'd kissed him on the cheek, he reminded himself. Yeh, and after he fell in the Dang, too. She was probably incubating typhus. No, she wasn't. Stop.

Bort was wearing a slightly bemused expression. Had that succession of thoughts taken longer than he realised? Had he said any of them out loud? Hmm. Hopefully not. Never mind. No good worrying about it now. Press on. 'Have you had a drink?'

'Yes. The old ladies gave me lunch on the house.' She threw him a coquettish smile. 'You've got them well trained.'

The Pan laughed, picked up the glass from the table and took a swig of his beer. 'It feels as if it's the other way round.'

'I've come to collect you.'

'What for?'

'Duh. Your fitting, idiot.' She started laughing but it was definitely with him, not at him. The Pan was a bit nonplussed, or possibly just a little fazed from being around Bort. Arnold's cobblers, he hadn't noticed this before. Not properly. 'Christine has cut out everything she can for the boots. Now she needs to measure your feet so she can sew it all together the right way.' She stopped and her face dropped a little. 'If you don't want them, it's OK,' she said. She sounded disappointed though.

'Actually, I would very much appreciate the boots. I need them.' He raised an eyebrow at her. 'You may have noticed, this being a small room, how much my current and only pair smells of the river.'

'I'm glad it's just your boots.'

'You mean you thought it was me?'

'I hoped it wasn't.'

'No human could smell that vile.'

'Believe me, I've met some who do. Come on, get that pint down you and let's get going.'

'If I down this pint I shouldn't be driving.'

'So?'

'So, young lady, Lower Right is a long walk.'

She gave him a bit of a look when he said 'young lady'. Maybe mock formality wasn't her thing. It seemed she'd decided to let it slide though, as she merely shrugged. 'It's a lovely day and we have legs, don't we?'

'Yes,' he said absently, trying not to look too obviously at

Bort's because she ... yes, she definitely did.

There was a knock on the door and Ada appeared along with Humbert who flew into the room shouting, 'Wipe my conkers!'

'Humbert!' said Ada.

To The Pan's complete surprise, Humbert circled the room once and then, with a single, 'Norks!', disappeared out into the hall.

'Well, that's a first,' he said.

'Isn't it, dear!' Ada winked at him and handed over a packet of sandwiches wrapped in greaseproof paper. 'You might want something to go with that beer, dear, but I do appreciate that your young ...' she stopped and felt around cautiously for the right word, 'friend has been here half an hour already. Gladys and I thought you could take these with you.' She beamed at him. 'They're on the house.'

With another ridiculously theatrical wink, she left the room. The Pan smiled to himself and shook his head, 'She means well,' he said.

'She's worse than Mum,' said Bort giggling. 'You alright eating those on the way?'

'I certainly am. Give me a minute to get rid of this,' he added and downed the beer in one. 'Right, me lady,' he told her, suppressing a burp because that would have compromised his attempt to sound chivalrous and suave. 'I'm ready if you are. Shall we?'

The burble of conversation in the Parrot and Screwdriver's main bar stopped for an instant as The Pan and Bort walked in from the direction of the snug but—fair play to the punters—it carried on as normal straight away, albeit at a slightly lower volume. Bort looked up at him and smirked. Gladys was either upstairs or down in the cellar as only Ada was looking after the bar. Despite their continued conversation, The Pan could feel the eyes of the punters on him and Bort as they walked up to it and put their glasses on the pristine wooden surface.

'Thanks for the beer,' he told Ada, 'and these.' He held up the packet of sandwiches.

'A pleasure, young man,' said Ada. Thank The Prophet she didn't wink again, but just gave him a cheery wave as he said a hasty goodbye and escorted Bort out of the door.

'Well, that's given them something to talk about,' he said as they wove their way through the tables of the Parrot and Screwdriver's outdoor drinking area and onto the street.

'They always that nosey?'

'Always, but they mean well.'

'Yeh, you said, and I did realise. I liked them.'

'So where are you parked then?'

'Moored, you dolt,' said Bort but she was teasing him. 'We moved but we're still in Lower Right. It's just a bit further along the canal, near where it joins the River Linnet. D'you know it?'

'Of course.'

The Pan knew pretty much all of Ning Dang Po. The River Linnet was one of the many tributaries of the Dang which ran through the city. The canal had been built to bypass a very bendy part that fed into a reservoir, then extended to improve transport links to other parts of the city. These days both routes took about the same time, unless the river was busy, but neither reservoir nor bendy bit were particularly appropriate for commercial boats. The reservoir because the boats weren't the cleanest things in K'Barth and it was supposed to be drinking water; the bendy bit because it took too long to manoeuvre the zed bends. Not only that but there was always a kerfuffle when boats going in different directions had to try and pass each other. There was only room for them to do so between bends.

'Well, it's a beautiful day for a walk.'

'It is.' He mentally planned a route from Upper Left,

where the Parrot and Screwdriver pub was situated, to Lower Right, where Bort's barge was parked. No. Moored. Get it right, man. There were several options. 'Which way d'you want to go? Quickest or scenic?' he asked her.

She smiled up at him and put her arm through his. 'Scenic.'

The Pan was a bit thrown. That was ... almost as if she *liked* him. Scenic was pretty spectacular; into town, along the river Dang over the Bridge of Eternal Glory and then along the canal to the wasteland. Apart from the last bit, that would involve all the most attractive and dramatic parts of the city. How long would it take, though, he wondered, a couple of hours? The Pan was fit—he spent a lot of his time running—but he was aware that not everyone else might be.

'Scenic is quite a long walk,' he warned her.

'I'm a mudlarker. I walk all day. And I've nothing else planned this afternoon. Christine and Mum aren't expecting you until half three.'

'Really?'

He raised an eyebrow at her. Well, it wasn't as if *he* had anything else planned for the next couple of hours either. 'Come on then.'

The Pan and Bort walked along the towpath by the river Dang. To start with he was very much on edge. But it was a hot day and it was soon apparent that both the police and the security forces had better ways to pass the time than sweating about outdoors. He began to relax and as he walked beside her, pointed out the landmarks of the city. She, in turn, showed him the places where she, Terri and Christine had been mudlarking. The Pan listened with interest as Bort explained how the water eddied and dropped things as the tide and the currents flowed in and out. He thought about how he enjoyed looking for fossils on the beach as a child and wished he'd known the things she was explaining back then. He reckoned, if he had, he'd have found a lot more. His thoughts turned, for the briefest moment, to his childhood in Hamgee.

Nope. Not that. Not now. Definitely not now. It wasn't often The Pan got to do something that felt normal. Walking along the towpath, arm in arm with a girl was more than he dared hope for, even if it was just for an afternoon. He wasn't about to stuff it up by letting himself get maudlin on her.

'You sound as if you love your life,' he said, trying to keep the envy out of his tone.

'Mudlarking is kind of addictive, wherever you do it. I miss Glardy though. We're part of a community up there—we all look out for one another. Well, all mudlarkers everywhere do that but it takes a bit of time to earn the trust of a new bunch.'

'You don't have much of an accent.'

'No, I wasn't born in Glardy but ... I dunno,' she shrugged, 'I guess it's where we fit in. A lot of us winter on barges moored up in the same place, along Vintner's Quay.'

'Sounds quaint.'

'No. Believe me, it's the crappest place on earth. It makes your Turnadot Street look posh. But I like it. It's a community up there.'

'What d'you do in the summer then?'

'Travel, mudlark in other places, see the waterways and sell Christine's boots and shoes.'

'You three not settling in Ning Dang Po then?'

She stopped and turned to face him. As she looked up at him, the sunlight sparkled off the unnaturally viscous waters of the river Dang as it oozed along in the background behind her. It reflected off her hair, too, giving her a kind of halo.

Wow, he thought. The world slowed down for a moment. If The Pan had been brave enough, he might have tried to kiss her. No. Not in broad daylight. She'd probably slap him.

'It was only ever going to be for a while,' said Bort. 'It's summer, so we're on the road, or at least, the water. But some of the best things are temporary, aren't they? Right?'

'I suppose so.'

The Pan had to concede that pretty much everything about his world was temporary. But he had a feeling Bort was talking about more than that. There was a whole subtext to this conversation that he wasn't getting. No surprises there.

'The thing is though, that doesn't mean they're any less good, the temporary things, or any less worthwhile. Or that you shouldn't enjoy them while you can.'

That sounded deep. The Pan was definitely lost now. 'Are you trying to tell me you ate the sausage?'

'No,' she said patiently. She gave him a bit of a 'you what?' look and started walking again.

Right. The temporary things stuff wasn't about the sausage then. 'Are you taking it back with you?' he asked before he could stop himself. No, no, no you idiot!

'The sausage?' she seemed a bit exasperated. 'Duh. No, we sold it.'

'You did?'

'Yep. I guess we just got lucky. We got rid of two by slicing them up and selling them to restaurants. Word got out and there was a bit of a bidding war. Then this weird Blaggysomp turned up and bought the other one. She was a go-between for some businessman. Apparently he has a house up in The Planes.'

'Ah,' said The Pan.

Bort shrugged. 'It meant nothing to me but she obviously thought we ought to know. I'm guessing it was her way of telling us he's posh.'

'Rich more like. If he lives there, he's loaded. He's probably also Grongolian. Hardly any K'Barthans can afford The Planes anymore.'

'This one can. Apparently he's a Swamp Thing.'

Oh. He would be, wouldn't he? 'A Swamp Thing with a Blaggysomp go-between?' asked The Pan, just to check.

'Yeh.'

'I see.'

'Yeh. Christine reckoned he was a gangster.'

'I'd say it's very probable,' said The Pan. He was pretty certain he knew exactly who'd bought the sausage but he wasn't going to speculate. Not aloud, anyway.

Bort gave him a bit of a sideways look. As they started walking again she continued, 'That's why you have to come and be measured today. Mum and Christine have to deliver the sausage first thing tomorrow so we're leaving straight after.'

'Flog it and leg it?' said The Pan.

'Too right. Haven't you sold yours yet?'

'I'm ...' should he admit what had happened to his sausage? No. 'I'm working on it.'

'I bet Bob'll buy it. I don't know her number but Mum has it, she'll give it to you.'

'The Blaggysomp was called Bob?'

'Yeh, it's short for Roberta apparently.'

Bob the Blaggysomp.

The Pan's wages were usually paid by a Blaggysomp called Bob who worked for Big Merv, chauffeuring his snurd and working behind the bar at The Big Thing night club. Her full name was Roberta as well. Could there be two Blaggysomps called Roberta who went by the name of Bob in Ning Dang Po? No. Not working for a businessman who lived in The Planes.

Mystery sausage buyer identified for certain? Check.

'Did she know it was fake?'

'It's not fake, it's a *replica*. It's made exactly the right way with the best ingredients the guy could get.'

'Which aren't the right ones ...'

'You got yours valued then. Good, I was beginning to

think you'd lost it. We told her it's a replica but her boss reckoned his Grongolian business contacts wouldn't know the difference.'

The Pan shrugged. 'That's true. They probably won't even eat it.' He wondered if he'd be delivering sausage slices to Big Merv's customers come next Prophet's Birthday, rather than Mrs Dingleton's traditional pastries. He sighed.

'We're meeting her at 10 o'clock tomorrow to hand it over.'

'Oh? Where?' asked The Pan. Surely it wouldn't be The Big Thing night spot.

'At Joe's internet cafe near the Botanical Gardens. D'you know it?'

'Vaguely,' said The Pan. He was happy for them, he really was, but she must have noticed that his heart wasn't quite in it.

'Cheer up. If Bob doesn't buy yours you'll find a restaurant that will, I bet.'

'Mmm.' The Pan heaved another sigh. He didn't want to think about what he'd lost. Time to change the subject. 'Talking of luxury foods, I'd better eat these sandwiches,' he said.

They were making good time, so he found a bench facing onto the river and sat down. Bort joined him, sitting closer than he expected, her leg warm against his. Despite the liberal helpings of chutney that Gladys and Ada had put into the sandwiches, he made short work of them.

'You're just a human bin, aren't you?' she told him.

'I'm hungry.'

She seemed disappointed that he finished them so fast. As if she'd enjoyed being so close to him. As if she liked the contact. It was almost as if she fancied him. Could she though? Really and truly? She was way out of his league, he knew that. Then again, he'd saved her life. Maybe she was grateful.

'I reckon you're always hungry,' she said.

'You have me there.' Should he tell her the sandwiches were the only thing he'd eaten in twenty-four hours? No.

'If I didn't know any better I'd be wondering if you ate your sausage.' There was a pause. 'Tell me you didn't eat it.'

'No,' said The Pan as he folded the greaseproof paper in half, tipped it up and poured the last few breadcrumbs into his mouth. Except it came out more like 'mnpfff'.

'Something happened though, didn't it?'

'Why d'you think that?'

'You still want the boots.'

She was smart, was Bort.

'There might be another reason for that,' said The Pan as Bort looked into his eyes. Arnold, yes. There was a very compelling reason to collect the boots sitting right next to him. Had she got there? She flashed him a smile. Mmm. Looked like it. Good.

Chapter 14
Subtle signals

As The Pan and Bort made their way along the canal towpath, the buildings around them gradually became more and more derelict. Eventually there was nothing but the canal, the towpath and the green grass of the embankment either side cutting its way through a bombsite. There were a lot of bollards for tying up but no boats were moored there. In the distance the remains of the old power station stood proud and, in between, fragments of other wrecked buildings stuck up among the rubble.

Bort walked very close beside him, occasionally linking her arm through his. But she kept stopping to pick aromatic leaves growing among the grass. Several different varieties, one garlicky, another minty and one which she told The Pan tasted like spinach. Larks ascended from the ruins around them into the summer air and gulls circled high above.

'Stay close,' he said as he looked around him. 'I normally fly over this. It's a while since I've seen it from down here.'

'Why not?'

'It can be a bit rough.'

'It's been safe enough for us.'

'Hmm ...' said The Pan as he scanned the rubble around him.

'And it's quiet.'

'Quiet. Yeh, I guess it's that.' Although it felt more like a restless silence to The Pan. There was a tension to the atmosphere which was less than tranquil. Bort strode breezily along, apparently oblivious. Or maybe she was just used to surroundings like this.

Here and there, where sections of buildings remained, The Pan could see the signs of furtive habitation. The beings living here would be those with nowhere further to fall; GBIs, the insane, the vulnerable, the lonely and the damaged. Beings even the Grongles wouldn't bother with. This was the kind of place where it was the inhabitants who howled at night and the wild dogs who stayed well clear.

Were Bort, Terri and Christine really so naive they didn't realise? Possibly. No. More likely the boat had armour cladding and was very secure. Or maybe they anchored it in the middle of the canal at night. Yes. That might discourage the locals. It was a wide waterway. The area had once been very busy, the waterway built to accommodate the huge barges coming and going from the factories. There was room for two or three of them to moor side by side without obstructing other traffic, and of course the presence of the locals might discourage other unwanted visitors.

'What made you choose this ... lovely spot?'

'No mooring fees,' said Bort.

'Ah.' Yeh, well, that figured.

'Also, people have to go a really long way out of their way to get to us on this side of the canal.'

They rounded a bend where a group of scrubby trees had grown up, obscuring their view of the path ahead for some distance. When they passed the trees, the canal ran straight again and there, about half a mile away, a single barge was moored. A little further on, out of earshot The Pan presumed but still in plain view, an overpass on stilts carried one of the open sections of the Outer Ring across the wasteland and away into the distance. The canal they were following merged into another, larger waterway there.

The *Happy Doris* was about ten feet wide with a long sloping roof which also doubled as a deck. Small channels cut along each side collected the rainwater that ran off it. There were portholes below it, and, underneath those, six-inch wide gunwales. At the edge of the roof, beside the run-off water channels, there were grab rails for anyone venturing along the gunwales to hang on to. He supposed the whole thing was about thirty feet long, although it was hard to tell from their angle of approach. Towards the front end, which, being a seasider, The Pan knew was officially called the prow, he could see fenders of plaited rope and a small triangular lower deck, one side stacked with neatly chopped firewood. Halfway along the roof he spotted a chimney. Perhaps they heated it with a wood burner in the winter.

The barge had a black mohair awning over the deck like the ones he'd seen on narrowboats; it was folded back and he could see double doors into the main cabin. The whole roof was covered in pots, mostly with edible plants growing in them. It looked as if a lot of the living accommodation was in the space which had originally been the hold. As well as the portholes in the side, there were a couple of glass faceted domes sticking up in the roof, about a foot in diameter, which The Pan recognised as light pipes. The sides of the boat comprised gaily painted wooden panels in red and blue; the red ones had a series of pictures and the name of the boat, while the blue ones contained the portholes with ornate decoration around each. As far as The Pan could see there was a lower deck at the back, too. Presumably they would drive the boat from that one.

Among the plants on top The Pan recognised tomatoes, and what might have been spinach or lettuces—probably some of each. There was curly kale and pots of herbs; basil, thyme and a small bay tree. There was even a stacking tower containing something that looked as if it might be strawberries.

'Wow,' he said, 'that's a pretty impressive crop coming on there.'

'Mum does the gardening,' said Bort. 'Christine makes shoes and boots. Every summer we come down south. She takes orders for boots and measures any new punters on the way down, then we moor up somewhere nice for a couple of weeks while she makes the boots, and deliver them all on our way back.'

'I wouldn't call this "somewhere nice".'

'No, we don't normally come this far in. Usually we stop at Lark Locks. D'you know it?'

'Not well. It's beyond my patch. I know roughly where it is and that's about it.'

'Your patch?' She rolled her eyes at him. 'You should try going further than your back door some time. Lark Locks is an amazing piece of engineering.'

'You don't strike me as an engineering buff.'

'I'm not! But you don't have to be a geek to realise something's cool.'

'That's true,' he conceded. They carried on walking. 'Have you always lived on a barge?'

'Most of my life, although Mum and Christine only finished it recently. They bought it as a rusty old hulk and converted it.'

'Arnold's trousers, that's impressive. Your parents are epic.'

'Yeh,' said Bort proudly, 'they are, and so is Christine.' She arched her eyebrows at him. 'Mum is mum, Christine is Christine. My *dad's* a getaway driver and he's Dad. He was kidnapped by the Resistance. We're hoping to buy him out one day.'

'Right, gotcha,' said The Pan. They hadn't a chance in a million of buying out the dad. The Resistance would just take their money and keep him. The Pan didn't say anything though.

'I didn't mean to sound waspish there,' said Bort. She seemed anxious.

'It's fine, you didn't.' He put his arm around her, hugging her as they walked. She leaned against him. 'I'm sorry if I was tactless.'

'It's OK. And you aren't tactless.' She smiled up at him.

As they approached the boat, what had become the

familiar smell of Goojan sausage wafted towards them on the breeze.

'Mmm, I can see why you had to moor up out of the way,' said The Pan.

Sitting on the roof on cushions dangling their legs over the side, sat Terri and Christine. They jumped off onto the grass as, arm in arm, The Pan and Bort approached.

'Ahoy there!' Terri called out to them. 'Would you like some elderflower cordial?'

Bort leaned up and whispered in The Pan's ear, 'Say yes, it's to die for.' It wasn't a normal whisper—her voice sounded low and husky, and he felt her lips brush against his skin. Arnold's nasal hair! He was thinking about all the wrong things now and his beats per minute had just about quadrupled.

'It is?' He looked down at her and without meaning to, ended up gawping straight into her cleavage. No, no, no. That's not where a gentleman should look! He shut his eyes for a second and when he opened them again concentrated on keeping his gaze on her face.

'Yeh, Christine makes it.' She looked up at him from under her eyelashes. There was definitely more than a hint of what Gladys and Ada would have called 'come hither' about her expression.

OK, so that was a pretty clear signal. In fact, he'd been getting pretty clear signals all day. But that one was so obvious that even *he* could believe it. He was sure, or at least, as sure as a young man with very little confidence dare be, that Bort fancied him. Possibly. Yeh. If he ever got her alone again, The Pan made a mental note, he would definitely kiss her. Almost certainly. Probably. Maybe. Yes ... of course he would. Perhaps. If he could gather up the courage.

Chapter 15
The *Happy Doris*

The boat was compact but surprisingly well designed inside, allowing the four of them to move about in relative ease without tripping over one another. Not that they had to. Terri and Bort turned to the left as soon as they entered, where Terri retreated to a galley at the far end of the cabin and set about preparing supper. It wasn't at the end of the barge—there was an open door behind her into a narrow passageway. Christine went to the right, where the barge extended four or five more feet.

Bort spread a mat on a low table in the middle of the long living area and then sat on a cushion, sorting the leaves she'd been picking into piles. She patted a low upholstered stool that had been placed against the wood panelled wall. 'You sit here,' she told The Pan, as Terri handed him a glass of the famous elderflower cordial.

He did as he was told, sitting with his back against the side of the barge, facing the entrance doorway, and looked around him. Christine was busy rummaging in a locker set in the wall in the space to his left. To his right, the other side of the barge's entrance door, was a middle relaxing and dining space where the table at which Bort sat was situated. She looked up from her pile of leaves and smiled. He raised his glass. 'Cheers,' he said, and drank some.

'How d'you like it?' she asked.

'It's fabulous.'

'And do you like the *Happy Doris*?'

'Is that the name of this boat?'

'Barge,' Bort corrected him with a wink.

'Yes. It's very smart,' said The Pan. 'Homely, too ... although it smells a bit.'

'She,' Terri laughed from the galley area. '*She's* very smart. All boats are called "she".'

'Right,' said The Pan who knew that but just felt awkward doing it. 'Well ... *she* smells of Goojan sausage.'

'It's amazing how quickly you get used to it. We hardly notice it anymore. And it's not for long,' said Christine.

The Pan drank his cordial and relaxed. The portholes and doors were open, and as the air outside began to lose its heat, a cool breeze blew in off the water. He heaved a sigh. He felt a comradeship with the three of them; they lived in this boat and took their home with them wherever they went. He lived in his snurd. Was it so different? Yes. Of course it was. Idiot. He mostly slept under the stars, or, in cold or inclement weather, in a very small vehicle which wasn't designed for that sort of thing. This was a proper living space. Even so, the pang of jealousy he sometimes felt, mixing with beings who were still on the inside of society, the settled ones, was less keen. As he watched Terri stirring something in a pot that smelled utterly heavenly, he took in the cupboards, the hanging bunches of herbs and bulbs of garlic. Though the galley was at the end of the main room, it was only about halfway along the length of the barge.

Through the open door behind Terri he was pretty sure he could make out the doors to more rooms in the corridor behind and stairs up, presumably to the wheelhouse. The second door along was open slightly and he could see into what appeared to be like a tiny, cupboard-sized bedroom. Bort noticed where he was looking.

'The bathroom's through there, if you need it.'

'You have running water on this thing?'

'We have a tank for drinking water which we fill,' said Christine. 'The hot water system is filtered canal water. It comes in through the engine intake just below the waterline.'

All engines in K'Barth ran on water—they split the H2 from the O.

By this time Christine had opened another stowage locker which took up half of the back wall of the barge. Inside were panels of wood which swung out in various directions. Unfolding and twisting them like some complicated piece of origami she latched them together with clips and bolts. Within a few minutes, where there had been empty space, there was a work table, tool bench and seat.

'Arnold's nostrils, that's impressive,' The Pan said once she'd opened it all.

'It is, isn't it?' Christine said with obvious pride. 'This is my personal cobbler's corner. But you haven't seen it all yet. Here's the best part.'

She swung a specialist heavy-duty sewing machine up from the dark interior of the locker and bolted that into position too. After that she rotated the middle of the table, flipping it up and locking it steady. On it stood a bizarre foot-shaped contraption made of brass and copper.

She gestured to the metal thing. 'An adjustable last. Your average cobbler makes wooden lasts to the shape of the client's feet. I can't store them so I've made this. I take the same standard set of measurements for each different foot and adjust the settings. Then all I need to keep is a list of measurements. Much more compact than lasts.'

The Pan looked closer. It was made up of small panels of copper, about an inch square. Each one was attached to a strip of steel and the steel strips, in turn, ran down to a bank of adjustment screws at the bottom.

'That's amazing,' he said.

'Thank you. It's my own design.'

The Pan risked a glance at Bort who'd finished sorting her leaves and was handing them to Terri, who was adding liberal handfuls to the pot meal she was cooking. Both were smiling at Christine proudly.

'Christine is the brains of this outfit isn't she, Mum?' said Bort.

'I'm afraid so,' Terri laughed. 'I just grow the veg and do the cooking.'

The Pan turned his attention back to Christine's machine. 'Is it very complicated?' he asked.

'I suppose it is, but it feels natural to me. Now that we've sold the sausage, I'm thinking of having one made in polymorphic metal.'

'You should, Christine,' Bort chimed in.

'It depends if we can afford it,' she said. Then, to The Pan, 'we have other things to do with the money first. Now, take off your boots.'

He did as she asked. She picked up his black suede elastic-sided boots and put them to one side by the open door. Neither of them mentioned the tang of the Dang but it hung in the air like a ... well ... yes, The Pan supposed, it *was* a bad smell. As she returned to her seat The Pan cracked.

'Sorry about those. It's the river,' he said.

'It's our fault you fell in,' said Terri from the galley.

'Put your foot on here.' Christine gestured to a tray on the floor. It was covered with lines and numbers. She adjusted his foot so his heel was flat against the back and began to take measurements with a pair of compasses. The Pan didn't know much about boot making but suspected Christine's method of measuring was as unconventional as the adjustable last she used.

'Yes,' she said quietly as she wrote down the numbers. 'Polymorphic metal would be the answer. It's just a question of finding a way to interface with it ...'

He watched, with interest, as she turned the screws and the pieces of copper shifted and changed. It took a while and by the time she'd finished it was nearly seven o'clock.

'Right, I have all I need from you. Terri? Are we ready?'

'We sure are! Let's eat!'

They moved to the low table and Terri placed a bowl of steaming stew in front of them. It smelled heavenly, almost as good as something Gladys and Ada at the Parrot and Screwdriver would cook up. The Pan remembered The Prophet's Birthday celebratory banquet they'd made the previous winter. That had been an amazing meal and the curried squid course they'd produced was so good it was the standard by which he now judged all other food.

He waited patiently while they said a quick prayer of thanks to Arnold, The Prophet, and then everyone tucked in. Terri was a fantastic cook and the stew tasted every bit as good as it smelled. The Pan nearly asked what was in it and after a bit of thought to his surroundings decided it was better not to.

'Rabbit stew,' she told him, as if reading his mind.

When they'd finished The Pan helped with the washing up and then decided that it was time he left.

'Thanks for supper,' he said, 'I think I'd better get going now.'

He looked outside. The sun was beginning to set. If he summoned the SE2 he could be back at the Parrot for last orders.

'When should I come and pick the boots up?' he asked Christine.

'I can make them now—it's just trimming and stitching. Wait a moment though.' She went over to the shoemaking area, turned to open a second, smaller locker and pulled out a piece of folded leather. 'I was going to use this.' She put it on the table. In the light he could see that it was black with a massive splash of yellow paint across it. 'Spoiled, as you can see but,' she flipped one corner over so he could see the other side, 'you seem to like suede. If you want something like the pair you're wearing this will last you a good long time. It's decent quality and I can get you two pairs of boots from it.'

The Pan met her eyes for a brief moment and smiled. 'Thank you. That would be wonderful,' he said.

'Splendid,' said Christine. 'It'll take about an hour and a half to stitch them up. I've glued the soles already so it's just a question of trimming and piercing them, stitching the insoles in and the uppers on. I was going to put a rubber sole on the bottom too—that'll help them last. I'm sorry, I thought I had more glue mixed up. I can only do the rubber sole on one pair now but if you're a regular at that pub, I dare say I can send the second on.'

'Thanks, you're an angel,' said The Pan.

'Happy to help aren't we, Terri?'

'Aye aye!' said Terri from the galley. 'Off you go then. Anchors aweigh! Bort, take him for a walk to look at the sunset or something, will you?' and to The Pan she said, 'You'll be staying over, I presume?'

'You have room?'

Terri and Christine exchanged glances.

'We have room,' said Christine.

'Then yes, please ...' said The Pan.

'Come on then,' said Bort.

She passed him, much closer than she needed to, and with a brief smile over her shoulder, stepped outside.

'I'll see you later, then,' The Pan told Terri and Christine, and, grabbing his old boots from the step, put them on. He tried not to be so uncool as to actually run after Bort.

Chapter 16
Almost lucky

The Pan and Bort climbed through the open front of a ruined building and picked their way across the rubble to the first floor. An old beam lay across the concrete, against the wall. Bort sat down and patted the space beside her. The Pan joined her. He leaned back and closed his eyes. It was surprisingly comfortable and the plaster still held the heat of the day. In front of them, the sun was setting over Ning Dang Po. The sky turned a vivid red and the lights of the city twinkled on, one by one. In the far distance it was just possible to see the Bridge of Eternal Glory suddenly appearing as the floodlights came on.

The Pan couldn't ever let his guard down completely. But this brief, humdrum day spent with Bort was about as close as it got; about as close to normal as his life could ever be. It didn't happen often. She shuffled up and leaned against him. He put his arm round her and they looked out at the city and then up at the sky. He noticed a solitary star had come out. 'Do you come here often?' he asked her.

'Will you shut up!' she teased him, but she was laughing.

They sat there looking up at the sky without talking. Time seemed to be elastic and slowed down.

'Mum reckons you're bad news,' said Bort.

'She's right.'

'Lone wolf, eh?' she said, with a certain amount of relish.

'Abandoned puppy more like.'

'Christine thinks you're blacklisted.'

The Pan was seldom asked this question up front, but on the few occasions he was, he could never think of a convincing way to avoid answering. Perhaps he should try

the truth—she would likely think it bravado and that would
be the end of it. 'I am.'

She started giggling. 'OK, some things I'm prepared to
believe but not that. Not even after seeing the way you drive
a snurd.'

Bingo. Maybe he should try the brazen approach more
often. He said nothing more and the conversation lapsed.

Given the time to get to know her better, The Pan
imagined he and Bort might easily be friends. It was pretty
clear they could also be a lot more. But an affair with Bort
would be pretty intense and it wouldn't be permanent the
way a friendship would. Except that The Pan being The
Pan, permanent anything was impossible. She would move
on, he would be murdered by someone; the authorities, or
Big Merv. No, let's try to think positive—he might not be
murdered but he had to be vigilant. Except he was tired of
living on tenterhooks the whole time. And here, in the
present, somehow, all that seemed far away and irrelevant.
Bort and The Pan had narrowly escaped death together and
it was a surprisingly strong bond. It was easy to sit there in
silence. Except that her hair was tickling The Pan's chin
and it was taking all his concentration not to sneeze.

He thought about their earlier conversation—when Bort
was talking about her itinerant lifestyle—what she'd said
about the temporary things; how their transience didn't
make them any less good. Everything in The Pan's life was
temporary, right up to his existence itself, which was
probably one of the most temporary things in it. OK, so he
was proving a bit longer-lasting than he'd expected. But his
continued presence in the land of the living was definitely
threatened regularly.

Bort hadn't *just* been talking about life on the river
though, had she? There was more to it than that; something
else. And after the way she'd whispered in his ear as they
approached the boat, he was beginning to think he might

possibly understand what she *had* meant.

Maybe.

'Bort?'

She turned so she was facing him. 'Yes?'

'Thank you.'

In the orange glow of the sunset he could see her brow furrowing in puzzlement. 'What for?'

'A lovely day. I don't get many days like this. It's been ...' he hesitated, trying to think of the right word. Not 'fabulous'—that was too gushy—nor 'marvellous', because that sounded like his grandfather. Arnold's trollies! Think of a word! '... great.'

So lame.

'Any time,' she told him, except she seemed to mean something else, the same way she had earlier. Their eyes met. Did she want him to ...? It looked as if she might. He put his hand up to her face, a shy caress. She tensed. Arnold's socks! Was that a good sign? She relaxed against him a little and breathed in. Mmm ... OK maybe that was a good sign. Her eyes closed and her lips parted. Alright, yes, that was definitely a good sign. Probably. He took a deep breath, leaned forward ... and then Bort put her arms around his neck and kissed him, passionately, hungrily.

Blimey.

She slid herself onto his lap, sitting astride him.

Arnold in the skies!

He pulled her against him, holding her close, eagerly returning her kisses with some pretty ardent ones of his own. He felt her legs around his back, her hands on his body, under his shirt. By The Prophet! This was so dangerous. But it felt so good. He shouldn't relax, not for a moment! He must stay vigilant. He *would* stay vigilant, he told himself, but he also wanted to be normal, to be like other beings. He wanted Bort and he wanted this tiny slice of a real life that the normals took for granted. He wanted it more than he'd imagined possible.

The Pan abandoned the promises he'd made himself, and for the first time since he'd been blacklisted, let his guard down. Completely. He surrendered to his desire, not just for Bort, but to be normal. He'd let this perfect day be the one when he got to do the things everyone else took for granted; go for a walk, talk to someone and kiss them; and if that meant it was the last day he lived, so be it. He and Bort lost themselves in each other and—as Gladys and Ada at the Parrot and Screwdriver might have euphemistically put it—one thing led to another. Several times. They didn't notice the unforgiving concrete floor. They were lost in the moment and in each other. The Pan doubted his parents, and more to the point Bort's parents—or Christine—would approve. Then again, none of them was there, while Bort was. And she was clearly enjoying herself as much as he was.

He never noticed darkness had fallen until the two of them were lying back against the wall, arms and legs entwined, gazing up at the inky blackness above them, and the stars.

They straightened their clothing and lay back again, together. As they contemplated the night sky, the moon rose, bathing everything around them in a silver light.

'I wonder if moonlight gives you a tan?' she said.

'Maybe,' said The Pan.

He introduced her to a dumb game called *Making Up Constellations*. He'd played it as a child with his brother and sister. He and Bort rechristened one cluster that was normally called 'The Small Stars' as 'The Zits' and another, more well-known constellation as 'The Happy Terrier' because it looked like a small dog. They were now working on the name of a third, which Bort wanted to call 'The Big Spade' while The Pan argued that 'The Giant Spoon of Doom' sounded better. Things were getting flirtatious again. He propped himself up on one elbow and looked down at her. Christine and Terri would be expecting them back at the boat soon, but surely they had half an hour or so...

Her thoughts were clearly running along similar lines because she reached up and ran her hands through his hair. Oops, careful or she'd discover the eyes in the back of his head. That would take a lot more explaining than he was ready for. He shut them, anyway, just in case.

'Ouch,' he said, pretending that what had actually been a very pleasant caress had pulled. She withdrew her hand at once.

'Sorry.'

'It's fine.' He leaned forward to kiss her but something in the distance caught his eye and distracted him. A light. 'Hang on,' he said.

'What's up?' she asked him.

'There are lights on the towpath.'

'Where?' She sat up.

He pointed. 'Along there, about where we joined it I'd say. Do many people come along here?'

'Not this side, no. It's a dead end when you're on foot.'

'Then, what are they doing?'

'I don't know.' She sounded worried.

It was more than one light—there were several. And they were bouncing up and down the way lights do when they're being carried by people who are walking.

'Is that normal? You know, visitors?' he asked her.

'No.' She sounded alarmed and The Pan suddenly had a feeling that both of them should be elsewhere, fast. He never, ever ignored feelings like that. Bort clearly felt the same because she stood up. Instinctively, the two of them moved to the shadows. The lights seemed to have stopped. They were circling. Perhaps they were waiting for something. Or someone. As Bort and The Pan watched, the lights went out. Now, he could make out shapes on the water.

'Hang on. Bort, are those dark things boats?'

'Smeck! Yeh. I think they are. Oh no!' Her hand went to her mouth, 'It'll be King Milo!'

She made to go but he pulled her back into the shadows. 'Careful!' he whispered. 'They look like they're waiting for something. I think there might be an advance party, you know, coming to check that everyone's at home.'

'Smeck!' she said again.

'Yeh, pretty much. OK, stay still and wait here. I'm going to try and get a better look,' he whispered.

Quietly, he crept forward and scoped the lights in the distance. Yes. There was a crowd alright and yes, they were waiting. He tried to remember how long he and Bort had taken to reach the barge; twenty minutes, thirty? He'd been right about the advance party though. Just past the trees where the canal cornered he could make out some more dark shapes on the towpath. They'd chosen a dumb route of attack. He could easily see them. Was that the point then? Were there others, already there, waiting to pounce when least expected? Arnold! He hoped not.

The Pan didn't know much about King Milo—as a member of Big Merv's staff he tended to steer well clear of his counterparts in other gangs—but from what he'd heard and seen of the fellow, he was street-smart rather than clever, and a bit weird. He was also a lot nastier than Big Merv. Although, The Pan supposed, that was all relative. But Big Merv was reasonable, for a gangster. He asked questions and he listened to the answers. He was smart and he learned fast, that much was obvious. It was easy to tell how Big Merv had ended up running such a big chunk of Ning Dang Po.

As The Pan looked out into the darkness he wondered, fearfully, if it was as easy for King Milo and his goons to see him as it was for him to see them. He hoped not. Having checked out their target, the scouts appeared to be heading back towards the others. Maybe they were going back to tell King Milo that his quarry was still in place. As The Pan watched, the advance party signalled the rest of them with a torch and waited.

Arnold's nostril hair! It looked as if they were about to attack.

How long would the lot of them take to arrive? Ten minutes? Fifteen? Less if they ran ... and what about the boats? It was best to underestimate the time in hand for a situation like this. As quickly and quietly as he could he made his way back to Bort. 'We have to go,' he said, taking her hand.

Chapter 17
Prepare for departure

The Pan silently thanked The Prophet that the canal ran through a raised embankment at this point. He realised it would have made things a lot trickier if he and Bort had been forced to go along the path.

'Keep low to the bank and follow me,' he said as they scurried along in the shadows.

When the two of them arrived back at the barge Christine and Terri were sitting on the deck again, dangling their feet over the side like before. They each had a glass of wine in hand and the bottle stood between them, along with a tealight burning in a jam jar.

The Pan and Bort scrambled up the bank.

'Where did you two spring from?' said Terri.

'I've finished your boots, lad!' said Christine.

'There are people coming,' blurted Bort.

'King Milo?' asked Terri.

'Yeh. I'd say so,' said The Pan. 'They're up to no good.'

Christine and Terri were on their feet in a trice. They leapt onto the towpath beside The Pan, undoing the mooring ropes and throwing them onto the deck where Bort was already in place to catch and stow them.

'How long do we have?' asked Terri in a low voice.

'They're a fair way back so I'd say we have ten or fifteen minutes. But less if they run. There's an advance party though. They came as far as the bend and headed back to join the others. If they've seen us and followed they'll be here in no time. I'm pretty sure they didn't—we tried to stay out of sight and I think we succeeded—but it pays to be cautious.'

'That it does, lad,' Terri agreed.

He noticed Bort was priming the engine. 'Wait, don't do that,' said The Pan. He glanced up the towpath. No sign of anyone yet, but that didn't mean much.

'The lad's right,' Terri told Bort. 'We'll punt her to start with and wait until we get close to the outer ring. There's still a bit of traffic about. It may mask us.'

'They'll hear the bass engine note of the barge above the other traffic, though. It'll carry,' said The Pan.

'That it will and they might,' Terri conceded. 'It's a chance we'll have to take though. Hop on, lad.'

'We need to get a head start on them,' said Christine.

'Yes, we do. But we may be too late. How fast does this thing go?' asked The Pan.

'About ten knots if the tide's with us.'

'And without the tide?' Silence. 'What I mean is, can it go faster than a running man?'

There was an even longer silence broken only by the gentle sloshing of the water, the sounds of Terri, Christine and Bort stowing ropes and making sail, so to speak, even though there weren't any actual sails. No-one answered but in the background The Pan could hear distant shouts.

'I'm guessing that's a no. That's not good. Especially as I can't help noticing that we're facing the wrong way. Is there anywhere you three can hide? Maybe I can pretend I own the boat. You sold it to me. They can search and see you've left your stuff but you're long gone.'

'They'll never buy that. They saw you on the river bank. They'll think you're one of us,' said Bort.

'I know it's not a great plan but it's all I've got. Otherwise,' he held up his snurd keys, 'we take to the skies. Now.'

'And leave the boat and everything we've worked for? Everything we own?' said Christine.

'No,' said Terri and The Pan could understand her

reluctance to leave. 'There's no need to panic, laddio. We'll leave them standing.'

'That's right,' said Christine. 'You stay here with Bort. Bort, prime the fuel pump and be ready to start the engine when we get close to the bridge and the traffic. Full speed ahead when we say.'

'Yeh.'

Again, Terri and Christine seemed to understand each other's thoughts. Together they leapt onto the roof. Christine ran nimbly along the top of the boat to the prow and jumped down onto the small front deck. She picked up a long pole which was lying along the roof. As she did this, Terri stopped to pick up a similar pole from the roof at the back of the boat, where Bort and The Pan waited by the engine. With quick, neat strides she carried the pole to the other end and jumped down onto the deck beside Christine.

'What are they doing?' asked The Pan.

'You're not the only one who can make a quick getaway,' said Bort. She took the rudder, holding it straight. In perfect synchronisation, Terri and Christine began to punt the barge out into the waterway.

'That's impressive,' said The Pan as the boat began to pick up speed.

'Sometimes we just run along the towpath with a rope. It depends on our priorities.'

'Your priorities?'

'Yep. Fast or safe.'

'Ah. Right.'

It was a clear night and the moon was bright. That was a good thing as they'd be able to see their pursuers more easily; but it was also a bad thing, in that the beings tracking them would enjoy the same advantage.

The Pan kept his eyes on the water behind them, scanning for any sight of King Milo and his gang. So far there was none. In his mind's eye he tried to imagine where they were, gauge the speed they were travelling and determine how far along the path they were now.

The *Happy Doris* was picking up speed.

Bort seemed remarkably calm. The Pan thought for a moment. 'You said this thing goes at ten knots ... that doesn't sound very fast.'

'It is for a barge. And it's supersonic for one of their narrowboats.'

'What if they have other boats?'

'They don't usually.'

Usually ... but they did sometimes. 'How many knots are we doing now?'

Bort looked down at a dimly lit dial by the rudder. 'Five. Mum and Christine are really going it.'

'OK, so is there a point to the engine?'

'Shut up! I'm concentrating.'

'Do you do this often?'

'Not recently. A lot more before Dad left.'

'We're sitting ducks on this thing. You know that, don't you?'

'Chill,' said Bort. 'We'll be fine.'

Something about her confidence reassured him a little. Or was it blind stupidity? No. She said she'd done it before and Bort was anything but stupid—that was one of the reasons he liked her. Yeh, he thought, *really* liked her.

'If you want to make yourself useful there's a bag of rice in that locker down there, and a blunderbuss. Well ... it's more of a punt gun.'

He might have been pathologically afraid of guns, but as an employee of Big Merv it paid for The Pan to know about them. A punt gun was more of a cannon.

'Can you load it?' she asked him.

'The punt gun?'

'No, stupid, the vending machine on the docks.'

'I've never tried to load either,' he told her.

'This is no time for jokes.'

'You started it.'

'Get on with it, you nutter,' said Bort.

'You haven't any ammo, only the fuse and powder.'

'Duh. That's what the rice is for,' she explained.

'You ...?'

'We don't *kill* people! Rice is quite enough to get them rattled.'

In spite of his fear, The Pan smiled as a wave of relief washed over him. He could never kill another being either—not even in self defence—and he knew it. These were people after his own heart. 'Good,' was all he said.

'So *can* you load it?' Bort asked him.

'No. But if you need me to, I can drive the boat while you do.'

'You don't know how.'

'I'm Hamgeean. Believe it or not, I've been on a boat and I'm OK with vehicles, usually.'

'Yeh, but can you steer one backwards?'

'I expect so. I can fly a snurd backwards.'

There was a moment of silence. Down the canal, the lights and darker shapes which The Pan and Bort had seen from the ruined building, turned the corner, where the trees were. The lights went out.

'They're catching us up,' said The Pan as from the front of the boat, Terri let out a loud whistle.

Bort pressed a button and the engine roared into life. Well, now they and King Milo's bunch were in visual range there was no point trying to be quiet. It was obvious they were leaving. Bort pushed the throttle lever to the middle which meant it was just ticking over.

'Steer,' she commanded. 'Throttle forward to accelerate and back to slow down. Middle is neutral but you shouldn't have to do any of that yet. Just hold it steady while I get the blunderbuss.' The Pan took the rudder.

Bort opened a locker set into the gunwale and removed a huge and ancient gun. It had a round stock, like something a highway robber would have carried in K'Barth's earlier and more colourful history. The end of the barrel was flared. No rifling on this thing. Then again, it was designed to kill the maximum number of ducks at close range as they took flight, and it was there to act as a deterrent. The Pan had to concede it had size and presence. Yeh, and the less beings it actually hit the better, as far as he was concerned. It had a stand which Bort sunk into a brass-ringed hole in the gunwale that he hadn't previously noticed.

They were nearing the point where the canal merged into another waterway. 'Which way?'

'We're going left, I think, but leave it up to Mum and Christine, they'll turn us. Then, when we're facing the right way, we redline the engine and take off,' said Bort as she loaded the gun.

'Right,' said The Pan. The distant boats were gaining. They, too, were barges with what looked like the odd narrowboat thrown in for good measure. A crowd of beings on bicycles and on foot were running along the towpath on one side, the side on which the *Happy Doris* had originally been moored. 'They're gaining. Shouldn't we turn now?'

Bort was finishing loading the punt gun, ramming the 'ammo' into the bottom with a long thin piece of metal. 'Duck!'

He did as she asked and she spun the punt gun round so it was facing over the stern of the boat. There was another loud whistle from the prow and Terri came running down the roof, a dripping pole in her hands. Bort pulled The Pan to one side as Terri leapt onto the deck with them and jammed the pole into the water beside the keel. At the other end, on the opposite side, Christine was doing the same thing.

'Help me, lad,' puffed Terri as she heaved on it. Bort took the rudder back from The Pan and he did as he was told. He saw, at once, what Terri and Bort were doing.

'Are we handbrake turning a boat?' he asked.

'Barge,' Bort corrected him.

At the exact same moment her mother said, 'Yep.'

'It's about momentum,' said Bort.

'You're doing a rolling start in this thing?'

'Yes. Worth the time ...' puffed Terri as she wielded the pole.

'It gets us up to speed faster,' Bort explained.

'You mean, you can get it from zero to sixty, or at least six, under your own steam before it can?'

'Yep.'

'To get us up to ten knots that little bit more quickly?' asked The Pan.

'Exactly. We want to make a quick getaway as well as a quiet one,' said Terri.

'Right. Just thinking,' he said as he helped Terri haul on the pole, 'I'm a little sketchy on these things but am I right in thinking that ten knots is just over eleven miles an hour?'

'Yeh,' said Bort.

'That's not fast enough.'

'I'll be the judge of that,' said Terri.

'If we can get to the junction before they do, it will be,' said Bort.

'Are you certain?'

'Trust me,' said Bort. 'We've done this before.'

The boat was across the canal now, its speed slowing as it presented itself side on to the weight of water ahead of it. Then the stern was coming round with perfect precision, the front and back of the boat missing the banks by a few feet each end. Bort was revving the engine ready. Slowly but surely, the boat turned and though its momentum had fallen away dramatically, it kept moving.

'Ready?' shouted Terri as the stern came about.

'Ready!' Christine called from the prow.

'Now!' shouted Terri. She and Christine slid the poles out of the water again and stowed them quickly back in place on the roof, swapping them with two similar but shorter versions.

Bort pushed the throttle forward. For a horrible moment the revs dropped and The Pan feared the engine would stall. Then it chugged back into life, revving faster and faster, pumping thick clouds of white steam from its exhausts.

Chapter 18
Slow-motion flight

The *Happy Doris* began to pick up speed. Although in this case, speed was a relative term.

'Arnold's pants! Surely it goes faster than this!' yelled The Pan as he took in the leisurely pace at which the bank was sliding by.

'It takes time to get going!'

That it did. *Time we don't have*, thought The Pan. The other boats were bearing down on them but as if in slow motion.

'Looks like they're boats are souped too,' shouted Bort over the loud chugging of the *Happy Doris's* engine.

'Arnold, that's all we need!' shouted The Pan.

'Patience, young uns!' Terri yelled back. 'The forecast is fog tonight. We'll only have to hold them off for so long.'

How could she be so calm? OK, so she *was* shouting, but that was about combating background noise rather than panic.

The other boats were only a few hundred yards away now but, The Pan realised; they were no longer gaining. Unfortunately, the unruly band on the towpath were able to run, while others were equipped with bicycles so they were still making ground. One cyclist was ahead of the others and he bellowed across the thirty odd feet of water between them. 'Give us the sausage and no-one gets hurt!'

'We haven't got it!' Christine shouted. 'We sold it.'

'You sold two! We know you've still got one.'

'We sold that too!'

'No ...' there was a pause while he swerved to avoid a

lump of rubble on the path. 'You've still got one!'

'We know what we have and haven't got, me lad!' shouted Terri.

Something flew over their heads and landed on the towpath on the other side. It burst and threw a carpet of flame over the ground.

'A bottle bomb!' squeaked The Pan.

Bottle bombs were pretty simple—something combustible went into a glass jar with a rag stuffed into it. Then you lit the rag, lobbed it and when it smashed the burning liquid went everywhere.

'Bort, I'll take the tiller a minute, you know what to do!' Terri shouted as she grabbed it and Bort turned, at once, to the gun. 'Let 'em have it!' yelled Terri as her daughter pulled the trigger. It let off a thunderous retort and the pack on the towpath fell back. 'Hah! That showed 'em!' She seemed to be almost enjoying herself. She must be nuts. She turned to The Pan. 'Can you drift, lad?'

He cast a dubious glance at the water.

'No, *drift*. In your snurd.'

He nodded.

'Splendid! It's a similar principle,' she grabbed his hand and put it on the tiller. 'You turn the boat, and Christine and I will fend us off the sides. Not too fast though or you'll capsize us!'

How many tonnes was this thing? The Pan wondered. And how in the name of Arnold were they going to fend it off the sides? It was like trying to bounce the windscreen off the fly. Not going to happen. He looked back at the gaining pursuit. Never mind, needs must. He took a deep breath and set about steering the boat. It took all his strength on the tiller to push the rudder against the force of the water, and he heaved and sweated as he tried to hold it steady. It was working though. The barge began to turn, slowly. Drifting sideways as well as round. It wasn't like cornering on dry ground, but there was certain slow-motion similarity to the business of turning a snurd in the air. The Pan found he had the same instinctive understanding of the physics and his toes twitched in his boots making to press an imaginary rudder pedal, as if he actually was flying. He throttled back a tiny bit—no need to hit the side of the other waterway head on. The barge turned lazily like a cruising leviathan but with the same slow power as an uncurling mattress. The Pan hauled at the tiller to keep it on course.

They were approaching the junction now. The Pan throttled back a great deal more and let the boat float round, while Terri and Christine fended it off the sides and, where they could, used the poles to punt it. Bort had reloaded the gun and let off another volley of shot at the crowd on the towpath, who were now marooned on the wrong side of the wrong waterway, unable to follow.

'There! That'll hold them up a little,' shouted Terri.

The Pan doubted that. They'd just use the boats. He knew he could easily have jumped on or off a boat without trouble at these speeds. Presumably their pursuers were also as fit as he was or, at the least, close. Yeh, and they'd be smarter and wiser to boot. As he watched, to his dismay, some of them did indeed cross to the other side, leaping from boat to boat of the pursuing flotilla. On the upside, they could only use the larger boats. And not all of them had succeeded—The Pan saw a couple end up in the canal. The ones who'd crossed would take a minute or two to catch up again. Yep. He had a moment to take stock.

The Pan reckoned the waterway ahead of them was the river Linnet. He tried to recall how its extensive meanderings looked on a map. From what he remembered it wiggled crazily across Lower Right towards Lower Central before it hit the reservoir. It was a shorter route than the canal system but it was definitely going to take some navigating. Looking at the towpath either side, he realised that was different too. It was bisected at regular intervals with fences and gates. Huge trees overarched the water, their trunks providing another impediment to the members of the bottle bomb-hurling mob who'd crossed the canal and caught up, running and cycling alongside.

Smart, thought The Pan as he put the boat into another sharp bend. It was all he could do to control it as he fought the weight of the water. His face and clothes were covered in sweat and spray from where the hurled bottle bombs and other projectiles which, so far, had fallen short, hit the water.

'Well done, lad. It's all about the cornering!' shouted Terri, pausing as Bort let off another volley of rice over the heads of the mob on the towpath. 'Once we hit the reservoir we'll be out of range of the idiots on the side and we'll leave the others standing!'

After twenty fear-filled minutes of slow-motion, drawn-out action, The Pan realised that Terri's plan was working. Both groups of pursuit were falling back, but in the case of the boats, not as quickly as he'd hoped. Finally, as they came to open water, the yobs on the side stopped. The pursuing boats carried on but The Pan thought the *Happy Doris* might be continuing to get ahead of them ... slowly.

'I told you we'd leave them standing,' said Terri happily. The Pan looked over to the other side of the reservoir—trying to gauge the distance—and then back at the pursuing boats behind. This was hardly leaving them standing.

Something sailed over their heads and landed in the water with a fizzing sound. Another bottle bomb. King Milo's boats might be falling back, but they were still within the throwing range of a strong arm, it seemed. No. Wait a minute!

'By The Prophet's socks! They have a trebuchet!' said The Pan.

'A what?' said Bort.

'A catapult!'

Another bottle bomb came sailing over.

'Arnold's cleggnuts!' shouted The Pan.

Now that she was no longer needed at the front, Christine ran down the roof to join them.

The boat was going faster, but compared to the hectic nature of a snurd chase, it felt like racing glaciers to The Pan ... or possibly continents.

He watched the group of beings loitering at the water's edge as the towpath receded slowly into the distance. Some were wandering away, their shoulders drooping dejectedly, but another group were standing around on a flat piece of shoreline in front of the trees. They were waiting for something.

No time to think about that though. Another bottle bomb sailed over, glanced off the side of the *Happy Doris* and fell into the reservoir with a splash. It didn't break and most of the burning liquid went out as the jar hit the water. But some spread across the surface in a flaming slick of oil. Worse, a few splashes hit the *Happy Doris* itself. A patch along the side was peppered with burning spatters. In a trice, Terri leapt onto the roof, grabbing a metal watering can which was painted with gaily coloured flowers and upending it over the flames. They went out.

Phew.

Another bottle bomb came over.

Uh oh. This one was right on target.

'Smecking Arnold!' muttered The Pan, his knuckles white on the tiller as he held the barge steady. The bottle bomb was heading, inexorably, towards the *Happy Doris*. And there was nothing he could do. This was it.

He watched in horrified fascination as the bottle bomb flew at Terri, on the roof. But then, the most extraordinary thing happened. She flipped the watering can round and, holding it by the spout, as if it was some kind of weird bat, she stepped up and hit the flaming missile! As if this was a sport and the bottle bomb was a ball. She was smart enough not to give it a head-on smack but instead, fended it off with a glancing blow that deflected the bottle into the water behind her, on the other side of the boat, without breaking it.

'Yes!' shouted The Pan. 'What a shot!'

More bottle bombs came flying over and landed in the water either side of them.

'Uh-oh, that's range finding,' said The Pan.

'I could do with a little help up here!' Terri shouted.

Bort turned to The Pan. 'Keep steering!' she told him before shouting, 'On it, Mum!'

She leapt onto the roof, snatching up a short-handled paddle that was normally used for close manoeuvring or to row a smaller boat.

Christine loaded the punt gun and then turned to The Pan. 'Keep us on this heading,' she said, climbing onto the roof with her wife and step daughter.

'They're going to hit us eventually,' muttered The Pan.

'No, they're not!' said Bort, who'd stationed herself at his end of the barge and had heard.

The bottle bombs rained down and The Pan watched in terrified awe as Terri, Christine and Bort deftly deflected them into the drink on either side of the *Happy Doris*. Terri had ditched the watering can now and grabbed another oar like the one Bort was using, while Christine wielded one of the shorter barge poles.

The three women leapt and jumped, flicking and swiping at any flaming missiles that were on target while The Pan grimly held onto the tiller and kept the *Happy Doris* on course. As he watched, Bort swung the oar, flicking a burning jam jar right round her and high into the air. It flew back in the direction from which it had come, landing with a splash in front of the leading barge.

'Fantastic shot! You nearly got one!' he shouted.

She glanced down and nodded a swift acknowledgement before turning her attention back to the task in hand. Blimey, Bort was something else! She could do anything, be anyone she wanted ... well ... if she survived this. If they all did. The Pan checked back at the pursuers as another bottle bomb flew straight and true and ... fell short.

Christine whooped. 'Yes! We're out of range,' she shouted.

The Pan kept one hand on the tiller and the other on the throttle, pushing the lever as far forward as it would go. As he looked towards the exit of the reservoir, he could see wisps of white rising off the water. Was it mist? Fog rising? Forecast or not, could they be that lucky? The Pan could hope but he knew it wasn't worth relying on.

Looking the other way back at the boats following them he could make out the same wispy pieces of fog rising off the water. The pursuit was definitely falling back now and the numbers of bottle bombs flying at the *Happy Doris* seemed to be dropping.

It's not going to be this easy, The Pan thought. *They have something else planned, I know it.*

He scanned the water, further back. He could also just see distant figures on the bank where the *Happy Doris* had entered the reservoir. Not all of them had given up, it seemed. Some of them were standing around, as if waiting for something. The Pan's stomach turned over as he realised exactly what that something was.

'They're waiting for snurds,' he said to himself.

Arnold's nostril hair! It would be. And he had nothing to

pit against them but the SE2, which hadn't been checked over since the horrific flight from the Grongolian security forces. At the same time, though it had sustained substantial cosmetic damage, the engine had been running perfectly the one time he'd used it since. Could he risk it? The Pan was willing to bet his life King Milo had access to snurds ... and they'd have perfectly proficient drivers. Proficient but not exactly good, because anyone with any ability was working for the Resistance whether they wanted to or not. Except for The Pan.

He knew he could drive. And he was definitely proficient compared to the security forces—but that didn't take much. He had no means of comparing his skills with other K'Barthans though, so it was hard to tell if he was proficient enough. Would he be able to outrun King Milo's drivers? He didn't know. He risked taking his hand off the tiller for a moment to pat his back pocket and feel the reassuring shape of his snurd keys.

Bort jumped down onto the deck beside him, giving him a shock. 'Hi!' She sounded happy, energised. Well, she, Terri and Christine had just got themselves out of a pretty tight spot.

'Hello.' Despite his nerves he managed to flash her a smile.

'Round one to us, I think,' she said.

Round one. Good. So she realised it was only a reprieve. King Milo wasn't about to give up. 'Let's hope so.'

'Teamwork gets you everywhere, right girls?' said Terri, as she and Christine climbed down onto the deck to join them.

'That was ... amazing,' said The Pan.

'It took all three of us to keep those bottle bombs off. We'd be in a different place without you there to steer, lad,' said Terri.

'Well yes, you'd be off course.' He scanned the water

ahead. 'Although even with me here, you still might be.'

'No. You've done well,' said Christine.

'Grand job, lad,' Terri agreed.

'Thanks.' He looked down at the deck and smiled. 'I think you three did the lion's share of the work though.'

'Well, *I* think we should celebrate with a cup of fruit tea,' said Christine.

The Pan felt more inclined to suggest a stiff drink but didn't say anything.

'Here, let me do that,' said Terri, taking his place at the tiller.

He stepped gratefully aside and looked out over the waters behind them. King Milo's boats were still in pursuit.

'What happens now?' he asked as he leaned against the gunwale. 'This isn't over, is it?'

'No. We keep going—we haven't lost them yet,' said Terri. He was amazed at how relaxed all three of them seemed to be. Relaxed but at the same time, pumped, clearly, after their bout of bat-the-bottle-bomb.

'Look, I think there's trouble brewing,' said The Pan. 'What do you do to fend off snurds?'

'We try not to get attacked by them,' said Bort.

'True, and the kinds of people who chase us don't usually have snurds,' said Christine.

'They will here, trust me.' King Milo was a gang lord like any other, The Pan reasoned.

'If they do, they won't have any drivers,' Bort said as the four of them looked backwards towards the receding boats behind them and the outline of the shore.

Visibility definitely wasn't as good now—the view was a little hazy. The Pan turned and gazed in the direction in which they were moving. The water ahead of them wasn't glistening anymore and although he could still see the trees at the other side of the reservoir quite clearly, along with the moon and the stars, the surface of the water seemed to have faded and disappeared. A blanket of fog lay on top of it. Except blanket wasn't quite the right word, The Pan thought. That would have implied something thicker. This was like a three-foot layer of dry ice. Vaguely in the distance, The Pan could make out the figures on the bank.

'Hmm,' he said thoughtfully. 'They won't have any *decent* drivers but it hardly takes a genius to hold steady above us while someone lobs a few bottle bombs out of the window, does it? They might even have APTs.'

'All-Purpose Torpedoes? No-one can get those.'

'Not officially, but you do hear about the odd beings who do. Let's hope King Milo isn't one of them. It's academic anyway. They'll have something. Rice shot might have kept those gits on the towpath at bay, and that thing with the bats!' He laughed in spite of himself. 'Arnold's ear wax, that was impressive, I have to say! How did you learn to do that?'

'Expediency,' said Christine.

'I can imagine. Well the thing is, that might have kept us in one piece for now but I don't believe we're edging ahead. I think they're dropping back. I reckon they're waiting for something.'

There was silence.

'You might be right, lad,' said Terri.

'I hope I'm not, but if I am, it's got to be snurds. You're not going to deter snurds with rice from this thing,' he said, waving a hand at the blunderbuss. 'It's not going to reach them for a start—and you can't smack back a bottle bomb when it's falling from the sky at terminal velocity.'

'You're right,' Terri nodded. 'We'll have to zigzag,' she said.

'It'll take more than zigzagging at the speed we're going,' said The Pan.

'Every little helps!' she replied.

'Really? Maybe if I give you a tow in my snurd it might

give us a couple of extra miles an hour but I'm certain we'll need more.'

'They aren't going to damage the boat. They can't risk it. They want the last sausage,' said Terri.

'Yes,' Christine agreed. 'They know we've got it and they know they won't get it if they sink us. They're just trying to make us stop.'

'You think?' retorted The Pan. 'I'm not so sure. What if they're just trying to kill you? They might decide they'll take losing the sausage if they get to murder you.'

'They're gangsters,' said Bort. 'Even if they are trying to kill us, they'll want to catch us alive and then lecture us about how nobody disrespects them and gets away with it first. *Then* they'll kill us.' The Pan threw her a look and she shrugged. 'That's what gangsters *do*.'

'Yes, well, that's a fair point,' The Pan conceded, as a brief image of Big Merv popped into his head.

'We'll be off their patch soon and they'll give up on us,' said Christine.

'We're already a long way off their patch and they're showing no sign of that,' said The Pan. 'But I have an idea which might work.'

'Go on then,' said Terri.

Chapter 19
Desperate measures

As the *Happy Doris* chugged across the waters, The Pan shared his plan with Terri, Christine and Bort. 'OK, look. Before I start, honestly now, is he after the sausage or you?'

'Both,' said Christine.

'I reckon he'll take the sausage though,' said Terri.

'So if they saw me take it from you, get into my snurd and fly away, would they give up on you and come after me?'

'They might. But that doesn't help you,' said Christine.

'And, me laddio, we're not letting you gallivant off with our sausage. We offered you a quarter, not half. You have one of your own.'

'I know but I didn't—' The Pan stopped. Should he tell them what had happened? No. He glanced back at King Milo's boats which were now a couple of hundred yards behind and slowly but surely losing ground, or at least, water. 'Here's my plan. I take the sausage, or if you like, I take something that looks like the sausage, and I fly away.'

'Where does that leave you?' asked Bort.

'Home free, I hope. As you know, I can drive.' So cocky. Arnold's plums, he hoped he could live up to his boast. 'I get that you don't know me but things are getting a bit hot for you lot. I'm guessing King Milo will have goons on every street corner looking out for you. Even if you escape, I assume you've sold it to someone in Ning Dang Po. It'll be difficult to come back and deliver it.'

'That could be true,' said Christine. She, Terri and Bort exchanged looks.

'If you trust me, I can deliver the sausage for you. If you don't, let me take something sausage-shaped and draw off the airborne pursuit. Whatever happens, you need to get away from this lot as fast as you can. But if they think I have the sausage, you might, possibly, have a few hours' grace until they're sure they can't find me. Then they'll come to ask you where I am.'

'And they won't find us—we have friends on the water,' said Terri and she put one finger on the side of her nose, the way Gladys at the Parrot and Screwdriver always did. Despite his fear, The Pan almost laughed. 'Also,' Terri continued, 'we have a protocol for this.'

'It'd better be a good one,' The Pan said, taking his keys from his pocket and pressing the button.

'Tried and tested.'

'Then, at the very least, let me give you a tow. What else I do is up to you. You need to decide quickly, though, because I reckon King Milo's airborne division has just arrived.'

Sure enough, in the distance five small dots had appeared in the sky. A sixth came from a completely different direction; The Pan's snurd SE2.

The three women seemed to come to a decision in a moment of silent assent, then Bort ran through the doors into the cabin. He saw her rummaging in a cupboard in the kitchen and pull out something about the size of her forearm, wrapped in cloth.

'There's no time for a tow,' said Christine as Bort stepped back out onto the deck.

The Pan realised she was carrying the linen bag which had contained the largest of the four sausages. Presumably the sausage itself was hidden safely somewhere on the barge and she'd stuffed a rolling pin or something similar into the bag for effect.

The Pan checked behind them. King Milo's barges were

a couple of hundred yards back now, but the snurds were gaining. The Pan had to make sure they'd all see the handover. 'OK, I'm going to get into my snurd. Then I'm going to motor past you and you need to hold out the bag. I'll pretend I can't grab it and you throw it to me, alright?'

'Why?'

'Because they need to see you hand it over. That's the whole point. It needs to be really obvious. Otherwise, between you and me, I'd just take it from you now and fly off.'

The SE2 had arrived. It came in low and flew past, clearly expecting The Pan to jump into the seat. When he didn't it turned and landed on the water cruising towards the *Happy Doris* at speed.

'Good luck,' said Bort and gave him a hurried peck on the cheek.

'You too,' he told her and leapt up onto the gunwale. He was about to jump into the snurd when he stopped. 'Wait a minute.' He stepped back onto the deck again. 'Where will I find you?'

The five snurds had fanned out and were approaching them, fast, across the water.

'What?' asked Bort.

'Where will I find you?' he asked again. 'And where are you meeting the buyer? You can't come back into Ning Dang Po. Not with King Milo's goons looking for you. I have to turn up in your place and bring the buyer to you.' The SE2, motoring along beside them, pooped its hooter. He turned to glance at it. 'In a minute.'

'It's a machine,' said Bort.

'Yeh. I know.'

'Why are you talking to it then?'

'It makes me feel better.'

'But—'

'No time. Where will you be?'

'Tell them to come to the Hungry Boatsman, tomorrow at three. It's on the second marina, the one just after Lark Locks,' said Terri.

'And you're meeting Bob, the Blaggysomp I told you about, at ten o'clock tomorrow morning outside Joe's Internet Cafe, opposite the Botanical Gardens. It was supposed to be us with the sausage,' Bort added.

This was going to be tight. The other snurds were closing now, still lined up in attack formation. He bundled into the SE2 and as it started to move Bort climbed onto the roof waving the sausage bag at him, as if he'd forgotten it.

'Here! Take this,' she shouted.

'Nice touch,' he said and had time to smile to himself as he tried to drift the snurd closer. But he couldn't get near enough and the other snurds were upon them. Bort flattened herself against the roof and The Pan ducked down in the seat as they swooped low over him. Why weren't they shooting?

Ah yes. Can't have Bort drop the sausage in the drink, The Pan thought. The snurds flew up—it would take them a few seconds to turn and make a second pass. The *Happy Doris* was entering the blanket of fog. Good, that might help, although it was only hiding the bottom half for the moment. Bort stood up again and as The Pan turned the SE2 in a circle, at speed, it threw up a cloud of spray.

No, slow down, they have to see this. He throttled it back, stood up in the seat so he showed above the blanket of fog and shouted, 'Throw it!' as he passed the barge. Bort did, almost too hard. He reached up and just managed to make enough contact, with his fingertips, to bat it into the footwell. Then he flung himself into the seat and pressed the button to put the bulletproof polymorphic metal roof in place. King Milo's snurds made a second pass, machine guns blazing this time and The Pan floored the accelerator. The SE2 began to pick up speed, bouncing across the water as the airborne snurds turned again to follow. They were going to try and trap him so he couldn't take off. They were in the air, which made them miles faster than him. It should have been easy for them to block him and keep him on the surface where they could surround the snurd and capture him. Luckily they didn't know what they were doing. Instead of spreading out and closing in from the sides, they stayed in formation, like a gang of bikers on a Sunday ride. Yeh, and bikers was probably what they were.

'Schoolboy error,' said The Pan as he pressed the aviator button, turning sharply to avoid them as the SE2 rose above the waves. He made one last pass over the *Happy Doris*. The whole area was covered in low fog now—it looked as if it was disappearing into a rising sea of cotton wool. So weird. Waggling the wings to say goodbye to his friends, he headed off.

The snurd drivers chasing him hadn't a clue. The Pan reckoned King Milo's gang had been even more badly hit by Resistance's need for drivers than Big Merv's. They were Sunday-driving bimblers by the looks of it. Pretty much anyone could have got away from them. Bob would have shown them a clean set of heels without breaking a sweat.

'Yep,' The Pan muttered to himself. 'These blokes are definitely not skilled operators.'

That was a relief.

Clearly King Milo's tactics had been more a case of grabbing any being who could drive and putting them up in the sky, with a lot more hope than conviction. Then again, they were chasing a boat with a top speed of about eleven miles an hour. It was hardly taxing flying. Yeh, King Milo wouldn't expect them to have to do much. Keeping up with The Pan clearly lay beyond their capabilities so he slowed down and let them chase him around for nearly an hour until he'd led them across the city to Upper Left. The fog wasn't so bad in the city so he gave them the slip by flying down into the narrow streets of the Goojan Quarter where they lacked the skill to follow him.

It would take them a while to get back out to Lower Right and find King Milo. Hopefully long enough for the fog to have hidden Bort, Terri and Christine's boat from sight. Arnold let them have enough 'friends on the river' to hide them, at least for the time being. Yeh. And their boat.

There was a very strong smell in the snurd, a combination of Goojan spiced sausage—because the bag reeked of the sausage it had contained—and The Pan's unpleasantly Dang-infused boots. He opened the window a little.

OK, so he'd ditched the pursuit. Not so hard in the dark. But it would be dawn soon and he had to be bright and chipper for meeting Bob the Blaggysomp outside an internet cafe at ten o'clock. He glanced at his watch as he drove. It was one o'clock in the morning. Time to take stock and work out what he was going to do next. Sleeping would be handy as well, he thought. He was getting very tired.

He landed the SE2 on a flat roof. Switching off the engine, he got out and wandered over to the edge where he sat down, his legs dangling off the side. He heaved a sigh and gazed out over the city. The fog had rolled in now although it was still lying low. It obscured the streets but the roofs of the taller buildings stuck out of it like islands in a cotton-wool sea, except the moonlight turned it silver. The Pan had seen something like this once before, looking out over the sea from the cliffs in Hamgee. But that was just fog and sky. This ... this was weird but also, kind of cool. He drank it in for a while, enjoying the strangeness of it and letting his mind settle.

Now what?

He yawned and stretched. This might be a good place to stay parked overnight. He could sleep in the snurd, undisturbed. Tomorrow, or at least, later today, he would head off to the Botanical Gardens and meet Bob, with the bag so she knew he was genuine. Then Big Merv would go and get his sausage from the Hungry Boatsman pub.

Except that wasn't going to work.

King Milo's people believed The Pan had the sausage. After losing him they and their boss would be turning to other methods to find it. The Pan wasn't big on planning ahead but he knew that if he'd been in King Milo's current position he'd start looking for Terri, Christine and Bort. They could never stay ahead of him, but could they hide from him until three o'clock the next day? The Pan suspected not. No matter how many 'friends on the water' they had. They'd be alright while it was dark, but come daylight King Milo would just put snurds up to look. Yeh, and he'd find them in a couple of hours. He might not be in Big Merv's league but that was no reason to underestimate his intelligence. 'Yeh, just because his drivers are crap, doesn't mean his network is. He'll know people, ask questions and he'll find them,' said The Pan aloud.

Quite right. And you know what that means, said a voice in his head. When The Pan was trying to think things through, or stuck for ideas, he liked to imagine his parents in his head, when they still got along—before it all went wrong. He called it 'virtual parenting'.

'I know, Dad. I'm with you on this. I have to rescue Terri, Christine and Bort,' he said.

Yeh. Bort especially. He thought of her with a pang of longing. It had been the most wonderful day, and Bort was utterly lovely, but a day was probably all he could expect. Yes. And he was extremely grateful. If only it had ended differently though, perhaps with them falling asleep in each other's arms in her small cabin on the boat. Oh Arnold. No. Don't think about that.

Mooning about a girl isn't going to help, the voice of his father told him.

'I know, Dad, but you have to admit, it's a lovely way to pass the time.'

Will you concentrate, you feckless oaf!

'Alright.'

He stood up. He knew what he had to do. He had to tell Big Merv what had happened to his sausage supplier and he had to tell him now. Bort, Terri and Christine had showed The Pan great kindness. Now they were in danger and since he couldn't get them out of it himself, it was time to hand the matter over to someone who could. He swallowed. Big Merv. He looked at his watch. If he was quick about it and got to The Big Thing nightclub before it closed at two, he could probably give all the information to Bob and let her pass it on to whoever needed to know without any further involvement from him. Yeh. That would be a bonus.

'Right. No time for futtering about here,' he sighed, got back into the snurd and took off into the night.

Chapter 20
Awkward interview

The Big Thing nightclub was buzzing. There was a long queue at the door and The Pan walked straight up to the front. He wasn't going in this way—he was going to use the back door—but he wanted to be sure Bob was there before he did that.

'Hop it, pond life,' said the peanut-headed bouncer policing the entrance. Oh no! It was the ironically named Smart Dennis. Thick as two short planks. Hobbies: being stupid, and making life as difficult as he possibly could for The Pan of Hamgee.

'Is Bob in?' asked The Pan.

'You what?'

'Is she working the bar?'

'Yeh, she works here.' By The Prophet, Dennis was a git! 'Yes, we both know she works here,' said The Pan, 'but is she working here *now?*

'Might be.'

Was that a yes? Arnold in the skies! The Pan knew that the trick with Dennis was not to show any signs of losing patience or ask too directly. He didn't appreciate giving straight answers, or at least not to The Pan. Clearly he was different with Big Merv or he'd have been thumped into next week by now for being irritating.

'Can you give her a message?' he asked.

'Ner.'

'Right,' said The Pan patiently.

'Yer. On account of that she's not 'ere.'

'So she's *not* working?'

'Ner. She's workin' but I'm not givin' 'er no message. I

ain't your lackey, you wussy little smeck! You want to give 'er a message, *you* can do it.'

'I can?'

'Yer, when you come in. If you can before closin' time. You ain't nothing special, so you can queue with them other nobodies,' Smart Dennis waved a hand at the long line of beings waiting to enter the club. 'The end's round the corner.'

'Couldn't I just pop in and ...?'

'Ner,' Smart Dennis paused for a moment to unclip the red velvet rope and let in an eager group of wannabe trendsetters, all bar the last one who he grabbed and pulled back into the night air. 'No trainers, pal,' he said.

The being looked at the dark oblong of the entrance into which his friends had already disappeared. 'My friends have trainers on too.'

'Yeh, but they aren't those trainers, see?' Smart Dennis pointed at the tattered shoes the lad was wearing.

'Oh,' he bent down and began to undo his laces.

'No bare feet and all! Sling yer 'ook before I give you a slap!' Smart Dennis watched with evident satisfaction as the guy trudged dejectedly into the night. Then he reverted his attention to The Pan. 'You're not gettin' in neither. Scum like you don't get to go customer side. Specially not when you honk like a tramp's armpit.'

Oh yes, The Pan remembered, his Dangy boots—not to mention the cotton bag which had contained the Goojan spiced sausage, humming away merrily from his back pocket.

'Thanks Dennis,' said The Pan blithely and walked away in the opposite direction.

'Wait up you little turd! I told you! The queue's round there!' bellowed Dennis, pointing.

'Yeh, whatever,' said The Pan.

'Why you little…!' began Smart Dennis, but he couldn't do anything because he couldn't leave his post.

The Pan turned the corner into the service road that ran behind the club. He made his way to the fire exit at the back of the building. As usual, it was ajar. Brilliant, he'd just slip in and—

Unfortunately, just as he arrived at the door it was thrown back, hitting the wall with a slam. Frank the Knife and Smasher Harry, Big Merv's two right-hand henchmen, strode out into the night.

Arnold's trousers. The Pan tried to duck back into the shadows but they noticed him at once. They would, wouldn't they?

'What you doin' 'ere?' snarled Frank.

'Yeh,' growled Harry.

By The Prophet this was unlucky. 'I need to see Bob.'

'She ain't here yet.'

'Smecking Dennis! He told me—'

Frank grabbed The Pan's collar and pulled him so close that their noses nearly touched. 'You badmouthing my friend?'

The Pan knew that Dennis wasn't Frank's friend, but he also knew not to argue. 'No. I—'

'Wossat smell?' Frank wrinkled his nose. 'You stink!' he snarled, pushing The Pan away so he staggered backwards.

'Yeh, it's my boots.'

'It's smeckin' disgustin',' said Harry.

'Yeh ... it is a bit rich. Sorry about that, lads,' said The Pan.

'What d'you tread in?' asked Harry.

'What you want to see Bob for?' said Frank.

The Pan skipped Harry's question as it seemed more pertinent to answer Frank's.

'It's about one of her deliveries, there's been ... a bit of trouble and the supplier needs to—'

'What you two Herberts doing out here?' demanded a voice.

Arnold's ear wax, no! Weren't Frank and Harry enough? The Pan had so hoped he could just tell Bob and run away. Then again, he thought, heaving a resigned sigh, that would never have worked out. They'd have needed him to lead them to where he last saw the *Happy Doris*. Yeh. Grim though it was, this was the only way he could help Terri, Christine and Bort.

Big Merv stepped out into the night. He was still wearing his usual pin-striped suit but in a lighter material, and he'd taken off the jacket and waistcoat to reveal a white shirt with red braces. The shirt was tight, not so it would split or the buttons would gape, but enough to highlight the formidable array of muscles on the body underneath it. Somehow, it made him seem even more intimidating than he did with the jacket on—and that was bad enough. He took in the scene; The Pan, Frank and Harry, standing in the shaft of light falling from the door.

'Whatcha doing?' asked Big Merv.

The Pan guessed, correctly, that this question was aimed at him. He took a deep breath to compose himself and tried to sound calm and manly when he replied. 'I have a message for Bob,' he said. Not bad. A bit squeaky but less of a fearful wobble than sometimes.

'Well, she ain't here.'

'It's from a ... supplier she was dealing with.'

'Then I reckon you gotta to deliver it to me.'

Smeck. 'It's about—'

'Yer?'

'About—'

'Yer?'

Arnold's armpit hair! Why did he always have to do that?

The Pan took another deep breath. 'It's about ... this ...' he blurted, taking the sausage bag out of his pocket and holding it up.

Big Merv's felt-tip green eyes narrowed. The Pan knew that with beings of his boss's genus, Swamp Thing, it was possible to gauge their moods from watching their antennae. Right now Big Merv's were sticking straight up from his head, as if they were statically charged, an unmistakable sign of rage. A few seconds into the conversation and the blue touch-paper was already fully lit. Marvellous.

'Have you been messin' with my business?' asked Big Merv quietly.

'No, absolutely not.'

'But you got that bag.'

'Yes, but as you can see, not the sausage, so technically that's not interfering it's just—'

'Lads, take 'im up to my office.'

'No, it's alright!' squeaked The Pan as Frank and Harry bore down on him. 'No, really. You don't have to drag me. I'll go myself.'

As Smasher Harry and Frank The Knife made to grab him, The Pan ducked past them, side-stepped Big Merv and scuttled up the stairs. At the top there was a landing which had been furnished as a waiting area with chairs and a table. It was like visiting some kind of very scary dentist. Except with Big Merv in this kind of mood, The Pan felt that anaesthetic-free root canal would probably be preferable to the interview he was about to have.

Frank, Harry and Big Merv clattered up the stairs after him. Arnold knew what Big Merv would do if anyone went into his office without asking, and The Pan had absolutely no intention of finding out. Ever. He stopped on the landing and waited. Big Merv strode past him and opened the door.

'In here. Now,' he stood in the entrance and pointed.

The Pan walked past his boss, into the office beyond. Big

Merv followed him with Frank and Harry bringing up the rear and closing the door behind them. Big Merv threw the bag that had contained the sausage onto his desk and stood behind it, legs slightly apart, arms folded in a manner that made his biceps bulge. It was a standard intimidation tactic, but despite the fact The Pan knew this, it still scared him.

Frank put a chair in front of the desk, the usual one; a metal-framed, stacking affair with plywood seat and back. Harry went and stood in front of the door blocking off any escape. The Pan supposed there was the window…? No. There wasn't. Anyway, in theory he was being helpful. He sat down, Frank standing close behind him. Big Merv nodded and said, "S alright lads, I got this.'

Frank and Harry left the room in silence and the door closed. The Pan was now alone with fourteen stones of angry Swamp Thing. He took a deep breath and tried to calm his nerves.

Big Merv put his hands on the desk, one either side of the bag, leaned forward and glared at The Pan. When he spoke his voice was quiet, controlled and deadly. 'What's goin' on pal? An' you'd better be straight with me. No monkey business.'

'Your suppliers have run into trouble.'

'What sorta trouble?'

'King Milo.'

'How d'you know?'

'I was with them.'

'What's my suppliers got to do with you?'

In a flash of inspiration The Pan said, 'One of them's a cobbler, and she's making me a new pair of boots. I went for a fitting and while I was there, King Milo turned up.' Excellent answer—all the salient facts covered without revealing anything else.

'Oh yeh?'

'Yep,' said The Pan breezily, except even to his own ears,

his unfazed facade sounded brittle and forced. He was beginning to sweat as well, but with a gargantuan effort, he stopped himself from saying anything more. The last thing he needed right now was for Big Merv to start asking difficult questions like who, exactly, had eluded the cream of the Grongolian security forces above the Arboretum the previous day.

Big Merv stood back and blew the air out through his cheeks. Had he swallowed The Pan's story?

The silence lengthened.

'That ain't the whole truth though, is it, mate?' he said eventually, without letting up on the glaring.

'Yes, it's ... pretty much it.'

'Yer. Pretty much. But like I said, I reckon there's a lot you ain't telling me, and if King Milo is messing with my suppliers and my business, I gotta know more than that. I gotta know what's going down. All of it.'

'Right.'

'Yer. See, them boots you got on, they don't look tailormade to me.'

'No. They're not the ones I—'

'Shut it, son, I'm talking. I give you, you got style, it's your own interpretation, but for all that, you got it. But you ain't got no cash and that shows. If you could afford a cobbler, you wouldn't be poncing about in the crap you got on. I can tell you something else, too. I don't reckon a bloke who lives on the streets and runs errands for me is the type of geezer what buys flash boots.'

'They last ... a very long time.'

'I pay your wages, son, remember? I know what you earn. And I wasn't born yesterday.'

'No. I—'

'King Milo's paying you to keep schtumm then, is he?'

The Pan could feel the colour draining from his face. 'Smecking Arnold! Come on! You know that's rubbish!' The power of Big Merv's felt-tip green glare intensified.

'Alright. Then I gotta know the rest. Everything you can tell me. If you got some handmade boots on order, I know for a fact you ain't paying cash. I reckon we'll start there. What you done to get free boots, you little numpty?'

Now what? If The Pan admitted he'd been there when they found the sausage Big Merv might put two and two together about certain aspects of his delivery man's life. Things it would be better he didn't know. 'OK, I helped them. They were grateful and they wanted to thank me with a pair of boots.'

"S a big thank you, son.'

'Yeh,' The Pan was glad he hadn't mentioned the other pair of boots. 'It was ... quite a big hand.'

'Yeh?'

'Yes.'

'What you done to earn that kinda thank you?'

The sweat was running down The Pan's face now and his shirt stuck to his back. 'It's difficult to say.'

'You're gonna try though, ain'tcha?'

The Pan took another deep breath and summoned up the courage to meet those felt-tip green eyes for a couple of microseconds. 'I don't think I can,' he mumbled.

By The Prophet what was he doing? This was asking for a good kicking.

'You what?' growled Big Merv.

'Believe me, I wish I could but ... I really, really— Look. You asked me to tell you what I can. That's what I'll do. If you're willing to overlook the,' he swallowed, 'the details of my involvement, I think I can tell you enough to— I think I can tell you what you *need* to know.'

'Alright.' Big Merv sat down in his desk chair and leaned forward. 'I'm listening.'

The Pan took a deep breath.

'I was at the river when they came along and started

poking about on the mud. You know, looking for—'

'I know what mudlarkers do, you giant skipping rope! Get on with it. We ain't got all day.'

'They asked for my help. I agreed in return for a reward. I helped them pull a box from under the jetty to the bank.' The Pan almost hiccupped as he remembered the hideous stench of the box in question. 'To be honest, I thought it was a coffin.'

'Then what?'

'The box was full of rotten meat.'

'Yer, then what?'

'Then they took some plastic containers out of the box and—'

'How many?'

'I'm not sure, I was too busy trying not to hurl, three? Four?'

'And ...?'

'A mob turned up and we all escaped and ... I helped them with that and they were ... grateful.'

Big Merv's antennae tied themselves into a knot and untied themselves. 'What was in them boxes?'

Dare The Pan admit that he knew? No. 'I don't know, but ... looking back on it, the sausage they're selling you, I guess.'

'And they didn't give you none?'

'Er ... no,' The Pan wiped the sweat from his face with a shaking hand as Big Merv watched, missing nothing. 'I expect they wanted a whole one.'

'I thought you said there was three or four boxes. That's more than one sausage, pal.'

'I guess it must have been. I didn't really think about it.'

'You didn't?'

The Pan cleared his throat. 'No.' Arnold's ear wax! OK, so The Pan had managed to survive some years on the blacklist, but he must definitely learn how to lie in a more convincing manner if he wished to survive any more. 'I told them where to find me so they could bring me the boots,' he added.

'You don't look like you got none.'

'No. I didn't. Christine, the one who makes the boots ... she'd got as far as she could with them and she needed to measure my feet to finish them.'

Big Merv nodded. 'And ...?'

'Bort came to get me from the Parrot and Screwdriver yesterday, so I walked back to the boat with her and Christine did just that. Then we had supper and she sent Bort and I off for a... ' he hesitated a fraction, '... walk, while she finished them off. We saw boats approaching and—'

'A walk,' said Big Merv flatly, doing air quotes with his fingers either side of the word 'walk'.

The Pan adopted his best expression of wide-eyed innocence and said, 'Yes.'

Big Merv clearly knew the score but he was decent enough not to enquire further. That was a pleasant surprise. 'What then?'

'We saw boats and it didn't look good so we went back to Terri and Christine at the *Happy Doris*, their boat, and they didn't think it was good either, so we took off. After we escaped, they thought it might be a bad idea to come back into Ning Dang Po so they sent me to meet Bob tomorrow in their place and ... ask you to meet them somewhere called Lark Locks instead, at three. They gave me the bag to show that they're genuine.'

'They know who you work for, then?'

'Not as such, no. Begging your pardon, Big Merv, sir, but that's not the kind of thing I own up to among the ... you know ... normals.'

'Yer. 'S understandable,' Big Merv leaned back in his chair. 'Them mudlarkers are a rum lot though, hardly normal.' His antennae twisted themselves together and untwisted again. 'I wanna know something. They was meeting Bob at ten a.m. tomorrow. Why d'you suddenly reckon you gotta deliver that message now instead of waiting?'

'Because they're ...' what to call them? '... river people. They live on a barge. It goes at eleven miles an hour and that's only because it's souped. It's all they have. If King Milo catches up with them and attacks them, they'll lose more than a sausage. They'll lose everything they own.'

The Pan met Big Merv's scary, felt-tip green gaze. He wanted to look away but he couldn't.

'So?'

'So, King Milo has drivers, in snurds. Tonight, he also had people on the towpath with bikes. The people on the towpath and the snurds ... all of them can go faster than the boat. Bort and her family, they told me they'd lose the pursuit, no problem. They went up the bit of river that the canal bypasses. It's all bends and fences and overhanging trees, then it runs through the reservoir which is long and wide. And if you're following a boat on a bike or on foot, you can't get all the way round it. When I left the boats were dropping back but still following. There was a fog coming up and they were confident they'd be at Lark Locks to meet you. They said they had a foolproof escape protocol and friends on the river—but it's not like they can duck up a side alley. There's no hiding there and no hiding the boat.'

'So what d'you think I'm gonna do about it?'

'Well, you want your sausage, don't you? They haven't a clue what they're up against. As soon as it gets light, King Milo will put his snurds up and they'll find the boat in a jiffy.'

Big Merv nodded. "S a good point.' He paused and his antennae waved to and fro as he thought. 'Them snurds, are they still followin'?'

'They might be. It depends.'

'What d'you mean it depends?'

'I ... well, the reason I have the bag is because Bort threw it to me with a rolling pin in it. We hoped that if we pretended I had the sausage the snurds would all chase me—'

'Yer an' you got a snurd. You drivin' a silver SE2 these days?'

'You must be joking! No way!' It wasn't silver. It was metallic grey. Anyone could see that.

Big Merv's eyes narrowed. 'Oh yeh?'

'Definitely.' Yep. Metallic grey, for sure. Grey, grey, grey. NOT silver. 'Then again, I guess at night, they couldn't tell what I was driving, because they did follow me. It took me ages to lose them,' The Pan added, hoping Big Merv would believe he had found it tricky. 'I finally dumped them somewhere over Upper Left.'

Big Merv gave him an appraising look. 'That's a smart plan, son, you done alright.'

'Not so smart. King Milo will know his snurds have lost me by now, along with—he thinks—the sausage. He'll be straight down to Lark Locks looking for the others so he can ask them where I've taken it. I don't think he's going to ask nicely either. From what I understand, he seems to think it's his.'

'Yer, well, finders keepers. But if he heard the same rumour as them girls and looked in the wrong place, that's his bad and their gain innit? And you ain't wrong. He's gonna be after them three birds of yours like a rat up a pipe.'

Big Merv stood up suddenly, which made The Pan jump, and went to a filing cabinet at the side of the room. After a few moments' rummaging he took out a large piece of folded paper, which he brought back to his desk and spread out. It was a map. He looked at it for a few moments, his brow puckered in a frown.

'Yeh,' he said, jabbing at the paper with an orange index

finger. 'There's Lark Locks. It ain't far. Right.' He put on his jacket.

'Are we leaving?'

'Course. C'mon, look sharp!' said Big Merv as he folded the map and shoved it in his inside jacket pocket. 'Let's get some of the boys together. We gotta find that boat.'

The Pan stood up. 'You want me to—'

Big Merv grabbed him by the lapel and frogmarched him towards the door. "S right. I do. Them birds are gonna need reassurance. That means they gotta see a familiar face. So *that* means you're gonna introduce us.'

The Pan's heart sank. He'd hoped that maybe he'd get to see Bort one last time but if he turned up with his boss in tow she'd probably go off him forever. 'Are you sure that's a good idea?'

'P'raps not for you pal, I dunno. It's the way it's gonna play though. See, I don't like it when people get above their station. It's time King Milo learned to show some respect. If he thinks he can nick my sausage from under my effin' nose he can think again.' He pushed The Pan out of the room and pointed to one of the chairs on the landing. 'Wait there,' he ordered before bellowing down the stairs. 'Frank! Harry! Up here! Pronto.'

Chapter 21
Escape at last

Bort watched The Pan of Hamgee's snurd fly away into the night sky. She hoped he'd be OK. No, of course he would be. He could fly like a pro. He'd escape alright. That wasn't the issue. The big question in Bort's mind was whether he could be trusted to deliver her mum's message to Bob the Blaggysomp. It would be a big disappointment if he couldn't. Yeh. Especially after the things they'd done earlier.

She settled back, keeping a hold of the tiller, making the odd minor adjustment occasionally to keep the *Happy Doris* on course. Now that The Pan of Hamgee had drawn off the airborne pursuit, no zigzagging was required. Terri stood beside her, keeping the blunderbuss aimed at the boats following behind while Christine stood at the ready to fend off any more bottle bombs with the paddle she'd used for that purpose earlier. Not that either party was in range of the other anymore—but it didn't hurt to be at the ready. The three women stood in silent concentration, lost in their own thoughts. After twenty minutes, not only were King Milo's boats dropping further and further back but they were disappearing into the mist. The strange blanket of fog covering the water was rising and beginning to envelop the boat. Bort was using the compass to steer, so it was only when she looked up again that she realised how thick the fog around them had become. 'Yes!' She almost punched the air.

'You only just noticed?' Terri asked.

'I was concentrating.'

Terri reached one arm round Bort's shoulders and hugged her. 'It's providence, that is!'

'Maybe.'

'Definitely,' said Christine. 'Anyone fancy a brew?' she added because even in the most fraught pursuit on the water there was always time for a cuppa. Things happened a little more slowly than on land, even in a souped-up barge with such a mighty top speed as the *Happy Doris*. When Bort and Terri eagerly accepted her offer, Christine stowed the paddle back where it lived, next to the grab rails along the side of the roof, and then went below to put the kettle on.

Bort and her mum maintained their stations in companionable silence. Bort thought about the differences between the chase they were embroiled in now and those action-packed moments over the Arboretum in The Pan of Hamgee's snurd. Where would they be if they hadn't run into him? Back to normal, she supposed. Or would the Grongles still have turned up? She glanced briefly at her mum, beside her. Ugh. She shuddered as she thought about the creepy one and his mate. She didn't dare think about what might have happened with them. Or would the third one have saved them from that? He'd seemed alright ... for a murdering Grongle smecker. No, her mum would still have lost her ID for good and been blacklisted. Putting aside the fact that Bort liked The Pan of Hamgee, she reckoned all three of them had been lucky to run into him. She smiled to herself. This trip to Ning Dang Po was turning out to be a bit dangerous in some respects, but that just made it more exciting. Yeh and The Pan of Hamgee was an unexpected bonus. Except that it was difficult to steal enough time with him when there was all this going on. Life was annoyingly complicated sometimes, she reflected and sighed heavily.

Terri was scanning the waters behind them, but when she heard her daughter sigh she reached out and patted her arm. 'You OK, darling?' she asked.

'Yeh,' said Bort.

'If you need to talk to your old mum about anything you know I'm here.'

Bort thought about it but decided that while she might talk to her mum at some point, now wasn't the time. Christine came back.

'Brew's up,' she said putting a cup on the gunwale beside Bort and handing another to Terri. She ducked back inside and returned with another cup for herself and sat beside Terri. 'Herbal tea.' She looked up at the sky. 'Looks like the weather is with us tonight. But the forecast's clear for tomorrow. It's going to make it tricky. We'll have to get to Lark Locks as soon as possible, and we'll need all the help we can get.'

'Yeh,' said Bort. 'We're going to hide the cash we got for the other two sausages, right?'

'Yeh, with Mrs Spurdle at the Hungry Boatsman.'

Bort sighed. 'I hope they didn't catch him,' she said, talking about The Pan.

'Me too,' Terri replied, realising exactly what she was talking about. 'He's a sweet lad.'

'Yesterday morning at breakfast, you two told me he was bad news,' said Bort.

'We did,' said Christine. 'But that doesn't mean we don't like him.'

'Yep. He's very charming,' agreed Terri. 'But I reckon he comes with a lot of baggage. *That's* the bad news. *He's* an absolute poppet.'

'And even with the baggage, he's perfectly alright for a fling,' added Christine, 'if you like that sort of thing.'

'Arnold! Will you two shut up,' said Bort. 'You're such stirrers.'

But now Bort was thinking about The Pan again. He *was* charming, but possibly a bit too frivolous for her taste, long-term anyway. Even so, the prospect of him becoming, say, a medium-term thing held a fair bit of appeal.

'For all his bravado, I'd say he's shy,' said Terri.

'Yes, he is,' said Bort. Surprisingly shy really. She'd

thought the chemistry between them was totally obvious. Clearly not to him though. In the end, she'd had to practically throw herself at him, which would have been horribly embarrassing if he hadn't, eventually, got the message. Because a woman has pride. Thank The Prophet the penny had finally dropped. Then again, thinking about it ... 'He's not shy in a crisis,' she said.

'Nope,' said Terri. 'Very incisive. Clear thinker.'

Yeh. In a crisis The Pan of Hamgee was something else, Bort reflected; calm, in control, quick, confident and a little bit manly in a way that was so, so hot. Why couldn't he be like that all the time? She sighed. She wondered if she'd see him again—she hoped she would. Somewhere secluded where they could be alone, preferably. Yeh, and with any luck he wouldn't be so shy next time, either.

Arnold's socks! What was she doing? This wasn't the time to think about that sort of thing. She was supposed to be concentrating. Now was the time to keep them on course and at top speed. It was challenging enough, with the fog obscuring the entrance to the canal and the eddying of the current also catching the boat a little. She was driving blind. She had to keep making minute corrections to stop the *Happy Doris* from drifting off course. It called for concentration and vigilance. And while reliving her day, and especially the evening, with The Pan of Hamgee was an enjoyable way to pass the time, it wasn't being vigilant. Not really. She rolled her eyes at herself.

She was pulled out of her thoughts by Christine. 'I can't see hide nor hair of them anymore, not that it means much with this fog, but I can't hear them either which might. The fog could be deadening the sounds of their engines, or we could've lost them,' she said as she scanned the fog behind them for any sign of King Milo's boats.

'I'd say we're gaining,' said Terri. 'If we're far enough

ahead at the next lock, we'll lose 'em.'

As the *Happy Doris* pulled away from her pursuers, Bort dared to hope that the three of them could disappear. Terri finished her tea and put the blunderbuss back in the secret compartment in the gunwale. 'We'll have to clean that tomorrow,' she said. 'Can you do it, Bort?'

'Sure.' Well, it was better than some of the other jobs.

The air was still, but the movement of the boat through the water ruffled it enough to waft Bort's hair against her face. The fog was really thickening now. She could hardly see the surface of the reservoir let alone any boats following them. The fog had come to their rescue. Bort had been scared King Milo would call up speedboats from somewhere. It looked like he wasn't going to though. Not tonight anyway. Then again, why would he? There were only so many places they could go. She supposed they could have the *Happy Doris* lifted and taken to another waterway far from there. But lifting a boat wasn't something that happened often, so when it did people noticed. Yeh and people would talk, too. If King Milo wanted to, he would find them.

'If he's a true being of the river, he'll give up soon, go back to his lair and put his ear to the ground,' said Terri quietly.

Bort sighed. 'It won't stop him though, will it?'

'Nope,' said her mum.

'We've given smarter minds than his the slip before,' said Christine.

'Yeh, but the stakes weren't so high were they? He thinks we have a Goojan spiced sausage.'

'We won't by the time he catches up with us,' said Terri.

'Yes,' Christine agreed.

Bort shrugged. 'He'll find us before we meet Bob the Blaggysomp.'

'Yes, but I think the Hamgeean lad is clever enough to arrive early. If we're lucky he might even bring the cavalry with him.'

'D'you think he will?'

'I'd say so. If Bob wants that sausage for her boss, she'll be at the locks by eleven,' said Terri.

'What if King Milo gets here sooner?' said Bort.

'It's a worry,' Terri conceded. 'But if we can get up the locks before he arrives I'd say we can get the sausage sold and get out before he finds us.'

Bort heaved a sigh. She knew the *Happy Doris's* disappearing trick worked. It had worked every time so far. Then why was she so worried?

'There's so much that relies on this,' said Christine.

'Yes,' said Terri with a sigh. 'I expect that's why we're all so jumpy.'

Chapter 22
Time to regroup

Gradually, as the *Happy Doris* reached the other side of the reservoir, it was swallowed up in the fog. Visibility was down to fifty yards or so now.

At the head of the pursuing barges King Milo watched from the deck in irritation. He was called King Milo because he was known for being a 'gentleman thug'. That said, he was a Blaggysomp, one of K'Barth's mountain species, and so was not strictly a man as such. He was covered in blue fur, except on his face. And though his features were human—but sky blue—his neck was a tiny bit longer than that of other species.

When it came to his behaviour, the epithet 'gentleman' was definitely ironic. King Milo was a great deal more ungentlemanly than most. As some of the beings who served him pointed out, although not to his face, he just went about his thuggery with airs. He called it 'class'.

He certainly looked the part. He wore evening dress at all times; today it was a white tie, tail coat, spats, white shirt and red cummerbund. It was topped off with a red silk-lined opera cloak, a monocle and a top hat, to add character. He also spoke with a ridiculously posh accent which he'd affected after watching old films.

These days the sleeves of his coat were worn shiny in places and the whole get-up was beginning to look a bit frayed about the edges close up. His ridiculously posh accent didn't come naturally and every now and again, if he wasn't concentrating, his street urchin origins could be heard in his speech. Nobody was going to point that out to him though, because for all the tatty nature of his clothes, King Milo was still a bona fide psychopath.

At this precise moment, he'd discarded the tailcoat and the cloak. This was one of the hottest summers ever, after all. While the fog-laden air should have been cooler, in theory, it was all relative. He was still sporting the shirt and cummerbund, of course, and the monocle.

'If those foolish females wish to risk pressing on to Lark Locks in this pea souper then, I aver, we shall let them.' He clicked his fingers. 'Halt the Royal Barge and call the others alongside,' he ordered.

Someone pressed a klaxon and the water behind the barge boiled as the engines were thrown into reverse. It slowed to a halt. Gang members ran officiously up and down the gunwales making the other boats fast. When the activity had settled down a little, King Milo beckoned to the enforcers skippering the largest barge.

'Hopper and Spannock, take the *Rosalee*—*Rosalee* being the name of the vehicle in question—'and block the canal entrance. I believe they have proceeded onward to Lark Locks but it pays to cover every eventuality. The rest of us will go back to base and regroup. If you catch them doubling back, hold where you are and send a runner.'

King Milo's senior commanders also wore their own version of evening dress. Hopper and Spannock were no exception. However, they were only ever going to look like a pair of brick outhouses with some dark material draped over them. Never mind, King Milo reflected, only Arnold was perfect. They were doing their best, and for a couple of henchmen—or at least henchman and henchThing because Spannock was a Swamp Thing—it was probably the best he could expect. They stood smartly to attention and a group of the thugs under their command gathered round them, and their leader, to listen.

'Er ...'

'Yes, Hopper?'

'Is that a good idea, Your Majesty?'

'Of course it's a smecking good idea, you poltroon!'

'Shouldn't we continue after them? I mean, what if they get away?'

'Where to? They have to negotiate the locks and to do that they have to wait like everyone else. We'll arrive at dawn, kill them and take their home and everything they own.' King Milo chuckled nastily to himself. 'That barge of theirs will fetch a fine price even before we add the sausage. They know they haven't a hope so they'll double back and you'll capture them.'

Hopper's brow furrowed. 'We will?'

King Milo examined his fingernails for a moment and then looked up suddenly. 'Yes. They won't escape. Not now. And if they do I'll have you killed.'

'But ... they *have* escaped, already, Your Majesty,' said Spannock glancing nervously about him as if for potential executioners.

'No. They've gone to Lark Locks, and—as we have discussed—that's not allowing them to escape, it's letting them walk into our trap. I think you'll find there's a difference.' Spannock's antennae curled up as he computed this information. King Milo waited until they uncurled, signifying that the penny had, in all probability, dropped before continuing. 'It may be busy there, and they may disguise their barge, but we'll find them.'

'What if they're gone, your Majesty?' asked Spannock.

'As I explained less than thirty seconds ago, I believe it most likely they'll be queuing for the lock. And if by some miraculous fluke, they get through it before we arrive, we will apprehend them before they leave the upper marina, I swear it.'

'What if they're in disguise?' asked Hopper.

'Then we ask where we can find three people on a thirty-foot barge. I am confident there will be plenty of loose mouthed beings at Lark Locks who'll tell us where they are.

Especially if you shake them hard enough.'

Spannock's face brightened as he finally understood. 'OK, Your Majesty,' he said.

'Your Majesty? Begging your pardon,' asked Hopper.

'Yes,' sighed King Milo heavily.

'I don't wish to speak out of turn, King Milo, Your Majesty—'

'But you're going to,' said King Milo tetchily.

'Yes, Your Majesty. See, that snurd was an SE2.'

'Yes, a silver one.'

'Begging your pardon, Your Majesty, but I thought it was more of a sort of, metallic grey,' ventured Hopper.

There was silence as King Milo gave him an intensely withering look and continued. 'It looked silver and since it's dark, we can't be sure. Hopper, if you interrupt me again, I will be forced to stab you in the eye. Don't make me do that, there's a good fellow.'

'Sorry, Your Majesty.'

'I'm so glad, because you really are too useful to maim. If I may be so bold, I'm assuming that what you wish to tell me is that a group of silver-*coloured,*' he glared at Hopper, 'SE2 snurds gave the security forces the run around a few days ago. Am I correct?'

'Yes, Your Majesty,' said Hopper.

'Official word is that they were all downed. However, since the number cited varies you're right to raise this. We can't be entirely sure. BUT ...' he raised his hand, one blue index finger extended. 'Both the rumour mill and the Grongolian News Network agree that they were all the same colour.'

'Yes, Your Majesty. Word is they may be members of some kind of gang, see? And I thought...'

'You wonder if, perchance, there *are* more and the SE2 we've just seen is one of them?' Hopper nodded. 'Well, if it is, I'd guess the fellow who went off in it can drive and, that being the case, our airborne colleagues may not catch him. You're wondering if that might not cause us a problem, yes?' Spannock and Hopper, along with a group of other sundry heavies who'd gathered round to listen, nodded like an amazed audience watching a mind-reader's act and muttered that yes, indeed, they were. 'I'm so delighted we are all of one accord. And I congratulate you on your intelligent thinking. Here is our plan B. We watch and wait. He has the sausage. He will have to return to them, either with the sausage or, if he's their delivery mule, with the money they've been paid for it. He'll have to meet them somewhere, soon, to make the handover.'

'Will they trust someone else to take the money, Your Majesty?' asked a voice. Spannock, this time.

'Oh no, my friends, *they* will make the sale,' King Milo said. 'He'll bring back the sausage for them to sell, and if things pan out the way I anticipate, we may even get our hands on their buyer. And if he's who I think he is, then I—and by association you, my friends—will have everything. All we have to do is be patient.'

The assorted heavies gathered around King Milo snickered nastily and he felt a glow of pride. He was going places. They all were. Even if some looked the part a bit more than others. Spannock, especially, bore more resemblance to a bus with a tarpaulin draped over it than an actual being. A bus with antennae. Never mind. It was nothing a decent tailor couldn't fix. King Milo knew that if his plan worked, he'd be very, very rich. Oh yeh, and the Boss of Ning Dang Po, or at least, a sizeable chunk of it. And he'd be king of the rest of the city in no time. He smiled to himself. Wouldn't that be fine?

His reveries of city-wide domination were interrupted when he noticed that Hopper and Spannock were still there. 'What are you waiting for gentlemen? Go!'

'Yes, Your Majesty,' they said and went.

Chapter 23
Disappearance

Bort, Terri and Christine steered slowly through the fog. They kept the lights of the *Happy Doris* off. When switched on, the headlamp beams merely bounced off the fog, surrounding them with a dazzling glow of white. So it was easier to see without them. More to the point, without the lights nobody could see *them*. They slowed as much as they dared as they left the reservoir behind them. Three more miles of meandering river lay before them. Then there was a lock where it re-joined the canal. It wasn't beyond the realms of possibility that King Milo would have people waiting there, but it was a chance they'd have to take. Beyond that lock was another short stretch of water; the canal, then the locks: a series of fifteen over a mile-and-a-half stretch, with a basin and a marina at the top and bottom. The Hungry Boatsman was situated on the bank of the far marina at the top, but it would be easy enough to walk up there as soon as they arrived. And they could hand the cash and any other valuables over to Mrs Spurdle who would keep everything safe.

Lark Locks was always a busy stretch with plenty of other boats queuing, waiting in the locks or moored in rows in the marinas at each end. It was a good place to stop for a while. There were shops, boat yards and repair stations, and a little village.

A drip fell from the overhanging branches above and landed on Bort's shoulder, making her jump. She looked up. The ancient trees lining the meandering river Linnet seemed to be trapping the fog, making it denser. In a way it was eerie, but mostly she was just glad it would help hide them. Bort knew that the *Happy Doris* needed to be out of sight from prying eyes for at least two minutes. Ideally, it should be longer, more like five. Then they needed to be through the locks and out the other end before there was any chance of King Milo making visual contact a second time. It would be a tough ask and it depended on a lot of outside factors.

Yeh. She finished her coffee and yawned. She was so tired.

'D'you want me to take the tiller for a while?' asked Christine.

'Go on then. I'll do the cups.' Christine had given her some time alone with her mum; now it seemed only fair to give her a bit of time alone with her wife.

Bort left her at the tiller and took the cups inside to wash them. She pulled down all the blinds before she put on the light and even then, kept it to the one small spot above the sink. She'd already checked the escape options in this area. She and her mum had spent a day checking and marking all their routes out of Ning Dang Po in the map book during the first week after their arrival, while Christine was busy making and selling boots. Mudlarkers were usually solid, but every now and again they could be a bit suspicious of newcomers. Other times there were beings like King Milo in their ranks who thought the community owed them a living and extracted it from them by fair means or foul. Both kinds of mudlarking community were close knit and stuck together. That was great if they accepted you, but not so great if they didn't.

The first thing Terri, Christine and Bort did on arrival anywhere, was to make sure they could leave in a hurry if they had to. Just in case. Perhaps it was a hangover from the days when Bort's father had been living with them. Before he'd moved out; before Christine. In those days, midnight flits weren't uncommon. But that was more about the driving he did than the mudlarking his wife and daughter were engaged in.

Bort ran a little water in the bottom of the sink and squirted in some washing-up liquid.

With just the three of them it was quieter. Disputes in mudlarking were rare although when they did happen, they seemed to be fiercer now than when Bort had been a child. Perhaps that was because she understood more of the undercurrents in adult interaction that her childhood self had missed. Possibly. But she guessed that in these lean times of institutionalised poverty among the K'Barthan population, a valuable artefact meant more to the finder. These days, even something of moderate worth could make or break the lives of the folks who found it. When everyone lived hand to mouth, she supposed that was how it worked.

Bort picked up the kettle as she mulled this over. There was still some water in it so she emptied it into the sink, put it back on the stove and started washing up. The water was warm against her hands. As she stirred it about the soap made an impressive layer of foam. It wobbled like a crackly white jelly as she scrubbed at the cups beneath.

'We shouldn't have to be running,' she muttered to herself. Mudlarking had rules, after all.

Yeh, she thought, *but it's a fact of life that some people ignore the rules or write new ones of their own.*

These days, if they had a big enough gang of thugs ready to bash dissenters, they tended to get away with it. King Milo being a case in point. Bort felt they'd been unlucky in Ning Dang Po. She liked the city and was sad they were leaving in a hurry.

Then again, she thought as she dried the cups and stowed them safely away in the cupboard, the three of them would have means soon. They'd be in a different world, with any luck, a world away from that sort of malarkey. Yeh, well ... she could hope. She put out the light and returned to the rear deck.

'Alright?' asked Christine.

'Yeh, can't see much now though. Are you OK there for a few more minutes?'

'Of course, sweetie. It's quite dense but there's a full moon above it. Your eyes will adjust soon enough.'

'What are we going to do now?' Bort asked.

'The usual,' said Terri. 'Disappear.'

'I mean after this. What will it be like?'

'We'll have a home.'

'We already have a home,' said Bort.

She liked their gipsy life. She thrived on change and travel; just enough of their existence was predictable. The rhythms of their summers travelling through the waterways of K'Barth and their winters in Glardy were always the same. Yet each time was also different, comfortingly familiar yet pleasingly different; enough to be interesting but not enough to be alarming. The change and the constant movement suited Bort. Itinerant was easy. It usually meant staying in places long enough to find a boyfriend but not so long it got serious. Bort was only young and she didn't want serious. Well no, one day she did, but not yet. Itinerant meant uncomplicated; it meant that life, and love was like a series of holidays and holiday romances. It meant there was always something new just around the next corner.

Could she settle down? Should she? Even if her mum and Christine did. She was officially an adult, now. Should she strike out on her own? If she did, what would it be like? Would she be lonely? She liked living with her mum and Christine—the bond between the three women was deep and abiding—but she couldn't live at home forever. She would have to do something with her life at some point.

'We probably shouldn't make any plans until we've sold the last sausage and we know for sure how much money we have,' said Christine.

Bort had got used to the darkness now and took the rudder again. The fog seemed to be thinning because every now and again the moonlight broke through, illuminating the blanket around them with ghost-like speckles of light, or casting a thin grey sheen, a hint of a reflection, on the water.

For a few minutes they journeyed on in tense silence until Terri spoke.

'We'll be at the lock soon. There might be someone there watching out for us. I think it's time to say goodbye to the *Happy Doris.*'

'Right.' Christine cut the engine and let the momentum carry the barge onwards.

The three of them stood listening.

Bort could hear no sound but the slapping of the water against the hull and her own breathing. After a few moments Terri and Christine got to work. Bort kept watch as the pair of them ran along the roof of the boat, flipping up the grab rails which had been put there to make walking along the gunwales at the sides a little safer. The *Happy Doris* was clad in wood, painted bright red and inset with decorated panels. These had a mostly blue background, with illustrations at their centre; bunches of gaily painted flowers, four river scenes depicting the water during each of the seasons and, of course, the name of the boat. What no-one knew was that if the grab rails were flipped up, these panels could be removed and turned round. The scenes on the back were different and painted on a green background. The panels bearing the boat's name also had a different one applied: *Frolicking Maiden.* In dire straits it was even possible to remove the panels completely, revealing yet another set of scenes painted on the metal hull and a third name: *Fancy Mermaid.* But that involved hiding the panels under the floor in the main cabin and there was no time for that.

Tonight, the *Happy Doris* was going to disappear. And the barge mooring up at Lark Locks in a few minutes' time was going to be the *Frolicking Maiden.*

Panels duly switched, Bort flipped the grab rails back into position shore side, while Christine did them along the other. Meanwhile Terri used a similar procedure to change the name on the plaque at the front of the boat and ran to the back to change the name there too. Grab rails done, Christine ducked into the cabin to switch the paperwork. All three of the boat's 'identities' had the legitimate licences required. The one in use was always kept out, in the desk, while the other two were hidden under a plastic cutlery canteen in the drawer where the kitchen utensils were kept.

A few minutes later they sparked up the engine again and arrived at the junction with the canal proper and the lock. Beyond it lay a short stretch of canal and then the basin. This lock had no lock keeper. Even if there had been, it was unlikely they would have come out to work the gates at this time of night, so in theory the three of them were alone. Terri and Christine stayed on the barge while Bort opened and closed the gates. Once the barge was through and out onto the water on the other side, she ran along the towpath to catch up, leaping nimbly back onto the boat as Christine steered it closer to the side.

Now that the *Doris* was disguised and they'd been through the lock without incident, Bort felt a little safer. Even so, she knew that when they arrived and moored up, she, Terri and Christine must disguise themselves the same way they'd disguised the boat.

****

From the darkness of the bushes a few yards away,

unknown to the three women, someone watched. As the boat headed off, he turned and began to walk back down the towpath towards the reservoir. He was certain those were the women he was looking for. And that King Milo would pay handsomely to know that the *Happy Doris* had changed its name and livery.

****

By dawn the barge formerly known as the *Happy Doris*, now the *Frolicking Maiden*, had made it to the basin at the bottom of Lark Locks. There'd be no travelling any further until the lock keeper woke up. Then again, Bort reflected, that was only a couple of hours away.

'Right,' said Terri, rubbing her hands together, 'time to turn in.'

'Shouldn't one of us keep watch?' said Bort.

'Yes, but Christine's going first, then I'll do an hour and come and wake you. It'll be six by then and Zeb will be up and about. If nobody else is ready he might let us jump the queue for the locks.'

Zeb was the lock keeper, an elderly Galorsh, his purple fur flecked with grey. He wore dungarees most of the time with good solid boots made by Christine. She re-soled and heeled them every time they came through, and gave him a new pair every ten years or so, long before the others wore out, just to keep in his good books.

'It's only a precaution,' added Christine.

Yeh, Bort realised that. Lark Locks was a busy junction in the canal system. Routes all over K'Barth converged just above the locks at Lark Junction, and hundreds of boats used the basin there. They bought supplies from the boat chandlers, and there was a yard that fixed their boats—plus they could have a meal and some excellent beer at the Hungry Boatsman. It wasn't a smart pub, but in the summer it was alright, especially if you stayed in the garden. It was owned by Mrs Spurdle. She was strictly front of house though; the nitty-gritty was done by a Blurpon couple called Norman and Helmut. They didn't take any crap from anyone.

There was a community up there, and the beings were largely friendly. The regular travellers, even seasonal ones like Bort, Christine and Terri were known to them.

'Go on then, off you go,' said Terri.

Bort knew the right thing to do was argue and take watch first—after all, she was the youngest. She tried but her heart wasn't in it and she soon acquiesced, went to her cabin and sank gratefully onto the bed. Before she'd even thought of putting on her night clothes she fell into a deep sleep.

She was woken, almost instantly it seemed, by her mother.

'Time to get up, sleepy head! Come on, sluggabed! Up you get!'

'What time is it?'

'Five. Zeb was out watering his garden, and he says he can get us through the locks ahead of all the other boats if we go now.'

Yawning, Bort took the cup of coffee her mother proffered her and had a gulp. Perfect. She stood up, put the cup on a nearby shelf, stretched and went to the bathroom. There wasn't time for a proper shower so she washed her face and hands, brushed her teeth and went back to her bedroom. If the boat had changed, the passengers had to as well. So she put on a pair of wide canvas trousers and rolled them up. She balled her blonde hair up under a hat and finished the look off with a baggy t-shirt. At first glance, if someone wasn't really looking, they might mistake her for a lad. Even if they didn't, she hoped the frumpy clothes would make her harder to recognise as Bort.

That done, she went barefoot onto the deck to help Terri

and Christine get the boat underway.

The canal at Lark Locks went uphill for quite some way, a feat that would have been impossible without a row of fifteen locks to allow boats to move from one level to the other in manageable increments. It took four or five hours to go through but on the other side they had a choice of seven canals to escape in to. The marina up there was just as full of boats as the one down here, the shop and pub bustling with other beings, so it would be easy for the *Frolicking Maiden* and her crew to blend in unobtrusively. Especially when the beings searching for the *Happy Doris* wouldn't have expected it to have made such good progress, and would probably start looking at the lower basin.

As Terri steered the boat into the first lock, Bort felt something like relief.

Chapter 24
Who? Me?

The Pan was escorted downstairs by Big Merv, who was now sporting the trilby hat he habitually wore. They arrived in the car park at the back of the nightclub where a band of Big Merv's other enforcers had gathered to wait. The Pan recognised a couple of regulars from the club, but these ones were clearly picked for their brains rather than their brawn. Smart Dennis was missing, for starters. They were of all genera, including three Blurpons, a Galorsh and two Swamp Things, like Big Merv, only they were the usual green rather than their boss's unique orange. With Big Merv, Frank, Harry and the other enforcers The Pan counted eighteen—twenty if he included himself and Bob. Not so many considering the numbers of beings he'd seen chasing the *Happy Doris*. He hoped Big Merv knew what he was doing.

With a quiet crunch of tyres on tarmac, Big Merv's sleek midnight blue MKII snurd arrived, along with two other similar models.

'You know what you gotta do?' asked Big Merv to the group.

The assembled posse nodded and shuffled their feet. A couple said, 'Yer'.

The Pan heaved a sigh. He hoped Bort, Terri and Christine would forgive him for bringing Big Merv and all of this lot to their barge. Yeh. He was bound to be overreacting and they might not take kindly to it. They were probably fine.

Probably.

Except something in the pit of his stomach, a small knot

of tension, told him he didn't believe it.

Bob stepped smartly out of the snurd's driver's door to open the back door of the MKII. She stood beside it, ready, waiting for Big Merv to get in. It seemed she'd arrived for work while The Pan was being grilled by his boss. It was a relief to see a friendly face.

'C'mon then, let's go,' said Big Merv.

Phew, job done. The Pan turned to walk away but with lightning speed his boss reached out and grabbed him by the collar. 'Whoa there! Wait a moment! W— what—'

'You're coming with us, son,' he replied as he dragged The Pan over to the MKII. 'Get in,' he added, shoving him towards the immaculate, shiny snurd. Frank and Harry climbed into the back seat.

Straightening his clothes, The Pan headed for the front passenger door.

'Nah, you pillock! In there,' said Big Merv grabbing him by the collar again and shoving him towards the back.

'What with—'

'Frank and Harry. Yeh.'

The Pan took a deep breath. 'Right.'

It would have to be Frank in the middle, wouldn't it? Harry might dislike The Pan, but Frank loathed and detested him. The Pan squeezed in on the end trying not to touch any bit of Frank, at all. Frank and Harry were clearly even less enthusiastic about the prospect of sharing the snurd with The Pan than he was about sharing with them. He almost wished he was driving. No, trying not to scratch Big Merv's MKII? That would be terrifying.

With a smile and a reassuring wink, Bob shut the door on The Pan, walked round and held the passenger door open for Big Merv. Finally she went round and got into the driver's seat.

'Alright, you know where you're goin'?'

'Yes, sir, roughly. The canal, where it bypasses the river

Linnet down in Lower Right,' said Bob.

"'S right. Good. Drive,' said Big Merv, 'If you do have any trouble findin' it, this little scrote'll give you a hand.' He jerked his thumb backwards in The Pan's direction. 'We're goin' to a place called Lark Locks, somewhere in the sticks beyond there. You know it?'

'Yes, sir,' said Bob.

For the first time ever, in the months The Pan had known Bob, Big Merv ordered her to fly. She didn't seem to need directions but The Pan gave them anyway. Mainly because he needed to do something to take his mind off the fact he was sitting next to Frank the Knife. She didn't seem to mind. Maybe she understood.

A handful of other snurds carrying the rest of the group flew alongside them in formation. Out of the window the city stretched away into the distance, a sea of white cotton wool with the silver, moonlit roofs of the taller buildings sticking out of it like islands. Occasionally The Pan spotted a twinkle of light from a window as it flashed past.

Bob flew low, a few hundred feet above the ground. The Pan watched the MKII's shadow, and those of the other snurds, as they skipped over the surface of the cloud beneath them. The sky began to lighten. Dawn was coming. It was difficult to tell from above but the fog seemed to be dissipating the way it had risen—it was still thick but the tops of trees were beginning to appear now. At the end of the reservoir, the treetops lining the river were clearly visible. Another stretch of meandering river, then, somewhere ahead, The Pan knew it rejoined the canal.

He explained this to Bob and she followed the trees for a couple of hundred yards or so before Big Merv spoke to her and the MKII peeled away over several acres of sugar beet fields. They landed on a road which ran more or less parallel to the river and Bob drove on for a few hundred yards before turning onto a concrete hard standing. Later on it would be piled with beet but the crop wasn't ready yet. Right now, barring a couple of pieces of farming equipment, a rusty trailer and a strange conveyor belt like thing on wheels, it was empty.

As soon as the snurd came to a stop, Bob was out and round to the passenger door to open it for Big Merv. To The Pan's horror, before he could think about getting out himself, his boss wrenched open the back door.

'Out,' he growled, grabbing The Pan by the lapels of his jacket and hauling him onto his feet while Frank and Harry got out the other side.

The fog was still thick but it had now sunk to the point where there was a layer about four feet thick across the ground. The Pan looked around him at the heads and torsos of his boss and enforcers, sticking up, proud, from a sea of white. This was the weirdest thing he'd ever seen.

The other snurds landed and then they waited while a second group arrived. Many of the hardest enforcers in Big Merv's employ were there, including Fists McDermot, who'd reported The Pan to the security forces at one point. That had been down to a misunderstanding, of course. Even so, The Pan tried not to get too close to Fists, who appeared to be even less appreciative of his presence in Big Merv's organisation than Frank and Harry. If that was possible.

Big Merv sent a couple of the lads off to keep a look out, then spread the map across the bonnet of one of the other snurds. Everyone who was left gathered round to look at it. The Pan hung back, preferring not to jostle with the throng of bigger and scarier beings for a view. Big Merv consulted the map for a moment or two and then addressed his assembled enforcers. At the back, The Pan couldn't see much. He took a step away from them to give himself a bit more personal space, and listened.

'Here's how this is gonna go down,' said Big Merv. He pointed down the canal, into the distance. 'Lark Locks is about four miles up there. The canal goes up hill there and—'

'How's it do that, boss?' someone said.

'The magic of science, pal. As I was saying,' Big Merv continued in a tone that clearly brooked no interruption. 'There's a whole bunch of locks—that's the science, Johnno,' he explained to the enforcer who'd interrupted him, 'and how it goes up hill. Anyway, them birds want us to meet 'em at a pub at the top to pick up the goods. I reckon it'll take a good few hours to get through them locks. I reckon that's why they wanna meet at three. If I was King Milo, Lark Locks is where I'd strike. Now, I reckon he and his boys are behind us. They ain't got no clue who they're messing with so they'll reckon they got all the time in the world. They'll get themselves sorted and come for the goods at dawn while them ladies is still asleep. That means we gotta go check out the lie of the land and get ourselves into position, quick and quiet like. We're gonna fly on ahead in the snurds and gets ourselves fixed up, you get me?' The assembled crowd nodded and mumbled their assent. 'Sweet.' Big Merv folded the map stuffed it in his pocket and straightened up. He pointed along the road. 'Them locks is a few miles down that way. We're gonna drive there, case the joint and get set. We gotta be proper subtle, you get me? We don't want no-one knowing who we are.'

The assembled heavies nodded.

'While the rest of us does that, someone else has gotta go on foot and check them birds didn't double back.'

'Right, boss,' said Frank.

'Yer, see, if *I* was them, I'd backtrack quick smart, take another route outa the city, park the boat and get a ride up to the locks in a cab. But, King Milo ain't stupid, so he might've put some blokes in place back at the reservoir to make sure that don't happen.'

'We gonna bash 'em then?' asked Harry.

'Ner, I just gotta know if they're there. This is how it's gonna go down. Someone's gonna go and check the exit to the reservoir, nice and subtle like, someone who ain't gonna get themselves noticed. Then, someone is gonna walk to Lark Locks. Follow the river, in case them birds is stopped half way. If he finds them ladies, he's gotta persuade them they need to be at the basin at the bottom of the locks, pronto.'

'You want me to go, boss?' asked Frank.

'Nah. It's gotta be a bloke what they'll trust. Also, it's gotta be the kind of slippery little bleeder that no-one'll catch up with, even if something goes down.'

There was a short silence.

'Who's gonna do that then, boss?' asked someone. The Pan thought it was Fists McDermot but he couldn't be sure.

'Him,' said Big Merv, jabbing a pointy finger.

The crowd of enforcers stepped back, turning as they did to look where their leader was pointing. Straight at The Pan of Hamgee. He had, sort of, seen it coming but he looked behind him anyway, just to check.

No-one there.

Arnold's armpits! It seemed he really was the target of Big Merv's pointy finger.

Arse.

Chapter 25
Unwilling accomplice

'Me?' The Pan asked anyway, because there was no harm in making sure.

''S right pal.' Big Merv walked casually over to The Pan and jabbed him in the chest with his finger a couple of times for emphasis. 'You.'

'Are you sure about this?'

'Yeh. See, them boats, we all know they ain't that quick off the mark. I reckon there's a chance your mates ain't even got to Lark Locks yet. What's more, even if they have, I reckon they'll have disguised themselves, their boat and all, if they're able.'

'How would they do that?'

Bit Merv shrugged. 'I dunno. But I reckon they will. Like you said yourself, sonny, them boats ain't that quick and it's not like they can pull into a side road and disappear. If they're hiding, it's gonna be in plain sight. You know it an' I know it. And that means you're the only bloke what can find 'em.'

The Pan sighed because Big Merv was right. 'OK.'

Big Merv continued. 'You gotta walk up there.' He pointed to a track across the road. 'I'd keep low and all, coz if King Milo's got blokes up there, they might be watching. When you hit the towpath if you see a bunch of likely lads lying in wait, you're gonna signal.'

'How?'

Big Merv yanked something out of his pocket. It was hard to see the detail but what The Pan could see was that it black and cylindrical and oh please Arnold, let that not be the barrel of a gun. Such was his fear of guns, not to mention his boss, it took all The Pan's self control to stand his ground and not run. He managed it, which was a bonus. He even controlled the urge to cower, but a small squeak of fear escaped before he could stop it. Big Merv froze, black metal thing in hand, with a look of complete disdain. Then he held the thing out to him. 'With this torch,' he said.

Arnold. That was a bit embarrassing. But at the same time, kind of, phew that it wasn't a firearm.

'Right,' said The Pan, taking the torch from Big Merv's outstretched hand. It was heavy and the metal was warm from being in his pocket.

'Yer, "right". If they got someone there, you're gonna hide where they ain't gonna see it and flash the light on and off at us three times, you get me?'

'Yes.'

'If there ain't no-one there, you're gonna wave it backwards and forwards.'

'OK.'

'Either way, once you've given us the signal, you're gonna walk along that river to the locks.'

'Right.'

'You clear, son?'

'Yeh, check for King Milo's people, signal and then look for the boat.'

'And?'

'Bring them to Lark Locks, unless they're already there.'

'And if they are, what you gonna do?'

'Tell you?'

'"S right, and you ain't gonna make contact with 'em neither. You leave 'em where they are and report to me.'

'Right. Um ... Big Merv, sir?'

'Yeh. What?'

'What if King Milo and his gang are between us and Lark Locks?'

'That ain't the way King Milo works, son. I get that it's

a risk but it ain't a big one. Specially not when it's you what's giving them the slip.'

Was that a backhanded compliment? The Pan wondered as it zinged past.

'Thing is, it's gotta be you, mate. Coz it's gotta be someone them ladies knows.'

And someone who's expendable, The Pan thought. 'Fair enough. I understand that but what if, I dunno,' he shrugged. 'What if King Milo fancies a change? What if he *is* there?'

'Then you stay low, outa sight and follow 'em to the locks. We'll be up there before you are an' we'll all be waiting. You gotta report to Bob when you get there.'

'Right,' said The Pan. 'What if I don't find them?'

'You still report to Bob.'

'What if I can't find her?'

'Arnold's conkers, you spotty little Herbert, we ain't got time for this. You *will* find her, mate. Coz if you don't I'll punch your effin' lights out. An' also coz we'll leave her somewhere so bleedin' obvious that even *you* can't miss her, you great wazzock! Alright?'

'Right.'

There was a pause.

'On you go son.'

That was it.

'Okaaay,' said The Pan.

He took a deep breath, crossed the road, climbed over the gate and slunk up the track to the towpath, keeping to the shadows and staying low, as instructed, to hide under the layer of fog. As he neared the trees flanking the canal he slowed his pace and trod lightly. But there was no-one around. When he reached the towpath he turned to his left and stopped. Even from here he could see there was a barge moored up, blocking the entrance. Should he go closer?

No, no point in going looking for trouble. Arnold knew he was in enough already.

He positioned himself behind the trunk of one of the larger trees, where he couldn't be seen by anyone in the moored barge and gave the signal with the torch. Big Merv and his gang got into their snurds. As The Pan watched, Bob and all the other drivers pulled off the hard standing and disappeared into the night. But a handful of figures remained, and were making their way up the track. He waited and in a few minutes, Fists McDermot arrived with a bunch of heavies.

'What you still doin' here, you pathetic little cleggnut?' McDermot whispered. 'It's not like we need no-one to run messages an' the boss gave you a job to do. Hop it!'

One of the others—The Pan thought it was Johnno who'd asked the question about the canal going uphill—had something in his hand. The Pan realised, as he saw the glowing green of a display, that it was a mobile phone. Blimey!

'Yer, we don't need you coz we got this, see? You're all set,' Johnno whispered, not unkindly.

The Pan nodded in a way that he hoped made him look taciturn and manly rather than the frightened wimp he was, waved a hand in acknowledgement and walked away.

The canal stretched into the darkness. If anyone lay in wait they'd be difficult to spot in the weird waist-high fog. Then again, that worked both ways.

As he walked, he kept his eyes peeled for shadowy pursuers. The eyes in the back of his head were always handy in a situation like this, but there was no sign of anyone behind him and no sign of any boats moored on the water, even though there would have been room for them at this point. As he walked he checked his watch. The fog persisted but it was definitely thinning now, and the sky was beginning to lighten with the first hints of dawn. The birds drew his attention to it first. There were still no boats moored along the path. Yeh, and judging by the volume of the dawn chorus there was a reason for that. He liked it though. He never heard anything like this back in Ning Dang Po, not even when he slept in the Botanical Gardens or the Arboretum.

By the time The Pan reached the point where the trees thinned out, it was much lighter. Not one hundred percent daylight, but there was a definite crepuscular tone to everything that heralded imminent dawn. He passed a lock, and a few hundred yards further on, the water widened along with the towpath. The trees were set further back and there were a couple of houses and a hostelry, but it was called the Frog and Whistle, not the Hungry Boatsman. Ah yes, he remembered, the Boatsman was at the top of the locks. As it began to get lighter, The Pan realised that the fog had sunk even lower—but a three-foot layer of dense cloud still hung over everything. Trees, fences, people and bits of boats poked out of it. The air above was clear and he could see ahead of him. There was a basin with the roofs of a number of narrowboats and barges sticking out of the fog but none that looked like the *Happy Doris*. As he stopped to take in his surroundings, he saw the locks.

'Wow,' he said.

He knew there were fifteen of them stretching over a length of about a mile, maybe further, running up a hill. What with the strange fog, the bottom two were difficult to make out. He could see the handles of the lock gates though, tall metal poles with a bobble on the end of each one, sticking out through the low-lying cloud. As the line of locks rose up the hill they also rose into clear air. The Pan had never seen anything like this. Each lock took the boat a little higher until it had completed the full seventy-five foot change in height between the level at which he stood and the one at which the canal continued. It was an impressive piece of engineering.

He followed the path and as he reached the Frog and Whistle, noticed a familiar figure leaning against the fence of the beer garden.

'Hello, stranger.'

'Hi Bob.'

'You didn't get lynched by King Milo's mob then?' she said.

'Not funny,' he said, raising an eyebrow at her. 'It was actually a surprisingly pleasant walk. If I have to be up and about at this ungodly hour there are worse places to do it.'

'Have you seen your friends?'

'Not yet.'

'No worries. Big Merv said you were to wait here for instructions.'

'Right,' said The Pan. Instructions? Arnold's plums! Really? The Pan wanted to see Bort again but he didn't want to get involved in any shenanigans between Big Merv and King Milo, especially any that took place in her actual presence. Arnold, no!

Again his eye was drawn to the locks; the sun began to rise turning the soft cotton wool surface of the low-lying fog a delicate baby pink. 'Wow,' he said.

As he watched the locks, someone's head rose slowly up through the layer of fog over the bottom lock, followed by their body, as the water level rose and the boat beneath their feet rose with it. Was that Terri? The Pan squinted to try and see better. Not sure. Bob saw where he was looking. 'What d'you reckon, lad?' she asked.

'The locks? They're pretty impressive.'

'Yeh,' said Bob. 'That's the biggest incline any canal covers in the world. Even the ruddy Grongles can't top that. Makes you proud to be K'Barthan.'

'Mmm, it does a bit.'

He watched for a while. Even this ridiculously early there appeared to be a lock keeper up there, although, in the strangely low-lying fog The Pan could only see their top half. There was someone doing something near the gates as the boat moved slowly through them. Two figures appeared on deck, bustling to and fro, while the third stood at the tiller. They seemed familiar and certainly looked about the right ages and sizes to be Bort, Terri and Christine. Although, from what The Pan could see the younger one was a lad, and the older two had different hair styles, not to mention hair colours.

'Look familiar?' asked Bob.

'Yeh, a bit. But I'm not sure. If it *is* them, they're in disguise.'

'Want to borrow these?' Bob held out a pair of binoculars.

'Thanks.'

After a bit of a kerfuffle and some coaching from Bob The Pan managed to get the binoculars to work. But the boat had disappeared again.

Bob glanced at her watch. 'Five. Big Merv said he'd be here at quarter past.'

'Any sign of King Milo?'

'Not as far as I know. If he turns up, we'll be waiting and ready.'

The Pan and Bob chatted, and he watched the locks as he waited, hoping to catch a proper glimpse of the boat with the binoculars. What would he do if he were Bort, Terri and Christine? The Pan wondered. Easy, he'd repaint the boat, change how he looked and get up those locks as fast as he could. It wasn't as if the three of them could leave the boat behind. It was their home, after all, and presumably the money they'd earned from selling the Goojan spiced sausages was stashed away in it somewhere.

It was full daylight now and the sun was up, even though

it was still low in the sky. He couldn't see any other boats working the locks. Surely, if it took a while to get through, there'd normally be a boat in each one. They'd be queuing up, ready to get away early. Unless the lock keeper had started before hours just for this one.

Why would he do that then?

Because someone needed him to. Surely, for him to work that early, they'd be paying extra. Yeh and if they were paying extra, they were in a tearing hurry ... or desperate.

Hmm, kind of the same thing, The Pan thought. As he watched, the boat began to appear again on the rising waters of the lock. He glanced at his watch. It was five fifteen.

'Want the binos again?' Bob asked.

'Thanks.'

The Pan held them to his eyes and looked. The boat wasn't the *Happy Doris*; it was called the *Frolicking Maiden*. It had a similar haphazardly arranged garden of edible plants in pots on the roof. Similar, yes, but they were in different places to the ones on the *Happy Doris*. It would be easy enough to move those about though. He watched the crew. The way the lad moved reminded him of Bort, as if she'd had a brother. He smiled. Yeh, something inexplicable, a slight lifting of the spirits, told him that disguise or no disguise, it was her.

'I think they're in the boat that's going up the locks. It looks as if they've changed the name somehow and Bort's disguised as a boy.'

'I'll tell Big Merv.' Bob took a walkie-talkie out of her jacket pocket.

'Is that legal?' The Pan asked.

'Course. It's the kit we use at the club, sweetie. All the bouncers have earpieces and the rest of us have radios. Means we can sort out any trouble before it gets out of hand, you know if some perv gropes one of the Big Ms or something.'

The Big Ms were The Big Thing's entertainment; an all-female erotic dance troupe.

'Blimey, I see ...' said The Pan.

Bob pressed a switch on the side and there was an abrupt bust of static after which she spoke into it. 'Happy Frog to Big Boy, over.'

'Big Boy 'ere,' said the tinny voice of Big Merv.

'Target located. Over.'

'Roger that. Tell that little numpty to wait. Over and out.'

The radio clicked and went dead.

Bob shrugged. 'Dunno about you but I reckon we may as well go sit in the beer garden.' She opened the gate. 'After you.'

The Pan stopped, his gaze drifting over to the locks. 'Shouldn't I warn them?'

'Big Merv said to wait here.'

'I know, but—'

'They're safe enough, sweetie. There's no sign of King Milo yet. And if he does turn up, he'll have us to contend with.'

That just made The Pan feel even more nervous. But he know Bob meant to reassure him. 'That's ... very comforting,' he said.

Chapter 26
Catastrophe

Bob went and sat at a table. But before The Pan had a chance to join her Big Merv arrived, jogging along the towpath with Harry and Frank a few paces behind.

'There you are, you little nerk. Sweet. You ready?'

'Ready? For what?'

'To pick up my goods. I reckon 's best if I don't go up there. We don't wanna scare 'em.'

'Right,' said The Pan.

'Yer,' said Big Merv. He held out one hand and Harry handed him a battered briefcase. It was made of soft leather and opened at the top like a doctor's bag. 'So, you give this to your mates and they give you the goods.' He shoved the bag at The Pan and then handed him the fabric bag which had originally contained the sausage.

'What if King Milo turns up?'

'I got your back.'

'That's a comfort,' said The Pan weakly.

'Yer, innit,' said Big Merv.

The Pan clutched the bag to his chest and felt the weight of something drop from one end to the other as he upended it. Probably a bundle of used notes, maybe two? He didn't dare shake it again to check. Hopefully not a brick. Arnold's earwax, if the people on that boat were Terri, Christine and Bort please let him not be handing them a brick in a briefcase. Please let Big Merv not be like that. No. The Pan trusted Big Merv—he might be a gangster but his word was his bond. He was a Thing of honour.

'Am I going alone?'

"Course. 'S no danger.'

'Right,' said The Pan. Of all the beings from Big Merv's organisation currently in the area, The Pan knew he was the most expendable. Was he about to become the bait in a trap? There were no obvious signs of King Milo and his lot, but that didn't mean they weren't there. Clearly The Pan's doubts showed in his face because Big Merv was now wearing the type of vexed expression he always wore when he realised his delivery man was about to argue.

'It's just that ... is it safe?' The Pan asked, glancing over at the boat on the locks which was just disappearing into the next one.

'I already said so, you giant plank! You ain't got nothing to worry about. Unless you're reckoning on doing a runner with my cash.' Big Merv's voice switched abruptly to sinister. 'You wouldn't do a runner with my cash, would you mate?'

Once again the image of Finicky Bert hanging upside down flashed into The Pan's head: an image which kept haunting him and one he heartily wished he could un-see. He blinked it away but he could feel the cold sweat starting on his palms at the mere thought. 'No,' he whispered. 'Absolutely not.'

'You're thinking about it though, ain'tcha, you shifty little nerk,' said Frank.

'Yer, I reckon,' Harry agreed. 'Look at the state of 'im.'

'No, I'm just...' The Pan swallowed, '...nervous.'

'You're goin' up there coz them birds know you. And also because if you gotta keep me up all night and drag me up here this bleedin' early, you're gonna do the donkey work.'

'OK.'

'Yer, "OK". Now get on up there and get it done. Pronto,' said Big Merv.

'Right. Yep. I'll be off then.'

Shakily The Pan set off towards the locks without looking back.

To get to the first of them he needed to walk round the marina. The path was lined with bushes and trees, not to mention the small front gardens of houses, a workshop with an open entrance and plenty of other places for anyone waiting to attack him to hide.

Yeh. Not going that way.

After a moment's thought, he took the direct route, treading lightly across the roofs of the moored-up boats so as not to wake the occupants. Although if King Milo turned up and it all kicked off between his gang and Big Merv's, they'd wake up pretty fast anyway. Using the handy eyes in the back of his head, he could see his boss was watching him, along with Bob, Frank and Harry. The wave of disapproval coming off them merely pushed him forward. A quick hop off the last boat and then onto the towpath. He'd noticed that the boat in the locks seemed to be choosing the left-hand side to wait every time.

As he started up the towpath his senses were on full alert but he could see nothing untoward—not that it was easy to tell. The towpath was flanked by bushes; about ten feet back his side and twenty or thirty from the opposite, left-hand bank. Good move on their part to keep to that side then. He noticed a couple of small movements in the foliage to his right which reinforced his view. It could be small woodland creatures, birds or even one of Big Merv's enforcers. Please Arnold, let it be something simple, or one of Big Merv's heavies, rather than one of King Milo's.

Whatever it was, The Pan was taking no chances.

He ran at the open gates of the nearest lock, put a foot on the top railing and leapt across the canal. Kicking off the top of the gate on the other side he landed in what should have been a crouch, except he got tangled with the briefcase and ended up on all fours. Oops. Never mind. He stood up and brushed the dirt off his knees and hands before picking up the briefcase again. He should have known not to try and pull a move like that when there might be people watching. Indeed, the fact he'd failed to pull it off just proved he had an audience. He took a deep breath and started up the path.

How had he got himself into his mess?

Always thinking with your trousers, said the voice of his Virtual Dad.

Smeck, there was no time for that right now. 'Shut up,' he muttered.

Blanking his thoughts, The Pan put his shoulders back and gripped the briefcase. 'Right. Fingers crossed,' he said quietly and began to walk up the path.

It didn't take long to reach the boat; it was only a few hundred yards away, although he passed four or five more locks to reach it. As The Pan drew near, it was just entering the next in the series. From what he could see, it bore a striking resemblance to the *Happy Doris* but only if you'd examined that boat in detail and knew what to look for. It was red and green now, rather than red and blue, and as he'd seen through Bob's binoculars, called the *Frolicking Maiden.* On closer examination, he was certain it *was* the *Happy Doris.* The scratches on the roof were the same, the poles Christine and Terri had used to punt the boat were there, along with the shorter paddles they'd smacked the bottle bombs with, not to mention the watering can. Although looking at it, he still wasn't sure if the plants were the same. Perhaps they'd swapped with other boat owners? No. They wouldn't have had the chance. It was the same collection of plants. It had to be. They were just grouped differently, that was all.

Then there was the crew. He almost didn't recognise them. Terri's salt and pepper hair had blue highlights now and her skin was a darker shade of brown. Christine had short hair and Bort, at first glance, looked like a boy. Hmm, but only at first glance.

No, no, no ... don't think about that sort of thing now. This patently wasn't the time.

The lock keeper closed the gates and The Pan lost sight of them again. He picked up his pace.

'Ahoy there!' he called as he approached.

The lock keeper, who'd finished closing the lock gates behind the barge, grabbed something that was leaning against the rail beside him and turned to face The Pan. He was a Galorsh, which meant he was covered in purple fur—a full coat of it by the looks of things, as his shirt had a lumpy look that gave it away. Blimey, he must be boiling in this weather. Normally both Galorshes and Blaggysomps, their fellow mountain K'Barthan species, shaved their hair off if they were in the lower regions of the country during summer. Gerry, the Pan's favoured mechanic at Snurd who was also a Blaggysomp, had explained how they still had to wear long sleeves, even so, to avoid sunburn.

However, the thing about the Galorsh which really had The Pan's attention wasn't that he was sporting a winter coat of fur midsummer. Nope, it was the item he'd just picked up: a shotgun.

'Can I help you, young man?' he said coldly.

'I—' The Pan put a hand up, one finger extended, his best, most polite 'excuse me' demeanour in place and took a step back. The lock keeper took a step forward. 'I'm here—' he began but his voice cracked. By The Prophet, why did it always do that to him? He cleared his throat and tried again. 'Hello there.'

'It's alright, he's with us,' said the voice of Terri breezily, from behind the closed gates.

The Galorsh nodded and stepped aside. The Pan took a deep breath and moved cautiously past him to the edge of the lock. He peered down at his friends.

'Hi,' he said trying to make eye contact with Terri and Christine first when, really, he only had eyes for Bort. The 'boy' outfit just made her even more alluring than usual.

'This is Zeb,' said Bort waving a hand at the scary lock keeper who'd opened the gates in front of the boat a fraction, to let the water in.

The Pan turned. 'Hi Zeb,' he said.

'What are you doing here, you absolute idiot?' said Bort sternly, but her eyes were shining. She was pleased to see him, he was certain of it. Good.

'It's complicated,' said The Pan. Blimey, wasn't it just? 'OK, there are some things you three need to know about me.'

'You forgot your boots,' said Christine and before he could stop her she ducked into the cabin and reappeared, said boots in hand.

'That's very kind of you but—'

'Want a cup of coffee, laddio? We're just about to make Zeb one,' said, Terri.

'No, I really— I—' He stopped. 'OK, you need to listen; this is about your message, the one you wanted me to deliver to Bob the Blaggysomp later this morning, about coming here to collect the sausage.'

All three women looked up at him with questioning expressions; he had their full attention now, though, so that was progress.

'I happen to know Bob—'

'How the—?' began Bort but he spoke across her.

'And I delivered it,' he said, 'sorry to talk over you, Bort.'

'Are they coming?' Christine asked.

'Definitely, well ... sort of. That's the thing, I need to explain. They— I'm here with the ...' he cast a sideways look at Zeb, '*item* you requested.' He held up the suitcase.

'Why would they send you?' said Christine.

'Yeh, you don't look like the kind of guy who's employed by a multi-millionaire.' Bort frowned up at him. 'I didn't think you worked for anybody.'

'Yes, about that—' he began but before he could get any further there was a massive bang. Zeb's arms flung out sideways and he was thrown off his feet. He landed on the towpath on his back and lay still.

'Smeck! Something's poleaxed Zeb!' squeaked The Pan and he ran over to the lock keeper's prone form.

'Arnold,' he whimpered. He was pretty sure he knew exactly what had poleaxed Zeb, and as he knelt down beside him, his worst fears were confirmed. There was a hole in his shirt. A small, round hole.

The Pan scrambled to his feet, almost in tears, and was confronted by the sight of a Blaggysomp in spotlessly clean—but tatty—evening dress. The lining of his jacket and the undersides of his coat tails was a rich crimson. He also sported a monocle and a top hat. The hat, like the suit, had clearly seen better days but was also meticulously clean and cared for. Where the material had worn it was darned, like the suit. He had a cruel set to his mouth and his eyes were dark brown. He reminded The Pan of some mountain species vampire who was down on his luck. A gangster then. But clearly not as successful a gangster as the one The Pan worked for. The new arrival was flanked by six large beings, Swamp Things and humans of similar size. They were also wearing evening dress, although not with the same style and panache of their boss. They were of a similar shape and there was a set to them which reminded The Pan of the beings Big Merv employed to bash people. Enforcers, for sure. They fanned out on either side of their boss. Four had their arms folded in the standard technique used by thugs everywhere to make their biceps look bigger. And two were wielding sawn-off shotguns. Arnold's conkers! In broad daylight.

The Pan wondered if one of them had shot Zeb. No, the sawn off was lethal at close range but hopelessly inaccurate at distance. These guns would be locked and loaded—someone else had shot Zeb.

Like their boss, King Milo's enforcers were a little shabbier than the ones The Pan was used to dealing with. But he doubted that would make a significant difference to anyone on the receiving end of their ministrations. They looked just as double-hard and dangerous.

Chapter 27
King Milo

This was extremely bad. Shaking with fear, The Pan stood and faced King Milo.

'Smeck,' he whimpered. He tried to stand straight and tall but then he realised he'd dropped the bag and hurriedly snatched it up. As he clutched it to his chest he stared at Zeb. Arnold's knees, he was definitely dead. The Pan hiccupped. Arnold's Y-fronts, no! This was not the time to hurl.

His throat was so dry he could hardly speak, 'He's dead,' he croaked.

'Absolutely,' said the Blaggysomp, laughing. 'I'd say he is.'

By The Prophet, something about that laugh made The Pan feel even sicker. Zeb lay on the ground, immobile. The sight of his body made all the more horrific because his fur seemed to be soaking up the blood, unless, somehow, he wasn't bleeding. Arnold's trollies, no! Of course he was smecking bleeding. He'd just been shot. The Pan turned away before he actually had to see the blood because if he did, he knew he definitely would throw up.

Arnold! This shouldn't be happening. Where was the cavalry? Where was Big Merv? He took a couple of shaky steps towards his friends on the boat and turned to face the new arrival from what felt like a slightly safer distance.

The Pan looked up at King Milo, trying to hide his fear and revulsion, trying to meet his eyes or, since he couldn't do that, look vaguely in the direction of the face. *Arnold's trollies, say something.*

The Pan's throat was even drier now and, at first no

sound would come out of his mouth. But finally, he managed to speak. 'Are you King Milo?' he squeaked.

'The same. And these ladies have my sausage.'

The Pan turned to where the heads of Terri, Bort and Christine were beginning to appear over the lip of the lock as the water level rose.

'Rubbish!' said Terri. 'We found it fair and square.'

'You found it on my turf, and you knew I was looking for it,' said King Milo.

'So what? The first rule of mudlarking is finder's keepers.'

'That's absolutely right, ladies. Especially if I say *I'm* the finder.'

'You didn't.'

'I don't need to. Anything that falls into the river round Graden End Bridge is mine. What's more, you knew that because you knew my people were looking for it.'

King Milo had a weird accent, mostly old-film style posh but with the odd hint of street creeping in here and there, presumably when he wasn't concentrating.

Christine calmly countered him. 'Everyone was looking for it,' she said. There was a lot of natural authority in her voice, a power that commanded attention. 'The salient point here,' she added and the authority in her voice notched up another level, 'is that *we* found it.'

There was silence as King Milo and his six goons digested this. The Pan looked from them to the three women on the barge and back.

'And *my* point is that you found it on *my* river,' said King Milo, his voice hard like ice.

'No, it was *the* river. It belongs to everyone. It's not yours,' said Bort. 'Finders keepers, that's the first rule of mudlarking, unless you can trace the original owner.'

Arnold no! Shut up, Bort, shut up all of you! thought The Pan.

'Maybe I am the original owner.'

The Pan reckoned King Milo was going to take the sausage and the money, and probably kill Terri, Christine, Bort, and rather more disconcertingly, him too, unless somebody explained just who'd bought the sausage. Christine, Bort and Terri didn't know The Pan's boss was a gangster and unless they really had to, he'd prefer to keep it that way. On the other hand, he also wanted to live, and if he intended to do that it was time to let the cat out of the bag. He took a deep breath, gathered all his courage, which wasn't much, and spoke. 'Look, do none of you realise who this sausage belongs to?' he asked.

'Yes. Me,' said King Milo. Well, that was predictable.

'I understand, Your Majesty.' The Pan turned to Christine, Terri and Bort. 'Ladies, I'm guessing *you* would say it's yours. The thing is, it fell off the back of a cart, didn't it?'

'The side,' said Terri.

'Right.' He turned back to face King Milo.

'So?'

'Could it be, Your Royal Highness, sir, that what you might be wisest wondering, in this case, is whose cart? Who's going to be running a fake sausage racket?'

'This sausage is not fake,' said King Milo.

'Well, that's true in a way. Officially, it's a copy, but it isn't *quite* the real deal, if you see what I mean.'

'Yes, it is.'

'I hate to contradict you because I'm aware that it might make you kill me and I really don't want that. But I promise you it *is* a copy.'

'Shut up, you little smeck, unless you want to go the same way as the lock keeper,' snarled one of the heavies.

'Your Royal Highness, before you take the sausage from these ladies, there's something else you need to know.'

'Not from you, you little piece of pus.'

The enforcers tensed. Arnold in heaven, this was it, they were going to kill him. 'W— wait! Please ... Look, would I be endangering myself like this if what I have to say wasn't important? Please listen to me.'

King Milo put up one hand. 'Alright,' he said.

'The sausage is part of a batch made up in Driesch somewhere by a bloke who also makes the real thing. The point is it's crafted: not bodged together by numbers in a mass production workshop. The only reason it's not real is because the guy who made it can't get all of the right stuff. The ... the saffron is from a different plant, stuff they grow on the plains near Glardy ... not the mountains. The herbs and spices are the best he can get, but they're not from the right places to be the real deal. It's good, so good that even K'Barthans are taken in, but not good enough. The point is, it cost money. A lot of money and it fell off the side of a truck loaded with similar sausages.'

'It was a cart.'

'It doesn't matter if it was a unicycle, does it?' No, no, no! He shouldn't have said that. Never mind, too late now. He took a deep breath and ploughed quickly on. 'It's one of many expensive, high-end copies to be passed off as real to buyers who don't know any better.'

'So what?'

'So, maybe what we should all be thinking about here, Your Royal Highness, is what kind of being has that kind of cash, and what he's going to do when he finds out we've got one of his sausages.'

King Milo laughed. Not what The Pan expected at all. It was a nasty sinister laugh too.

'Well now, young fellow. I believe that, were I to be in possession of that kind of cash, and were I to be running the type of racket to which you refer, I wouldn't wish to be found. And if I had a truckload of high-quality merchandise to sell, I would write off a handful falling from the sides as collateral damage.'

Smeck. The Pan flung a helpless glance at Terri, Bort and Christine and turned back to face King Milo. 'I—' he began, but King Milo spoke over him.

'Although, I believe that's academic because if something happens to you and these ladies, your millionaire sausage forger is never going to know.'

'It's not a forgery—'

'That's academic as well,' said King Milo.

The Pan's stomach sank and he could feel himself going white. King Milo stepped up to him, snatched the briefcase from his clutching hands and held it out sideways. One of the heavies, a hefty bloke whose evening bib and tucker made him look more like a particularly oversized and malevolent penguin, stepped up and took it.

'If something happens to us you'll never get the sausage. It's hidden,' said The Pan as the penguin-like heavy opened the bag and looked in. King Milo cast him a quick glance and he nodded. 'Seriously,' The Pan warned him. 'You'll never find it.'

'Won't I?' King Milo sniffed the air. 'Maybe I'll just follow my nose. I'd say it's not that far away. Not when you're here to collect it. And you *are* here to collect it, aren't you?' He waved a blue furry hand at the briefcase his enforcer was holding with a flourish. 'Otherwise, why all that money? Deny it if you dare.'

'Fair enough, I am, but before you kill us, you should know I'm collecting it for Big Merv.' The Pan blurted. Damn, he'd tried so hard to keep his voice calm and clear, but it was difficult when he was so petrified. He was afraid he might actually hurl, or worse, lose control of what Gladys would have called his nether regions. Arnold's hair, please no. If he had to die now, could he not manage to do so with, at least, a modicum of dignity?

King Milo threw back his head and guffawed. 'You lying snot-faced weasel!' He looked past The Pan, to Terri, Bort and Christine and said, 'I want something from you, mudlarking scum; my sausage and I want it NOW. This little turd might be history, but I'm going to give you a chance. Give me the sausage and I'll let you go.'

'Wait,' began The Pan.

King Milo grabbed the briefcase from his acolyte and held it up, laughing. 'If you really work for The Big Thing maybe I should let him deal with you. Then again, no. Boys, you can go play with him for a while if you like, but we're leaving in half an hour. I want him dead by then. I'll be taking this.'

'I don't think so, pal,' said a voice.

The Pan had never, ever, believed he would be relieved to see his boss. But then, he supposed, everything has to happen once.

Big Merv stood, alone, behind King Milo and the group of thugs gathered round The Pan. The thugs moved away from their intended victim and turned to face this new arrival. Then as Big Merv stood there, calm, unmoving and oozing complete confidence, Zeb the lock keeper suddenly stood up, very much alive and also, very much armed with that shot gun. Of course, The Pan realised, it hadn't been fur under that shirt; it was a bulletproof vest.

'You shouldn't have come here on your own, Big Merv,' King Milo said. 'I have people all round us. Maybe this is where you make your final mistake and I step into your shoes.'

'You reckon?'

'Oh yes. I'm going to make sure you go down. Right. Now.'

'You can try, pal. But it ain't gonna happen.'

'Really? D'you think you and some elderly dotard stand a chance against me and my entire staff?'

Big Merv shrugged. 'I'd say so. See, this elderly dotard,' he nodded at Zeb, 'I get that he looks like a doddery old gimmer but he's got a black belt in hoo-flung-yoo. You can have a go if you like. 'S not a smart move, though. I wouldn't wanna try and take him down. As for your blokes…' He raised one arm and suddenly the bushes and undergrowth seemed to be alive with other beings. It wasn't just the group who'd travelled there with The Pan and his boss—there were even more. 'These your blokes?' asked Big Merv, ignoring the fact that several of the beings surrounding them were patently female.

King Milo looked around him in growing agitation. His face rapidly paled from its normal Blaggysomp-coloured sky blue to an altogether lighter version. A shiny slick of sweat appeared on his cheeks and forehead. 'You know they aren't,' he said. His voice was calm but the fear in it was audible.

'Yeh. 'S right. I do.'

'What have you done with them?'

'Nothin' mate,' said Big Merv, annunciating the word 'mate' through clenched teeth in a way that was very definitely not friendly. 'I sent them home.'

'You killed them?'

'What? Nah. Why would I do that?'

'Because if you don't they'll come after you.'

'You reckon?'

'They're loyal.'

'Nah, they're scared of you. That ain't the same thing.'

'It will be, for you.'

'I don't think so. See, they're smarter than you. They know the score. You may be the king of the river, sunshine, but you ain't the boss of Ning Dang Po an' they know that. Unless you're gonna tell me different? Are you gonna tell me different?' Big Merv's voice had a sinister edge that made all the little hairs stand up on the back of The Pan's neck.

King Milo sounded even more strained when he said, 'No.'

"'S right pal, coz I'm the boss of Ning Dang Po, ain't I? Although ... it looks like that mighta slipped your mind these past few days. It hasn't slipped your mind, has it? You remember who's boss, don't you, mate?' Again, the way he said the 'mate' made The Pan's blood run cold.

'You hurt me and you're done for,' Milo said.

'Who said I'm gonna hurt you, pal?' He gestured to The Pan. 'You back off an' give the briefcase back to the snotty little bleeder there an' maybe we can have a chat about what *is* gonna happen to you. Course, a lot depends on how you answer my question.'

'W-what question?'

'I asked if you remember who's the boss of Ning Dang Po.'

'You, Big Merv, sir, definitely.'

'Sweet. I'm glad you ain't forgotten. So now you're gonna go with the lads ain'tcha, nice an' easy like, without causing no trouble, while I finish up my business with these ladies. And when I'm done, you and I, we're gonna have a talk.'

King Milo swallowed noisily. 'OK,' he said. The Pan almost felt sorry for him.

'Smooth,' said Big Merv. 'I'm lookin' forward to it.' He pulled the briefcase from King Milo's shaking hands. 'I'll look after this.' He clicked his fingers and pointed an imperious finger. Frank and Harry appeared from the crowds of beings surrounding them along with Fists McDermot. Smart Dennis had also arrived and joined them. While Frank and Harry grabbed King Milo by the arms and hauled him away, Fists and co escorted his heavies off down the hill. Heart hammering, The Pan waited.

'Ladies, I reckon you got some merchandise for me?' Big Merv said.

Silently, Bort went into the cabin and came out again.

'Give her the bag, son,' said Big Merv.

The Pan removed the fabric bag from his pocket. With a look of desperate apology he handed it to Terri as Bort returned with the sausage. Terri took the sausage from her daughter, put it in the bag and handed it back to The Pan who turned and gave it to Big Merv.

'Sweet.'

Big Merv stood at the side of the lock, and looked from Terri to Christine to Bort and then at The Pan and back at Bort.

'Alright son, I reckon I'm done here.' His gaze flicked to Bort again briefly before he concentrated his attention on The Pan. 'I'll see you tonight, at the club, seven pm.'

'Yes, boss,' said The Pan.

'Nice. Don't be late son; you know how insulted I feel when people waste my time.'

'Yes, Big Merv, sir, I won't be late.'

'You'd better not be,' said Big Merv. 'Alright. Later then, sonny,' he added, slightly less sternly, but still in a tone of voice The Pan found scary. 'Thank you, ladies.' He nodded at the three women as they stood on the barge roof, raising his trilby hat a little, but not so much that his antennae were visible. 'Pleasure doin' business with you.' And with that, he turned and walked away. As he passed Zeb the lock keeper, he patted him on the shoulder. 'Thanks pal,' he said. Then he took Zeb's hand and shook it as he added, 'I owe you for that.' The Pan couldn't say for certain, but he reckoned there'd been a couple of crisp bank notes folded up in that handshake. Zeb put his hands in his pockets as the five of them watched Big Merv walk away.

By the time The Pan had the wit to look around, all the enforcers, male and female, had disappeared—even the strange low-lying fog had gone—and the area around them was empty.

Chapter 28
Aftermath

Zeb was the first to speak. 'That's this one finished. We're making good time. Give me one moment and I'll open her up.'

It took The Pan several seconds to realise that he was talking about the lock. Zeb laid the gun carefully on the concrete while he went and hauled on the lock gate. The Pan stood on the side of the canal with his most contrite expression in place. Terri and Bort stood on the roof of their barge. Christine was now standing on the small deck at the back, holding the tiller as the engine idled. All three of them were staring at him.

'I'm sorry about that,' he said. He was shaking so much he could hardly speak. 'Are you OK?'

'Better than we could have been, worse than we might have been,' said Terri.

It took The Pan a moment to compute but he guessed that was basically 'so-so'. Bort rolled her eyes and The Pan was tempted to smile. It probably wouldn't be tactful though. He was pretty sure Terri and Christine liked him, but as Bort's parents, or at least mum and guardian, he doubted they saw him as potential boyfriend material. Then again, he suspected Bort didn't either, hence all the stuff she'd said about 'temporary things'. It was one thing liking the man, but The Pan completely understood that, in his case, the baggage that he came with was a bit much for anyone. That was alright though; he didn't have the kind of existence that allowed for long-term commitments. He ran his shaking hands through his hair and it stood up, as usual, in tousled spikes.

The four of them stood in silence. It was slightly awkward but not nearly as much as it should have been. Then again, after that run in with King Milo and Big Merv, it would be difficult to feel remotely negative about anything else. Yeh, awkward was for wimps, or at least, other wimps. The Pan nodded in the direction of Zeb the lock keeper. 'I've no idea if he really is a black belt in hoo-flung-yoo but I think he might need a hand,' he said.

'Yeh, even this early it's warm to be doing all that in a bulletproof vest,' said Bort.

'On you go then, me hearty,' said Terri.

'And when we're safely into the next one, you'd better come down here and get your boots,' Christine called from the back.

Weren't they angry with him for bringing all that lot to their door, or at least, boat? Hmm. It seemed not.

'Perhaps we should thank you too,' Terri added, giving The Pan a searching look. He could see the conflict between the side of her that wanted to mother him and the other one, the one that really didn't want her daughter getting involved with someone who worked for a gang lord.

****

A few minutes later, the *Happy Doris*, or at least, the *Frolicking Maiden*, was safely positioned in the next lock. Zeb nodded a thank you as The Pan stepped up beside him and took hold of the gates. The gate had metal pull bars sticking out each side for leverage. The Pan wrapped his fingers round them, felt the coolness of one side contrasting with the other, which was warmer from the sun. It was real; the smell of the metal as he gripped it, the sound of the water. All of it pummelled his senses with a lurid intensity. But it also helped him; undid the sense of disconnect he felt with existence after the horror of meeting King Milo, a horror so vivid it felt unreal. Thinking about King Milo, what would happen to him now?

No. Don't even go there, he thought.

He concentrated on the way the metal pull bar felt beneath his hands; the sunlight on his skin; the weight of the wooden gates on his arms, or at least a bit of it—Zeb didn't seem to need much help. These things were real and they were there. Grounding himself was part of the trick, The Pan knew that.

He nearly jumped when someone arrived beside him but managed to confine it to a slight twitch.

'Touchy,' said Bort as she joined him.

'Sorry.' Arnold, what was he apologising for? She nudged him to make sure he realised she was joking and when he glanced at her she treated him to one of her ravishing smiles.

'I don't think you're making much difference. You should try harder,' she said with another mischievous smile. He laughed. It felt surprisingly good.

'I don't think Zeb needs much help,' he told her.

'That I don't,' said Zeb. 'I do this every day, all day. It's not such heavy work. It's all about leverage, son, working with the water rather than against it.'

'Ah,' said The Pan because he wasn't sure what else to say.

Gates sorted, Terri steered the boat into the next lock.

'I'm alright, kids,' said Zeb, when The Pan and Bort stepped up to help him close them, 'if you are.'

'You've just been shot. It must smart a tad,' said The Pan.

Zeb laughed. 'Nah. It's true what your boss told you, I practise hoo-flung-yoo. I can take a tap in the guts.'

The Pan frowned and scratched his head. 'It was a bit more than a tap.'

'Nah, I was playing dead. There was only one of me so I needed to get the jump on them. I didn't know your boss was going to turn up with the cavalry but I knew these ladies were in a hurry and ... you get an instinct for trouble brewing in this line of work.'

'Whoa, are you really a black belt?' Bort asked.

'I dabble.' Zeb put one purple furry finger on the side of his long dog-like snout and winked.

'At the least have a cup of coffee while we do this one then,' said Christine. 'We're going to have breakfast, would you like some toast and an egg?'

'I'll take the coffee, but I have to open the gates down below for another boat. Today's first booking. Might have to calm 'em down a bit too. Doubt they were expecting a little caper like the one you lot have just been involved in, even if I was. I'll be back to let you through to the next lock when this one's full.'

'I'm sorry. I hope the folks in the other boat weren't too alarmed. Big Merv can be a bit heavy-handed sometimes,' said The Pan.

All four of them stared at him for a moment. Arnold in the skies, what was he doing? Fine, so he felt he had to apologise for his boss but somehow that had made it sound as if they were friends. Big Merv was not The Pan's friend. Some kind of scary collateral damage caused by his efforts at staying alive? Yes. Friend? Definitely not. 'Sorry, that sounded quite weird, didn't it? I just meant that ...'

Zeb nodded. 'No need to explain.'

The Pan smiled weakly. Zeb was right. There was absolutely no point in trying to explain. It would only make things worse. Yeh. Best to quit while he was ahead, he decided, or at least, not quite so far behind. Oh well, at least helping with the gate seemed to have processed some of his excess adrenaline. Such a normal and straightforward task had made him feel a bit calmer; he'd stopped shaking now, and no longer felt as if he was about to throw up.

Zeb went off to check on the other boat, coffee in hand.

The Pan jumped down onto the roof of the *Happy Doris*, although it was more of a plummet, and he didn't make the lightest or smoothest of landings either.

'You look all-in lad,' said Terri. 'The sofa's yours for an hour or two if you want it.'

'Yeh, we'll be going through the locks most of the morning,' said Bort.

'I don't want to put you out. I should take the boots and be on my way.'

'Are you sure?' asked Terri.

'Bort's right. It'll take a few hours to finish these locks, and you're safe here,' said Christine.

'Won't you stay for breakfast?' asked Terri. 'We'll do you a bacon butty.'

'At the least you're welcome to have a shower,' said Christine.

The Pan wondered if he smelled. Yes, he decided. He'd been utterly petrified—which had made him very sweaty—so he probably did.

'We have big fluffy towels,' said Bort. 'You can borrow Dad's old pyjamas, catch a few zeds and we'll wake you at breakfast time. You can kip in my bunk.'

He was facing Bort and through his other set of eyes, the ones in the back of his head, he saw Terri and Christine, who were standing behind him, exchanging glances. 'I think I should be getting on,' he said.

'Where will you go?' demanded Bort.

'I—'

'What are you going to do?' she interrupted him.

What *was* he going to do now? He hadn't a clue. Park his snurd somewhere quiet and sleep probably. He shrugged. 'Stuff.'

'Why you utter ...' Bort glowered at him. 'Words fail me.'

Hang on. What had rattled her cage? Why was she annoyed? 'I—' The Pan began.

'You think we're going to dob you in to the authorities, don't you? Mum! Christine! After all we've been through this loser,' she flung her arm out at The Pan, to indicate exactly which loser she was referring to, 'thinks we're going to dob him in.'

The Pan smiled ruefully, 'No, that's not what I think, I'm just worried that—' he yawned.

'You're in need of some decent sleep, that's what you are,' said Terri. 'You can worry all you like when you've had a kip.'

'Exactly!' said Christine. 'When did you last sleep in a proper bed?'

Arnold! A bed—so, so tempting. The Pan scratched his head. 'It was quite a long time ago,' he said.

'Off you go then, me laddio. No buts,' said Terri firmly. 'Breakfast when you wake. We'll all eat then and we'll be very insulted if you refuse to join us.'

'If you're sure,' said The Pan.

'Yes. Now, crewman Bort, will you show our guest to his quarters?'

'Aye aye, Captain,' said Bort.

'And hurry up, Bort,' said Christine. 'I know Zeb said he didn't need a hand with the gates but I still think we should offer.'

Chapter 29
Safe, for now

The fluffy towels were as luxuriant as Bort had promised and when, freshly showered, The Pan made his way to the cabin she'd shown him, the bed had clean sheets on it. A pair of pyjamas was folded up on the pillow—standard checked cotton bottoms and button-up t-shirt top, like an old fashioned vest. He put them on. They were very comfortable. He dried his hair as best he could with the towel. As usual it stuck straight up, and out, in a kind of natural tousled spiky look—no gel required. The Pan's hair was one of the few things about himself he liked. He yawned and lay down. It was warm in the cabin so he didn't bother getting under the covers. Anyway, if he lay on top, it would save his hosts the hassle of having to put on another bottom sheet later.

He closed his eyes and slept, half waking when he thought he felt the warm soft form of Bort joining him, before drifting back off to sleep. When he finally woke the room was a lot warmer and bright sunlight shone through the porthole.

'Arnold,' he muttered and looked at his watch.

'Yeh. Time to get up,' said a voice.

'Bort?' He rolled over.

'Yeh. Come on, sluggabed!' She was standing beside the bunk holding two cups of coffee. She was wearing a towelling robe and by the looks of it, not much else.

'Sluggabed?' he asked her.

She laughed and rolled her eyes. 'It's a word Mum uses on me. It's nice to have a chance to use it on someone else for a change.'

He shuffled up the bed, plumping the pillow and sitting up before checking his watch again. 'I can't believe it's eleven.'

She grinned mischievously. 'Yep.'

'Arnold's socks!' He ran his hands through his hair.

'D'you feel better?' Bort asked.

'Yeh. Thanks. I can't believe I slept all that time. Arnold! I must have been knackered.'

'Too right. You didn't even wake up when I got in. You just kissed me and went back to sleep.' She sounded a little disappointed and he didn't know how to react.

'I'm sorry. I'll make it up to you, I promise.'

'Yes, you will: after breakfast. We're going for a walk; somewhere quiet, peaceful and secluded. And then you'll have to go and see your boss.' The way she said the word 'boss' was loaded with meaning. 'First, you'd better take one of these.' She handed him a cup of strong coffee with a bit of milk but not too much. He took a sip.

'That's heaven.'

'Yeh, I make a wicked cup of coffee, though I say so myself. Budge up.'

The Pan moved over. Bort kicked off her slippers, walked over to the bunk and leaned over, close but not quite touching, while she put her cup on a shelf inset into the wall. A small part of The Pan's brain noted that the shelf was there and probably designed for just that purpose. The greater percentage of The Pan wasn't really listening to it though. He was distracted by the close proximity of Bort, which made him feel pleasantly giddy. She took his cup and put it next to hers. Coffee taken care of, she sat next to him and leaned back, her head on his shoulder. He put his arm around her and felt her relaxing against him. Arnold, this was wonderful, like being normal. He closed his eyes, took a deep breath and let it out slowly.

'You alright?' she asked him.

'Yeh. I feel as if I've slept for a thousand years. You?'

'Yep. Mum sent me to bed shortly after you. Christine says we hit the top lock by nine fifteen, were moored up by twenty past, and she and Mum were snoring their heads off by half past. That's the upside of starting so early. It took nearly the same amount of time, but because we started when we did, we still have the day. It was quicker, too, because we had all Zeb's attention for the first few locks.'

'Didn't you just?' said The Pan.

'That's not what I meant.'

'I should apologise—'

'No, you shouldn't. Really. You did us a huge favour. It probably doesn't feel like it, but you did.'

'Well, then ... I'm sorry I stole your bunk,' said The Pan although he was apologising for so, so much more than just that.

'You didn't though, did you? I shared it with you. And,' she turned over and readjusted her position so she was lying on his chest, 'I'd say that works pretty well.'

His eyes met hers as she beamed at him. Noooo, he was thinking about all the wrong things now. He made to kiss her and stopped. *Arnold's nostril hair, what will Christine and Terri think of me,* the Pan wondered. *Not much.* 'Your mum and Christine are they ... OK with this?'

'I'm eighteen! I'm a grown woman and this isn't the dark ages.'

'Yes, but we might be about to ...'

'Yeh. So what?'

'That's ... pretty cool of them,' said The Pan and regretted it at once. Pretty cool? Arnold's snot! He sounded like some ageing rock star or one of Big Merv's more eccentric employees—the ones that did the thinking rather than the enforcing. Bort didn't appear to notice though.

'Yeh, they're not bad. They've gone to the launderette and while the washing's on they'll probably have a walk and get some supplies. Mum said they'll be back by half twelve.'

'Ah.'

'Yeh, so that means you and I are on our own.'

'Hmm,' said The Pan. 'And they left you here unchaperoned?'

'Yep.'

'And they know what we might do?'

'Yep. Amazingly, they really like you.'

'They do? Even after meeting my boss?'

'Yeh, even after that.' To his disappointment, she sat up. 'Anyway, they know this, you and I, is only a fling. It's not like we're going to get married, is it?'

'No. Of course not,' The Pan agreed hurriedly. OK, so he fancied her, a lot, but this wasn't actual love, was it? 'Surely the fact it's just a fling merely makes it worse. You know, a petty criminal taking advantage.'

'I seduced you, if you remember.'

'That *is* true.'

'So, why are you a gangster?'

'I'm not.'

'You work for one.'

'No. Well, yes, but I'm ... I'm just a delivery man.'

'Why? There must be loads of honest work you can do. You're,' she coloured a little and looked down at her hands, 'a lovely guy.'

'I'm not really employable.'

She leaned in close and took her cup from the shelf again. 'Drink up, it'll get cold.'

They sat in silence and The Pan watched as she sipped the coffee. She was lost in thought for a moment, turning the cup round and round in her hands. 'Christine and Mum reckon you're in deep trouble. We can help you if you like. You can come with us. Although ... this would have to stop.'

'What, the drinking coffee?' he asked as he drained his cup and put it back on the shelf.

'No, silly, *this*. Nobody living on the boat full time gets it on except Mum and Christine because they're married and—'

'Whoa,' The Pan put one hand in front of him in a don't-go-there gesture. 'That's not a mental picture I want.'

'It's important that you understand,' she said.

'Well, I promise I do.' He raised an eyebrow at her. 'Not even a snog?'

'No,' she sounded stern but there was a smile in her voice and the corners of her eyes had crinkled up a little. 'This is fun but it hasn't got legs. That's what I meant about temporary things, right? You and I? We're not a long-term thing, but short term we can have a lot of fun. You got that, didn't you?'

'Yes, I did.'

'You have the best intentions but you're ...' she stopped clearly searching for a way to put it politely.

'Trouble?'

'Yeh.'

He laughed dutifully but he felt a little flat. Not because she was, sort of, throwing him over—he knew this was just a fling—but because he was a GBI and it couldn't possibly be anything else. It hurt that she was right about the trouble. There was a lot of stuff legal beings got to do which he never could, and one of those things was date girls. On the other hand, if Bort, Christine and Terri were happy to let him stay a couple of days, that would be good. Especially if things were really as quiet as they seemed. It depended how reliable the locals were, of course, and how regularly the Grongles checked the place. He didn't want to get the three women into trouble.

She looked into his eyes. It was difficult to hold her gaze. Her words had hurt but he would never be able to explain the reason why; this wasn't about his feelings for her. Well, no, it *was* a bit, but for the most part it was because of his life, generally. She picked up on his mood though because after a moment's thought she said, 'Shall we change the subject?'

'It's got *some* legs though, hasn't it? Us?'

'I dunno, it probably has. It's the baggage that hasn't and I reckon you come with a lot of it.'

'Correct.'

'Yeh, so let's talk about something else.'

'Go on, then.' He waved one hand in a carry-on gesture. 'Why?'

He raised an eyebrow at her and gave her his best quizzical expression. 'Why ... what?'

'Why this? Why us? You had no reason to save our skins from King Milo, or even the Grongles who got us in the first place. In fact, you could have left us to be captured on the riverbank.'

That wasn't really a question The Pan could answer. 'I dunno,' he shrugged. 'I can't really tell you why I do anything. It's all spur of the moment—my whole life is. Stuff happens, there are repercussions and I sort them out; rinse and repeat.'

'That's not a straight answer.'

'Well, it's the truth. I could have done a lot of things differently but I got you into trouble in the first place by whisking you all away without your mum's ID. Maybe I felt responsible. Who knows? I certainly don't.' He held his hands out either side of him in a typically Hamgeean 'search me' shrug. 'I acted without thought. Most likely, I wanted my sausage.'

'You'd have had all four. We left them in your snurd. That's why I know I can trust you, by the way. But aside from that, we listened to the K'Barthan Broadcasting Corporation the morning after we found the sausage—'

'And?'

'KBC reckoned the Grongles chased two snurds over the Arboretum. But GNN was saying five.'

'Yeh, I heard that too. As far as I know it was just us.'

'Yeh. And GNN and KBC are *both* saying a gang from the Resistance found one of the sausages and was captured just after they sold it.'

'They could be lying, or getting it wrong, like they did with the number of snurds,' said The Pan, trying to brazen it out.

'Yeh, but in this case, I don't think so.'

'You don't, why?'

'They agree.'

'So. It happens occasionally.'

She rolled her eyes, 'Yeh, whatever but I think the Resistance *did* find a sausage.' A beat. 'It was yours, wasn't it?'

'Why d'you think that?'

'Because you're here. If you'd got the money, you wouldn't have cared about your boots.'

'I told you, it might not have been *just* about the boots.'

'OK, maybe it wasn't. But you're a lot shyer than I'd expect a man who's just earned himself a fortune to be.'

'It isn't a fortune though, is it? Not even when you sell three.'

Bort sighed. 'No.'

They sat in silence for a moment.

'Is it going to be enough to spring your dad?' The Pan said.

'I hope so. But you're changing the subject.'

'Sorry, carry on.'

'OK, so usually people who are talented at something have this kind of inner glow, this confidence. You don't. I mean you do when you're taking control in an escape situation. Then you're, like, totally lightning speed and on it. But the rest of the time you're unbelievably shy.'

'I am?'

'Duh, yeh. I thought you were never ever going to make a move on me yesterday. I had to practically *beg* you.'

'I thought that was just a lot of feminine allure.'

'Stop it, you muppet!'

'I'm not *that* shy, I'm just ... not a good prospect. So I never expected you to be interested. GBIs don't get to go on dates—we're too much of a risk.'

She looked at him with such a supremely ironic expression that it made him laugh. 'Wait a minute, are you actually, really, a GBI?'

'Yes. I told you I was.'

'Yeh and I thought that was bravado. Although after this morning, I guess it's easier to believe. You're so not the kind of guy who joins a gang. No way you'd be working for Big Merv unless something had gone really, really wrong.'

'He might have made me.'

'Yeh and I bet he did, but that would also come under the heading of "something going really wrong". You wouldn't have been around a being like him unless you were already in a massive amount of trouble, that's what I'm talking about.'

'Yeh, well, you have me there.'

'How long?'

'Three years.'

She grabbed a cushion and threw it at him. 'You total liar. Why can't you be straight with me? Nobody lasts three years on the blacklist! Nobody lasts three weeks.'

'Some do.'

'Oh yeh? As if ...'

'It's the honest truth. Have they an internet point round here?'

'Yeh, there's a machine at the chandler's they let people use.'

'Right. Then, if you really want to know the truth, pop in there, and type my name into a search engine. I'll come with you if you like. I haven't looked at my record for a while, I'll be interested to see how it's getting on.'

'Seriously?'

'Seriously.'

'And the sausage?'

'Unfortunately, you're dead right about that. I went to see the same expert you did. He told me you'd been round, or at least not in so many words, but I knew. He also told me that the Resistance were watching his place. Maybe he's the best, or maybe he's the only expert prepared to look at a sausage with no provenance.'

'It has provenance. We found it in the river.'

'Yeh, but I think normally there are bills of sale and stuff. I get the impression he didn't see many found items, let alone four in one morning.'

'Did he dob you in?'

'I doubt it. If he did, he had no choice. The Resistance were waiting, watching his place and although he warned me, well,' he shrugged, 'what with the Grongles doing a house-to-house search at the same time, I missed the signs. I let them mug me basically. I'm still kicking myself. On the upside, they didn't dob me in to get the reward or at least, if they did, I'd managed to leave the area by the time the Security Forces arrived. They didn't kidnap me and carry me off to be a getaway driver, either. Two out of three isn't bad. In fact, in my world, I'd call that a win.'

'Don't you want to be a getaway driver?'

'Arnold, no! Especially not for them. I'm a coward. I don't do bravery.'

'You did this morning.'

'What are you on about? I ran squealing to my boss. It was hardly brave and I'm only here because he dragged me back.'

'You still came to the boat.'

'Yeh. Because he was pretty much poking me in the back with a pointy stick ... and probably a loaded gun, knowing him. I didn't dare check, I consider myself allergic to fire arms.'

'Oh yeh?'

'Well ... I'm a bit less scared when they're full of rice.'

'That explains a lot.' She looked down at the empty cup

in her hands with surprising shyness. 'Thank you, anyway for all the help you've given us.'

The Pan bit back the urge to say, 'my pleasure' because it really hadn't been, not for the most part, even if the bits with Bort had been extremely enjoyable. There was another long silence and she cocked her head on one side and looked at him, biting her lip. He thought about kissing her.

'Can you cook?' she asked him.

'After a fashion.' He raised an eyebrow. 'Some people call the results food, others call them charcoal. It depends what you'd like me to make. I can do a handful of dishes quite well. Others are ... a bit dicey. These days, I don't get much practice.'

'If you think you can handle a fry up, I ought to get dressed.'

'Do you have to?'

She gave him a look of mock disapproval. 'Yes. I told you, we're going to go for a walk. If you have time. I've looked out one of Dad's shirts and a pair of shorts.'

'What's wrong with my kit?'

'I thought you might want some clean clothes.'

'Do the others hum that much?'

'Like a rhino's armpit.'

'Do rhinos have armpits?'

'I dunno but if they do, trust me, that's how it would smell. The t-shirt's even worse. Well, it was, it's in the wash now—Mum and Christine took your stuff to the launderette with ours. They'll bring it back in a while and we can all have brunch.'

'Alright.' He got out of bed. 'Show me to the stove.'

'Wait! First, there's something else. I'll be right back.' She jumped up and ran out of the room.

Chapter 30
A rare gift

A few seconds later Bort returned to The Pan with some clothes; a red, yellow and orange paisley shirt, a pair of boxers and some light brown knee-length shorts. She put the shorts and boxers on the bed and held the shirt up in front of her.

'Don't ever wear this when you have a hangover,' she warned him.

'No ...' he said slowly. 'I'll try not to.' A shirt like that was a rare gift though. He *liked* it. A lot.

'Sorry. It's a bit stoury,' she said.

She was right—it did have the faintest hint of mothballs and detergent, and clothes that have been in a cupboard for a long time. But, as Ada would have said, 'nothing a couple of hours on a washing line in the fresh air can't fix'. He smiled to himself as he imagined her saying it. Bort cocked her head on one side and adopted a quizzical expression.

'What's so funny?' she asked.

'Nothing, I was just ... laughing at the shirt. I expect the smell will blow off as I wear it.'

'Yeh well, Dad did have a bit of line in shirts. Clothes full stop, in fact. Mum says that when they were young he dressed like something between a rock star and a pimp.'

'Always cool if you can get away with it,' said The Pan.

'Yeh,' she said and then gave him a bit of a look as if to say, 'not'. 'Looking at your shirt, we reckoned that you might like to borrow this one while yours is drying. It was the first I found but I was going to dig the rest out for you. If you can do breakfast, I can do shirt hunting. Then when

Mum gets back I'll just check there aren't any she wants to keep.'

'Won't your dad need them? When he comes back.'

'He might but I don't think so. I can't remember him ever wearing shirts like these so it must have been ages ago. I dunno, they might even be *his* dad's and he died before I was born. They're really well made but ... I mean,' she held it up, 'they're pretty rad.'

The Pan raised an eyebrow at her, 'Rad?' he said flatly.

'Yeh, but good material. This one's silk. They're all natural fibres, silk or cotton mostly. I think a couple are wool. We'll probably have to wash them first.'

'Don't you like it?'

'I kind of do. It's just ... loud. They all are.'

'But they remind you of your dad.'

'Yeh, but I don't *need* that. My dad's still around and I'm going to see him soon. It's different for you because I'm guessing yours isn't, is he?'

'No.'

'Sorry.'

'It's OK.' He took the shirt from her, along with a white t-shirt she'd offered to go underneath. 'I think it's brilliant.' He put the t-shirt down for a moment and held the silk shirt up.

'Yeh, I thought you might.'

'You did?' Wow. She'd clearly taken note of the way he dressed. Was that a good thing? Yes. Probably. She seemed to anticipate what he was thinking.

'It's not hard to figure out. I've seen the one you were wearing, remember?'

The Pan was about to tell her that the shirt he'd been wearing *had* belonged to his father but decided against it. His dad had gone in for loud shirts every now and again. He supposed that was why he did. However, his father had mostly worn them as an ironic thing, in competition with his work colleagues. He was a professor of random mathematics at the University of Hamgee, after all. Science lecturers had a reputation for dressing in eccentric clothing—or just plain badly. There were dress-down days when all the science departments would attempt to reinforce this misconception by arriving in the most bizarre attire they could find. The Pan's father contented himself with vividly patterned shirts, mostly paisley. He was rubbish at it because they suited him and he didn't look odd enough. Indeed, in his youngest son's view, he looked like a rock god, which wasn't exactly the satirical image he was attempting to achieve. These days, a shirt like that, while no longer fashionable, was alternative and niche. That's what The Pan thought, anyway.

'Christine's left your new boots by the door,' Bort said. 'She and Terri took the old ones away with the rubbish when they took it up to the bins earlier. I told them they should ask you first but—

'It's fine.'

'Really? We weren't sure but—'

'They stank?' She blushed a little and looked down. Yes. Clearly. The Pan had never seen Bort blush. It was endearing, especially when she seemed bombproof usually. 'It's brilliant, really, exactly what I would have done. Thank you.' He pulled her into a hug and kissed her.

****

Shortly afterwards The Pan dressed in the clothes Bort had looked out. The shirt was a good fit, but the shorts were a tiny bit big round the waist. Bort found him a leather belt with a brass buckle after which they were fine.

He'd raided Bort's father's wardrobe a second time to look out a pair of jeans for later because the shorts didn't really go with his only footwear; the black suede elastic-sided pointy boots Christine had made him. Then he set about preparing breakfast. By the time Terri and Christine returned there were bacon, sausage, tomato halves and fried potatoes ready to go. He cooked them an egg each while Bort made more coffee. Then the four of them sat down to eat. The three women teased The Pan about his cooking but they had no trouble finishing the meal he'd prepared, he noticed. He drank more coffee, transferred the belt to the jeans, which were purple canvas, rather than denim. He put on his new boots and some socks after which, as promised, Bort took him for a walk. They spent most of the afternoon lying in the long grass in a hay meadow, far away from prying eyes, doing things The Pan's parents—and possibly Bort's—would definitely have frowned upon.

Pity he was so conspicuous, The Pan thought, because he reckoned the country would be a good place to live. There was probably some casual work he could do for food or cash in hand. He'd be noticed at once though. Small communities were tight knit and strangers were notable and, more to the point, newsworthy. At the least people would gossip about his arrival, knowing his luck, where the wrong people could overhear. Bummer.

After an idyllic day with Bort, pretending they were girlfriend and boyfriend, behaving like the couple it was impossible to be, The Pan said goodbye to Terri and Christine and again refused their offer to stay. He had an orange Swamp Thing to go and see. The mere thought filled him with nerves—Big Merv would probably find something to be angry about. But at the same time, he'd clearly been pleased to get the sausage.

The Pan and Bort walked to a parking area, where the towpath met the road. No point in being too conspicuous taking off in the SE2 from the water. And it would make him look a right poser as well. They walked in silence, neither of them talking until they reached the waiting SE2.

Then he pulled her into his arms one last time and kissed her.

This was it. 'I'd better go, Big Merv will be waiting.'

'Will you come back tomorrow?'

What? She wanted to do this again? That was blummin' brilliant. 'Will you still be here?'

'I hope so.'

'What about the temporary thing?'

'You're digital, aren't you? On or off, all or nothing.'

He glanced down towards the ground. 'A bit, yes.'

'When I said "temporary" I was thinking of something like a holiday romance—you seem to be thinking of a one-night stand. I mean, it can be a one-night stand if you want but—'

'No, really, I don't. I'm sorry, don't mind me. I'm a bit slow on the uptake.'

'It's OK.' She smiled up at him. 'I just meant, I guess, that maybe one day, when you came to see me, we wouldn't be here. That's probably how it'll end.'

'Right. Well ... I'm happy to keep visiting until you aren't. I don't get to be this normal this often.'

'Then you'll come back tomorrow?'

'If Big Merv doesn't kill me or give me a pesky delivery to do I'll definitely be here. In fact, I *have* to come back.'

'You do?'

'Yeh.' He hugged her. 'You have my shirt and trousers, remember? I still haven't got that second pair of boots either.'

'Nine o'clock tomorrow morning, then. Don't be late.'

'I won't.' He hesitated. There was no-one around. Yeh, why not? He held her close and kissed her again, for quite a long time.

When they finally stopped, she said, 'Go, or you'll be late.' She sounded a little breathless.

'My wish is your command,' he replied.

She rolled her eyes at him and he walked away, turning to wave one last time as he got into the SE2. As he drove off, he pooped the hooter. She raised one hand and waved back. Then she stood watching him, a lone figure in the middle of the road, until he reached a corner and she was lost from sight.

Chapter 31
Words of warning

When The Pan arrived at The Big Thing it was a hive of activity. Nobody was saying what had happened to King Milo but he'd disappeared, leaving his patch without a boss. Someone had to take over King Milo's turf. And in the absence of anyone brave enough to stand up to him, it looked as if that someone was going to be Big Merv.

The Pan went round to the back of the club, as usual. It was hot and the fire door was open. Some of the enforcers were outside taking the evening air (but luckily not Frank or Harry). He stepped inside and immediately Big Merv appeared at the top of the stairs. 'There you are, you little scrote. Up here, now.'

The Pan followed Big Merv into his office. The usual plywood and metal chair was in position in front of the desk, but Frank and Harry were still absent. Phew. That was a relief.

'The boys are busy so I gotta deal with you myself. Sit down,' he said. He was wearing the same get-up as he had been in the small hours and The Pan reckoned his boss hadn't slept. Big Merv ran his hand over his bald head and his antennae looped and un-looped.

'You alright, Big Merv, sir?'

'Yer. Better than your pal, I reckon.'

Here we go, thought The Pan. He wasn't sure what to actually say. But he knew that if he was going to have to beg for his life he needed to pick the right time. This wasn't it. So he stayed silent. 'I gotta have words with you, mate.'

Smecking smeck. Did he really? 'Right,' said The Pan.

'Yer, "right". First, I gotta thank you.'

Say what? 'You have?'

'Yeh. You solved a couple of problems for me tonight. That little squirt King Milo for starters—that's one thing I ain't gotta deal with no more.' The Pan started to sweat. Arnold's socks please, please don't say Big Merv had chucked King Milo in the river. Yes. Of course he had. He was a gangster. Mmm. Best try not to think about it. Big Merv continued. 'On top of that, I got the finest fake Goojan spiced sausage money can buy. That's a good day in anyone's book.'

'Yes. Congratulations,' said The Pan weakly.

'Yer, 's right pal. Lucky me. And coz you was loyal to me,' Big Merv opened his desk drawer and pulled out an envelope, 'I got you this, as a token of my appreciation.' He walked round the desk and handed the envelope to The Pan. It was the same kind of brown envelope the payments for his deliveries came in—only it was thicker than usual.

'There's something else and all.' Big Merv perched on the desk and The Pan looked up, a long way up, into his boss's face. 'Something important what you need to take on board, sonny Jim.' He pointed an orange finger at the envelope The Pan was holding. 'And it's worth more than that. I got some good advice for you.'

'W-What?'

'Advice. It ain't gonna cost you nothing. But you need it son. See, you're a slippery little bleeder. There ain't no-one what can catch up with you coz you got nous and you use it. I like that,' said Big Merv.

The Pan stared at him. Was that a compliment? Yes, apparently it was. Although it was clear that in this case, there was a big difference between grudgingly respecting something about someone and actually liking them.

Big Merv continued. 'I ain't stupid. I know you don't

wanna work for me. But you ain't got no choice. You've accepted that, coz you're a realist, an' you do what I ask with no complaints. I like that and all. You got a lot of pragmatism. 'S a good thing, that.'

'Thank you,' stammered The Pan.

'Yer. And ... although you do stuff your way, which is a right pain in the arse, you do it good. You done good last night and all. I know it wasn't about loyalty to me, it's coz you're shagging the young one, innit?'

There was a pause and The Pan realised he was expected to answer. 'I— we—'

'Yer, thought so. If you wanna stay alive in this world, mate, you gotta learn what you can get away with.'

'I'll try,' whispered The Pan. Arnold, this was difficult. The envelope had money in it—that was good. But on the other hand Big Merv was extremely serious and this, this would have looked more like an I'm-going-to-throw-you-in-the-river moment if it wasn't for the compliments.

Big Merv's face was hard and his expression uncompromising. 'Yer. You gotta listen to what I'm gonna tell you, son.'

'I will.' As usual when those felt-tip green eyes met The Pan's he felt as if he was being read, and read with complete accuracy.

'Yer, I reckon you will if you wanna stay alive.' Big Merv shrugged. 'I reckon you're a good judge of that ... usually. Right now, though, I'd say you gotta learn some serious smarts about the way folks are.'

'I have?'

'Yer. Otherwise, it don't matter if you're the slipperiest bleeder in Ning Dang Po. It don't matter if you're the slipperiest bleeder in the entire effin' world, you're toast.'

'I am?'

'Yer. See, it's like this.' Big Merv folded his arms and

glared down at him. 'You reckon you're well in with them birds?'

'They helped me out and I think they like me.'

'That ain't the same as a yes. You got doubts?'

'Not exactly but—'

'You ain't gonna push it too far?'

'Something like that,' The Pan said quietly.

'Do they know you're on the run?'

The Pan's head snapped up sharply, 'I'm not on—' he began but Big Merv spoke over him.

'There's a reason no-one catches you, son. It ain't all smarts. I reckon a lot of it's practice. I seen your moniker on posters before now. I reckon a fair few folks want you dead. Folks who would pay them birds good money.'

'*They* don't know that,' said The Pan, realising that he'd told Bort he was a GBI. Despite his suggesting it, the pair of them hadn't got round to looking up his record at the chandler's. But that didn't mean she wouldn't take the initiative and check on her own. He could feel himself going pale.

'It ain't so tricky findin' out. I know what you are, son.'

'Then how come—'

'I said. Simple business decision, innit? You might be worth a lotta cash.' He shrugged. 'I dunno. Thing is, you're worth more to me alive than dead.' He paused. 'And I don't owe the Grongles nothing. They want you, that's their business. If they think I'm gonna concern myself with that they can shove it. That ain't the thing, though. What you gotta learn, sonny, is that with a price on your head, you got to know who you can trust,' he put an orange thumb against his chest, 'in 'ere. Them ladies up at the lock, does it feel the same hanging out up there as it does down the Parrot and Screwdriver with them old ladies an' them punters?'

Thinking about it, The Pan realised that ... no, it didn't. Was that difference a good thing or a bad thing though?

There was nothing about the three women that rang The Pan's alarm bells. His gut instinct was to trust them, and he'd learned to trust his instincts. But Big Merv's warning rattled him a bit.

Putting instinct aside, The Pan knew that Christine, Terri and Bort needed money. And he was also aware that when people need money badly enough they'll do a lot of things they might not normally do.

Was that it? Was that the tiny seed of doubt? Or was it just the whole thing with Bort? He'd completely let his guard down and he regretted it because it made him feel vulnerable. Could his misgivings be so simple? The control freak in him throwing a hissy fit? Maybe. Or was it simply the way they'd accepted him and shown him such kindness? Was that just too good to be true? No, because Gladys, Ada and Trev, and the punters at the Parrot had been kind to him too.

'Them folks down that pub,' Big Merv continued, 'I'd say they got your back—'

'Yeh. They have,' said The Pan, utterly certain as he answered, that he believed what he was saying.

'Yer. Them three birds on that boat, though? I dunno.'

'I know they like me.'

'Yer, they like you.' Big Merv unfolded his arms and wagged a warning finger as he glared down at The Pan. 'I reckon you like them too. What's more, I can tell you for nothing, that if any bit of skirt as hot as that Bort set her cap at me the way she done at you, I'd have shagged 'er and all.' The Pan looked down, trying not to cringe. And anyway, how did he even know? 'It's bleedin' obvious, son,' said Big Merv answering The Pan's unspoken question. 'But that ain't my point. What I'm sayin' is that *I* wouldn't let my heart,' Big Merv pressed one finger to his chest, 'get in the way of my thinking apparatus.' He pointed to his temple.

The Pan thought about it. He'd rescued Christine, Terri

and Bort and they were definitely grateful to him. They also liked him—especially Bort—and Terri and Christine didn't seem to mind her liaison with him, or at least, not short term. But The Pan knew that 'like' wasn't enough. After all, he was on nodding terms with a lot of beings around Ning Dang Po, and did he like them? Well yes, of course, but did that mean he could trust them? No.

'Yer,' said Big Merv as he watched The Pan thinking. 'They gave Bob some sob story about needing cash for springing a much-loved family member outa the Resistance. That true?'

'Yeh, I'm pretty sure it is.'

'You reckon?'

'Yeh, I reckon.'

'Why?'

'The way I found out.'

'Their guard down?'

'Something like that.'

'Big time down?'

'Yeh, I'd say so.'

Big Merv nodded. He seemed a little sad. 'Poor bleeders. I paid a hefty whack for that sausage but all the money in the world ain't gonna spring no-one from the Resistance.'

'They had—' The Pan began and stopped. They might not want Big Merv to know they had three. He ran his hands through his hair and tried to concentrate. He didn't want to give away any more than he had to but needless to say, his boss had already picked up on it.

'Yer, I know there was more. Four missing, one found. I reckon the reason that gang of Resistance fighters what was caught with it escaped was coz they bought their freedom, and I reckon we both know what with. An' you just told me, right there, who got the other three. 'S like they divided up the loot with someone, innit? If I was you, I'd wanna know who.'

Arnold's armpits! Did Big Merv actually realise The Pan had been given the other sausage?

No. Calm down, The Pan told himself, his boss was smart enough to guess a lot of things—and probably guess correctly—but he couldn't possibly *know* anything like that. It was a shot in the dark. It had to be. The Pan did his best to keep his expression noncommittal and refuse to be drawn. Big Merv looked down at him, antennae waving backwards and forwards in thought but also with a hint of impatience.

'Way I reckon it goes is like this: if their bloke's in the Resistance, maybe they got contacts. 'S no tellin' what happened—too many rumours flying around obscuring the truth—but we all know something big went down at the Arboretum. Like I said, no-one's got no clue what it was and we ain't never gonna know. But one thing it tells us, for deffo, is that they've got the inside track with a tasty getaway bloke.'

'Possibly,' The Pan said cautiously. Arnold's trousers, where was this going? Please Arnold, not in an I-know-it's-you direction. He was beginning to feel a bit sweaty.

'Yer, sunshine, so maybe they gave their getaway bloke a sausage.'

Arnold's hair, Big Merv was very, very smart. 'Hmm. I guess they might have done,' said The Pan as noncommittally as possible.

'Uncanny, innit? The bloke, or the lady, what helps them gets rolled over and loses *their* sausage. Meanwhile your mates get to sell the other three. What does that say to you, son?'

'That the one who lost their sausage did something dumb, maybe?'

Big Merv shot him a look and his eyes narrowed. 'Maybe,' he said quietly. 'Or, maybe he wasn't like you.

Maybe he was proper smart but he lost it anyway, coz they dobbed him in.'

'What? To the Grongles?'

"S right,' said Big Merv. 'Or it mighta been the Resistance. What if it was part of the payment? "We can give you cash and, if you fancy helping yourself from this geezer we know who's got it, there's a Goojan sausage on top." 'S a thought that, innit?'

The Pan shook his head, 'No, they wouldn't do that.'

'How can you be so sure?'

Easy. As the geezer in question, The Pan was certain his getting mugged had been an unlucky fluke. Except he couldn't tell Big Merv that. 'They're not the type. They're honourable,' he said. How useless did that sound?

'You gonna bet your life on that, son? Coz if you're gonna hook up with that bird again, that's what you're gonna be doing.'

'Yes.'

'One hundred percent?'

'I think so.'

'That ain't yes.'

'No. But from me it's the best you'll get. I don't buy them dobbing anyone in. For starters, they wouldn't know where h— this person would be.'

'They mighta done.'

'Maybe but we can't tell.'

"S right. We can't tell,' said Big Merv, 'and that makes it a risk. Have I got you thinking yet?'

Surely Christine, Bort and Terri weren't like that? The Pan was as certain as he could be that Big Merv was wrong. After all, he didn't know the facts; that The Pan had saved their lives, that it was The Pan who'd been at the wheel above the Arboretum. Even so, deep down, a tiny, tiny seed of doubt germinated.

'Well?' Big Merv demanded.

'Yeh, a bit,' The Pan admitted.

'Yer. See, I know you like them ladies. I get that. They're proper likeable. But if you're gonna get close to other beings, you can't afford to let it blind you. Not in the game you're playing. You let your heart rule your head and you're dead meat, sunshine. That's why you gotta see people straight, even if you like them so much that you don't wanna. Specially then.'

The Pan looked into Big Merv's scary green eyes, searching for a reason for this to be artifice, or a game, or for his boss to be wrong. All he saw was the usual stern authority and very little else.

Big Merv continued. 'Listen, son.' He leaned down and poked The Pan in the chest for emphasis. 'I told you. You're worth more to me alive than dead. While it stays like that, then, if anyone gets to dob you in to the Grongles, it's gonna be me. Not some bunch of birds out at Lark Locks. You get me?'

'Yes,' said The Pan.

"Cept it ain't gonna be me, coz you're doing alright.'

OK, kind of reassurance. That was novel. Now what? Big Merv was definitely expecting him to say something. 'That's good to know.' No, not that. Something less lame. 'Thanks.'

'Yer, thanks,' said Big Merv drily. For a moment his eyes held the tiniest hint of something that might have been a smile, were it not for the fact that he never cracked the remotest hint of a smile, ever. He went on. 'If you gotta go back there for a second helping, just remember what I said.'

'I will,' said The Pan.

'Good. Coz if you get yourself arrested, you're on your own. I ain't schlepping out there to save your sorry arse. You get me?'

'Yeh. I get you.'

'Sweet. Now hop it, coz I've got stuff to do.'

'Yes, boss,' said The Pan and he went.

Chapter 32
Let fate decide

It was a quiet and thoughtful Hamgeean who sat in The Parrot and Screwdriver soon afterwards.

Trev was collecting the glasses while Ada and Gladys prepared sandwiches. Betsy Coed and the girls from the guest house more or less opposite, which was really a bordello, were having a night off. The Pan watched them laughing and having fun together. His thoughts were disturbed by a chinking noise as Trev put the three glasses he'd collected on the table and sat down opposite him. 'Does you know you is staring at them girls like they is from outer space?'

The Pan heaved a sigh. 'Sorry, no.'

'Yer, I reckoned not. Is you alright, lad?'

'Not really.'

'Girl trouble?'

'No.' The Pan raised a suave eyebrow but his heart wasn't in it so, unsurprisingly, it cut no ice. 'Alright, I suppose it is, sort of. But it's general trouble, really.'

'Isn't you used to that by now?' Trev winked.

'You'd have thought I would be, wouldn't you?' said The Pan.

Trev waited without saying anything else and, as he often did when presented with silence, The Pan filled it. 'You three—you, Gladys and Ada—how do you know who you can trust and who you can't?'

'Well, now.' Trev leaned back and rubbed the stubble on his chin with a scritching sound. 'I reckons a bit of it is instinct. Usually, folks what hurt others is damaged or unhappy, or carrying a heavy load. And a lot of times, that shows.'

'How?'

'They gets brittle. They is spiky, or they laughs a bit too long an' a bit too loud. Y'know, tries too hard. 'S more than a feeling. Sure, it feels like it's a gut instinct but I knows it isn't. It's my subconscious working, see? Funny thing is, I doesn't reckon I could list the signs cause it's stuff I doesn't consciously notice. I dunno. Maybe sometimes it's down ter telepathy or some quantum cobblers.' He chuckled to himself. 'I couldn't tell yer. I isn't up on all that kind of malarkey!' He held up one hand and made a whooshing noise as he passed it over the top of his head. 'Sometimes, you just knows they're a bad 'un an' time proves you're right. Like that Killer Mike bloke, or that Marcella the Pirate.'

'Arnold, don't remind me!' The Pan thought for a moment, digesting what Trev had said. 'Thanks. That makes a lot of sense.'

'I'm surprised you is asking. You is a good judge on that score, I reckons. Better 'an most I has seen.'

'Thanks. I suspect you flatter me. I think my method is similar to yours, though. A lot of it feels like instinct but it probably isn't. The rest of it's a case of making sure I go in with my eyes open, or that I think things through. If there's time, that is.'

'Yer, 's the best way I reckons. Why is you asking?'

'I guess I have a conundrum right now. Usually my instinct and my thinking line up but someone's said something to me this time and now ...' he sighed.

'They doesn't?'

'Yeh. I'm pretty sure that all's well except ...' he held out his hands either side of him. 'Not completely certain.'

'This someone has said something which has got yer thinking?'

'Yeh. Does that ever happen to you?'

'Yer. Sometimes.'

'And when it does?'

'Depends what I has heard and who from.'

'A warning, from someone reliable.' Was Big Merv reliable, though? The Pan wondered. Yes, in that he completely trusted him to behave in a certain way. The Pan knew exactly where he stood with his boss even if it was, mostly, on shaky ground. He heaved another sigh. 'The thing is, he doesn't know the whole story, and I can't tell him. I think if I told him the truth he might take a different view. Except there's no way I can do that. On the other hand, he's also a very shrewd judge of character, so if he *is* a bit suspicious then even if he doesn't know the whole story, he's probably onto something.'

'Tricky.' Trev sucked the air in through his teeth. 'If I has heard from someone reliable then either I walks or I takes a gamble and I trusts 'em, but with my eyes open.'

'Right. So when it happens, what d'you usually end up doing?'

'Depends. I has a soft heart, like Mum and Aunt Ada. If it's a being needing a hand, I keeps my wits about me and wades on in.' He stopped to think, pulling one earlobe absently with his finger and thumb as he mulled it over. His eyes gazed, unfocused, into the middle distance for a moment or two. 'Yer. Usually. But I has to weigh up the risk. Y'know, if I gets it wrong, is some other bloke going to get hurt—or lass,' he added hastily, 'or if I has to rely on the delivery snurd and it isn't running right, is I going to take the risk of it letting me down at the wrong time? Or p'raps I has to be somewhere I doesn't know, so I isn't sure of the way out. Them's the times I might walk away. Them's the times when you has ter be careful.'

'Yeh, I can imagine.' *If I has to rely on the delivery snurd and it isn't running right.* Arnold's sandals, it was as if he knew.

''S that helped, lad?'

'Yeh. It has. Thanks.' The Pan thought for a moment. 'D'you have a pen and paper I could borrow? An envelope, too if you can run to it.'

'Yer, sure,' Trev rose to his feet. 'Things is going ter get noisy round here soon though. I reckons you is best off in the snug. I'll bring them through.'

****

The Pan of Hamgee strode through the cool summer night with a bottle of water in his hand. The air was surprisingly fresh and clean for Ning Dang Po and he inhaled deeply. Every now and again he stopped to admire his surroundings and take a drink of water from the bottle.

Eventually he reached his destination, a quiet part of lower left near the river. Nobody was around so he climbed over some railings and walked across the grass to the shadows under the trees. He wouldn't be seen here. At least not until first light, but he intended to be gone by then.

He summoned his wheels, and when the SE2 arrived took his wash bag out of the boot. Using some more of the bottle of water, he cleaned his teeth and washed his face. Under the cover of the trees, hidden in the shadows, he could relax. He was safe here—or at least, reasonably safe—behind the locked gates and railings. He wasn't the only person who could climb a fence but he was probably the only person who'd bother. Seeing as he was pretty much invisible where he was, nobody was likely to come after him. He put the bottle into the boot, removed his cloak and hat, got into the passenger seat, reclined it right back and settled down for the night, cloak wrapped round him as a blanket, hat over his eyes.

It wasn't chilly—he didn't need a blanket—but the cloak had been his father's and this was more about comfort than anything. Beside him, nestled in the inside pocket of his neatly folded jacket was the letter he'd written to Bort. He

257

wanted to see her again. But after a great deal of thought, he decided it might be smart to wait, just in case his three new friends were that desperate that they decided to sell him to the authorities. The Pan was self-aware enough to realise that waiting was not his strong suit though. He might well crack unless he took measures. This would be an excellent way to leave things to fate. He'd take the SE2 to Gerry to check, and wait until it had the all-clear, or any problems were fixed, before he went back to see Bort.

As The Pan lay in his seat, he enjoyed the luxury of some thinking time. Hearing his thoughts articulated aloud tended to make them clearer somehow, but he only talked to himself quietly, in places where he knew he couldn't be overheard. As usual, his thinking took the form of a conversation with his Virtual Parents.

Your priority is to stay alive, said the voice of his Virtual Father.

'You think so?' asked The Pan quietly.

Yes, and so do you. Or do I have to take you up to the Bridge of Eternal Glory to remind you?

'No, that won't be necessary.'

Good. You need to get the SE2 checked before you expose yourself to any more risk.

'Yeh, I know. I guess I was just caught up in the moment.'

Thinking with your trousers, I'd say! As ever.

Go easy on him dear, he's still young! said Virtual Mum. *I remember when we were that age! You were just the same. Remember that night we—*

'Whoa! That's a bit too much with the realism,' The Pan sat up suddenly, his hands out in front of him in a stop-right-there gesture. 'Back off,' he told himself, or at least, whatever bit of his subconscious had just been speaking. 'That is stuff I do not need to think about.'

Well, you had to come from somewhere— began the voice of his Virtual Mum.

'La la la, not listening!'

He knew it wasn't really his Mum and Dad. In fact, from the way they often bitched at him, he presumed his Virtual Parents were his self-hatred. But, when they managed to be civil, 'talking' to them did help sometimes.

What did you tell her?

'Who?'

He could almost hear Virtual Dad casting his eyes heavenwards in exasperation. *That slip of a lass! Bort.*

The Pan thought about the letter in his jacket pocket. 'That I can't see her tomorrow, but I'm going to, as soon as the SE2 gets the all clear.'

You shouldn't go back at all, said the voice of his Virtual Father.

'I realise that, but I need to. I need to get my shirt.'

Don't be so bloody ridiculous! Shirts are two a penny.

'Yeh, but this one isn't.' The Pan ran one hand through is hair. 'This one's yours.'

You will be careful then, won't you, dear? That was Virtual Mum. She understood even if Virtual Dad didn't.

'Yes. I will. I have to sleep now.'

He heaved a sigh, rolled up his jacket and lay back down again with his head on it. He was beginning to think that Terri, Christine and Bort were on the same side of the law as he was. Not outlaws, but definitely people who were a bit more louche than average with the concept of 'legal'. To The Pan, that almost made it easier. If they were criminals of a certain type, like Big Merv, that was good. Because for all his scariness, on the whole, Big Merv was fair and could be relied on to do the Right Thing. But if they were like King Milo or Marcella the Pirate ... yeh, that would be a different thing entirely.

No. He'd have picked that up, wouldn't he?

He closed his eyes and in what seemed like an instant, woke up again. The dial on his watch read four thirty a.m.

Time to go. It was still dark but once it got light his presence under the trees would be obvious and would definitely raise some eyebrows. He put the seat upright, got out and walked about for a few minutes. It was early in the year and for the moment—despite the heatwave—the grass, and the leaves, were still green. Under the cover of darkness, and his father's cloak, The Pan put on clean underwear and socks. Then he strolled round to the boot of the SE2, removed the bottle of water, cleaned his teeth and washed his face. Finally, he dug out a long blonde wig. He put it on and tied it back with an elastic hair band.

'Not great,' he said as he took his shirt off so he was just wearing one of the white t-shirts he normally wore as a vest. He checked his reflection in the wing mirror, in so far as he could. 'Hmm ... definitely better without the shirt.' For the purpose of disguising himself, it always was.

He opened the filler cap at the back of the SE2 and poured the rest of the bottle of water into the tank. Like all snurds, The Pan's ran on water. 'There. That should keep you going for a while,' he told it quietly.

It was still cool, so he put on his jacket and got in. 'Lark Locks, here we come.'

He ran his thumb over the reader on the dash. 'Ident confirmed,' said the SE2.

As always, the sound of its voice lifted The Pan's spirits. It really was very sexy. He pressed the starter and the engine purred into life. Hmm. It sounded pretty good. You couldn't be too sure though. Yeh. What he wanted to be doing in a few hours' time, at nine o'clock, was meeting Bort at Lark Locks. What he *should* be doing at that time was arriving at Snurd with the SE2 to get it checked. On the other hand, The Pan tended to arrive there at nine because he wasn't a morning person. Gerry was often around by seven so if The Pan turned up then, and Gerry checked the SE2 and gave it the all clear, it might just still be possible to make Lark Locks to meet Bort at nine a.m. like he'd promised.

In the meantime, he'd written a letter explaining which he'd deliver to Bort. He'd thought about delivering it to the *Happy Doris* himself, but he knew that if he went there in person the temptation to throw caution to the wind and spend the day with Bort would be overwhelming. Yep, he'd whizz up there in the SE2 and post the letter through the door of the lock keeper's cottage. Then he'd be back at Snurd for seven and fate would decide. He wrote an apologetic note to Zeb on the envelope, asking if he'd be able to drop it off at the barge next time he was passing. The lock keeper had come across as a kindly being. Hopefully, it wasn't too cheeky a request and he'd deliver it.

The Pan checked his watch. It was now a quarter to five. Mmm. OK. A bit early but he wanted to get up to Lark Locks and back with the letter before it got light. He also wanted to hit the sweet spot—after any late revellers at the Hungry Boatsman had gone back to their boats to sleep, but before the nutters who got up at dawn, to go fishing and the like, were up and about.

'Right. Let's try not to get killed, shall we?' he told the snurd. 'We're just going to post a letter, then I'll take you to Gerry for seven o'clock opening and get you checked over.'

Chapter 33
Difficult decision

At half seven, in the once *Happy Doris* now *Frolicking Maiden*, Bort was preparing breakfast. She'd always been a morning person—her mum less so, and Christine definitely not. Even so, all three of them liked to start the day with a hearty breakfast, and because she was the brightest and best in the morning, it was usually Bort who cooked it.

She diced bacon, potatoes and onions, then heated some oil in a skillet, and put the whole lot in to heat up along with a few wild garlic leaves. She'd cook it a bit, then put the lid on, turn the gas down and let it do its own thing. If she checked it didn't catch from time to time, it usually browned up nicely on its own while she did other stuff. Then it was just a case of smashing a couple of eggs over it, giving them time to cook and serving it up.

'Morning darling.'

'Hi, Mum.'

Terri came over and gave her a hug. 'Are you seeing The Pan of Hamgee again today?'

'Hopefully, unless Big Merv gives him stuff to do.' Bort realised she'd be disappointed if The Pan didn't show. She was fonder of him than was sensible. No. She wasn't. It was just a massive crush. He'd saved her life, for heaven's sake! And more importantly, he'd saved her mother's life. And Christine's. How could she not have a crush on him after that? It was only a crush though, she knew that. He wasn't compatible with her at all. OK, so in a crisis he was; a lightning-quick thinker and utterly sure of himself. But in real life he had absolutely zero confidence, which was less appealing. She wanted a man who'd take charge, but who'd also be in tune with her enough to insist she do the things she actually wanted to do anyway. The Pan was ... well, yes, OK he was lovely, but he didn't know what she wanted by instinct. Not at all. He had to ask her, or worse, he was too shy to ask and she had to tell him. That wouldn't do at all. Not long term.

Yeh, she told herself. She had a thing for The Pan but it was nothing more than a crush. A big one, but she'd be over him in a few weeks.

Terri looked at her thoughtfully. 'We need to talk about him.'

Bort turned, fish slice in hand. 'Mum, it's just a fling.'

'Does *he* realise that?'

'He should, I've made it *very* clear.' Maybe a bit too clear. If he didn't show at nine when they'd arranged, Bort reflected, it would be entirely her own fault.

'I see,' said Terri.

Bort stirred the mixture in the skillet and stuck a fork into one of the diced spuds. Hmm. Time to put the lid on. She turned down the heat, put the fish slice neatly on the chopping board beside the stove and turned to face Terri. 'Mum, is something wrong?'

'While you were both off by yourselves yesterday, Christine and I went to the Hungry Boatsman and looked him up on the computer.'

'So?'

'He really is a GBI.'

'So what?'

'Sweetheart, to get your dad out, we're talking to some very jumpy beings. I'm not sure if they know about Big Merv turning up here yesterday. I sincerely hope they don't. But if they thought we were harbouring a GBI they'd walk.'

'We're not "harbouring" him.'

'We sort of are, we've fed him, clothed him—'

'We haven't. He left his stuff behind.'

'He's wearing a pair of boots Christine made him. Also … it turns out he's worth a lot of money.'

Bort was shocked. 'You're not going to dob him in? You can't. He saved our lives, Mum. And he's a good person. He waited for us, with four Goojan spiced sausages in his snurd, when he could have just taken off.'

'I know, but what I'm trying to—'

'You can't dob him in!' Bort almost shouted but she didn't want to wake Christine. 'If you do, I'll never speak to you again.'

Terri heaved a sigh. 'Bort, my dear, if you'd just listen. I'd never dob him in—he's a lovely lad. Lovely enough that I invited him to join the crew, if you remember. Although it's probably lucky for us that he refused. Now that I know more about him, I think it would be a bit difficult. I suspect he did too. That's probably why he said no. From what Christine and I could tell, there was another Pan of Hamgee, his father, who was, quite clearly, a vocal critic of the Grongles. It looks as if they've muddled the records up a bit because it says The Pan of Hamgee was blacklisted three years ago. I can't quite tell if it was him, or his father, or both. Thinking about his behaviour the day we met him, I'd say he is a GBI. And even if he isn't, he acts as if he's on the run and has been for a while. It's probably how he learned to drive like that.'

'Does it matter? It's only a fling and it doesn't look like they can catch him, does it?'

'That may be the case, darling, but they could catch *us*. We've drawn a lot of attention to ourselves. People will have noticed us, and they'll have noticed The Pan of Hamgee here with us. Sooner or later one of those people is going to look him up, too, the way Christine and I did. They're going to realise who he is, and what he's worth and call the authorities. In theory, we've been harbouring him.'

Terri stopped. Bort knew she was waiting for that to sink in.

'Mum, are you saying I shouldn't see him again?'

'Not exactly. You're eighteen now—in the eyes of the law you're an adult. But you're still my daughter and you know what the punishment is for any contact with a GBI.'

Yeh, Bort knew. Everyone did. It was being blacklisted, becoming a GBI yourself. She went pale.

'Come and sit down, love.' Bort followed her mother over to the home-built sofa and they sat down. 'I'm so sorry darling.' Terri took Bort's hand in hers. 'Really, I am.'

'It's OK.' Bort wanted to cry. Arnold's navel fluff! What had got into her? The Pan of Hamgee was a temporary thing; he knew it and she knew it. He couldn't be anything else.

'It's just a massive crush,' she said. Even so, she felt the first hot tears falling. Her mum wrapped her arms round her and hugged her close. For a short time, she cried and Terri hugged her tight, whispering reassurances in her ear. Then she sat up, got out a hankie and blew her nose.

'I'm OK now,' she said.

'I'm so sorry, sweetheart.' Terri wore a look of genuine anguish. 'It's awful. I can't bear to see you get your heart broken because of some petty rule. It's bad enough that there's a blacklist at all, but that lad is such a good and kindly soul, and so are you. It's wrong on every level.'

'I really like him, Mum.' She rolled her eyes. 'We're completely incompatible though. I knew it couldn't be long term. He did too but ... I guess I just thought we'd get more time together than this. I know he's not the right guy for me.' She looked down and smiled wryly. 'But he helped us. And he left his shirt and the other pair of boots. He's got nothing. He needs them.'

Terri smiled. 'He does, and that's something we can fix, at least. We can send them on.'

Bort brightened a little. 'Yes. There are plenty of boats who'll take them. And I can write him a letter and explain.'

'That's the spirit.' Terri hugged her again. 'There's something else. Smurfit is coming today…'

'The Blurpon who introduced us to Goldy McSpim?'

'Yes. He's coming round this morning to finalise the details. When he's done we'll know when and where we're to meet Dad. And,' Terri heaved another sigh, 'when we know that, we have to leave.'

'What? Straight away?'

'Yes.'

'Will we ever come back here?' asked Bort. Her voice sounded smaller than she'd wanted it to.

'One day, yes, I hope so. But there's something else,' her mum continued. 'Oh sweetheart, I don't really know how to tell you this but,' she took Bort's hand, 'if we want to get your dad out, we have to sell up.'

'What, sell the *Happy Doris*?'

'Yes. I'm terribly sorry, my love.'

Bort felt another tear run down her cheek. *Oh no! Not more tears—you're supposed to be an adult!* 'But she's our home. We've been through so much together,' she said.

'Yes, she is and that's the trouble. A lot of folks know that, folks who might say the wrong thing by mistake to the beings trying to get your father back.'

'He's not going to live with us, is he though?'

'He might if he needs somewhere to stay at the start, while he finds his feet. We were always friends more than anything, he and I. It's why we never had rows, I suppose. Then he started driving and I was more of an accomplice than a wife …' She smiled. 'I've probably made a bit of a mess of my life but it turned out to be a surprisingly happy mess. He's a good friend still, your father—and he was always a good dad to you. And it's down to him that I have you. I met Christine through him, too.'

Bort remembered the rows her friends' parents used to have, back in Glardy, before the *Happy Doris*. She was twelve then, and still going to school. Her parents hadn't ever rowed—they'd just gone their separate ways. Her dad had moved out and rented a succession of places. She'd been livid with both of them to start with, but her father had visited often. Even when Christine moved in he'd come over and hang out with them, like a friend would. She stayed over at his rented places too, treasured daughter-and-father time. She was aware that he'd had girlfriends but he hadn't had a steady relationship. But then he was driving—perhaps that was why. He was doing more and more jobs and Bort, Terri and Christine saw less and less of him. Then one day, he disappeared.

'I suppose I wouldn't mind if Dad lived with us, so long as you and Christine are OK with it. It'd be fun. Is she alright with the idea of Dad staying?'

'Yes, I've spoken to her. She's fine with it. She gets on well enough with your dad and she knows he and I are just friends.' She smiled. 'He and I really can't be anything more than friends. I wanted to speak to you about all this, though. I wanted you to know everything. I don't want to do anything you'll be unhappy with. Not unless it's something like selling the *Happy Doris*, where there's no other choice. For what it's worth, I'd say we're all unhappy about that but,' she shrugged, 'needs must. As far as possible, though, I want the three of us to agree on what we do. Do you understand?'

'Yeh, Mum, of course I do,' said Bort.

Part of her felt a little thrill of happiness that her father would be around again. But part of her felt sad at the end of it being just the three of them, and something approaching bereft at the idea of selling their home—she didn't want to see the boat go. They'd made so many happy memories there.

Terri was watching her intently. 'So ... you're alright with it all?'

'Yeh, I guess I'm OK. I get it about Dad, and The Pan. But why sell the *Happy Doris*? Do we need cash?'

'Some. But we need the anonymity more than anything.'

'We can repaint, change the boards.'

'No. We need a different-sized barge. Your father may have to pretend to be someone else. The Resistance ... it's not an organisation you can walk away from. If your dad leaves, they'll come after him and they'll come after anyone who knows him to ask where he's gone. It doesn't matter where he lives; whether it's with us, or anywhere else, I'll always be his ex-wife. I'm the first person they'll come searching for. Christine and I reckon it will be a lot easier if the three of us are miles away, either on the main waterways to the west, where we're just another boat passing through, or in the back of beyond, somewhere really hard to trace.' She ran one finger along her eyebrow. It was something she always did if she was feeling insecure, or sometimes if she was just thinking. 'The other alternative is to join the mudlarkers in Ning Dang Po and lie low there, you know, get lost in the crowd, the way our friend The Pan of Hamgee has done. But if *he's* in Ning Dang Po and anyone makes the connection, it might make people come searching for us there. We can't go back to Glardy because that's where we're from and it's the first place anyone would look. We have to disappear and make a fresh start. The waterways are a good enough place to do that, but we have to sell the barge and start afresh. New places, new boat, new customers.'

Bort had to take a few deep breaths to stop her lip wobbling before she was able to speak. 'When?' she asked.

'When we get word from Smurfit that your dad's on the way. That means we'll have to put the boat on the market today. If you agree.'

'What if I don't agree?'

'Then we're in trouble. We need a bit more cash and we'll only really have enough if we sell Christine's shoemaking equipment, or the boat.'

'I guess we'll need the equipment—we'll need Christine to keep making boots and shoes, won't we? Unless it's too conspicuous…? Anyway, it would break her heart to see it go.'

'Yes, it would and yes, we'll need her to keep working. She's the only one of us with a real skill. If we sell the *Happy Doris*, we'll take her equipment with us, and all our things. But we'll still have to be careful. We'll have to sell the boots and shoes as ready-made to start with. There aren't many floating cobblers and we don't want to stand out like a sore thumb.' Terri smiled ruefully.

'I can believe that,' said Bort. Smecking Arnold! This was the pits. She wanted to throw a tantrum but she knew her mother was right. They were going to have to sell up and leave the home in which they'd had so many happy times. And on top of that, there was no way in a million years that she could ever see The Pan of Hamgee again.

Chapter 34
Problems

Bort and Terri sat in silence, broken only by the slapping of the water against the boat and the spitting, bubbling sounds of their breakfast cooking on the stove.

'I think maybe that needs stirring again,' said Terri.

'Maybe it does.'

Neither of them moved.

'We'll be alright, Bort, we always are.' Her mum hugged her, but it felt as much about reassurance for Terri as for her daughter.

Bort took a deep breath. 'Yeh. Shall I get that or d'you want to keep an eye on it while I make the coffee?'

They stood up and immediately there was a sharp rap on the side of the boat, just by the entryway, which made them both jump.

'Arnold! I hope that's not the Grongles,' said Bort.

Terri looked out of the port hole. 'No, it's Zeb the lock keeper.'

She unbolted the entrance and opened it.

'I got a letter for the young lady,' said Zeb. 'It's from Big Merv's lad, I reckon. Someone put it through the letterbox overnight. I found it this morning.'

'Brilliant! Thank you,' said Bort, trying not to actually snatch it from him. Terri stepped outside to chat and Bort left the two of them talking for a moment while she returned to the kitchen. She put a fresh pot of coffee on and looked at the envelope.

Bort, The Frolicking Maiden, Lark Locks. On the back it said, *Zeb, very sorry to put you out but please could you pass this on?*

Bort opened the envelope, unfolded the pages inside and absent-mindedly stirred the bacon, onions and spuds on the hob with one hand while she held the letter in the other and read the contents.

The Pan of Hamgee still hoped to be with her at nine a.m. as he'd promised. However, he explained, he'd rather have his wheels checked before he came out to Lark Locks as he lived the kind of life where a reliable escape option was essential. He'd have to go to Snurd first and get the SE2 checked and then, if there was something wrong, he'd have to wait until it was fixed. He hoped that wouldn't take too long, but warned her that, if it was serious, it might take a day or two. If the SE2 was given the all clear, he believed he should arrive on time, or at the latest, around lunchtime. He apologised and promised that if he was late, he'd drop in at the Parrot and Screwdriver and buy some cheese sandwiches. He also warned her that Big Merv might give him some deliveries to do—but if that was the case he'd still try to come and see her that evening, after 'work'. If he didn't make it by then, he warned her, it might be a day or two before he could get to see her. Bort thought about what her mother had said. It sounded as if they were going to leave as soon as possible. Would they still be there at lunch time?

Zeb put his head in through the open door. 'Everything alright, lass?' he asked Bort.

'Fine,' she said.

'If you need to send a reply, I've an errand to run in Ning Dang Po the day after tomorrow. I'd be happy to take it for you and drop it in. It'll be much cheaper than sending it by post, quicker too.'

He didn't say what Bort suspected he really meant; that it was more secure, the Grongles being less likely to find or check hand-delivered packages.

'We don't want to put you out,' said Terri.

'You're not. I'll be going right there. I'm hitching a ride with Big Jim in the post van.'

Bort was pretty sure that wasn't allowed but she didn't say anything. She didn't actually know The Pan of Hamgee's address but he did spend a lot of time in that pub, the Parrot and Screwdriver. Also, she remembered that, on the day of their flight from the security forces above the Arboretum, he'd told her, her mum and Christine that they should leave a note there if they needed to contact him. She was beginning to suspect he didn't have an actual address per se. No. If he was really blacklisted, he probably lived on the street, or in his wheels.

'I should know by tonight if I need to write back,' said Bort. Except she should probably write anyway, because it looked as if she, her mum and Christine were about to do a disappearing act. She'd know more once Smurfit had been to see them, she supposed. 'The best place to take it is to the pub he goes to. It's somewhere called Turnadot Street in Left Central.'

'Not the Parrot and Screwdriver?' asked Zeb.

'Yes.'

'Ah, I know it well. I think they used to supply guest beers to the Hungry Boatsman. Sound fellah delivered them.' He flicked his long purple tail over his shoulder and smoothed the fur absently as he cast his mind back. 'I reckon he went by the name of Trev. Yes, that's it. Trev Parker. He went to the same school as me, in Upper Left but about a hundred years after I did.' He winked. 'Anyway, it's on my way, so I can drop it straight in, no problem.'

'If you're OK with doing that, I think I may have to write back,' said Bort.

'Righto, take your time. So long as you drop it round at the cottage by end of tomorrow I'll take it. Otherwise it'll have to be next week.'

Would she even be there tomorrow, let alone next week,

Bort wondered. Who knew?

'Thanks. Would you be OK taking a parcel as well? He left his boots here, and his shirt,' said Bort.

'Not a problem.'

****

A few miles away in Ning Dang Po, The Pan of Hamgee sat waiting at Snurd while Gerry checked his wheels. The envelope Big Merv had given him had contained enough cash for a few repairs, so if Gerry gave it the all clear, he decided that he'd book it in to have a new windscreen fitted. He didn't fancy using submariner mode until the cracked one was replaced.

Gerry had shown him to the customer waiting room and offered him a cup of complimentary coffee while he waited. The Pan sipped it in silence and watched the goings on in the workshop through a large glass window built for the purpose. It was meant to give him a grandstand view of the mechanics working on his vehicle but instead it made him feel like a goldfish in a bowl.

Yeh, they just need to draw some pond weed on the window. He went up to the glass, opening and closing his mouth like a fish and just managed to close it and compose his features in time as Gerry turned round suddenly. The mechanic gave him a thumbs up, after which he held both hands up, palms facing The Pan, and opened and closed his fists; sign language for twenty minutes. The Pan nodded and sat back down.

There were a few magazines but most were several months old so he let them be. He couldn't sit still so he paced to and fro across the carpet. In the workshop beyond, on a stand specially designed for the purpose, Gerry morphed the SE2 from road to aviator, to submariner, speed boat and many other iterations. As he did so he checked it with a series of meters and other equipment whose function

The Pan could only guess at. It seemed to be going alright, although it was difficult to tell.

Soon it would be eight o'clock and Gerry would have to move the SE2 to one side and get on with work for proper customers who'd booked. The Pan sat down again and closed his eyes. Within a few minutes, he'd dozed off and was awoken as the door of the goldfish-bowl waiting room banged. Gerry looked a bit crestfallen.

Uh-oh. 'Everything OK?'

'Yes and no. It's running like a beaut, but you've ... something stuck in the fuel line.'

'Ah,' said The Pan. 'Can I drive it?'

Gerry shrugged. 'I wouldn't. It's fine so long as whatever's stuck there doesn't fall out but I can't guarantee it won't.'

'Ah. You'd better fix it then.'

'Righty tighty. And the windscreen? I'm guessing you don't want to be filling up with water if you use submariner—it doesn't have an airtight seal at the moment.'

'If I can run to it. How much to fix that lot?'

Gerry sucked the air through his teeth and scratched his head.

'That bad?' asked The Pan.

'Nah, I was just thinking,' Gerry said. 'When d'you want it?'

'I was hoping ... quite soon?'

Gerry gave him a look, 'Yeh well, I can imagine that. The thing in the fuel pipe looks like a bullet.'

'What?' The Pan adopted his best puzzled expression which cut precisely no ice with Gerry, who just laughed.

'Listen, I dunno what you get up to and I'm not going to ask. But if it falls out while you're flying, so will the fuel and then the snurd will fall out of the sky. You want it fixed.' He stopped and thought for a moment. 'I can do it a lot cheaper if I do it on the sly. It only needs a few hours and management doesn't mind but they don't like us being here after seven in the evening. I can start on it tonight. If I have time, I'll do the body work too. We've some dark-grey paint in at the moment. Not much but it's left over from a job last week so no-one'll mind if I use it. Not sure about the lighter colour but I can have a look. D'you want me to do that too?'

It would be sensible. The smarter the SE2 looked the less often it was stopped. There was nothing like driving about with obvious machine gun damage all along one side to arouse the interest of the authorities.

Yeh. Best it was fixed. 'You probably should if you can. How long will it take you?'

'Let me think ... tonight, then with tomorrow before and after work and a bit more the following morning. If I do the bodywork first, I can re-programme the dents out in a jiffy so that won't take long. Then I'll paint it and leave the panels to dry while I'm doing the fuel line and the windscreen.' He rubbed one ear with a furry hand. 'Yeh, it should be done tomorrow morning. It might run over to the next night but I doubt it. I won't know until I take the panel off to fix the fuel line—there might be more damage I can't see. There's no point guessing about that one until I know more. Can you wait that long, mate?'

'I guess I'll have to.' The Pan tried to put a brave face on it. 'I'm not getting you into trouble though, am I? If I am, I'll book it in.'

'Nah, it's like I said. They don't mind us doing our own thing—they know that's how we learn stuff. They just don't want us doing it on their time.'

'That's very kind of them.'

'Fly, more like. They get better mechanics that way. Their bread and butter is simple servicing—we buy clunkers and fix 'em up for our apprenticeships. Or we fix our friends' clunkers. There's a lot more learning on something that's got more to fix.'

'I guess.'

'I *know* there is, mate. Anyway, you don't want to book it in. They haven't got a slot for two weeks. I'd guess you'd rather not wait that long.'

'Well, I can,' lied The Pan, 'but I'd rather not have to. How much will it be?'

Gerry named a figure which, The Pan knew, was little more than the cost of the parts. He continued, 'Just to be on the safe side, pick it up at eight o'clock in the morning, day after tomorrow, yeh? Tell you what though, if you pay me now, then if it's ready the night before I'll lock the spare keys in the boot, leave it where it's able to escape and bell the pub.'

This arrangement suited The Pan. But he was also aware that for Gerry it was an excellent way of making sure he got paid while his client actually had some money. He opened the envelope, counted out the cash and handed it over. 'Cheers Gerry, you're a star.'

'Any time mate. Oh, you still have another set of keys, don't you?'

'Yes,' The Pan held them up.

'See you in a couple of days, possibly ...'

'Righty tighty!'

Bum! That ruled out going to see Bort but at least he'd had the snurd checked. If that bullet had come out of the fuel line at the wrong time things would have got ugly. Yeh, and he'd sent her a letter. At least she would know he wasn't standing her up.

Chapter 35
Waiting

The Pan almost walked to Lark Locks after his visit to Snurd. It would have been daft though. It was about fifteen miles away for starters. Driving was one thing, but walking would have made him look a bit too keen. He suspected Bort wouldn't go for keen.

Instead, rather than give in to temptation, he decided to distract himself by heading to Mama Jack's and offering to do a bit of cleaning for Jenny in return for a plate of scrambled eggs and toast. Then he decided that no, he'd head to the Parrot and Screwdriver first.

When he got there, he discovered a summons from Big Merv, and any thoughts of a day to himself disappeared. Big Merv had just taken over King Milo's patch. As a result, there was a seemingly unending stream of correspondence to be delivered until late in the evening.

Once this was done, The Pan returned to The Big Thing nightclub to report to Bob, who warned him as she paid him that his services would be required again the following day. He was to report at nine a.m. prompt. There was a lot to do, but after their previous conversation he also wondered if Big Merv was deliberately keeping him busy.

Time flew past as The Pan spent the best part of two days walking, and occasionally running, backwards and forwards across Ning Dang Po. He began to wonder if he'd walked the equivalent mileage of going to Lark Locks anyway. He was glad of his new boots though. They were unbelievably comfortable. Every time he looked down he thought about the time he'd spent with Bort. Arnold, he wanted to see her again. It had been so wonderful to do something normal. Like a dream.

Finally, at the end of the second day, they let him go and

he went to the Big Thing nightclub to collect his earnings. It was past two a.m. when he got there, so mercifully, this didn't involve any interaction with Big Merv himself. The Pan was so scared of his boss that there was a limit to the amount of time he could spend in his company in one day.

When he arrived at the night club, despite it being after closing, with only the staff in at this hour, the place seemed to be buzzing. 'What's up?' he asked Bob as she handed over the usual brown envelope, although again, it was thicker.

'It seems the beings on King Milo's patch are playing nicely. And what with him taking on all King Milo's business interests, it means the boss is in the money. He's given everyone a bonus. You've done him (and us) a good turn.'

'I have?'

'Yeh, but don't get too cocky. He still thinks you're a waste of space an' so do we,' snarled a familiar voice.

Oh great. The Pan took a deep breath and turned round. 'Hi Frank.' He smiled sweetly because he knew Frank hated it, and it was one of the few ways to get back at him without being thumped. 'Lovely to see you.'

'I'm not stoppin'. I got better things to do than talk to a little squirt like you,' said Frank having done just that. The Pan raised an eyebrow at Bob as they watched him stride away through the doors to the back of the building. If Frank was around, Big Merv was probably back in his office. Time for a sharp exit, The Pan decided, before he ended up with more deliveries to do. Bob clearly thought the same thing.

'Off you go sweetie,' she said and winked.

'Yep. Catch you later, Bob.'

Shoving the envelope in his pocket, he left by the front door. To The Pan's delight, when he found a safe spot and checked his earnings later, he found a note telling him he was no longer needed and that Big Merv would send word to The Parrot and Screwdriver by midday if that changed.

'Brilliant!' said The Pan. And with a new energy and a spring in his step, went to find somewhere quiet to sleep.

Chapter 36
Surprise parcel

The Pan awoke surprisingly invigorated after spending a night on a bench overlooking the river where it ran through The Planes. He hadn't seen Bort for three days. Now, hopefully, he could change that. All he needed was the SE2.

That hadn't gone so smoothly. Needless to say, Gerry had encountered problems. But he'd promised The Pan he'd have it finished in his lunch hour and ready for collection by two o'clock. The Pan didn't want to tempt fate so he decided to give Gerry as long as he could and go to The Parrot and Screwdriver first to check there wasn't a summons from Big Merv.

He hadn't seen Gladys, Ada and Their Trev since his chat with Trev and wondered whether, if he arrived at the right time, he could blag some sandwiches. Surely someone there would have ordered a round with pickle and found it a bit hot.

It was a beautiful morning and the clear blue sky heralded a perfect afternoon—hopefully one spent lying cocooned in long grass with Bort. Yeh, The Pan smiled to himself as he arrived at The Parrot for eleven o'clock opening. He realised he was the only customer in. Perhaps the punters had had a few too many beers the previous night. Well yes, it was Saturday. They were probably hanging gently over.

'Where has you been?' asked Gladys the minute he walked in. 'Yes, dear, Trev said he'd had a very worrying conversation with you and the next thing you just disappeared!' She threw her hands up in the air for emphasis as she said the word 'disappeared'. 'We've been worried sick!'

'I'm terribly sorry. I didn't mean to worry you. I had to run rather a lot of errands.'

Trev appeared from the Holy of Holies behind the bar wiping his hands with a tea towel. 'I told yer. Big Merv's taken over King Milo's patch and I reckoned the lad's had messages which has ter be taken.'

Arnold, they knew everything about him and yet they didn't seem to care at all. 'That's about the size of it,' said The Pan because he could see no point in denying it.

'Oh and someone called Gerry called to say your wheels are ready,' said Ada.

'Yes!' said The Pan adding a hasty 'thank you'.

'Apparently they're parked where they can escape. He says he's locked the spare keys in the boot so you can summon them with your set.' She looked a bit dubious, as if she expected him to have lost them.

'Thanks,' said The Pan again. Hoorah! He could go and see Bort.

'Hmph.' Gladys' voice broke into his jubilant thoughts. 'Does you know a Blaggysomp called Zeb?'

'Yes, I do. He's the lock keeper up at Lark Locks,' said The Pan.

'He brought you a package,' said Ada.

'Yer,' said Gladys.

'Hang on a moment. Trev, dear,' she trilled, 'be a pet and get us that parcel, will you?'

'Right you are.'

The two old ladies moved to the left of the door to the Holy of Holies as Trev went along the back of the bar, ducked inside, and came out with the package in question. The Pan heard a thump somewhere, followed by the flapping of wings. Uh-oh.

'Arnold's air biscuits! Wipe my conkers!' shouted a voice.

'No Humbert, dear, it's not for you,' said Ada as Trev carried the large brown paper parcel round into the main bar and put it on a table. Humbert circled round his head, squawking excitedly, until he saw The Pan, headed straight for him and settled on his shoulder.

'Windy trussocks!' the parrot yelled.

'Blimey, Humbert, keep it down a bit! I need that ear.'

'Yer. Stop deafening the lad,' said Trev.

Humbert made a keening noise and sidled along The Pan's shoulder until he was very close to his face. 'Wipe my conkers?' said the parrot quietly.

'Humbert, dear, come here at once!' said Ada. As usual Ada's efforts to control her wayward pet had no effect whatsoever. Humbert stayed where he was.

'Humbert,' said The Pan, 'Can you go over there!? You're digging your claws in.'

'Here.' Trev put the parcel on a nearby table and flapped a hand at Humbert. 'Go on, git!'

'Shroud my futtocks!' yelled Humbert but he did, at least, fly over to the bar and settle on one of the shelves behind it.

'If you soils my nice clean surfaces you is goin' ter be in trouble,' said Gladys sternly.

'Yes, Humbert,' agreed Ada, 'but you can watch if you're a *very* good boy.'

'I reckons you oughter open that while you has the chance,' said Gladys with an eye on Humbert who seemed to have decided to stay put for the moment.

The Pan untied the string. On the top, he found the shirt, t-shirt and trousers Christine and Terri had taken to the laundrette for him. Underneath them was a second pair of fabulous boots Christine had made him. And underneath those was another package, wrapped up in brown paper.

'I'll keep these for best,' said The Pan, putting the boots to one side and placing his freshly laundered clothes on a nearby table.

There was a sense of silent anticipation in the room as he opened the second parcel. It contained another seven shirts in virulent paisley patterns. Two were wool; the others looked as if they were a silk and linen mix. They appeared to be the same size as the one he was wearing and he reckoned they'd fit him well.

'Wow!' He held up a particularly bright one with a pattern in green, purple and blue.

'Arnold's conkers, they is loud!' Trev said.

'Don't blaspheme Trev, dear,' said Ada.

'Yer,' said Gladys.

'Sorry Mum, and Ada, but blimey.' He waved a hand at the shirts. 'Does they come with a volume control?'

'Pah! Volume control,' said The Pan. 'I'll have you know these are the height of good taste.'

'Melons in a hammock,' said Humbert although whether he was agreeing or disagreeing, The Pan wasn't sure.

'You Hamgeeans is nuts,' said Trev.

The Pan raised an eyebrow at him and turned his attention back to the parcel. That looked as if it was everything. Gladys and Ada had a habit of keeping things like brown paper for re-use so The Pan made to fold it. As he did so an envelope fell out from between two sheets and landed on the floor. He picked it up. Gladys and Ada came out from behind the bar and joined Trev at the table to examine The Pan's booty.

'They've got your taste in footwear off pat,' said Ada.

'Yep, that's Christine who makes those.'

'They is good boots,' Gladys was saying. 'Sturdy boots which I reckons will last for a long time.'

'Yeh.' The Pan held them up. 'They are.'

'Isn't you goin' ter try them on?'

'I'm already wearing the other pair.'

'She made you two?' asked Ada, her eyebrows almost disappearing into her hairline. There was a short silence as she and Gladys exchanged what they would call 'looks'.

'Yes,' said The Pan. 'I helped them out and the payment was two pairs of boots and—' He hesitated. Should he say anything about the sausage? No. It was too embarrassing for starters. 'Two pairs of boots.'

'I see,' said Ada.

'You has got them ladies eating out of yer hand then,' said Gladys.

'No, not really, they're just being kind,' said The Pan.

'Hmph, an' you said that is the other pair you is wearing now?' Gladys said, as if she was having trouble believing it.

'It is.'

'Let's have a look, dear,' said Ada.

He walked out into the middle of the room.

"S proper craftsmanship that is,' said Gladys approvingly.

'You're not wrong there,' said The Pan. 'I walked miles in them these last two days and they feel wonderful, as if they're made for me.'

'Well, they were, weren't they dear?'

'Well ... yes but ... you know.'

Gladys and Ada went back behind the bar.

'Would you like a beer, dear?' asked Ada.

'Yes please. I'll have a Gumpert's Sprocket.'

He opened the letter, sat down and silently began to read.

Dear Pan of Hamgee,

Remember I said that if you decided not to come with us you'd come to the marina and find us gone? Well, by the time you get this, we will have.

We have enough cash to get Dad out of the Resistance, but we had to pay someone to look the other way and smuggle him out. He's going to be a bit like you for a while. Although the Grongles aren't after him, the Resistance might be, so he'll have to lie low. He has to look different but he doesn't want to stand out either so there's no way he can wear these shirts anymore. Not ever. So, we're sending them to you, along with your own stuff. I love to think that you'll have them now. Dad would want them to go to someone who'd appreciate them. So I know he'll be pleased you have them. Also, you forgot the second pair of boots, so here they are.

I'm kind of hoping that you escaped from Big Merv, got away from Ning Dang Po and went North to Glardy. I'm kind of hoping this'll never reach you and that we might meet again up there one day—you know, as friends—but if I'm wrong, and you're reading this that's OK too. So long as you're happy.

Maybe you were right not to come back. We had to sell something else and there were only two things we had access to that were worth that kind of cash—one was the barge, but the other would have been you. LOL. Don't worry, it was always going to be the barge. So if the snurd's fixed and you're still staying away it's safe to drop in. Desperate people do crazy things and we're not good people, not really—I think you understand that—and we're desperate. But even we aren't that bad. You saved our lives—and Mum from blacklisting—which is the same thing ... What I'm trying to say is that even we wouldn't stoop to dobbing you in after that.

The barge has to go though. If the Resistance come looking for Dad they'll look for Mum first and that means they'll look for our boat. We got a fantastic offer from some people Zeb knows, who either have no idea about the trouble that might come with it, or don't care. We move into our new home tomorrow morning. It's totally knackered. A real restoration project. But it's going to be fun. We've been in contact with Dad and he's going to stay with us a while and help out. It's bigger than the Doris, which is cool, but it's called the Flubbering Mantis! *So, so lame. We're leaving to pick it up first thing tomorrow. I've insisted we change its name to* The Tall Dark Stranger *in your honour.'*

'I'm not tall,' said The Pan.

Over at the bar Ada looked up suddenly and threw him a nonplussed look. 'No dear, but you're not short either. Somewhere in between, I'd say.'

'Hmm?' he cocked a quizzical eyebrow at her.

'You said you weren't tall, dear.'

'Ah yeh, sorry. I didn't mean to say that out loud.'

He read on.

I know why you didn't come back. And I'm glad you didn't because that was the smart option and that's what's going to keep you alive.

'How is she gettin' on?' asked Gladys.

'Not bad, not bad,' said The Pan. They watched in silence as he continued reading. By The Prophet they were nosey, but he didn't really care and since no-one else was in, it didn't matter.

'She was a lovely girl, very attractive! A bit flighty for you though, I think,' said Ada.

'Yer, I reckons she is alright but I agrees with Ada. You needs someone deeper, if you sees what I mean,' said Gladys.

'Yes, I do hope you didn't do anything untoward with her,' said Ada.

Untoward? The Pan had never heard it called *that* before.

'Yer and if you has, I hopes you was careful,' said Gladys. She pronounced the word 'careful' with special emphasis as if she meant something else which The Pan realised, she did. Blimey. Even his grandmother had been up to date enough to call it 'birth control'. Then again, she'd probably been younger than Gladys and Ada.

'You know me, I'm a very careful man,' said The Pan with what he hoped was an enigmatic smile. Unfortunately he suspected he was blushing too badly to make it work. Arnold! Luckily, at this point, Trev clearly decided The Pan had suffered enough mickey taking.

'Mum! Aunt Ada! What is you both like? Leave the lad alone!' he said.

'Norks!' shouted Humbert from his station on the shelves, as if in agreement.

The Pan turned his attention to Bort's letter again.

We thought it would be helpful to tell everyone around the marina that you were going south for family reasons. We told them we'd got you a working passage to Tith on the Gipsy Maid. *The captain is called Genton and he's Zeb, the lock keeper's, brother. It runs a three-person crew. I think enough people saw you while you were here to make that stick for a bit. Zeb says his brother will report that you jumped ship and ran away when you got close to the checkpoint at Tith, just before the marshes. That way maybe they'll look for you there and the heat will be off for a while. I hope that's going to be useful.*

I'll always remember you. And I hope that you find a way out.
Mum and Christine send their love and so do I.
Stay safe and be happy,
Love,
Bort—and Mum and Christine—and even Dad because he's grateful to you for saving us. But mostly me, because I'm the one writing the letter.

The Pan chuckled to himself.
'Oy-oy,' said Gladys. 'Is she survivin' without you?'
He smiled. 'Yes, she's fine. They're all fine. Really, there's nothing going on.' The two old ladies stared at him. 'OK nothing major. It was just a fling,' he said. It made him feel sad, and a little empty.
The Pan stood up and walked back to the bar. He checked the date on his watch.
'Is you goin' ter want lunch? I reckons two pairs of boots is worth celebratin'. P'raps not the shirts so much but then, I s'pose you is happy with 'em. You can have it on the house, a pint of Humbert's Wallsmacker as well.'
'Yes please to the sandwiches and the beer, but not right now, in fact maybe at supper … there's something I need to do first,' he said. He took his snurd keys from his pocket, pressing the button as he ran out onto the street.

Chapter 37
The penny drops

The Pan of Hamgee circled the canal near the derelict ground in Lower Right. The SE2 flew like a bird and he flipped it into a victory roll with the sheer joy of being alive. He headed out over the glittering waters of the reservoir, followed the tree-lined waterway to Lark Locks and circled lower there. He could see the *Happy Doris*, except it was now maroon and green and there was a flustered-looking couple standing on the towpath talking to three Grongles. They didn't seem to be in any trouble, it was clearly just a spot check—but neither of them was Bort, Christine or Terri.

Banking away before he was seen, he flew round in a wide circle and, after checking for any more Grongles, landed in the car park. No squad cars or any other sign of the security forces. They must have come on a boat. He walked round the lower marina on the path this time, crossed the lock at the lock gates and noticed Zeb two locks up. He ran up the hill.

Zeb greeted him with a smile and a twinkle in his brown dog-like eyes. Noooo not dog-like. That was speciesism. Galorsh-like.

'Hello, young man. Good to see you're still around.' A definite euphemism for 'still alive' that one.

'Yeh, like a bad smell,' said The Pan and Zeb laughed. 'How's it going?'

Zeb tutted and scratched one of his purple furry ears. 'The Grongles were all over here like a rash last few days. Said some GBI had been up here, hell of a dangerous bloke apparently. Not that I'd say I'd seen anyone.'

'Apart from King Milo and Big Merv, you mean?'

Zeb laughed. 'They aren't blacklisted, son. Although I'll give you they're both dangerous.' He stopped to think. 'Although King Milo ... not so much now, I'd say.'

'The story is, he's moved to Glardy.'

'Yer, I s'pose you could call it that.'

The Pan cleared his throat. 'Mmm,' was all he said.

'Whoever this GBI bloke is, life must be pretty hot for him. You know what brought the Grongles up here?'

'No,' said The Pan with his most innocent, this-has-nothing-to-do-with-me expression in place.

'Apparently someone up here put his name into one of the computers up at the chandler's. That's all it took.'

'Arnold. Whoever he is, I don't fancy his chances,' said The Pan and he made a mental note that he'd have to be careful who he gave his name to from now on.

'Me neither. Anyway, I guess you'll be looking for Terri and her crew,' said Zeb.

'I am. Are they still here?'

"Fraid not. They've gone with Jim in the postvan first thing. He's taking them out to Hellman's Dip to pick up their new barge.'

The Pan had never heard of Hellman's Dip. 'Where's that?'

'About twenty miles south. It's where the Western Waterways connect up with the main system. Lots of traffic there.'

Yeh, a good place to disappear. That figured. The Pan sighed. 'I guess I've missed them.'

Zeb nodded. 'Yes, I guess you have,' he said.

'D'you reckon you'll see them again?' asked The Pan.

'I reckon I might,' said Zeb but there was a suggestion in the inflection that it was an, '*I* might, *you* won't.'

'If you ever do, will you tell them thank you from me? They sent my stuff on. I owe them.'

'Yes. I'll pass that on.' Zeb hesitated. 'If you take the South Road, turn left at Felton Spring and follow the signs to Grimpot Marina you might still have time to thank them yourself. The barge is a runner though, and there's not much paperwork. I reckon they'll make sail quick smart. You might be in time ...'

'Thanks Zeb, you're a star.'

'A pleasure, lad,' said Zeb.

It was a pity more of Big Merv's people in town weren't like Zeb, The Pan thought. Then again, he might not have been, specifically, Big Merv's man. No. He was a lock keeper. He probably had to walk the line and be everyone's man from time to time, or at least everyone's Galorsh. Why else would he have a shotgun and a black belt in hoo-flung-yoo? The Pan could imagine him turning a blind eye and a deaf ear to certain things and perhaps, dropping a word in the right place about others. Yeh. Probably.

He bade Zeb goodbye and headed off.

Since the directions he'd been given were to go by road, that was how The Pan had to drive to Hellman's Dip. He wasn't sure he could find it without following Zeb's instructions. No. He *was* sure. He wouldn't have a hope in hell. He'd never been there, and beyond Ning Dang Po, or Hamgee, where he grew up, he didn't have such an instinctive grip of the geography. Or any grip of much of it, if he was honest with himself. Then again, he could always ask directions. No. Scratch that. It was best he left no obvious traces of his presence.

He soon found the signs for Grimpot Marina and followed them for another twenty minutes or so until the road ended at a car park. Clearly traffic access was limited and most of the travellers who came here were using the canal. Having found it, The Pan selected aviator mode and took off. Flying high above the area in the SE2 he circled, searching for boats.

Hmm, he thought as he flew. *There are quite a lot of boats down there.*

What would he do if he was Terri, Bort and Christine? First he'd paint the barge so it looked in good condition on the outside. Maybe he should look for something with a new paint job. Except that this seemed to be some kind of boat mending and selling place. There were dry docks with boats in them being fixed and cranes with boats hanging having their undersides scraped. In fact, it looked as if pretty much all the boats there were having a new paint job.

Presumably Terri, Bort and Christine wouldn't have bought their new home until they got the cash from selling the *Happy Doris.* Would they have time to get it painted? Would someone have done it for them while the sale was being finalised?

As he dipped lower and checked the boatyard more thoroughly, he realised that none of the boats being fixed and nothing moored there was big as the *Happy Doris,* let alone larger.

He flew over the main waterway and followed it for a while. It was part of a similarly large junction to Lark Locks with canals and waterways heading off in several different directions. All were busy. Too busy for The Pan to be able to pick out Bort, Christine and Terri on a boat he'd never seen, even if, by some miracle, they were still there. Which one of the routes below had they taken? Good question.

'What am I even doing here?' he muttered. 'I'm never going to find them.'

It looks unlikely. You knew it was going to end like this. She pretty much spelt it out! said the voice of Virtual Dad in his head.

'Yeh. So why does it matter?' he asked himself.

He thought about it as he looked down at the green fields below and the brightly coloured boats plying their way up and down the sparkling water. He wasn't sure what he'd wanted to do. He didn't want to take up Terri, Bort and Christine's offer to join them. Not that it mattered—he doubted they'd want him to join them anymore, not now they knew who he *really* was. After all, he'd told Bort to look him up. It must have been her, Terri or Christine who'd done so on the computer at the chandler's and sparked an alert. If they'd seen the clamp-down at Lark Locks that Zeb had described, the last thing they'd want was for The Pan to stick around. He understood that. So what had he followed them for? He scratched his head. He supposed he just wanted to say thank you, or goodbye, or something.

He flew back to the car park and landed anyway, parked in one of the spaces provided and walked a little way along the towpath. The canal wasn't nearly as idyllic looking from up here—the glassy surface of the water no longer hid the colour, and it smelled a bit; definitely less fresh than Lark Locks.

Finally he found a place where the grass was more trampled than the rest and a tell-tale yellow patch where it had been starved of light suggested the possible presence of a gangplank. A little further on, a poppy lay on top of the mooring post. Beside it, in yellow wax crayon, someone had written, *'See ya later xxx.'*

Was he imagining it or did that writing look like Bort's?

He picked up the flower but it had wilted in the morning sun and the petals fell off. Oops.

'See you later. Not goodbye. Yeh.' He dropped the wilted poppy stem into the water. 'Be happy, you three,' he said.

What was he doing? Soppy git. Terri, Christine and Bort were a family. The Pan liked that. They'd asked him to join them, before they realised who he was. He liked that too. And he was keen on Bort ... yeh, OK, maybe a bit more than keen. From the sadness he felt, he guessed he might, possibly, be starting to fall in love with her. But he had to admit to himself that an equally big part of Bort's allure was the idea of being normal; of being free to love someone without his mere existence being a danger to them. Anyway, he doubted she was in love with him. Yeh. Even if he managed to find her—and the others—what would he say? It was a lot of effort to go to, just to say goodbye: a grand, sweeping gesture, for sure, but one that was also, possibly, the wrong side of the borderline between hot-headed romantic and scary nut-bar stalker.

He chuckled to himself and shook his head. 'Yeh, you absolute weirdo,' he muttered.

The sluggish brown waters of the canal swirled and gurgled as a narrowboat chugged past. The woman at the tiller waved. 'Morning,' The Pan called, waving back. And as he did so he realised, with crystal certainty, that the closest thing he had to a family wasn't in a barge heading west, but waiting for him back in Ning Dang Po, at the Parrot and Screwdriver.

'Mmm, along with a free round of cheese and pickle sandwiches and a pint.' Yep. And if he got a move on he could be back to claim them before lunch-time closing. He looked up at the clear blue sky and smiled. Just thinking about his friends at the pub felt like coming home.

He turned away from the water, walked briskly back down the towpath, past the boatyard to the SE2 and leapt in.

Back at the canal's edge the dried-out poppy floated slowly away on the current. All was quiet but for the cries of the gulls upstream and the glooping of the muddy water against the sides. In the distance a snurd rose up into the blue sky. Moving swiftly, it was soon nothing more than a tiny glittering dot, growing smaller all the time, until, with a wink of sunlight on metal, it disappeared from sight.

The end

Other books by M T McGuire

If you'd like to find out what happens next, look out for the other books in this series:

Small Beginnings
K'Barthan Shorts, Hamgeean Misfit: No 1

When your very existence is treason, employment opportunities are thin on the ground. But when one of the biggest crime lords in the city makes The Pan of Hamgee a job offer he can't refuse, it's hard to tell what the dumbest move is; accepting the offer or saying, no to Big Merv. Neither will do much for The Pan's life expectancy.

Nothing To See Here
K'Barthan Shorts, Hamgeean Misfit: No 2

It's midwinter and preparations for the biggest religious festival in the K'Barthan year are in full swing. Yes, even though, officially, religious activity has been banned, no-one's going to ignore Arnold, The Prophet's Birthday, especially not Big Merv. He orders The Pan of Hamgee to deliver the traditional Birth of The Prophet gift to his accountants and lawyers.

As usual, The Pan has managed to elicit the unwanted attention of the security forces. Can he make the delivery and get back to the The Parrot and Screwdriver pub in time for an unofficial Prophet's Birthday celebration with his friends?

Close Enough
K'Barthan Extras, Hamgeean Misfit: No 3

When The Pan of Hamgee encounters some mudlarkers trying to land a box on the banks of the River Dang he is happy to help. Having accepted a share of the contents as a reward he cannot believe his luck. It contains one of the most expensive delicacies available in K'Barth; Goojan spiced sausage. If he can sell it, the sausage might spell the end of his troubles, but knowing his luck it could bring a whole load more.

There will be more K'Barthan Extras soon. You can also read more about The Pan of Hamgee's adventures in K'Barth in a series of four full-length books.

The K'Barthan Series

All The Pan of Hamgee wants is a quiet life.

So why did he have to fall in love with a woman living a different version of reality, upset a murderous tyrant and then run out of places to hide?

Now all he has to do is face his inner demons, rescue everything he holds dear and save the world, or die trying.

Oh yes, and he's an abject coward.

Great. No pressure then.

Escape From B-Movie Hell

Bronze Medal winner, The Wishing Shelf Book Awards, 2015.

If you asked Andi Turbot whether she had anything in common with Flash Gordon she'd say no, emphatically. Saving the world is for dynamic, go-ahead leaders of men. And while it would be nice to see a woman getting involved for a change, she believes she could be the least well-equipped being in her galaxy for the job.

Then her best friend Eric reveals that he's an extraterrestrial. He's not just any E.T. either. He's Gamalian: seven feet tall, lobster-shaped and covered in marmite-scented goo. Just when Andi's getting used to that he tells her about the apocalypse and really ruins her day.

The human race will perish unless Eric's Gamalian superiors step in. Abducted and trapped on an alien ship, Andi must convince the Gamalians her world is worth saving. Or escape from their clutches and save it herself.

Find out more at: www.hamgee.co.uk/books.html

Author News

Never miss a new release again! Sign up for M T Mail. Just visit this link: http://www.hamgee.co.uk/freenbook

You can choose to hear about everything or just new releases. You can also keep up to date with all things M T McGuire by joining her K'Barthan Jolly Japery Facebook Group.

To join, go here: http://bit.ly/JollyJapes

Or you can follow M T McGuire on these social media:

Website: http://www.hamgee.co.uk

Blog: http://www.mtmcguire.co.uk

Instagram: @mtmcguire

9 781907 809361